Books by Howard Blum

FICTION

Wishful Thinking

NONFICTION

Wanted! The Search for Nazis in America

WISHFUL THINKING

WISHFUL THINKING

Howard Blum

Atheneum   NEW YORK   1985

Library of Congress Cataloging in Publication Data

Blum, Howard, ——
    Wishful thinking.

    I. Title.
PS3552.L837W5   1985   813'.54   84–45609
ISBN 0–689–11543–1

Published simultaneously in Canada by Collier Macmillan Canada, Inc.
Composition by Heritage Printers, Inc., Charlotte, North Carolina
Manufactured by Fairfield Graphics, Fairfield, Pennsylvania
Designed by Cathryn S. Aison
First Edition

To the memory of my father.

And, of course, for Annette.

"Oh, Jake," Brett said, "we could have had such a damned good time together . . ."

"Yes," I said. "Isn't it pretty to think so?"

Ernest Hemingway, The Sun Also Rises

. . . Abraham makes two movements: he makes the infinite movement of resignation and gives up Isaac (this no one can understand because it is a private venture); but in the next place, he makes the movement of faith every instant. This is his comfort, for he says: "But yet this will not come to pass, or, if it does come to pass, then the Lord will give me a new Isaac, by virtue viz. of the absurd."

Søren Kierkegaard, Fear and Trembling

CONTENTS

PROLOGUE
6 Rms., 3 Bths. of My Own

WAS THERE A WOMAN INVOLVED? Of course. Also a friend: the man I believed in; the man I betrayed. A trail of schemes and dreams leading back to the scene of the crime.

"HER HUSBAND DIED about six months ago and now her children are carting her off to some sort of Wasp burial ground."

Max Fox paused to poke questioningly with his chopsticks at a curiously shaped dim sum and then, with a gesture meant to suggest he was made of stern stuff, popped it whole into his mouth. A small comma of a swallow and he continued:

"You pledge your soul and all your earthly possessions to the church and in return the good reverends promise to give you a roof over your head and prayers twice a day 'til death do you part."

"Except the good reverends are praying your soul departs before your money," I interrupted. A trickle of controlled laughs came from Max; despite the nearly four decades separating us, we were partners in cynicism.

Our audience, or more accurately our target, remained impressively mute. It wasn't like Kate Warner to miss her cues. Though her days as a true believer had lapsed with her adolescence, Kate invariably gamely rose to our baiting challenges, never wasting a chance to counterpunch at us heathen. Yet this summer afternoon sitting in the disturbingly dark Chinatown teahouse, she chose not to be the defender of the faith. She realized Max and I were talking around some very serious—and costly—doings.

Finally, as a stoop-backed waiter rolled his cart over and began removing the small piles of blue-bordered plates we had eaten our way through, she went on the attack. Her battle cry, so Kate, was both dismissive and pragmatic.

"Russ," Kate succinctly explained, "we can't afford it."

Of course she was right. There seemed to be no logical way we could afford to buy the apartment in Max's building, no matter how fortuitous the circumstances. Kate's laconic argument scraped the very bottom of the bottom line: we had no money. I didn't even have a job. Russell Lewis was a twenty-seven-year-old out-of-work reporter.

When Max Fox had been fired from the magazine he had created, edited, and milked for an executive's (if not a king's) ransom, all us young Turks had marched out right behind him; we were hotheaded veterans of the sixties when, you might remember, slamming doors and breaking glass were the craze. But while Max had carted off his bundles of carefully invested loot, all I took with me were my principles. And my ambition, of course.

Nearly eight months later on that August afternoon in 1974 when we were lunching in Chinatown, I was traveling much lighter. Quick, guess which of those two heavy burdens I had jettisoned? A hint: Our meal was to celebrate my delivering to the typist the nearly four hundred yellow legal pad pages filled in longhand with a first draft of *Hit Man!*; my, as it was announced in the publisher's catalog under what then seemed to be the stupendously optimistic category of forthcoming, "true-life kill and tell account of a no-miss assassin plugging away for The Godfather."

Kate didn't have a manuscript, but she did have a job. And I wasn't too wild about the one she had. Despite the daily self-righteous exodus of Max's young, gifted, and moody protégés from *City* magazine, Kate refused to surrender her title as dance critic. Maybe it was Kate's being raised in Europe during those formative Wonder years when an authentic American mind and body are busy growing twelve ways that reinforced her total obliviousness to the whimsy of sixties pop culture. Or maybe it was, more simply, her nature: one part proudly self-reliant, to one part disagreeably stubborn. To this despairing day I am uncertain. But Kate Warner refused to march to any drum. The lady simply strolled. She had strolled into her job as dance critic after just one conversation with Max at a dinner party three years earlier, and she remained unwilling to march into the desert of unemployment.

At the time, her refusal was a matter of fierce and fiery dispute. Later, when a young man's deep guilt required he fork up an argument to justify a newfound passion, Kate's failure to slam the editorial door in the new regime's face would be seen as a symbol, a bad faith vein of cowardice that betrayed larger failures of vision. But those "insights" would come in another country; or at least in another restaurant.

That afternoon in the claustrophobic Chinatown teahouse, Max stared across the gold-speckled formica table and, gray-haired mischief-maker, ignored Kate. He knew to whom he was playing. With a mugger's dexterity, he reached out swiftly for the pressure points.

"The truth is," Max lectured, "old Mrs. Nicholas won't allow the apartment to go on the market until next week when she's completely moved out. She doesn't want to be there while strangers come traipsing in." An insider's nod of the head as he added, "You know how these old Wasps are."

For the briefest instant Max looked at my etiolated Semitic nose and I focused on a tired yet ruddy face that might have been comfortably worn by a shtetl tailor; and we both smiled silently, caught in the painful realization that neither of us had the slightest inkling of how an old Wasp really is.

Then Max plowed straight ahead:

"But I started talking her up in the elevator yesterday, saying how her maid had mentioned to my maid"—Max paused a bit too obviously to see if we grasped all the hard-won social mobility that chain of communication implied—"that she was moving, and I knew a young couple who might be interested in purchasing her apartment.

"Now, she started apologizing that the place was a mess, but I gave her an understanding shrug and she gave me a smile and finally she said it would be fine. Bring the young couple up any afternoon this week.

"Look," Max continued, "in five days she'll be gone and after that it will all be up to her lawyers. Russ"—Max's voice started climbing while his delicate, long-fingered hands now flew wide from the table as if throwing shuttered windows open to the panorama of opportunity—"I tell you if you move quickly, you can get it for a steal."

"We'd have to steal to get it," Kate moaned.

Still, I was jumping high for the bait. A mother who shops at Loehmann's and a father who ventures into department stores only to copy down surreptitiously the make and model number of the appliance he is determined to purchase at cost from the manufacturer cannot help but produce a son whose economic theory is equally visionary: A bargain is a bargain at any price. Even if you can't afford it.

Kate, however, saw my wheels spinning and shot me one of her cross, down-boy looks. Comfortable, if not moralistic, in her bohemian poverty, she turned obnoxiously judgmental whenever what she called my "hustler's mentality" became too dominant. Poor girl, she didn't understand that genealogy is destiny.

But Max knew. And he began reeling the sucker in.

"After all," he went on, "no matter what you paid for the apartment, you'd be moving into the best building in the Village."

When he mouthed "best," Max somehow stretched and compounded the adjective into a complicated, multisyllabic word. He even resorted to uncharacteristic body language, squinting his soft gray eyebrows as he spoke as if literally to underline his appraisal: the old editor making sure we realized he was speaking in italics.

Here the renowned radical journalist Max Fox, sitting in this subterranean Chinatown dive on a sticky August afternoon while decked out in his somber burgher's mufti of a vested, pinstripe suit—though lightweight in deference to the season, I will admit—and rep tie chokingly close around his throat, was getting down to what he considered the most affecting part of his pitch. "Best" was an Old World, a gentleman's value, a code word that signaled discreetly how Max wanted himself to be seen by others. We were sitting with a man who pretended to live his life as if his ancestral portraits were done in oils, not yellowing snapshots at Ellis Island.

Kate was a more complicated snob—a bit of the real thing. She had the family portraits, all right; only catch was, the stately walls where they had hung had been sold off cheap in debt-ridden panic generations ago. But my Kate had other things going for her. She was—her greatest gift? —always up for folly. And she loved me.

"Okay, okay, I surrender," Kate announced. A submissive shake of her head and a short curtain of her straight brown hair fell over her face: the end of act one. "Let's take a look."

THE DOORMAN WAS A huge sort who carried himself with the erect silver-haired dignity of a Brahmin secretary of state. August sun be damned, he was outfitted—this, too, surely part of the running arriviste gag—like a footman serving the court of a minor European principality. From the tails of his black frock coat to the tips of his starched wing collar, he was the white-gloved model of deference and civility.

He hurled the heavy entry door open without command and we followed as Max bounded through, his footsteps muffled by a royally red —the joke was turning a bit arch, I decided—carpet.

"Good afternoon, Mr. Fox," the doorman fawned.

Max, in his best upstairs/downstairs voice: "Good afternoon, William."

A splendidly proportioned lobby spread before us. The vast space had a frigid, museum quality, and I felt as if I were a gawking tourist making his way through a stately nineteenth-century home opened to the public: acres (or so it seemed) of marble checkerboard square floor, oversized Queen Anne chairs, unobtrusively positioned rosewood side tables, and fields of hunting prints. There was, however, one jarring, anachronistic touch. In a prominent corner of the lobby was a black lettered sign on a gleaming chrome pedestal: "All visitors must be announced."

Immediately my mind, caught in this rarefied time warp, was racing with imagined possibilities. The imperious William on the house phone: "There's a Mr. Henry James to see you, sir," or "A Mrs. Wharton downstairs, sir. Shall I send her up?" The young master responds: "Right you are, William. Do send her up."

Clearly, I was hooked on the place without even seeing the apartment.

Kate, once more obstinate, was fighting the building's charm. "A lot of pomp and circumstance, don't you think, Max?" she suggested.

Max smiled benignly. He had enough confidence in the surroundings to roll with Kate's little punches.

As we rode up in the elevator, it was clear his mute defense was amply justified. The elevator was glorious, a luxurious work of shiny brass and rich wood that provided the classiest way to the top since Jacob's ladder. Every day for the last thirty-seven years, Max proudly noted, its solid mahogany walls had been devotedly polished until the wood now glowed with a scrupulously well-bred patina.

"It's like a coffin," Kate complained in a voice loud enough to cause the liveried elevator man to grimace as though shot clean through the heart. Now Max frowned, finally annoyed.

"She's just obsessed with death, Max. Saw too many Bergman movies in college," I tried to joke, hoping to deflate the situation. But Kate, realizing she had drawn blood, was already quickly repentant. Raised a lady, not a fighter, she backed off.

"Well, actually it's more like a humidor," she airily conceded. God, she was a sucker for Max.

Once we entered the apartment, Max, though normally reserved, assumed a hearty tone, making all the necessary introductions with hail-fellow cheer. He needn't have gone to the trouble. Straight off it was clear old Mrs. Nicholas was a bit dotty and more than a bit in her cups.

"Well, hel-lo, hel-lo. So ver-ry nice to meet you," she erupted as she raised her highball glass toward Kate and me, part salute and part toast. Then with a deep gulp she drained the drink dry. Ice and all.

We exchanged the same knowing look: The good fathers were going to have a hell of a time with her, all right.

With courtly Max at her side and a fresh drink in her hand, Mrs. Nicholas gave us a weaving tour through the domain she was abdicating.

The apartment, like Mrs. Nicholas herself, was a well-preserved relic from a less complicated and more comfortable era. Its rooms were generous in size and accented with gracious architectural details—a working fireplace surrounded by an intricately carved black marble mantel; lofty beamed ceilings; panels of Georgian wall moldings; and hardwood parquet floors.

As we maneuvered our way through the Volkswagen-wide corridor which led to the white tiled kitchen, a quick glance into a tiny room beyond a half-parted door set my middle-class heart reeling. Over a narrow monklike bed covered with a liverish yellow spread hung a freshly pressed maid's uniform. My face must have betrayed my complicated, covetous excitement; and Max, my fellow traveler, threw me a conspiratorial glance.

But Mrs. Nicholas simply announced with an offhanded lèse majesté and a hiccup, "The maid's room. I'm sure it must have a bath." And the tour continued without even a pause to explore this stark corner of her turf.

As we moved through the place, Mrs. Nicholas dutifully opening every closet for our inspection, the apartment, to my mind at least, seemed not so much grand as it was solid—a home. In fact, irony of ironies, this is what months later Kate explained ultimately sold her: The six rooms were the sort of old-fashioned nest where one could raise a family.

The tour over, Max sat with Mrs. Nicholas on a Louis XVI fauteuil in the living room, smiling indulgently as his eyes furtively rolled heavenwards while he prayed, I'm sure, for an expedient rescue from her sotted loquaciousness. Kate and I took advantage of this diversion to huddle in the bedroom.

"What do you think?"

"We can't afford it, Russ."

"Forget about that. What do you think of the apartment? Do you like it?"

"It needs a paint job."

"True enough." Mrs. Nicholas had eagerly informed us that the month after her husband, Schuyler's, death she had the living room painted a "Nantucket sky blue." She had been taken: The walls were a Manhattan slush gray.

I went on: "So it needs a couple of buckets of paint. Painting's no big deal. But what about the apartment? Do you like it?"

Kate paused for a beat. Then another. Then she caved in. "Russ, we both know it's perfect."

I kissed her sweetly on the lips and said confidently, "Okay, now leave the rest to me." Hand in hand, we marched with celebratory deliberateness into the living room. Except now I was the one frantically thinking, "How the hell are we ever going to be able to afford this?"

THE ECONOMICS WERE rough but not impossible. Max, the old charmer, had negotiated a giveaway price from gin-soaked Mrs. Nicholas ("If she got any more for the place, it'd just go to the church," he rationalized). Still, the "giveaway" price—$22,500—was, after deducting the funds left from my $3,000 book advance, approximately $20,000 more than we had.

(Today the price seems like the deal of a lifetime: $22,500! Yet I was not impressed by the blue-chip opportunity Max had placed before me. Inflation, for me at least, was still a textbook, not a household word; and who could have guessed the sky's-the-limit spiral Manhattan real estate prices would start climbing within a few short years? Back then $22,500 didn't seem like a deal; it was just a lot of money.)

Once again Max rode to the rescue. He, without my even tossing out a hint, offered a $5,000 loan. My parents, much to my surprise and delight, loaned me half that amount, bringing our cash on hand to what seemed to me the astronomical total of $10,000. Yet we were $12,500 short.

That's when I found out about mortgages. Do you know you can walk into a bank and fill out a couple of forms saying that you're a college graduate, that you've never been arrested, not even for protesting ROTC, that you swear your future's as bright as any up-and-at-'em twenty-seven-year-old's and if the loan officer likes your Pepsodent smile and your prep school manners, then the check is—truly!—in the mail? I never knew that before. But it worked. Three weeks after I had resolutely pledged to Mrs. Nicholas' lawyer that we would come up with the dough, it was all, much to my colossal amazement, deposited into my checking account.

However, my acquisitive dream now coming true kept me tossing and turning each night. Here I was out of work and $20,000 in debt, my future mortgaged on the first of each month for the next thirty years. Only in America! I was beginning to wonder what Max and my grandiose ambitions—or was it pretensions?—had gotten me into. I was beginning to wonder if practical Kate had not been right all along. I was even beginning to wonder how to pay the movers, not to mention the $454 due for the first month's maintenance.

As it turned out, I needn't have worried. By the time we moved into the apartment two days before Thanksgiving, fate, acting through a couple of men talking in a hotel room in Germany, had turned my whole world upside down. I had a winner. Though the pub date was months away, people were already wild about *Hit Man!* The man jawing with my publisher at the Frankfurt Book Fair had, after just a read through a Xerox of the draft manuscript, pledged at least a quarter of a million dollars for the paperback rights to my book. More he promised, and the contract so stipulated, if the book did well in hard cover. "It's a true-life blood and guts adventure story that's more exciting than fiction," he decided. Who was I to argue? I might have been ashamed, but that's something else.

Oh, I knew what I had done: I had transcribed a few brief conversations with a small-time hood, persuaded myself to accept his obviously invented tales of macho gangstering, added some melodramatic embellishments of my own imagination, and then passed the whole thing off as a true story. Sure, the book was, as the paperback scout judged, a pretty snappy "blood and guts adventure story," but his insistence that *Hit Man!* was "more exciting than fiction" was not merely a publisher's hyperbole—it was a lie. Just about everything in *Hit Man!*, including the excitement implied by the title's attention-grabbing exclamation point, *was* fiction. Or at least exaggeration. But I simply let that remain my little secret. Besides, any misgivings I might have had were quite effectively washed away. When it rained that autumn, it poured pennies from subsidiary rights heaven.

So two days before Thanksgiving, our books still in cartons from the liquor store, our few pieces of furniture clustered temporarily in a corner of the long living room, we gathered in our new home to celebrate. Kate and I sat on the floor in front of the fireplace. Max, not the sort to sit cross-legged on any floor, stood above us, struggling to open a bottle of champagne. It was a production; Max pushing and pulling a bit too frantically. Finally there was the customary puckered *pop!* and the sparkling wine rushed out as Max belatedly remembered to look for glasses.

"A toast," I shouted as Kate distributed coffee mugs—everything else was still packed away, she apologized—brimming with bubbly.

"To Max, who made all this possible," Kate suggested. But Max would have none of that.

"Don't toast me," he insisted. "You don't even owe me any money."

I beamed at Kate: Max had been paid off with the first check from my paperback advance.

In a soft, almost morose voice Max continued, "Don't toast me. Everything I got in life came too late. When I was too old to enjoy it." Then he raised his mug toward me and, now more upbeat, said, "To

Russ, who was smart enough to meet up with success when he was still young."

A bit embarrassed by Max's praise, I turned to him and, my blue eyes radiating self-satisfied charm, my smile promiscuously sincere, confided, "I can't help it, Max, if I'm lucky."

"How about, To luck," I tried.

But Max overruled my squeamish false modesty. "To success," he shouted. Obediently I picked up his cue, and echoed, "To success." Only today do I suddenly recall that Kate remained silent; nobody wrote her lines. Still, she joined us as we wolfed down the bubbly. And then simultaneously, like three swells, we threw our coffee mugs crashing into the fireplace.

TO LUCK? To success?

Six harsh years later, the apartment is empty. Over the weekend, I packed up all that remained. The suddenly broom-clean 6 rms., 3 bths. await only the energy of some farseeing realtor to plunk down the next Adam and Eve into this empty, white-walled planet. Of course, how they work out their own particular Fall is up to them. That will be their story to tell.

But today, sitting on the uncomfortably hard wood floor in front of the naked fireplace, a beer in my hand for a farewell toast, there is no story to tell but Kate's and mine.

Oh, yes. And Max's. He wished me success and, always eager, I scrambled to the head of the class. My name was stenciled on his door. I sat at his desk. I became editor of *City*. And we are no longer friends. Russ Lewis made it big, all right.

Our story—Max's, Kate's, and mine—is not a tale of unusual daring and skill. It is simply a tale of how we made our way through life, three outsiders who felt their lives could become more than what they were. We set out to make our mark, and we did . . . only to wind up marking each other. A tale of schemes and dreams.

This is the story I have survived to tell.

If only I could . . . I have learned my limitations: The truth would never have a chance. I cannot be a camera.

But *he* can.

What I mean is, I am abandoning the narrative ship.

Regardless of what you think, this is no failure of will. It is an act of conscience; *Hit Man!* got away with bumping off the truth, but I still

suffered. Never again. Now, as the first person steps aside, I am granting
Max Fox, Kate Warner, and even Russ Lewis the freedom to go where
their lives actually took them, whatever the consequences. He can do,
say, and think things I can't admit to. They are now free to sin—without
my apologies. And anyway, it would be misleading if I lulled you into
accepting that the authorial I of today is the same Russ Lewis of yesterday. But enough! I must be careful not to give his plot away.

So as I sit here alone in this empty space, now seems as good a time
as any for me to sit back and let him, this third person, do the talking.
A bit of luck, there were five beers left in the fridge and I have lined
them up on the deep black marble mantel I once was so proud of; they
stand like divers awaiting their turn to rush off the board and take their
plunge. Let another of my beers dive off its high board and help your
narrator plunge into their rambling story, his story about them: the tale
I lived.

PART I
The Romance of Poverty

ONE

MAX FOX'S head was thumping. Struggling to sit up in the crumpled bed, he managed to open his eyes to buttonhole-narrow slits. His throat felt as dry as a stretch of tarpaper roof baking under the high noon Bowery sun. These weary symptoms, Max acknowledged with a sullen shake of his throbbing head as he shuffled to the bathroom, were despairingly familiar, if not routine. No, this was not an auspicious start to what was left of this momentous day: January 31, 1954.

The shock of cold water splashing against his face helped. Staring into the bathroom mirror, he ignored the jagged hairline crack that split the toothpaste-spotted glass like an avenging biblical thunderbolt, and he began to focus on last night's decision. Jonathan Trout and he had shaken on it: They would publish a magazine. "We have the advantage of being extremely naive," Jonathan had said. "There's nothing for us to live up to except our instincts. What can go wrong?" Max, always the cynic, had replied, "Everything." But before that reality could overwhelm their confidence, Jonathan took charge: "We'll make it all public and official at your birthday party tomorrow night." And Max, trapped yet eager, agreed.

Now another glance into the cracked mirror and Max quickly remembered that his concerns about vengeance were larger than casual metaphors. There had been a beer or two last night to celebrate their decision, he now recalled with a flutter of contrition, and then he had weaved his way to the pay phone in the back of the San Remo to make a hasty call to Janey. "I think I've found what I've been waiting for," he had told her, "and I want you to be the first to know." He would reveal no more until lunch tomorrow. "One-ish?" she suggested and Max, his ambition lubricated by drink, found no problem with such a civilized hour. But that was last night. The watch on his wrist today was more knowing: The little hand was pointing directly at the five and the big hand had darted past the three and just wouldn't slow down. He wondered how long Janey had waited before she had executed one of her well-practiced huffs. Oh well, he sighed. He'd catch up with her at the party. Perhaps she'd understand, he reasoned. But then he knew it didn't matter. Even if Janey Leventhal understood, she would still move in for the kill. There would be repercussions.

Once more a woebegone shake of the head. But this admonishment was short-lived; there was too much to do today, too much to set right to pursue dead ends. Reaching for an opaque plastic cup, he shook his shoulders furiously as if to throw off any remnants of self-criticism; and, as tepid water filled the cup, he let loose with a small but nevertheless celebratory smile. He gargled noisily, finally spraying the water about the sink. He was feeling better.

After another brisk slap of tap water against his face, he was prepared to take on the mirror once again. This time he could handle what he saw. His first thought: I don't look forty. A less tortured observer, though, might have noted the precisely parted thick black hair, the impish twinkle in the mocha-brown eyes, and the dimples flanking each corner of a tight but still quietly naughty smile and come up with another conclusion: What a rogue. Regardless, Max enjoyed wearing his charmer's face. It was his confidence; it reinforced what he pretended to be. Maybe, he decided in these last moments of reflected vanity, he might be able to pull this whole thing off. And, more than anything ever before in his desultory life, Max Fox was rooting for *City* magazine, his magazine, to work.

It takes, Max knew, a bold and foolish courage to wake up in the afternoon debilitatingly hung over just hours before your fortieth birthday party, fully understanding you're a failure, and yet still sincerely believing you're going to wake up cozy with stupefying success 364 days from now on your forty-first birthday. But this is precisely how Max felt on that dim January day in 1954.

As he padded barefoot back into the small bedroom, Max could find little support for his bravado in the surroundings. Nearly all the furniture in the two-room apartment on the top floor of a tenement straddling the border between Little Italy and the Bowery had been reclaimed from the streets, relics discarded by people getting on to better things. Nevertheless, Max had put some energy into one grand obsessive touch, a gesture he hoped was jampacked with the proof that while he might not be a man of means, at least he was a man of taste: a cherished distinction. Also, he truly adored his clocks.

Arranged with the mad precision of totems in an Oriental shrine—one had the feeling that to tinker with their positioning would somehow result in corresponding fluctuations in Max's karma—his clocks stood in a wide semicircle on a bronze but well-thumped chest emblazoned with an Austrian double eagle that he had found abandoned amongst less spectacular garbage on East 11th Street. He had bought most of the clocks on the cheap from selected antique stores hidden in the dark beneath the Third Avenue El. Still his collection—just being able to drop this hefty word in a casual conversation puffed Max up with the weight of at least some accomplishment—not only added a bit of sparkle to his austere digs, but also revealed a modest connoisseurship. There was a late-nineteenth-century mantel clock with a bemused Eve winking across its circular dial at a thoroughly confused Adam; a cumbersome Chinese teakwood clock on a fluted stand; an octagonal deco number with self-important black Arabic numerals and steel-blue hands; a hoity, many-tiered Empire model done up in gilt and displaying a fierce eagle, all wingspread and determination; and a silly Viennese standing clock enameled with Diana and Actaeon frolicking in a mythical countryside under the encouraging gaze of an envious satyr—to hit just the high points in Max's collection. Yet despite the careful eclecticism of his choices, Max's clocks had a common foible: None of them worked. Max preferred to pass off this shortcoming as a circumstance forced on him by economy. However, the truth was, it was a deliberate touch. Max already was a man painfully well aware of his heading into middle age; he didn't need further reinforcement of that annoying reality. He drew the line at the possibility of having to live with the constant ticks, chimes, and bongs of his youth loudly and mawkishly slipping away.

And yet while he had contrived to have his clocks stand outside of Time, mute *objets* reduced to display, there was little he could do about the view from his apartment: it looked out on a cemetery. The metaphysical implications of this small triangular plot of century-old headstones was irrefutable. So Max made the best of a depressing situation and positioned his mattress and bedspring to survey fully this grim terrain. "The Andrew Marvell seduction technique," Max had explained to Jonathan. "Satisfaction guaranteed." And this was no barroom exaggeration: there were too many coy Village girls who had first heard the liberating clippety-clop of Time's winged chariot as they lay stretched out on Max's bed.

But as Max now dressed for his fortieth birthday party, he realized he could no longer rely on symbols and techniques to assuage painful truths; that is, unless he was prepared to deal with the possibility that he was destined to be a nobody.

It wasn't that he had previously been afraid to get involved in the hectic errands of life. Rather, he had been reluctant, more a feeling of reserve than one of will. He was a short man, perhaps five six or seven in his wingtips, but he had never felt small. And he had no doubts that when necessary he could even be brave. Max had found the strength to bury his father, a humorless high school history teacher, when he was fifteen and had managed to hang around Boston (actually Roxbury, but Max never gave out many details) another eight years while cancer destroyed his mother. Then, dry-eyed and virtually penniless, he headed to New York. Of course he gravitated to the Village. The war came and, to his own amazement, Max found himself storming Pacific beaches with machine gun blasting gusto. Yet as a civilian Max had been sticking to the sidelines—letting the G.I. Bill pay for some courses at The New School; hanging out at Village bars; writing an occasional article for a hastily put together encyclopedia whose editor was a drinking buddy. And then—as if in an instant—he was forty.

Last night with Jonathan at the San Remo Tavern, Max knew the meandering had come to an abrupt end. As soon as they shook hands, the pact cemented, the plan for the magazine finalized, he had felt as if he were back in the overpowering reality of combat: the struggle to transcend huge fears and yet the rush of confidence that you'll find what it takes to do it. For all along, despite the years of aimless lethargy, Max had been certain he was just waiting his turn. Failure, and its depressing bunkmate, poverty, were too commonplace a destiny, Max felt, for a man who was so attuned to his own, however passive, uniqueness. *City* magazine, his vision, his idea, would also be his chance: His adventure.

Max finished putting on his well-worn tweeds and, heading out the door, wrapped a long scarf once, then twice around his neck. He walked west across the Village toward Jonathan's apartment. The glows of neon and electric lights were beginning to jingle through the sharp city night. That always made Max feel better. But as he approached the front stoop of Jonathan's building, his resolve began to fall apart. Still, he didn't turn back. Instead, he took a deep breath and, almost fortified, made a silent birthday wish: I hope I can get through the evening. Then he rang the buzzer. There was no turning back.

TWO

JONATHAN TROUT watched as Janey Leventhal made her way across the crowded room. There was an angry crackle in her walk as if she were grinding glass with each sharp crunch of her heels. He was painfully aware he wasn't up for this sort of confrontation.

"Where the hell is Max?" she blurted out while Jonathan stood a few safe feet away. And, moving closer, she continued: "He was supposed to meet me for lunch, but the bastard didn't show. Big talk last night on the phone, all right. But I should have known he was just killing time. The Village wiseman waiting for someone to buy the next round. Now where the hell is he? This is his birthday party, isn't it?"

"I saw him just a minute ago," Jonathan tried, all easy cheer. Janey stared hard, straight at him; and, immediately cowered, he now spoke more softly into the bottom of his glass of Scotch. "He's got to be around here someplace . . ." The unfinished thought drifted off into a small swishing sea of ice cubes and liquor.

"Well, he had better be here." Sharing her frustration served to inflame her anger; six short, tough words and Janey was out for blood.

"Now Ahm surah, Janey . . ." Jonathan began, his anxiety over spilling the beans tumbling out instinctively in a dash of ancestral southern charm.

But Janey's days of sipping juleps on Jonathan's rhetorical verandas had ended long ago. Tonight she was marching through Georgia.

"Fuck you, Jonathan." And the lady, showing no mercy, stomped off, blazing a trail of indignant, smoldering fury across the party.

Taking in this exit, Jonathan felt relief: He hadn't broken down under Janey's questioning. And he had to laugh: She had bumped so forcefully into Curtis, a mildew-complexioned poet obliviously blocking her path, that the innocent bystander was literally turned around in midsentence. Then, as she vanished into the next room, Jonathan had to wonder: What was going to happen when Janey discovered that Max— no longer just his friend but, for twenty-four hours now, officially his business partner—had been huddled in a corner talking and drinking steadily for the past hour with Diane Farrell?

TONIGHT WAS THE exception. There was solid reason for Jane Leventhal's anger. Usually, though, her mood was quickly rubbed raw without the coincidence of cause.

At thirty-one, Janey was convinced she had grown up into one of those unfortunate people who somehow always manage to miss. If things could have just gone the other way, she imagined as she lay alone in bed at night. With a bit of luck, it could have worked out. But it didn't. The last seat was always taken a minute ago; the last one in her size was always just sold. Janey knew she was being dealt a dirty deal: She was the daughter of a Brooklyn couple who could never seem to save enough money to buy a house on Long Island; the graduate of a middling women's college filled with the girls who were wait-listed by at least one of the Seven Sisters; a registered nurse who had almost made it into med school and never seemed to have more than a casual date with a doctor; and a woman whose nose was too sharp in profile, hair not really dark enough to be thought of as black, and lips too full to be sensuous. Life, Janey agonized, must have graded her B minus at birth.

Except what made Janey so socially dangerous (as compared to her more congenially repressed or socialized acquaintances who led their small lives with only small whimpers) was her desire to get the best seat in the house. She, though riddled with public insecurities, insisted to herself in tirades of private passion that she deserved better; and she never stopped finding someone else to blame for grabbing the slender piece of the good time that should have been hers. Regardless of the arena or the audience, she was determined to go down loudly swinging.

If one had the energy or the interest to think through her aggressive personality, one could be forgiving: Insecure Janey was going straight for the jugular because she was certain you were preparing to do the same number on her. But if you didn't take the time, you might walk away with a forlorn shrug: This woman was a real pill.

For the past eight years Max Fox had been alternating between taking the trouble to think his way through her wounding defensiveness and, as mood or the tantalizing promise of a new opportunity led him astray, curtly shrugging her off. Of course, this ambivalent behavior exacerbated all of Janey's problems; and, years later, Max's cruel casualness would be recalled by a vindictive Janey with devastating consequences. Twenty years from now, Max would both realize and admit his blame: In their tumultuous and mercurial courtship, their marriage—and their life together—was doomed.

It would be stitching the seams of their relationship too hopelessly tight, though, if one didn't suggest Max and Janey found something if not wonderful, at least comforting in each other. At first. To understand this, you have to consider the sort of rakish figure Max cut throughout the Village in the early fifties; and to understand that, it also helps to appreciate the mood filling Max and his friends.

Max came back from the Pacific with no larger plan than to watch life drift aimlessly by. He returned to Greenwich Village and, taking up with a group of laid-back thinkers and big talkers, found a window seat where he could glance out at the opaque muddle of the Cold War years. Mostly, the seat happened to be at a table in the San Remo, the Cedar, or the White Horse Tavern. With a bottle of Guinness in his hand—tweedy Max always liked a touch of British class—he would listen as his friends haphazardly kicked about wide-ranging ideas; say, the gist of a book that had to be read; or a political solution that seemed guaranteed to maximize the common good; or simply the name of a new girl who had to be seen to be believed. The very style and form of their casual lives was part of their thumbing their noses at those (to use the best-selling sociological nomenclature of the time) other-directed organizational men in their gray flannel suits.

Max would look back at those lazy days with a cynicism made more cutting by his subsequent success. "We weren't a lost generation," he complained. "There was just no place we wanted to go." His criticism was largely self-directed; he wondered what he might have accomplished if he had gotten more of a jump on life. And to Russ Lewis, more than twenty-five years later, he would put down the whole beat scene with a snarl: "You know why they called it the beat generation? Because we spent all our time beating around the bush. We never got anything done."

Yet Max Fox, though understandably bitter, was being too hard on himself. It was during these years of hanging out, of sitting around an oak table in a Village bar, that Max nurtured his greatest gift, the talent that would make his career and his fortune—the ability to listen.

This is no small skill. Max would sit back, puffing pensively on his pipe, his soft brown eyes warming up to the flow of the conversation; and then it would not be long before whoever was talking was convinced Max Fox—above all men—genuinely understood what he was going on about. Max was the one, even as a young man, to whom people chose to pour out their broken hearts and their brooding minds. And while most of the nation in the fifties was drawn tight-lipped into a stupefying silence,

Max, always lucky, happened to find himself in the center of vocal dissent. Greenwich Village was the one place where it remained still possible to hear America singing—however off-key.

Max listened attentively. He was always curious. He was the romantic who signed on with anyone going on a rhetorical expedition after any ideal. He was their barroom editor before he had a magazine.

This is what Janey found in him: A man who would listen to her the way no one had ever before. And a man who could elevate her life from the continuing despair of near misses; for, though she never trusted him enough to share her bruised faith and her unrealized expectations, she knew Max would someday be a winner. While Max, similarly unsharing, found in Janey a bit of what he needed: She would be the anchor, the solid girl with a conventional job whose normalness would be a comfort whenever the tumult of ideas or sharp edge of Village craziness seemed too destructive. Max, though it would have pained him to admit it, confronted life with the instincts of an editor—he relished adventure, but when the day was done he wanted to get a good night's sleep in his own bed.

So, considering the adjoining neighborhoods of their daily wanderings and the complementary proximity of their needs, when Janey and a group of giggling nurses from St. Vincent's Hospital walked across the Village on a wintry evening for a beer at the San Remo, it didn't take much cajoling of destiny to have Max, Guinness in hand, waiting there eager to meet her.

NOT THAT MAX and Janey hit it off right away. Actually, Jonathan Trout—would-be abstract expressionist by way of a Georgia plantation childhood (his father had been the Master of Fox Hounds), a Yale education (Skull and Bones) originally interrupted by a tour as a paratrooper, and then permanently abandoned as he decided to spend the postwar years either hurling paint at a cluttered canvas or with his elbow not far from Max Fox's glass—was first struck by the strange, testy charm of the nurse from Queens.

Jonathan and Janey went through a brief, no-hard-feelings affair; while there was never any of that waiting-for-the-phone-to-ring anticipation that rattles the defenseless heart, their three weeks together left enough tender moments to make a valued friendship possible. In this, Janey was like a lot of women who started hanging out in the Village. Having a short affair with aristocratically soulful Jonathan Trout was part of the Village experience, part of the passage from undergraduate to bohemian.

Max had watched it all happen dozens of times. He was convinced the secret of his friend's flypaper appeal was not really his looks or his graceful southern pedigree. Sure, Max had overheard women in the Cedar or the San Remo going on about Jonathan's sky blue eyes, his helter-skelter bushy blond hair, and his closely trimmed, almost auburn beard —a disconcerting shade darker than his hair. But, the way Max saw it, it was Jonathan's slow, confident, even sometimes pedantic manner that made him so irresistible to the sort of confused girl who would come to the Village looking for neatly paragraphed answers to still unarticulated questions.

Jonathan was so patient, so concerned. Not like Max, who was only a listener, a witness. Jonathan, a guru, gave answers. His complete absorption in the problems and troubled concerns of these women was no Lothario's put-on. Over a beer these young women would pour out heartfelt tales of woe or longing; and Jonathan would follow with a full-winded lecture bogged down with cumbersome yet rational advice. It was a mannered performance so many of these girls found magically reminiscent of the English lit or sociology professor with whom they had fallen into puppyish unconsummated love only a few short semesters ago. Now, feeling their ripe adulthood and kicky with their beatnik freedom, these women had a chance to show they were no longer restrained undergraduates. Lucky Jonathan.

Inevitably, these flings fell apart as the women came to a crushing realization—There was no future with Jonathan; he could only help you get over the past. His let-me-help-you-work-it-all-out manner was an authentic, but still drearily tedious preoccupation. It was no long-term substitute for the lover who would take them off to new, friskier situations. Once these girls had cataloged a piece of their pasts and got a sense of the high-bouncing possibilities now open to them, the time to shake hands good-by with Jonathan would arrive. There would be a kiss on the cheek and a pledge of eternal friendship; and then, feeling good about themselves, they would scoot off to find the someone with whom they would build a new and complicated future.

For Janey Leventhal, as well as for Jonathan Trout, this overwhelmingly complicated future would be with Max Fox.

THREE

IT DIDN'T TAKE Janey much searching through the party to find Max. She found him by the bar. He looked like he had been there for a while. And had been huddling with Diane Farrell even longer.

"You wanted to talk . . . or are you busy?"

"No, no. I've been waiting for you to get here."

"So I see," said Janey, fixing Diane with a merciless stare. But Diane stood her ground. And then they both looked to Max.

He was a magnet drawing fields of charged tension from their iron wills. It clearly would only get worse. "You'll excuse us, won't you, Diane," he said quickly.

"Birthday boy's prerogative," Diane agreed, though not without getting off a trouble-making wink. But before Janey could respond, Max got a firm grip on her elbow and led her to into the john.

"Now what are you up to, Max?" Janey complained as Max locked the bathroom door.

"Just wanted a spot where we could talk. Only place here where there's any privacy." Max, glass firmly in one hand, put his free arm loosely around Janey. He was feeling a couple of drinks, but it was a sincere gesture. Full of the occasion, Max wanted her to share it.

"I've reached a decision, Janey."

Still she taunted. "I know. Decisions and decisions. And in the morning when you're sober, there'll be revisions and revisions."

Instantly weary, Max removed his arm from her shoulder and then took a fortifying sip of Scotch. The liquor helped; he no longer hoped for the strength to deal with Janey, only the desire.

She moved across the narrow room and sat on the edge of the tub. Max, facing Janey, leaned against the sink; it took him by surprise as he realized he needed the support. There was a world of white tile between them.

"No, not this time," he said with a somber shake of his head. "Anyway, a forty-year-old man doesn't have the luxury of making too many decisions. He takes stands."

"Until he runs away from them."

"I've got nowhere to run."

Only now did Janey back off. She realized Max wasn't kicking around half-tight in despair; he was serious. His tone, his resignation punctured her defenses. Seeing Max so stripped, for once so vulnerable, she wanted to ache for him.

But still Janey remained ready to dodge the anticipated cross fire. He was an arm's length away, yet she kept her seat. Just as Max, even though pleasantly anesthetized by the quality Scotch, proceeded with similar caution. He knew better than to reach out to her. It was a stand-off: They were aware of each other's fears; and they both resented the accuracy of the other's insight.

Finally Janey, proceeding carefully, tried again. "Okay, what's the big decision?"

He didn't answer straight off. His eyes darted about the locked room as if, now his last chance, he was measuring the distance to the nearest exit. But he didn't run. Instead, hitching up his resolve, he tried to explain it all to Janey. This was his opportunity for a private rehearsal of a soon to be public speech.

"You remember," he began, "how Jonathan and I have been talking about starting a magazine. Well, we're finally going to do it. . . ."

ONE HALF HOUR LATER Max, waving about a fresh glass of Scotch, stood in the center of the packed living room as he asked and finally shouted for quiet. When the revelers managed to settle down, Max sensed their impatience; he knew he wouldn't have them for long. This wasn't, though, his big worry. He was more concerned about convincing himself he could pull off the staunch center-stage part he was—for the first time in his life!—attempting to play.

With Janey he had been honest; he knew he couldn't fool her, anyway. She saw he was shaking with both vague and specific terrors— terror of the size and appropriateness of his challenge; terror of sustaining the courage needed to make it work; and even terror of his being able to delve deep enough into his own mind to find the pure intelligence necessary to realize and convey his rebel's vision of journalism.

From this night on there would be no choice but to grapple with these terrors. Max understood he would have to stand up and challenge his fears. Just as he now, staring toward his restlessly quieted friends, had no alternative after another swallow of Scotch but to find an appropriately flippant confidence in his voice and give it his best shot.

"I bet a lot of you think I waste most of my time," he began with a tipsy smile.

"Of course we do. We're with you most of the time," someone called back.

Max, in no hurry, went along with their laughter. When there was quiet, he continued. "But one day I realized I wasn't wasting my time. I was thinking."

"You sure you weren't just hung over, Max?" challenged an irritatingly high-pitched voice.

"At first I figured I was," he joked, "but this same idea . . . a murky but still wonderful plan, really, kept on popping up even when I wasn't pretty deep in my cups. I couldn't get rid of it. That's when I decided to try it out on our host, Jonathan Trout. Big help he was. You're just bagged, he told me. Occupational hazard when you hang around bars. Sleep it off. You'll forget it in the morning. But come the next morning, while I damn well was sleeping. . . ."

"With whom, Max?" the high-pitched voice again broke through. And naturally the crowd hooted. That got to Janey; but she bit down on her lip and kept quiet. Max shared only a mischievous smile.

"Anway," he continued, "Jonathan called me up and told me maybe he was crazy, too; but now he couldn't stop thinking about my idea. Kept him up all night, he complained. So we figured we both couldn't be wrong. That's when the two of us starting scheming in earnest. We've been at it for the past month. And tonight we're making it official. Jonathan Trout and I are starting a magazine."

"Hear, hear," someone—probably a Rhodes scholar gone astray—shouted. There was even, Max noted with delight, some applause.

No longer hesitant, he went on: "The magazine is going to be called *City*. Jonathan's going to be the publisher. After all, it's his money we're risking. [A background of uneasy giggles at Max's frankness.] And I'm going to be editor." A stagy bow by the new editor was rewarded with drunkenly contrived applause.

"The titles sound a bit grand, don't they? But I figure if a man can get himself through forty years, he might as well get to call himself at least an editor." The audience was stepping into Max's playfulness; they serenaded him with catcalls.

He let their boisterousness run wild for a minute; and then he pulled them in tight. "Actually, the most important title on the masthead of this magazine is going to be writer. *City* is going to be a writer's magazine. Your magazine. Just as your ideas, crazy as they may seem to me and you, are going to make it work.

"I mean, look at us. We're sitting in the center of the universe."

Someone digged, "And thank God it's rent controlled."

"That's the only thing that's controlled down here in Greenwich Village," Max shot back. "This is the one place in America where ideas are still running wild. Where people are not sleepwalking. Look at us: We're hip. They're square. And the pages of *City* are going to drive this difference home to the rest of the country."

He paused for his punch line. "And what I'm asking all of you to do is nothing more than this: Help me reinvent journalism."

The unsuspected scale of his ambition was greeted by a faintly censorious murmur, but Max was too excited to stop:

"I want *City* to be filled with whatever people in the Village happen to be thinking about that week. Let it all hang out. I want someone in Iowa to read through the magazine and come away with the feeling that he spent a night hanging around the White Horse. Well, maybe not that sloppy. [Now the background laughter only encouraged his oratory; he decided he had the crowd hooked.] But I want that edge. That feistiness. That uniqueness of ideas, of sensibility. You can write about anything— anything as long as you can keep my interest for a page or two. And if I'm interested, I'm convinced there will be a hell of a lot of people who'll also be interested. So convinced, that I'm willing to bet the rest of my life on it."

"Not to mention my money." Jonathan hopped in. He had a glimpse of the sentimental destination where the liquor and the energy of Max's resolution were taking his friend; and he knew such mawkish public confessions would be regretted in the morning.

"Wooh now, Max," he intervened when the laughter subsided. "We've all heard enough for one night. I'm getting almost sober, my friend. Wasn't this supposed to be a party . . . a birthday party. Come on," he called to the crowd, "how about a toast to the birthday boy."

"Hey, let's not forget our magazine. To *City*," Max rushed in.

Glasses were clinked and raised. And then it was only moments before noise and new fun washed over the memory of Max's speech; yet, as the party moved ahead Max remained oddly isolated, a solitary figure leaning without even realizing it against the bridge table that served as the makeshift bar: A man silently celebrating his fortieth birthday, lost in the glory of his thoughts, pursuing the wonderfully exciting nearness of his suddenly important future.

A PRETTY FACE brought Max back to the present.

"Where *are* you, Max?" Diane Farrell teased.

For an instant Max didn't even hear her; he was triumphantly rounding some third base of the mind.

"Now, Maxie," she coaxed, "even birthday boys shouldn't have so much to drink." Diane casually traced a long-nailed finger along the lapel of his herringbone jacket; slowly the finger inched across his chest toward the fat part of his tie. He was becoming aware of her presence; and as his pensive mood slipped, his private ball game was abruptly called on account of stormy weather.

"I'm not drunk."

A finger was circling a button on his shirt. The very tip of an exquisitely chiseled nail traveled round and round. She enjoyed making it a slow journey.

"Of course not, Maxie."

". . . no . . . I'm really not." He tried to stand convincingly straight. It was a struggle, but he made it. He looked directly into her face.

It was a face worth his efforts—particularly tonight.

Everyone in the Village knew about Diane Farrell's famous face. Her well-scrubbed midwestern looks were so classically American, so profoundly wholesome that of course there had to be money in them. Diane's shining pleasantness was so refined, her genuineness so transcendent that she stood out as more than a type: She was an ideal. Staring at you from a page in a *Good Housekeeping*, Diane was the housewife fathers who knew best wanted to come home too. It didn't take her long to become a hot property. Account executives up and down Madison Avenue were convinced her easy smile gave any product a natural, calico appeal. Diane's blond-haired, blue-eyed beauty was already earning her as much as $75 a day; and it seemed to be only a matter of time before Diane, too conspicuous a success, would have to move uptown.

Tonight, though, Max was finding Diane's wholesome looks more thrilling. Her smile curled about the corners of her mouth like a backseat come-on. And the big blue eyes, normally the perfect blue of a suburban pool, were flashing a similarly provocative message: This woman wasn't just giving Max the eye; she was leering at him.

He had met Diane over a year ago when she had first come to New York hoping to be a ballerina. This remained her ambition, but not, thanks to her marvelous face, the way she was required to earn her living. Still, each day she practiced. And while Max was no authority on dance, he had long ago come to the hot-blooded conclusion that all those hours of sweaty practice must have been what made Diane's legs so perfect. She had fantastically sculpted, kick-'em-high legs; and Max had spent a tipsy evening or two wrapping them tight around his fantasies. There was also, Max had learned over these convivial drinking bouts with Diane, a 4.0 mind to go with the high-scoring body. She was a woman who cared about ideas; Max imagined her underlined books would have wise notes written in the margins.

Of course Diane was the sort of woman Janey hated. The only pleasure she could find in the company of such a knockout was in speculating about the cosmic price Diane would have to pay out to the easily conned devil with whom this midwesterner had apparently struck her bargain.

Yet Janey, mired in the rut of her own life, would never have guessed the downside to being Diane. She would not have understood what was eating quietly away at the woman. Diane was doomed simply because she was aware how special she really was. Invariably in all her relationships there would come the crucial late-night moment when she would measure all her beaux against the luxuriously special package which was her dowry; and in these quiet hours before dawn she would realize she was coming up with the short end. So, unsatisfied but still game, she would continue auditioning new co-stars, searching for the one man who could give her something as good as he would be getting.

And tonight, fresh from his birthday performance, Diane had decided to give Max his chance.

FOUR

MAX continued staring at Diane and, too drunk to work up an explanation, decided there was no choice but to lie. "I'm sober as a judge," he insisted.

"If you say so."

Max pulled himself up even straighter. He would at least try to look the part.

"Okay." Diane shrugged. "I'm convinced."

Then Max made his mistake. What started out as a decorous nod of agreement exploded into a full-scale alert: As soon as he tipped his head, his nose began to fly toward the floor like a yo-yo.

That did it. "Well . . . perhaps I'm a little tipsy," he admitted.

Diane rushed in to second this verdict: "Smashed."

"Uh-huh."

And this time Max remembered not to nod. Instead, he poured himself another four fingers of Haig and Haig. Maybe a pinkie's worth managed to make it into the glass; his shoes, to his embarrassment, were soaked. He hadn't expected it to be such a complicated procedure.

He tried to maintain some dignity, though. "Join me?" he offered, ignoring the puddle of liquor that was beginning to soak through his shoes.

"For a drink?" Diane answered; and her fingers resumed their slow strut across his chest.

Max was drunk, but not that drunk. He glanced about the room: Janey was nowhere to be found. He hoped she was in the john. And then, for no rational reason, he decided Janey must have already left; perhaps she had to be on duty at the hospital late tonight. It was an illogical deduction; but Max Fox, a pragmatist, found it truly liberating.

"For a start," Max threw out gamely.

So Diane saw him and raised him: "Why don't we skip the preliminaries."

Max put down his glass and looked deeply into the pool of blue shining in her eyes. Her adventurous fingers dancing across his chest continued to hit their mark unerringly: five tactile Rockettes kicking it high to each drumbeat of his heart. Her very nearness was excitement. Desire was no longer simply nudging him; a twenty-mule team was galloping out of control, shoving and dragging him along, while Diane, with just one cool look, was giving the team the whip.

"What do you have in mind?" Max asked vaguely.

But Diane could handle things. "I think we both could use some air," she announced.

Without another word, Diane walked—and Max did not miss a promise more valuable than words made by that swaying walk—across the living room. She held open the front door of Jonathan's apartment. He looked at her and understood she would wait only a moment.

Max didn't let her wait that long.

THE HALLWAY WAS LIT by a naked neon bulb. In this flickering light he kissed her once. And then again. And then with startling abandon. Diane gasped; the thrill spilled from her with a small, high moan.

"That felt good . . . mmn . . . very good," she whispered. They were still clutching each other; his fingers massaged a tiny sweet space beneath her ear. Max kissed her once again, a long deep kiss; and then he relaxed his hold.

"What do you want to do?" he asked. "Should we go somewhere and get a drink?"

"You've had enough to drink," she answered. "Hold me." And she urged, "*Harder*."

How can one explain what happened next? Is it enough to say Diane was right—Max had had enough to drink; perhaps he shouldn't be faulted for the way his mind was working? Or, simply that a proposition like the one Diane was suggesting could make anyone fuzzy? And there was precedent—of a sort. Often on a sticky summer's night Jonathan and Max would take their problems and a couple of six-packs up to the airy isolation of Jonathan's roof. Surrounded by the summer stars, the two friends would drink until their emotional inconveniences were resolved; or until they were happy enough not to focus on them. The stairwell behind the brown metal door at the end of the dimly lit hall where the eager couple now stood wrapped about each other had always served Max well in the past.

So given these happy associations, Diane's wonderfully lustful impatience, and Max's totally soused condition, it did make some sense when Max suggested that the shortest distance between desire and consummation lay, if not precisely in a straight line, at least in a rickety stairwell to the roof. Some sense, but not much. After all, the stars on Max's birthday were shining on a frosty January night.

This time Max held open the door. Diane reached out for the hand he was trailing behind him as, no words necessary, Max led the way up the tin-plated stairway toward heaven.

Up on the frigid roof, Max and Diane kept warm by feverishly tugging, pulling, unbuttoning, unzipping, and unlatching several nuisance layers of constricting clothes.

A centrally heated floor below, though, things were really beginning to warm up: Janey was once again interrogating Jonathan as to Max's whereabouts.

Jonathan never had a chance. His ignorance was unconvincing. She stomped away from Jonathan, determined to track down the facts.

After pestering enough people she found her answer. Even Diane Farrell's exits do not go unnoticed.

"Sure, Janey, I saw him," Curtis, the emaciated poet, revealed, taking his revenge. "I saw Max leaving with Diane Farrell about ten minutes ago."

"Are you certain?"

"Positive." The poet was very eager. "Our new editor just sparkled with the look of man suddenly seeing a new world to conquer. I took one look at Max heading off with the beauteous Diane and thought of Keats. You know, his wonderful line about Cortes staring out at the Pacific for the first time. How does it go . . . ?"

Janey didn't wait around for the recitation. She slammed out of the party in an angry flash. Her charged-up mind instantly grabbed and, with all her furious might, held on to a very tight decision: Max had abused her for the last time. She was reeling with regret, but standing in the hallway outside Jonathan's apartment, she made a silent vow: She would never speak to Max Fox again.

It was an intransigent oath she undoubtedly had every intention of stubbornly keeping; but forces were at work that birthday night which were even stronger than Janey's black anger. For just at the moment when Janey was blazing her vow of silence into the thick stone of her conviction, she noticed that the door leading to the roof was ajar. Maybe she wanted the succor of a starry night; or maybe it was a feminine sixth sense pushing her through half-opened doors. All that is certain is she was propelled up the stairway, her sharp high-heeled footsteps ringing clear on the tin steps as she rushed ahead.

Max, meanwhile, was exploring other areas; and circumstances were also getting beyond his control. Not that many men wouldn't have traded their most prized moments for the delicious anxiety Max was suffering.

Here's what Max—literally—was up against: Diane, her long neck arched splendidly back, her rosebud nipples frosty pink and high in the air, was sitting astride him. She bounced on top of him in the cold, moving forcefully to a private rhythm. She must have been listening to this secret beat very, very carefully, so intent, so concentrated was the glaze masking her face. Yet it was a moment and a position that was Diane's inspiration. Many men would have settled for this. But not this birthday boy. Before either the ruthlessly intruding cold or, more likely, the orgasmic burst which was preparing to rip through his entire being brought these *al fresco* proceedings to an abrupt end, Max, never a quitter, was determined to have it his way. Nothing was going to keep him from climbing on top and having Diane's two sensationally long legs laced around him reaching high for the stars.

Except Janey.

Max, twisting with body English, was finagling to turn his and Diane's whole world upside down when Janey walked onto the roof. Her eyes opened wide as they filled with the wretched scene. Two swift words broke her vow of silence: "You shit," while Max, suddenly no longer interested, felt Diane's legs wrapping even tighter around him. Poor girl, he realized; she was trying to curl up and hide.

But there was no place to hide. And Janey was all fury. If she had a gun, she surely would have shot Max dead. Fortunately, Janey had to resort to metaphor.

While the interlocked couple looked on in mute fascination, Janey quickly set about gathering armfuls of the clothing that had been scattered pell-mell about the connubial tar paper. The sloppy piles of inner and outer garments in her arms, Janey marched to the very edge of the roof. Grimly silent, yet smiling wickedly, she hurled the clothes over the top. As she watched the flapping garments fly toward the ground—a lacy bra; clunky wingtip shoes; the tweed jacket; pink panties; a silkish red dress; a button-down white shirt—she could not help wishing she had possessed the strength necessary to have cast the two offending lovers into this seven-story free fall.

But before Max's shirt had hit the ground, Janey had stormed from the roof; and, she was certain, out of Max Fox's life for good.

With the fierce slam of the roof door, Diane released her exquisite grip on Max.

"What the hell are we going to do now?" she asked. Her control had vanished with her clothes.

Max, no longer drunk, was complacent. There was just enough absurdity in the course of the entire evening to allow him to accept, perhaps even enjoy, the hapless mortification of the last few minutes. In the morning, he anticipated, life would breed its own excuses. But tonight was his birthday.

"Before we get too cold," he suggested, "I don't think it would do us any harm to finish what we started."

"Only way to keep from freezing, I guess," Diane agreed, and attempted a coy smile; it immediately gave way to a rickety shiver.

"Keep me warm, Maxie," she begged.

"Like this?" His hands began to move in smooth, even circles over her body.

"Yes . . . like that . . . yes."

Her flesh was as white and cold as marble in the night. It was a fantasy: The sculptor brings his statue to life.

". . . mn . . . Maxie . . . MaxieMaxie . . ."

All else was pushed away. The private circle tightened. And what had begun in a drunken frenzy was finished in a very icy recklessness.

"'I'M GOING TO marry Janey."

"Sure you are, Max," Jonathan said in a tone one would use to calm a dangerous man.

The last guest from the birthday party had left. The two friends were alone. Jonathan figured it was very late. Then, noticing the first rays of the morning sun making their way in between his loosely drawn living room curtains, he realized it was very early.

They sat on the floor, their back against the sofa, a half-full bottle of Wild Turkey between them. Only this bottle of bourbon had managed to survive the party. Jonathan and Max took polite, alternating sips. They were determined to drink the remains of the evening down to the last drop; at that unsteady time it seemed like a good idea.

It was Max's turn to take a swig. Then he spoke: "No kidding, Jonathan, I'm really going to marry her."

Jonathan let Max go stumbling on. He didn't want to argue. Besides, he was too beat to remind his friend that only a couple of hours earlier he had opened the door to find a sheepish Max standing naked in the hall wondering if he could borrow some clothes. And oh, he remembered Max's nonchalantly adding, was there a robe or something he could lend Diane Farrell? No, Jonathan didn't argue; but you can't blame him if he didn't take his friend seriously.

Now it was Jonathan's turn at the bottle. He swallowed; coughed as the kick of the bourbon found him unprepared; and then was even more surprised to hear himself say, "Okay, I believe you. But how come?"

"Because it's right," Max insisted hotly. "It seems to have been meant to be that Janey and I get together. Not that we're drawn together out of any passion," he went on. "But the relationship does have its touch of romance. I mean we have been breaking up regularly for the last six years."

"That's true," Jonathan agreed; and thought better of asking what breaking up had to do with romance.

Max, though, had a theory: "There must be something that keeps always bringing us back together. Whether it's love or guilt or . . . maybe simply that we just need each other . . . whatever. The reason doesn't seem too important anymore. Look, I'm forty years old. Do you know that?"

"Maybe we should throw a party?"

"I guess I have had a bit," Max said with the overly polite embarrassment of the drunkard forced to fess up. "Of course you know."

"After your performance tonight, I imagine the whole Village knows."

"Well," said Max, abruptly deciding there was no percentage in being shamefaced, "there's something I know for sure, too. I'm at least a decade too old for running about naked on rooftops. It's time I settled down. I have plans."

"We both have plans."

"You're right. Excuse me," Max corrected. "We both have plans. We're in this together. It's our magazine and if it doesn't work it's going to be our fault. I don't have the time anymore for one night stands."

"If you can call freezing your ass off on a goddamn roof a one night stand."

Max smiled. "Whatever. I don't have time for that either. I'm a forty-year-old man and it's high time to put my life in order. I told that to Janey earlier in the evening before all the craziness and I still believe it. That's why I'm going to marry her. It might not be the easiest marriage. She's tough. But she'll stand by me while I figure out how to make *City* work. And I'll stand by her, too."

"I'll drink to that," said Jonathan. And he did. Max took his turn with the bottle as Jonathan wondered: "But what about Janey? I imagine she might not think you're the most eligible man in the world this morning. She's not the sort of woman to forgive and forget."

Max went through a heavy silence that was almost sobering. "No," he finally decided, "Janey won't forgive or forget. She'll extract her price. But Janey understands she needs me to get on with her life, too. Besides, she'd rather have me around to fight with than not have me around at all."

"Sounds like a hell of a love story," Jonathan warned.

". . . it'll work."

Jonathan remained silent; if Max thought so . . .

While Max, full of determination, was suddenly in a hurry. "Maybe I should go see Janey right away. Propose before she makes too big a deal about Diane."

"If you want to."

Though now that there was no one to prevent his rushing off, Max began to waver. It seemed silly to leave before the bottle of Wild Turkey was empty.

By the time the bottle was drained, Max decided to go home. A couple of hours sleep wouldn't hurt. He would propose to Janey that evening with a clear head and a neatly shaved face. He was certain she would, after some talented convincing, accept. They would have the rest of their lives together to work things out. He would find a way.

Except when he went home that morning and fell into his bed, his dreams, hopes, and contrivances were all fixated on his one true love— *City* magazine.

FIVE

THE HALLWAY STENCH immediately grabbed Max Fox
and whirled him around. It was hard to take at a quarter after six in the
morning. Max, though, didn't retreat. He bounded up the rickety staircase leading to the second floor offices of *City* magazine. The time had
finally come, he decided, to lay down the law at the bar in the basement—
let 'em piss in the street, not in the hallway. And just as he realized he
had been meaning to set things straight with the crowd from the Cellar
for three years now, he also knew he wouldn't get around to it today.
Today was press day. By the time Max was at the top of the stairs and
turning his key in the red metal door his mind was already circling a
larger problem: What sort of issue would he come up with this week?

For the past three years, Max had been measuring out his life in
weekly issues of *City*. "And a week at *City*," Jonathan joked, "was seven
days, five nights of sleep, three love affairs, two brawls, and at least one
disaster."

These hectic weeks first began gathering their skittish momentum a
mere five months after Max's birthday party announcement. On the second Tuesday of June 1954, the thin inaugural issue of *City* hit the stands.
Across its black and white cover was a photo of three unkempt types in
sandals, jeans, and dark turtlenecks slouching against a lamppost on the
corner of Bleecker and MacDougal streets. The headline tittered: "Rent
A Beatnik." And inside—along with articles on how un-American the
House Un-American Activities Committee really was, a first-person account of a night spent crawling through the Village pubs with Dylan
Thomas, and a bitterly critical survey of the avant-garde activities at
Black Mountain College—the tongue-in-cheek cover story ran for a
page. Matt Waldman, a curly-headed grad school dropout who had mi-
grated downtown from Columbia to become an out-of-work bartender,
announced his service to "rent by the evening or the hour genuine Greenwich Village beatniks complete with beards, sandals, and grimaces of
conspicuous disdain" who would be "suitable for weddings, cocktail par-

ties, bar mitzvahs, or Tupperware gatherings." "Put a little angst into your next suburban affair," he urged.

This first issue even had a piece, of sorts, penned by Max Fox. On the second page, below the table of contents and surrounded by a solemn black border, ran a terse statement of purpose:

"Our magazine will publish what all the other magazines and news-papers leave out. We will tell you what is really happening and what people are really thinking in this city. We will be uncensored, offensive, combative, arrogant, and maybe even wrong. But we will never lie. We will never keep secrets. In that vein, a confession: We are amateurs em-barking on something new. We really don't know what to expect. There-fore, we can only make one prediction—*City* will be unpredictable. If you don't like what you read here, we're counting on you to pick up a pen and tell us."

It was signed Max Fox, editor in chief, and Jonathan Trout, publisher.

Only a depressing 214 copies of the first issue were sold, yet Max felt the tingle of bigger things. Waldman's facetious rent-a-beatnik scheme was noticed by an enterprising stringer for the United Press who played it straight-faced. By the end of the week 127 papers throughout the country ran the story about "a new radical Greenwich Village weekly that was renting out representatives of the great unwashed." And Wald-man, who found himself anointed by Max as *City*'s first staff columnist for $5 an issue, received dozens of serious inquiries. (His second column, in fact, was about the all-expenses-paid trip he made to Scarsdale to have six uncommonly dry martinis at a party hosted by a stockbroker; and how he was asked to leave after he made a drunken attempt to lead the stockbroker's wife into her pink chintz bedroom and show her how beatniks make love.)

But the real tip-off for Max that he was striking a nerve out there were the letters. They kept pouring in. From the first issue on, people were eager to talk back. "I'm sick and tired of your ruling class drivel," wrote a lady from Barrow Street after the third issue. "I feel like I've found a new, outrageous friend," a man from the Upper West Side boasted. And nearly every article provoked dozens of letters, a spectrum of hot opinions ranging from fierce praise to savage condemnation. By the end of the first month of publication, Max decided to harness his readers' energy. He printed, regardless of the adamant stands they were taking, columns of letters to the editors in each issue. He even gave a cou-ple of acres of newsprint over to a letter writer who had conceived an epic poem written in the meter of Tamburlaine which seemed (Max could never actually force himself to read through the damn thing) to be ad-vocating the restorative powers of the orgone box. "The more voices we can get in the magazine, the better," he told Jonathan. "Especially when we don't have to pay for them," the publisher shrewdly observed. "We don't even pay for the stamps."

From the start, working at the magazine was an unexpected pleasure for Max. He found, and here was a wrinkle that caught a lifelong outsider by surprise, he loved the power. He loved sitting in his small office, Zeus-like behind his gray metal desk, watching, directing, and advising, as writers stomped in and out with ideas, arguments, or simply ruminations about the new girl straight from Bennington who was just hired to sell classified ads. Yet while Jonathan and Matt Waldman, suddenly a celebrity in downtown circles with his weekly "Hip Talk" column, were avidly nailing every black-tighted female searching for a couple of hours of bohemian adventure who happened to gravitate to the *City* offices, Max kept his distance. It wasn't simply that he was now a married man. His drawing back was not merely a moral decision, but also an editorial one; he was busy shaping a new, more rigidly privatistic style for himself, one that he thought decorously fit a man who held the title of editor in chief of *City* magazine.

After nearly three years—143 struggles over weekly issues—Max had discovered only a small rub in the realization of his dream. *City* wasn't making money. Small . . . yet possibly fatal. Every Friday Jonathan would sit down with him and laboriously recount another tale of financial woe. Newsstand sales, despite all the talk the magazine was causing, remained low. The big uptown advertisers were still too cautious to take a chance on appearing in a magazine during a decade when radical was thought to be just a polite euphemism for Commie. The partners had no choice but, starting this week, to cut back their weekly salaries to $60. Worse, Max could no longer count on Janey's paycheck. She was pregnant. He could not help but feel his back scraping up against the wall. The pain of losing his magazine, the only thing in his life he really cared about, was becoming real.

I T   W A S   I N   T H I S   M O O D that Max bounded up the smelly stairwell in the early hours of that March morning in 1957. As always he was the first to arrive; now that he had ended his serious drinking days, he found himself having to deal with the trade-off—insomnia. This morning, just like all the others, there was a proprietary rush as he opened the door to *his* magazine and flicked on the lights. An unconscious pause as he took it all in—"all" consisting of four banged-up metal desks, an old Remington and a black phone plunked in the middle of each, though they were pretty well camouflaged by messes of yellow foolscap; and beyond this newsroom with its two casement windows looking out on Sixth Avenue was the door to the tiny office he shared with Jonathan.

He tossed the key debonairly in the air before catching it overhand and returned it to his righthand pants pocket. Then Max made his way through the newsroom, impatient to hide behind his closed door and get on with his routine: a cup of milky tea—Max was forever the Anglophile —brewed on the hotplate next to his desk, the milk kept on a window-sill; next the assiduous reading of the *Times*, skipping only the sports and the crossword puzzle, before taking on the *Wall Street Journal*; and then, the clock moving in on seven thirty, on to the struggle with his own magazine.

Today, like any Monday, the struggle was bound to be straight uphill. By ten this evening *City* had to be at the printer's. As he pushed open the door to his darkened office, this thought caused the day's first kick of anxiety. And then, suddenly, the editor's fears became more tangible.

Max heard a noise. He stood motionless and listened. A quick, high-pitched moan came from behind Jonathan's desk. He waited. The sound grew large in the small, dark office.

"Who's there?" Max tried to challenge, but his voice slipped.

Abruptly there was silence. Then hasty, scuffling noises from behind the desk.

"Who's there?" Max repeated, more in control this time. And he turned on the lights.

"It's me, Mr. Fox. Josh."

Max watched as a bare-chested black kid, he couldn't be more than sixteen, Max figured, stood up from behind the desk. The boy was fumbling with the buckle to the garrison belt around his jeans.

"Oh, it's you," Max said with relief. Josh was the building super-intendent's son; Max had talked with him the last time Josh had come around to help the father clean up the office. He remembered the boy, a good-looking, smooth-faced kid, telling him he wanted to be an actor. "You giving your father a hand this morning . . ."

But as Max took a step toward Josh, he caught a glimpse of an obviously frightened black girl—was that pink bra all she had on?— trying to stuff her ample body into the space between the legs of Jona-than's desk.

Max was if not amused, at least sympathetic; but three years at the helm of his magazine had made him used to playing the outraged editor. "What the hell is going on?"

"Well . . . uh . . ." Josh stammered. The would-be actor kept on stumbling until he found his idol Robeson's lordly bass.

"I was just in here emptying the trash baskets like my father had asked me to do," Josh tried. "And Janet came to get me so I wouldn't be late for school. And . . . uh . . ."

"Yes, Josh?" Max pressed. He hoped it didn't show that he was getting a kick out of this.

". . . you see, Mr. Fox, we had some studying to do. I didn't think anyone would be here this early. We must've lost track of time. We were studying pretty hard . . . You know, for our chemistry test."

"Now, Josh, I might believe you if you told me you were studying for a biology test," Max said not too sternly. And a giggle crawled out from under Jonathan's desk.

"Okay," Max continued. "I'm going to let you two finish your . . . studying. I'll go get breakfast down the street. But when I come back, I expect you to be gone."

"Sure thing, Mr. Fox. I promise."

"And, Josh . . ."

"Yes?"

"When you finish your studying, I hope you'll remember to empty the trash baskets."

And so, like any inflexible rule, the proof of Max's unvarying routine was demonstrated by that morning's flexibility: He sat in a luncheonette rather happily sipping his cups of milky tea and reading the morning papers. As if to celebrate these extraordinary circumstances, Max broke a bit further with form and ordered a corn muffin. The editor sat there dreamily dipping his toasted muffin into his pale tea; a quiet interlude as he contemplated with a curious aloofness what other unanticipated dramas and disasters today—a typical press day at *City*—might bring.

SIX

MAX'S detachment, though, was short-lived. He returned to the magazine at eight thirty and, immediately suffering a familiar anxious kick in his gut, found the spirit of the approaching deadline slinking around the newsroom like a mustache-twisting, rent-demanding landlord. His office offered little sanctuary. Jonathan had already arrived, the publisher twirling about madly in a swivel chair behind a desk catercorner to Max's. Max stood at the doorway listening as his friend, redfaced, shouted into the phone.

Jonathan had been grasping the receiver in one hand as if it were a weapon and with his other he had been absently tugging at a paisley wing of his bow tie, but his attention focused when he saw Max. Immediately the publisher slammed down the phone.

"You can forget about a magazine this week," Jonathan moaned. He didn't even give his friend a chance to sit down.

"Oh?" Max questioned; experience had taught him a light touch would guide him through these weekly crises.

"That's right," Jonathan insisted with huffing and puffing fury. "It's pretty simple. No ads. No bucks. No magazine." Jonathan offered a tiny vent to his large and recklessly escalating frustration by giving a destructive jerk to the fluffy wings of his bow tie. The paisley silk opened into two hapless strands.

"Now just wait a minute," Max suggested in the sort of quiet, reasonable voice fathers find to tell their loved ones that a particular disappointment doesn't necessarily mean it's the end of the world. "Someone must have bought an ad." And after a moment he added, very serious, "Certainly all those nudist camps in New Jersey took their usual weekly spots. Those places count on us to put them in touch with the other free spirits."

"Oh sure, all sorts of people took ads. Everyone from some wildeyed looking guy trying to pass himself off as a Reichian therapist to some woman on Jane Street who wants to give her kittens away—but only to Zionists. She said she wanted her babies to grow up in a self-sufficient yet moral environment."

"Typical *City* ads," Max agreed. "But then what's the problem?"

"The printer."

"The printer?" Max repeated blankly. If Jonathan wanted to go through this step by step, Max would play along.

"I just spoke with him on the phone . . ."

"Uh huh." Max enjoyed picturing Harry the cigar-chomping printer jumping high into the air when Jonathan had slammed down the receiver; had the old man finally lost his faithful cigar?

"And he told me that somehow someone had . . . I mean, they . . . or maybe . . ."

"Sounds like?" Max joked, hoping to coax the mystery out of his partner.

"Well, it's like this," Jonathan staunchly announced. But he took a fortifying gulp of air before continuing. Then: "The goddamn printer lost all the goddamn ad copy. I dropped it off at Harry's last night and this morning he called to say he couldn't find it. He thinks maybe the cleaning man threw it out."

Max's initial reaction was to consider that this was the second time in a brief morning his routine had been upset by cleaning men. Was this random accident or Freudian pattern? He kept his quirky digression to himself, though, and tried to deal calmly and logically with the more immediate problem.

"Okay, so Harry lost the ad copy," Max reasoned. "It's inconvenient, but it's not irrevocable. You have your carbon dupes of all the ads, right?"

"Wrong."

". . . I don't understand." Max's voice was suddenly skidding.

"I should have the dupes, but I don't. I left them by mistake in the same folder with the ad copy at Harry's last night. Harry figures the cleaning man made a clean sweep."

Max wanted to work out a logical solution to this disaster, but after an exhausting fifteen seconds of intense thought he gave up: This *was* the end of the world.

"Jesus Christ," Max cursed as he, with an unintentional touch of symbolic exactitude, lashed out at the conspiring demons plaguing him: He kicked the wastebasket next to his desk across the room. A comet of yellow foolscap fell from the flying object. "Fucking Josh," he bellowed. It was Jonathan's turn not to comprehend; he was forced to decide his friend had gone berserk. "Fucking Josh," Max repeated. "I'm going to ring his little neck." Jonathan's mystification and concern increased as his quickly hyperventilating friend announced, "It's a plot. It's a goddamn plot. They're all in it together."

A wild Max was now convinced it wasn't random accident playing around with his life.

It took the editor three uneasy hours to shuck off these furious musings and slide back into his usual, more restrained demeanor. With this calm, finding a way through the mess of events became easy. He decided simply to grovel. The two friends rushed to the printer's on 23d Street and, on their hands and knees, spent an hour and a half meticulously sorting the noxious, ink-stained cartons of trash awaiting pickup in the basement. Max finally found the well-buried ad sheets next to the greasy remains of a half-eaten corn muffin; and the hiding place of this buried treasure was additional proof, he noted with a shiver, of the malicious symmetry of the forces conspiring to keep this week's issue of *City* far apart from its ten o'clock deadline.

THE DEADLINE HAD crept still another couple of hours closer by the time Max had returned to his office. He was at his desk working through the moments when he normally would have been finishing his lunch while the next small crisis elbowed its way into the already too crowded room. Phil, the chief copy editor, was the diffident bearer of this bit of bad news.

"We g-g-got a pr-pr-prob-lem," he managed to explain as he made his cautious way into Max's office.

Max shrugged. "It figures," he said without anticipation. Max looked at the gangly copy editor who was nervously stroking his ever handy pencil sharpener in his pale left hand, and for a moment couldn't decide what ticked him off the most about taciturn Phil: It was an exasperating toss-up between his maniacal neatness—even a stray punctuation mark added to a bit of copy was a precisely drawn minor work of art—and his annoying stammer.

"Let me hear it," Max conceded.

As soon as Phil started talking, cranky Max reached a swift decision: It was the stutter that made the anxious editor want to shove the afflicted man into the broom closet and lock the door. In fact, Max kept him around only because he was impressed by how the copy editor spent his nights off: Phil was using his dagger-sharp pencils to create a lovingly detailed trilogy telling the story of the rise and fall of a mythical kingdom ruled by benevolent chipmunks. Although the 783-page first volume ("The Land Between the Stones") had been summarily rejected by every publisher in New York, Phil, undeterred, had completed, as of last night's session, page 467 of the second volume of his epic. Max, on days carrying less pressure, admired, even relished, Phil's weird spunk. And who else could he find to work killing hours for $45 a week?

"Go on," Max wearily insisted as Phil still grappled with his story.

"I-i-i-it's D-d-d-ot, M-m-m—"

Max cut him off without mercy. "What about Dot?"

After sufficient time had passed, Max was acerbically convinced, for Phil to have completed the third, maybe even a fourth volume of his chipmunk saga, Max managed to learn the dimensions of this latest setback. It seemed that Dot, the magazine's incomprehensibly witty cartoonist, had gone off the deep, or more exactly, the shallow end. Dot's wife had found him at 2 a.m. trying to demonstrate to a bar of soap that he could walk across the foamy water in their bathtub. Mrs. Dot (or Dottstein, as it read on the marriage license) was neither as tolerant nor as unimpressed as the bar of soap. She immediately took her talented husband by the hand and, after drying off his soaking feet, had him committed to his usual room at Payne Whitney. Unless Dot escaped, which the editor knew he was certainly capable of, Max would at this late hour have to find something to fill the half-page hole reserved for the cartoon.

Max figured it would be more prudent to find a substitute for the cartoon than to count on Dot's ingenuity. He was busily sorting through the articles on overset when Phil entered to announce the space could be quickly filled—for a price.

"T-t-there's a m-m-m-man here who s-s-says D-d-d-dot sent h-him t-t-to see y-y-you."

"Well, where the hell is he?" Max barked.

"He s-s-says D-d-dot s-s-aid y-y-you w-would g-g-g-ive him f-f-five dollars."

Max searched through his pants pockets and came up with $3.50; he suddenly remembered the unavoidable expense of breakfast. Jonathan promptly contributed the missing dollar and a half. "All right," said Max as he clutched the required sum in his hand, "I'm game. Show the gentleman in."

Phil escorted a short Puerto Rican with thick, vaselined black hair into Max's office. The man had deep brown eyes the size of saucers.

"I'm Max Fox," the editor explained and offered his hand to the new arrival. "Did Dot ask you to deliver something to me?"

"I don't give nut-thing," the Puerto Rican vowed. "I don't give nut-thing 'til I get my five bucks." He wouldn't even shake Max's hand for free.

Max handed over the money; and, the Puerto Rican's suspicions assuaged, he became exuberantly courteous, shaking Max's hand as if the editor were a long-lost relative. The man then gave Max a manila envelope.

While Jonathan questioned the messenger—the Puerto Rican had now crossed the room to pump the publisher's hand—Max opened up the envelope. Inside was this week's cartoon: A scraggly, nearly emaciated Salvation Army Santa was ringing a mournful bell as he slumped beside a kettle decorated with the words "Keep the Christ in Christmas." Studying the drawing, Max noticed the small button pinned to the ragtag Santa's breast—"Keep the X in Xmas."

"You know how our friend here got the drawing from Dot," Jonathan called to Max as the Puerto Rican now turned to a reluctant Phil and commenced shaking his hand; it was an awkward encounter, though, as the messenger found himself crunching the pencil sharpener the copy editor had been obsessively clutching.

"It seems," Jonathan went on as a tense, clock-watching Max silently hoped Phil's neurotic plaything would be ground by the Puerto Rican's goodwill into irreparable smithereens, "Bobby here works as an attendant on the fourth floor at Payne Whitney. Dot drew the cartoon this morning and asked Bobby to drop it off when he finished his shift." Bobby, still jovially pumping away at wary Phil's trapped hand with the nonstop motion of a piston in overdrive, turned to Max and smiled graciously as if to confirm the veracity of the account.

"Well, you saved the day," Max said to Bobby. The editor was now eager to get on with work; he felt as if the deadline were another lurking presence in the tight room. But Max asked, "How is Dot, by the way?"

"Looney tunes," Bobby quickly answered. He illustrated this diagnosis by pointing an index finger in the vicinity of his head and turning it in clockwise but obviously hopeless circles.

"I know what you mean," Max agreed. His tone betrayed a weary acceptance of the inevitable; it was that kind of day. "Thanks again for dropping the drawing off."

"Glad to help," said Bobby, who to Phil's great relief had released his hand and was heading for the door. "I gotta go downtown anyway. I work down in Wall Street. Nights."

With the sighing precognition of a gambler who knows he's stuck on a losing streak, Max played out the rest of the hand: "What sort of work do you do?" he asked.

"I'm a cleaning man," Bobby said as he waved good-by.

Max, though, made another gesture. It was his turn to aim one finger at his own head and he wound it in similarly hopeless circles. "Looney tunes," he whispered with knowing resignation. And repeating this despairing gesture for Jonathan's confused benefit, he added, "I should have thought better than to ask that question. Something is certainly up today."

THINGS DIDN'T GET better. The afternoon, weighed down by a continuing series of small crises, was, Max felt, heading pell-mell downhill. It was five o'clock and he still didn't have a cover story. The occasional nervous kick in his stomach was gone; the pain had switched to the constant spin cycle. His insides swirled about with topsy-turvy anxiety.

We aren't going to pull it off this week, Max glumly decided. It's too late. I still need a cover, I need a goddamn cover story, his troubled mind kept repeating with metronomic insistence.

He shoveled for what must have been the twentieth dispirited time through the copy Phil had trafficked to his desk. His original dismal assessment remained unchanged: This was a pile of very dull stories.

After almost three years of climbing atop their weekly soapboxes, his *City* writers were beginning to find the ascent routine. Time doesn't necessarily heal all wounds, but, Max was convinced as he thumbed through the evidence in front of him, it does certainly dull them. By simply managing to survive, the magazine was losing its uniqueness.

His aging bohemian writers' contentious private concerns—Village bars, homosexuality, McCarthy, banning the bomb, bullfighting—were becoming stale, even familiar. In the short time he had directed the magazine, its aggressive rudeness already hinted at mellowing into more genteel vulgarity. Max feared the worst: *City* would become predictably outrageous.

A depressed Max searched the stories spread across his desk for something intoxicatingly new. Something people would talk about.

But by a quarter after six he had found nothing. The deadline clock continued relentlessly ticking. His nervous stomach was flying all the way up and all the way down like a majorette's baton. Max was convinced this week's issue would be a tepid affair. Then, just as Father Time was winding up for the cleanup swing of his scythe, he found it. The provocative idea had been there all along, lurking clandestinely between the lines of rational typewritten prose. He read the chosen story one more time and with a yell as exuberantly triumphant as the Hallelujah Chorus, called, "Wendy!"

Wendy Parker trundled with thigh-scraping quickness into Max's office; on press day all the *City* writers hung around in what passed for the newsroom waiting—and hoping—for Max's summons.

"Wendy," Max began as the woman attempted to squeeze her considerable bulk into the steel folding chair opposite his desk, "let's talk about your story."

"Yes, Max," she answered eagerly. "Just let me find my pen." She started hunting through a canvas sack voluminous enough to sequester a typewriter.

While she plunged deep into the bag, discarding a puffy mountain of used tissues, two notebooks, a thick address book, a locked diary, powder, lipstick, and other assorted cosmetics on Max's desk, the editor was deciding how to play her.

Wendy Parker, to the envious dismay of the other writers who lived at least a minor part of their lives for Max's attention, was one of his favorites. She had been born into wealthy and horsey Wasps who managed through carefully inbreeding to lose first their wealth and then their horses, but who succeeded in keeping the woeful tale of their plundered heritage alive by carrying themselves with a seedy, *fin de race* haughtiness; and she was enjoyably, but nevertheless uncompromisingly, odd. Max, the snobby bohemian, was fascinated.

Nearly six months ago, just at the precise moment when her marriage was speeding to an increasingly violent end, Max discovered Wendy. He was strolling down a deserted early morning Charles Street on his way to the office when he suddenly spotted hurling around this tranquil corner a gargantuan form wrapped in an incongruously feminine pink robe. It was a woman in rapid pursuit. And she was victorious. Max watched as this great pink whale, gurgling frighteningly savage sounds, hoisted high a thick volume of the Oxford English Dictionary as she prepared to bring the full weight of English letters down upon the bald head of a black-caped, ascetically thin victim. Max felt each mean blow as this hulk of a woman repeatedly slammed her heavy weapon against the pale, unprotected head. Such fury, Max would much later learn, had been building for a long time: Each wallop further consummated the bitter end of Wendy's six-year marriage to the harrowingly gaunt would-be poet her mother had described as "looking like he had stood out in Harvard yard too long."

It was both her choice of literary weapon and the unmitigated venom of her attack that prompted normally shy Max, once the carnage was over and the ripped pages of the hefty dictionary were scattering esoteric messages in the wind, to make an uncharacteristically impulsive gesture. The situation was so fetchingly absurd that curious Max, for the good of his magazine, he rationalized, abruptly decided to step into it.

"I'm Max Fox," he announced as he crossed Charles Street and approached the now sobbing pink-robed Titan. She turned rapidly. For a moment she considered lashing out at this intrusive little man, but then thought better of it; and anyway, all that remained of her arsenal was a page headed "xenophobia."

Max caught the wild look in her eye. A few strategic steps backward were discreetly executed. Then he continued: "I run *City* magazine. We're always looking for people with fury and conviction. And, if you don't mind my saying it, those are two qualities you seem to possess in abundance. If you feel like channeling that anger onto the printed page, come on by. Perhaps we can work something out." Before the woman could speak or possibly reconsider her aborted attack, he walked off.

It must have been a month before Wendy Parker appeared at Max's office ("I think he'll remember me," she explained to a protective Phil. "Just tell him I'm the woman he met on Charles Street. The one who was smashing her husband over the head with a dictionary") and equally as long before Max decided she was ready to write. During this tutelage, they sat for hours in the editor's office: Max puffing pregnantly on his pipe and working his sly, quiet charm as Wendy talked nonstop about herself. He would mine her personality before he would touch her prose.

An English lit major at Sarah Lawrence, Wendy, Max learned, had come to the Village to find a room of her own and write her novel. Instead she found a literary husband and discovered she was intrigued not by fiction, but by the incredible reality of what made the city around her tick. As head of her block association Wendy had successfully engineered minor symbolic victories against the ruling Tammany hacks. But these triumphs—the right to plant a few soon moribund trees on Bleecker Street and a putsch against a porno theater that closed after one sordid week—were just the beginning. Wendy was after bigger targets. With the quick uncomplicated clarity of a true paranoid, she was convinced certain conspiring forces pulled all the strings. And Max, carefully poking into the twisted theoretical corners of her well-developed obsessiveness, realized he had found just the sort of investigative reporter he was looking for: someone who would champion causes.

Yet the piece he held before him this week was depressingly cautious. Max would have to talk the below surface rumblings out of Wendy and onto the page. To rake muck, Max knew, you first had to be angry enough to sling it.

"Wendy," he announced as she expectantly raised her long-searched-for pen, "the piece this week—"

"Yes," she interrupted, uncontrollably fawning.

"It stinks," Max blurted out. Instantly her large body visibly sagged. "It's too unemotional," he chided. His two small hands became tiny walls pushing earnestly toward each other as he emphasized the constraints of her prose. "You don't let loose. You could have written this for the *Times,* for Christ's sake."

"You see, Max," she offered with a whimper of apology, "what I tried to do—"

"I don't give a damn what you tried to do," he shouted, the angry blast of his words rocking Wendy back in her steel seat. Of course Max was acting. He was cranking himself up, hoping his wildness would rub off on her. He wanted dictionary swinging fury in her story. He wanted a conspiratorial Cassandra whispering inside political dope to his readers.

"Let me tell you what you did," he continued in a glass-shattering pitch. His face was flushing a dangerous scarlet, but he felt he was just doing his job. "You wrote a dull civics lessons about how some politicians plan to plow a superhighway straight through the middle of Washington Square Park. Oh, it's all Wasp Sarah Lawrence goody-goody"—Max was a malicious genius at incisively salting the most telling wounds— but who's going to give a damn except some mothers who'll have to find another place to take their kiddies? What I need from you, Wendy"— and now the pitch of his temper was really ricocheting about the room— "is a piece that tells me who really is behind this highway. That points fingers at all the wheeler-dealers who'll make out like bandits." The editor leaned across the cluttered desk toward his reporter. "Let me teach you a cardinal rule of journalism," he said, though smiling to himself because he realized he had never before given much thought to any of the rules of journalism. "If you want people to help you move immoveable forces, then you had better make 'em fighting mad."

". . . I get your point," she surrendered.

But Max continued. "Look at this graph." And then he stole a look at his watch. It was later than he thought. He moved quickly now.

He began reading in a contemptuously singsong voice: "A proposal quietly introduced at the City Planning Commission last week calls for the building of a four-lane roadway with a five-foot-wide center mall across lower Manhattan and Greenwich Village. The proposed route of this superhighway will go straight through Washington Square Park.'"

"Damn it, Wendy," he said as he crumpled the paper in his menacing hand, though taking care not to rip it. "What a story this could be. But you've got to write it so that people care. You say the highway was 'quietly' introduced. Hell, it wasn't just quiet. It was a sneak attack.

"And the only way to stop it," he went on, "is to strike back—with emotion. Let me hear the voices of people who feel the bulldozers breathing down their necks. Don't just give me numbers. Tell me about the homes that will be destroyed by this monster road. About the families who'll be dispossessed. Sent to God knows where. Tell me what the banks and the local bosses and their union cronies will get out of this fiasco. Goddamn it, Wendy, the real story here is about a bunch of hack politicians setting out to destroy a community. And figuring to make a nice profit, I bet, while they're doing it. Tell your readers just how *you* feel, Wendy. Shout to them. And get them to scream with rage along with you."

Max paused a calculated moment to let his message sink in. "Come on, Wendy," he asked, rapidly changing routines; he was now the soft-spoken confidant, the one man a woman could trust. "What do you really think is behind this highway? Let me hear the *real* story," he purred.

"You're just going to tell me I'm paranoid," she complained.

"You're not paranoid, just precocious," Max shot back; but he wasn't sure if he were lying or simply hoping.

A rationale, however, became unimportant. His ploy worked.

With a great deal of cumbersome effort, Wendy, not bothering to rise, tugged her chair inches closer to Max's desk. Now it was her turn to lean forward, trying to close in on him. Her body was rocking over the editor's desk at a sagging, obtuse angle; her heavy breasts, Max noticed, shoved his mess of papers into even further disorder. So settled, she started telling her tale. Her voice took on a crazy cackle; a shrewd witch gleefully stirring her cauldron of trouble.

Wendy told a wonderfully libelous tale of what made the city government run. She sketched for a mute Max a complicated organizational chart that had the decision to build the highway ultimately running from a clique of politically well-connected developers and bankers. Throughout a prophetically lucrative year before the highway had even been proposed to the Planning Commission, these developers, with the help of suspiciously obliging banks, had begun (or at least this is what the downtown rumors, Wendy's largest source of information, speculated) purchasing vacant lots and slum buildings. Coincidentally, these once worthless properties stretched (according to the same rumors, that is) in a three-mile trail across the part of downtown Manhattan that happened to be precisely in the path of the proposed highway. And just as coincidentally, certain politicians suddenly began righteously shouting about the need for "slum clearance" and "urban renewal." It was good government, so the Tammany line went, to raze these urban eyesores and cover it all with four lanes of blacktop. There was, however, an irksome pothole in the middle of this potentially golden road—Washington Square Park. But this was a problem, Wendy explained, the power brokers had no trouble solving. They simply shoved enough dollars into the proper pockets and campaign chests. A whole crowd of city fathers now shook their hoary heads and sighed that the loss of a park was regrettable, but still a small price to pay for necessary progress.

"So," Wendy concluded with an angry chortle, "the rich get richer and the poor get highways. And everybody in Greenwich Village is supposed to sit back silently while they lose a park."

"Now that," ordered Max in a stentorian voice sprinkled with equal dashes of both amazement and enthusiasm, "is the story I want you to write." He stood up behind his desk to give his final command: "Write it just as you told it to me. Let me feel your anger." A final military gesture as he synchronized the watch on his wrist before instructing, "You have twenty-seven minutes to get it done."

"That's impossible, Max," she started complaining. But Wendy was already rising with some commotion from her chair.

"You finish it in twenty-seven, no, now it's twenty-six minutes," he announced as he followed the sweep of the second hand on his watch, "and it's the cover."

Wendy hustled out of the office with a determined but still bouncingly awkward speed as Max began writing the cover headline on the layout sheet in front of him: "The Rich Get Richer and the Poor Get Highways." The line—as infuriatingly simplistic as it was provocatively true—was vintage Wendy Parker muckraking; and it would become vintage *City*.

Max also shrewdly realized he had found a cause to rally his readers around: They, along with crusading *City*, would help save Washington Square Park.

Max was well aware of the dangerous journalistic game he was playing. It wasn't just the lateness of the hour that prevented him from quizzing Wendy about the sources for her incriminating tale. He simply didn't care if it were entirely true. In fact, he realized her agitated account was probably choked full of exaggerations. But it galled Max that the daily papers were ignoring this highway. For them, it was simply another unsensational $20 million construction project. Max, gliding on his outsider's anger, routinely believed nothing got built in New York without someone's making a fortune in dirty dollars. And why wasn't the *Times* or the *News* or even the *Village Voice* concerning itself with the neighborhoods that would be destroyed? If no other publication was going to point an incensed finger, then it was up to his unrestrained magazine to wave a couple of handfuls. He realized Wendy's attack was scattered. But he also had enough faith in her to believe she would be hitting the proper targets and raising powerful questions. Let her emotional paragraphs be dotted with small errors. Wendy Parker, the editor was convinced, was a unique, angry voice instinctively shouting *ultimate* truths about how things worked in New York. And that was the sort of personal and provocative writing Max Fox wanted in his magazine.

He was deciding whether to use a two- or three-column picture of Washington Square Park on the cover when Wendy hurried as best she could into his office.

"Fourteen more minutes to deadline," Max said sternly while she hovered near his desk.

"I know. I know. I'm almost done." Her voice was energized with her conspiratorial cackle. "I just remembered something I should have told you before. One of the union pension funds has also supposedly been busy buying up land in the area. Seems like they have a friend in high places, too. Should I put that in?"

"Give me all you got," he insisted. Wendy was making her eager exit when Max, filled with a strange sinking feeling because he was bewilderingly certain he already knew the answer, called after her. "By the way, which union is it?"

"The sanitation men's union," she answered.

Wendy was quickly out the door and hunched over the Remington at her desk so she never saw what Jonathan came upon when he returned to the office he shared with his friend: a maniacally grinning Max standing there, his index finger pointed at his distinguished head and turning in zany circles as he muttered, "Looney tunes. This whole place is looney tunes today."

But now he could smile about it.

SEVEN

WENDY, clinking the keys on her typewriter with the intensity of an Old Testament prophet hell-bent on sharing the Word, beat the deadline clock; and by 9:15 a weary Max and Jonathan scooted for the second time in that long day to Harry the printer.

"Where the hell have you been?" greeted Harry as he always did, his hunched cantankerous form hiding behind a dense cloud of stinking cigar smoke. "You've never been this late before," the printer added as he unfailingly did each week.

And Max, equally unfailingly, responded to the old man's barbs with the identical weekly burst of pride: "It was worth the wait, Harry. This is the best issue yet."

"Best? I should give a damn about best?" Harry barked, sounding at least a foot taller than his crumpled five feet two. "Let's just get the show on the road."

Harry grabbed the copy from Max's hand and shuffled to a rickety linotype machine. He sat down at the big brass-colored machine; a wizened and cranky child behind the controls of the monstrous, clickety-clacking device. Yet as the machine started up with an eerie, sharp noise, Harry's livered-spotted hands flew gracefully across the keyboard, the offensive cigar in his mouth jumping to the metallic rhythmn of the falling type.

Harry, lost in his own comfortably smoke-enveloped world, kept this up for hours, pausing only now and then when, as he complained, "the type lice are getting to me." The self-prescribed panacea for this invented ill was a fortifying gulp from the bottle of Johnny Walker he kept uncapped next to the noisy machine.

While Harry knocked out slugs of shiny metal type, Jonathan and Max put a shape to their magazine, cutting, pasting, and proofreading the articles for the dummy of this week's issue. Of course, they were prudent enough to interrupt their labors to take frequent doses of Harry's elixir.

The three men worked through a neon-lit night misted with the rotten scent of cigar smoke and into an unnoticed dawn filled with a similarly noxious thick dew. But at 6:12 a.m. Harry, celebrating the moment by shoving a new but still not fresh cigar into his puckered lips, announced with what he considered suitable formality, "Gentlemen, you may start the presses."

Max, as was the custom, pressed a blue metal button; there was a soft whirring noise and then the routine hesitancy as the machinery started to sputter, finally caught hold, and slowly began grinding out the 144th issue of *City* magazine. While the magazine spurted forth in high piles, the three men breakfasted on what remained of the medicinal Johnny Walker.

It was after eight in the morning when the presses finally coughed up the final copy of the eight-thousand-issue run. But while Harry could now go home to his smoke-filled apartment, Max and Jonathan, speeding into the twenty-eighth hour of their day fueled by the whiskey, still had more to do. The magazine needed to be delivered to the newsstands.

T H E T W O F R I E N D S lugged the tall piles of this week's issue into the back of Jonathan's station wagon. Reaching into the glove compartment, the publisher found his soft army cap with the still shiny captain's bars pinned on. Before he got behind the wheel, he put the cap on his head. Despite its jaunty angle, this was more than an attempt at fashion. He had learned long ago that newsstand dealers were a fervently patriotic bunch filled with suspicions about *City* magazine. "If it helps to get the magazine on the stands," he told Max, "I'll even wear my medals." Max, though, was uncomfortable with this sort of masquerade. He wouldn't wear his service cap (possibly because he had risen only to the rank of private first class) and he never drove (simply because he didn't know how; he remained convinced it was a silly suburban activity like golf). It was 8:45 when the car pulled away from the printing plant on 23d Street.

"We got the new issue here," Max announced to each newsie as the station wagon pulled up; and the editor, swallowing his shyness for the collective good, managed somewhat enthusiastically to wave a copy. The newsie couldn't miss the 12-point front-page headline, "The Rich Get Richer and the Poor Get Highways." "It's going to be a winner. It'll fly off the stands," Max promised, hoping he sounded convincing and yet not too shrill. Despite the previous hours filled with pressures and crises, this was the only part of the weekly routine he truly loathed. He found it profoundly undignified to hawk his magazine.

The newsies, however, were unconcerned with Max's discomfort. What mattered to them was business. And *City* was getting to be good business. Within the last year sales had been steadily building. Newsstands around New York were increasingly becoming willing to display at least a small stack of the brightly printed magazines.

Except this morning there was one dissenter. When the two friends pulled up at the Sheridan Square newsstand they learned that Willy, the friendly newsie who regularly took a weekly delivery of one hundred issues, was out with the flu. His obese stand-in refused to take even a single copy of the magazine. Actually, he wasn't merely refusing.

"Ya take ya goddamn buncha pinko magazines and git da fuck outta here," the newsie bellowed at Max.

Max shrugged. The long day had taken its debilitating toll. He decided he was prepared to lose his sale.

Yet just as abruptly, Max changed his mind. There was no reason he had to take this. His honor was being challenged. It was impossible to back down.

"I'm not going anywhere," he snapped back, surprising even himself. Max was instantly wide awake and delighted with his tough-guy pose.

The newsie, like some animal taught to walk on his hind legs, lumbered into the center of what had become a very small circle. Yet, now standing just an arm's length away from Max, he waited. It was slowly occurring to him that this glowering little guy, a man who had oddly chosen this moment to button the middle button of his herringbone sport jacket, was a bit crazy and therefore a bit dangerous.

"Hey, you talking to me?" the newsie dumbly questioned; if the troublemaker in the jacket and tie wanted to walk away, he was prepared to let him.

But Max was going nowhere. Instead, he bounced on his toes, hopping in place with a kinetic excitement. With a barfly's admiration for quick and direct working-class showdowns, Max took a giant step away from the reserved personality he normally inhabited. He relished letting an anger fueled by a day's frustration fly.

"I'm not going anywhere until you take a hundred issues of the magazine. That's what Willy always takes, and that's what you, my big dumb friend, will take."

"Why ya little fuckin' Commie twerp," the larger man lashed out. "I'm gonna shove ya and ya pinko magazines in da goddamn sewer."

The newsie cocked a beefy fist. In moments it would be bound for the bridge of Max's nose.

Max, though a novice and a bantamweight, eyed a fleshy spot just above the newsie's changemaker. He was determined that his small fist would drive a spigot into that keg of a belly.

Suddenly, there was a knockout.

But nobody had thrown a punch. The newsie was bounced flat to the sidewalk by an overhead smash from a yard-high pile of *City* magazines.

Jonathan, looking more embarrassed than enraged, stood above his felled and dazed victim.

"I fought and bled for my country, sir," he informed the downed newsie in a voice rigid with southern aristocratic indignation. "I saw too many of my friends die to allow anyone to impugn the patriotism of my magazine."

The newsie, though his consciousness was a bit rumpled, attempted to rise; his hands were set to push off from the concrete.

But Jonathan was in no shape for another round. "I think we'd better go," the publisher informed a truly stunned Max. The editor looked like a man who, on seeing the shattered pieces of the boulder which crashed inches from his feet, had all of a sudden realized what danger he had been in; and from what danger he had narrowly escaped. Jonathan led his still silent friend to the station wagon.

They drove three blocks before Max spoke. "Thank you," he said. And with a shake of his head as if to show he still didn't totally understand precisely what had happened, added, "I could have gotten killed."

"You could have gotten us both killed, " Jonathan shouted, trying to dredge up some anger to hurl at his partner.

"It's been a long, hard day," Max offered as an apology.

"It certainly has." Jonathan studied his rheumy-eyed and hopelessly drained buddy. "I think," he decided, "I'd better take you home. I'll make the rest of the deliveries myself."

"I'd appreciate that," Max sighed.

THIS WAS THE deenergized Max, all his grace and his emotion discharged in the tumult of the assorted activities his magazine had required in the past thirty-one hours, who walked in on a very pregnant Janey sitting behind the kitchen table of their Bank Street apartment.

"You look beat. That's a sign it's a good issue," his wife said while he pecked her perfunctorily on the cheek. "Can I make you a cup of coffee?"

"I just want to get some sleep." He started to undo his tie as he headed out of the small kitchen and toward the bedroom.

Janey followed, eager to talk. It was the lonely morning after a lonelier night. She felt trapped: trapped in a strange, swollen body; trapped, a caution necessitated by her condition, in their two-room apartment; trapped in the oppressive poverty of their narrow lives together. She looked to Max, a hero to so many strangers, to liberate her, to share the seemingly glamorous world he had created.

Max gave nothing. His tight unwillingness to share his vision or even his day with his wife had little to do with his present body-aching weariness. Whether his sharp attitude toward Janey had its strident roots in a protective vanity about the intricacies of his creation or in a simple meanness of spirit had long ago ceased to be the speculative concern of this battle-scarred three-year-old marriage. The routine concern of both partners was more sullenly direct—who would land the first vindictive blow.

What was so disturbing to friends who caught small glimpses of his private ugliness toward his wife was the contrast between this hard attitude and Max's normal concern and consideration for so many casual acquaintances. "It's so unlike Max," Wendy Parker decided after witnessing a no-holds-barred fight between her hero and his wife. Yet Wendy and the others were unaware of the conjugal pinpricks tormenting the man they admired. They could not have imagined that the editor of *City* carried around a rough load of concealed insecurities.

Despite the cocky, wise front the editor put up to the small world he controlled, Janey's very presence rebuked her husband with the less flattering reality: Max was forty-three years old without a penny in the bank; a man drifting into middle-age yet still hustling to support himself and a pregnant wife on a $60-a-week salary from a magazine that might be only an issue away from coming to an abrupt end. He resented Janey with a misplaced hostility approaching Dorian Gray's for the portrait which pictured his true despair; Janey was his maliciously accurate mirror mocking the confident strut he executed down the linoleum corridors of his public power. She knew—and she would tease—his secret fear of his own inevitable failure, of his own unworthiness for the task he had set for himself. As revenge, and as protection, he shut her out of his magazine; and as with all imagined dreams, this unseen world took on for her an impossibly sweet reality, an imagined wonderfulness that made her spiteful for the loss she suffered.

The tangled pattern of their lives together was, in a large disastrous way, predetermined by the parameters of their marriage contract. It was a union based not on joy or raptures of passion; rather, on Max's decision finally to insulate himself from his decades of dissipated, feckless hanging about. He had looked for an anchor; yet this anchor had been cast into a seabed of compromise. Such sands were bound to shift.

Janey, following him that morning into the bedroom, gave it one more cautious shot. "What's the cover story this week?" she asked.

Max, flopping down on the bed, complained, "Can't I just get some sleep? I've been up for the past day."

The battle lines were drawn and Janey, knowing that she could never win, went out to do as much psychic damage as possible.

"Go ahead, sleep. I really don't care what's on the cover. It doesn't matter anyway. You realize that, don't you? Even if you sold out the entire issue—what's that, five, maybe eight thousand copies?" she asked.

Max didn't answer. He was stretched out in bed, still dressed in his flannel slacks, his eyes tightly shut.

"So you sell eight thousand copies," she went shrilly on, now standing over his prone body. "You're still not going to make any money. You're still not going to bring home more than sixty dollars this week. The two of us can't even live on that. What's going to happen when there's three of us? How are we going to live?"

Max lay motionless across the bed. His eyes remained shut. "I don't know," he conceded.

Having wounded swiftly and deeply on one painful front, Janey closed in on another tender target.

"It's all fine for you," she badgered away. "You come home after being away for God knows how long and you want to go straight to sleep. Well, you might want to give me a hand at something. In case you haven't noticed, I'm pregnant and it's hard for me to do everything. You might offer to give me a hand."

"What would you like me to do, Janey?" Max asked. His eyes remained shut.

"Well, you . . . uh . . . could . . ." There was a stammer as she hurried to decide; she had not anticipated winning so easily. In an instant, though, she was rolling: "You know you could take out the garbage. You know I shouldn't lift anything. And the pail is damn heavy. You might offer to do that, you know."

Max managed a laugh at the pervasive symmetry of the small private joke plaguing his day.

"What's so funny?" Janey demanded.

But Max, smirking quietly to himself, wasn't sharing anything. He simply rose from the bed, went to the kitchen, and took the half full pail of garbage out to the hall incinerator.

It was only as he was shoving the refuse down the chute that his smirk disappeared; and for a long woeful moment he became sadly grounded in his wife's telling logic—struggling *City* would never support a family. But, Max decided as he walked slowly back to the apartment, there was really no honorable alternative but to continue putting out the best magazine possible: He would stick with *his* magazine until the failure which he feared was creeping up on him, and Janey threatened was at hand, brought him firmly down.

EIGHT

DESPITE JANEY'S unsheathed threat or Max's unarticulated fears, the walls of his incipient kingdom didn't come tumbling down. Instead, fortune beyond either of their get-even dreams came true. But it was a long, rough time in coming.

For eight anxious and scraping years, the magazine continued to lose money. The partners tried all sorts of stopgap schemes. Max's meager salary was cut by a third and ultimately by a woeful half. Jonathan took no salary at all; he got by on the income from his small trust fund. Even the writers' minuscule fees were slashed; top dollar was $15 an article, regardless of how long-winded its length. Still, Jonathan found it necessary to wait until after the banks were closed on Friday afternoons to distribute these salary checks; and even then the staff was asked as a favor to wait until Tuesday before cashing them. Despite these economies, by the arrival of *City*'s fourth anniversary in June of 1958, the magazine seemed headed for bankruptcy. But then Jonathan, shaving off his bohemian beard and swallowing a substantial bit of his natural pride, made a whirlwind summer tour of his southern relatives, borrowed a bit against his future inheritance, and came back north with $17,000 in new capital for the magazine. "The most brazen looting of Dixie since Grant took Richmond," Max congratulated his friend upon the publisher's return. Yet, within a year and half, as the magazine entered the sixties, the money was all spent and doom was once more just around the corner.

Not that there weren't some triumphs. Wendy Parker's original whistle-blowing article on the superhighway planning to zoom through Washington Square Park became, with Max's encouragement, a series of weekly battle cries. Issue after issue, Wendy poked obsessively into another corner of the corrupt deal. It wasn't long before her uproarious shouts, after some careful tonings down, were picked up by the New York dailies and even the less strident community weeklies such as the

Village Voice and the *Villager*. Wendy had instinctively and emotionally outlined the patterns of corruption, and now the more rigorous *Times* and *Herald Tribune* investigative reporters, convinced as much by her anger as by her logic, set out to uncover the irrefutable evidence. It didn't take them long to dig it all up: a twisting, yet incriminating paper trail of transferred deeds, joint bank accounts, and canceled checks. The highway plan was abandoned, two Tammany leaders were indicted, and a respected banker decided to retire to his upstate horse farm. When the smoke cleared, even *Time* magazine had to admit that "the first potshots against the Goliath of Tammany schemers were taken by a brash, beatnik David—little *City* magazine and its self-styled political scribe Wendy Parker. It was housewife turned journalist Parker, 33, who each week poured out her heart (and at least an innuendo or two) as she continued to lead her then lonely personal crusade against the power brokers. . . ."

This victory, though, while it gave struggling *City* some clout in uptown newsrooms and scared the daylights out of a lot of politicians, did little to increase circulation. Max, however, picking up on the nonstop weekly activity in his letters columns, came up with a plan that would not only get more local voices into his magazine, but would also require these writers to pay for the privilege of speaking their brief piece. He set aside a page of the magazine for a City Bulletin Board ("Just like the one near the door at the White Horse," he explained to Jonathan. "No one comes in without checking out those three by five cards to see if there's a cheap apartment for rent or at least a used Tarot deck for sale.") and Jonathan came up with the democratic rate of 15 cents a word. Now people started buying *City* for these personal ads as well as its articles. Starting with the April 14 issue in 1959, each week you could turn to the City Bulletin Board and read such notices as:

Joey: I miss your bongo playing. You can drum on me anytime. Come home. Cindy.

Gifted writer would like to contact interplanetary visitors. Eager to tell your story to the world. Subjects must be willing to sign release forms for domestic, foreign, and extraterrestrial rights.

I desperately need 12,000 feet of aluminum foil for an entertaining purpose too complicated to explain.

Wanted: Driver with diplomatic immunity to share life on the road with free-wheeling Barnard drop-out. No Dharma bums need apply.

Still, as Jonathan told the editor after the two weary partners had sat in their office going over the red-inked books till 2 a.m. on December 7, 1962, "The wolf is no longer at the door. He's huffed and he's puffed and he's blown our house down. I think maybe it's time we cut our losses."

Max remained silent. He knew the losses were more Jonathan's than his. But he just did not want to quit. How could he explain—even to Jonathan!—that there was no life other than his magazine for him to fit in to. When he finally spoke, he tried not to make his words seem too much like a plea. "There must be some money out there. Can't we raise enough cash for one more issue? Maybe just one more?"

"The banks won't even let us in the front door and we've already borrowed from everyone I can think of." Jonathan got up from his desk and began pacing. Unconsciously he stroked his beard. Perhaps, Max thought, he was already contemplating shaving it off and making another trip to the old folks down home.

"Look, if we can't raise the money, we can't," Max announced with little conviction.

"I didn't say that," Jonathan answered immediately. "We'll do it somehow," he insisted. "We're too close to give up now. I just feel it."

"So do I," Max lied.

But they were close. The partners, even as they sat that morning in their office worrying, were unaware of the two querulous sides just beginning to dig in across a bargaining table in a midtown hotel—the real-life thesis and antithesis that would rock their whole futures.

For at 4:17 that afternoon, Pearl Harbor Day 1962, the head of the New York Typographical Union, Local Number 6, took his Corona Corona out of his thick-lipped mouth; blew a puff of smoke into the stunned faces of the assembled daily press lords of New York; and then, ending twenty-seven hours of negotiations, growled, "That's our final offer. Take it or leave it." When the smoke cleared from their eyes, the press lords' response was a seigneurial, "We'll leave it." Thus began the longest newspaper strike in New York City's history.

For 114 days not a daily newspaper was printed. It was a duration Max always felt had some sort of numerological significance—the strike lasted precisely three months, three weeks, and three days. But the editor, like a graduate student poring over Faulkner, could never decide on what it really meant.

It was certain, though, that in the 114-day shutdown of New York's papers, *City*'s future was written and Max's nascent success was sealed. Max and Jonathan no longer had the problem of convincing either advertisers or newsies of the merits of their magazine: Nonunion *City* was the only weekly or daily coming off the presses. And news-starved New Yorkers, initially grabbing *City* from the stands out of desperation, continued buying it week after week when the strike was settled. The class struggle busting loose all around them had rescued the two bystanders. *City* was on its way to becoming a household word. And Max Fox, at forty-nine, learned that he was not too old to be fortune's child.

NINE

SILK BLOUSES. The crisp, rich rustling through drawers layered with many deep-hued silk blouses. Each day now began for Janey with this private and affirming gesture: a luxuriously abundant love song played out in the staccato sounds of crinkling silk; each enjoyed note a measure of her husband's tardy success; and, by extension, her own newly realized position.

Not long after the money from *City* first started rolling in, Janey made an excursion uptown—in those tentative days, anything above 14th Street was part of the grander uptown world—and wound up at Saks Fifth Avenue. It was an impetuous journey. She had suddenly decided she needed tangible proof of the change in her fortunes.

Janey wandered, antsy with covetous wonder, through the wide aisles of the great store. Taking it all in, she became excited by the activity around her, a promiscuous hubbub of women intimate with wealth and glamour; the rainbow scents of perfumes huddling about; the dismissive clink of steel hangers as rows of dresses were perused; the displays of erect, unshrouded lipsticks, so many subtle shades of the simple red on her lips that Janey silently marveled at the imagined ingenuity of the women who could coordinate a day's events with the proper inflection of color; and, wherever she looked, display cases of clear glass filled with careless stacks of fancy goodies—the brightest of scarfs, the sheerest of nylons, the softest of lingerie. Envy and desire were romping through her. Yet, as eager as she was to cut loose on an expensive field day, she was being roped in by the iniquitous restraining tug of her own insecurities— she didn't know how to play this uptown game.

Fortunately, her first lesson in the manners of success was quickly delivered. As Janey continued working her way through this shiny ground floor maze of fashions, she noticed a woman standing in front of the blouse counter. It was the woman's nonchalance that attracted Janey. She was a rigid, swept-back blonde who Janey decided—adding an additional crease to her troubled mind—had to be years younger than she; still, this young woman's effortless manner presented a maturer confidence, her lazy slim-fingered hand absently resting on the countertop as if on the head of a favorite beagle just in from the morning's hunt. To amuse this poised young blonde, an avid salesgirl paved the top of the display case with a long and winding road of silk blouses. Each blouse was clearly green, yet each blouse was clearly unique. A palette inspired by emeralds and limes and meadows of fresh-cut summer grass was being dutifully spread.

"I think this one might go nicely with your coloring," the salesgirl suggested, choosing a dark, moody green shade of heavy silk.

The blonde almost offered a smile, then reconsidered.

But the salesgirl's officious zeal went undeterred. "It would really be quite lovely on you," she insisted and tried to demonstrate her point by holding the blouse up against the customer's chest.

The blonde pulled back as if assaulted. It was a quick, instinctive reflex. Janey, peering wide-eyed through a strategic gap in a neck-high wall of atomizers crowding the adjacent perfume counter, thought it was terrific stuff. She silently cheered the blonde's crass but protective arrogance. And, to Janey's edification and delight, the performance continued.

"No, I think not," said the woman with just the slightest nod of her blond head. Yet, Janey saw, it was a gesture complete and condemning in its disdain; if only, Janey wished, she had the confidence to speak such a terse body language.

"Of course," said the salesgirl.

Then, with a clipped burst of words and motions that would forever live in Janey's mind, the woman walked the length of the display counter, a lone finger tracing a swift cedilla in the air as she announced, "I'll take this." The cedilla accented a pale green blouse. "And this." The moving finger fell on a green silk just a shade darker. And so she proceeded, her steps paralleled on the other side of the counter by the attentive salesgirl. Her decisiveness thrilled Janey: It was so godlike in both its authority and its arbitrariness. When the blonde had reached the end of the silken line, she had accumulated by Janey's count seven varyingly green blouses. Such casual extravagance made Janey giddy. And, as Janey was about to overhear, it was an even more indulgent performance than she had imagined—the blouses went for $112.50 a pop. A plastic credit card was produced.

"I'd like them sent."

Janey, tingling like a spy who has just pocketed a secret formula, hurried from Saks. So this is how it's done, she thought.

And on the very next day that's how she did it. Down to the vague cedillas she drew in the air as she indicated her two (she was still a novice, after all) choices. When she got around to instructing "I'll have them sent," and reached for her credit card, Janey felt like a new woman. She had power.

From this accidental encounter, a bit of Janey's personality was filled in. She believed she had found a way to confront a life which had gotten the better of her. The aches, of course, had all been dug painfully deep even years before life with Max had further scraped these anxieties to their tender roots; as a teenager in Brooklyn she was already displaying the tense fragility that made her quiver like a stranded songbird that had stayed up north too long into winter; way back then she was already surrounded by tormenting insecurities that made her feel that everyone was just a bit thinner, a bit wiser, a bit luckier. But in an afternoon at Saks Janey latched on to a battle plan to deal with them. Janey, now a woman in her early forties with a wealthy and successful husband, set out to prove to herself she was as good as everyone else. And that blonde in Saks became her mentor.

The silk blouses became her obsessive metaphor for making it. Janey dressed to kill her bleak past. Methodically, she worked her way through an expensive spectrum. First the basic colors; then she did shades; then she went after the seasons; until she finally wound up buying without even caring. Her drawers were layered with silks. With each purchase Janey felt she was buying another cloak of dignity, of confidence. These acquisitions served as her proof that she was Mrs. Max Fox, the wife of the editor of *City* magazine.

But that was not all Janey learned from the blonde in Saks. Janey did her best to mimic the woman's nonchalant arrogance. And not simply with salesgirls. She started to do her imitative high-hat routine with everyone she met. She even stretched this white-gloved act to the point that she developed an oddly affected English accent.

Max, beyond caring, found her new behavior ludicrous; it was added to his mental list, a further charge against her. "You know where she learned her king's English?" he told Jonathan. "Kings Highway."

CHARTS. BRIGHT RED arrows starting out in the dumps and then gradually reaching for the sky. Bar graphs where the stubby black ink bars kept on working their way up toward the top of the page like steps in a stadium. All over the walls in the corner of the office he shared with Max, Jonathan had hung these homemade testimonies documenting their magazine's newly achieved success. And just as Janey had her silk blouses, these charts were Jonathan's obsessive metaphor, his self-affirming proof he had finally made it.

At first Max thought Jonathan was putting him on. The newspaper strike had dragged into its ninth week (and the *City* gang was praying for at least nine more) when Max discovered Jonathan hunched over his desk, a ruler and a red crayon in hand.

"Arts and crafts? Or simply vocational therapy?" Max asked.

Jonathan never heard him; he was that wrapped up in his creation.

Max stomped theatrically over to Jonathan's desk, but the publisher continued, oblivious.

"Jonathan!" Max yelled.

Jonathan looked up. "Oh, I didn't hear you come in."

"Helping your kids with their homework?" Max attempted this time.

"No, no, Max. This is serious. Important. Take a look." Jonathan held up the now finished chart. There were all kinds of minute but carefully written words running up the left-hand margin and across the bottom of the page. A bright red thunderbolt flashed through the middle of the cardboard.

"I don't get it. Does this mean the patient's dying, or is he going to live to pay his bill?" The past two months of unanticipated success had made Max very loose.

"Oh, the patient's going to live all right. Better than that. He can even afford to pay his bill. Here," Jonathan continued, as he grabbed two thumbtacks off his desk and used them to hang his cardboard chart on the wall, "let me explain."

"Please do, doctor."

"You can joke all you want, Max," said Jonathan, "but I'm proud of this. And you should be too. Hell, you made it happen as much as me. More."

"Let me hold off taking any bows until I know just what this is all about."

"I ahm trahying to explain, Max." The South had crept unconsciously into his voice, a sign Jonathan was struggling with his temper. There was also an impatient frown.

"So what's stopping you?"

Jonathan ran his hand through his thinning hair; it was a mannerism he resorted to in those moments when another person might count to ten or bite his tongue. But in a flash he recovered, his voice racing with delight: "You see these numbers here refer to circulation figures for the last twelve weeks . . ."

Jonathan hurried into a scrupulously detailed recitation of the statistics of *City*'s current boom. Except for nodding eagerly whenever Jonathan seemed to slow down, Max listened without even trying to figure out what it all was about. Jonathan insisted, however, in demonstrating how precisely he was on top of everything. He displayed sheets of exact and complicated figures. These numbers added up to nothing for Max.

The editor did notice, though, that when Jonathan in the course of proving some esoteric point marched his fingers about the chart, the nails were brutally chewed; Max realized his friend, now also a husband and the recent father of twin girls, must be having quite a time of it at home.

"What it all comes down to," Jonathan concluded as he patted the chart on the wall as if it were the broad back of his best buddy, "is that with each of the last six issues circulation has risen an average of twelve thousand copies a week. And wait till you see the graph I'm putting together on the increase in ads. The department stores are booking full pages for months in advance."

"So the bottom line is that after all these years I can finally afford to buy you a beer?" Max asked.

"You can even spring for the imported stuff."

"I'll drink to that."

And they did. They were sitting in a booth at the Cedar Tavern putting away what Max felt was either their fourth or fifth round of Heinekens when he got around to asking Jonathan, "How are things at home?"

"The twins are great," Jonathan answered quickly. "They're starting to walk."

"And Rochelle?" When Jonathan had turned forty-two, he had told Max he was beginning to think it was time he got married. A couple of months later he met Rochelle. The red-haired daughter of a screenwriter blacklisted because he had once spoken too loudly at a party about wishing he had fought with the Abraham Lincoln Brigade and a mother who had religiously paid her Party dues until Stalin inked his pact with Hitler, Rochelle had grown up on the unsuccessful fringes of Hollywood. She left California—where at five ten in her sneakers, she had perfected a devastating cross-court shot—and came to New York singularly intent on marrying the first doctor or lawyer who asked her out on a second date. There weren't many second dates. But she did meet the handsome, well-bred publisher of *City* at a dinner party and it wasn't long before she was looking with more than casual interest at the fur coats advertised in the Sunday *Times Magazine*. Three months after they met, Jonathan had his wife and Rochelle had a beaver coat.

"She's a good mother," Jonathan eventually managed.

It took another round before Jonathan blurted it all out: "I know you think I'm crazy with these goddamn charts. Of course I knew you weren't paying attention." Though closing in on fifty, Max could still come up with the same charmingly sheepish grin he had perfected as a youngster when he was perpetually being caught in some red-handed act by his chagrined mother. Jonathan fell for his friend's repentant smile and agreed, "Sure, you're probably right not to take it all seriously. I can understand that, Max. But the numbers, the goddamn charts—I tell you, they mean a lot to me.

"It's not just that they mean money. You know I've always had some money and I always will. I've never claimed to be poor."

Max agreed: "That's the first thing I ever liked about you. You didn't go on about being down and out like a lot of phony trust fund bohemians we hung out with in the old days." Immediately, and with surprising warmth, Max found himself flashing on all the times Jonathan had reached for the bill.

"Whatever," Jonathan continued, brushing aside his friend's compliment. "But I spent my whole life living with the luck of having a wealthy father who was the son of an even wealthier daddy. The only thing I did to deserve that was to be born. I'm not complaining . . ."

"Only a fool would," Max interrupted.

"But I'm not taking any credit for it either. You understand that, Max?"

There was a swift nod of the editor's head.

"Okay," Jonathan went on. "So then I got married because it seemed easier than not being married. I have two girls and I love them, Max. I sincerely do. But I never really wanted children. Rochelle and I had children because there seemed to be no reason not to have them. I tell you, Max, the only thing I ever really wanted was some kind of success of my own. Something that I, Jonathan Trout, did all by myself. And now it's finally happened. Sure, I didn't do it all by myself. I did it with you. But I don't mind sharing anything with you, Max. Just as long as it's ours and no one else's. You can laugh at my charts if you want. But I tell you every time I look at them I think Jonathan Trout has finally accomplished something. So c'mon, Max, let me have my goddamn charts. Okay? Let me plaster the fucking walls with them. We worked hard, didn't we?"

"And somebody must have prayed hard for us, too," Max said, more seriously than his friend realized.

"Well, our prayers were answered. Now I want to have my fun. All right?"

"I'll even buy the cardboard," Max said. Just as he would pay the bills each month for Janey's silks.

But as they were leaving the bar, a tipsy Jonathan turned to his friend and asked, "Now truthfully, Max, what do you hope to get out of all this? The ship has finally come in—what's it brought you?"

Max, though normally talkative when a bit tight, smiled. One of his mystically devilish smiles. He was glad his secret didn't show.

"C'mon, Jonathan," was all he offered, "it's time to weave our way back to the office. We still have an issue to put out this week."

CLASS. THAT'S WHAT the editor wanted from all the fuss fate was suddenly making out of his life. That was the improbable gift Max—a man who didn't have a real job until he was forty—was hoping the polish of accomplishment would bestow. Max, not unlike his wife and best friend, was desiring a sort of confidence: the public recognition that he was no longer an outsider. People would no longer judge him as another bohemian superciliously posing above the fray; success would make Fox *better* than the fray.

This ambition was really nothing new for Max. The hints were always there. He had his clocks and he had his instinctively detached mien and, even when he was down and out, he always tried to dress like a tweedy squire. Now he also had money.

Of course Max didn't pretend his making it in a loud, worldly way would automatically deliver the sort of respect he secretly wanted. "The fact is, anyone can make a million in America," Max would lecture a mute and uncomprehending Janey with the swaggering logic of a man who was zeroing in on doing just that. "But the real challenge is how a fellow carries himself with his dough. How a gentleman spends his brass."

Money, then, was the necessary but not the sufficient in his personal equation. Now that he had the "brass"—and by the way he hesitated before he rolled the word from his lips, it was apparent he suspected there were people around town referring to his "shekels"—he set about, very circumspectly, to acquire class. Poor self-tormenting Max. Not that he missed catting around Village bars with Jonathan or fighting with newsies; such behavior was largely put on, anyway. But from the start, he understood his aspirations were a waste of time. A victim of the instincts and ambitions that made him a snob, he realized he was doomed in his own terms always to be a bounder. It just was not done in one untidy generation. Yet his vanity required he play out his game; it was, now that the dust of his hectic life was clearing, the only blessing he still lusted after.

He began to follow some rather eccentric self-prescribed rules of

conduct. Of course he realized anything flashy is bad form. But Max—
like Janey and Jonathan in their off-the-wall ways—did get a bit rigid
in his privatism. People who did not know him thought he was simply
neurotically shy. How were they to know he was attempting to behave
like a gentleman? Consider this one small example.

The 1964 Senate race in New York State was a pretty rough-and-
tumble affair. Bobby Kennedy, heir to his family's philosophy, fortune,
and—most detrimental, considering the circumstances—broad Massa-
chusetts accent, was pitted against a vituperative conservative field, first
in the Democratic primary and then in the general election. The opposition was taking lots of telling swipes at both his Vuitton and carpet bags.
Working people of New York were being warned against voting for a
staggeringly wealthy man who, though he kept a pied-à-terre (this foreign phrase made it seem all the more illicit!) in Manhattan, actually
lived in another state. The early polls forewarned toothy-grinned Bobby
going down for the electoral count.

Enter Max the kingmaker. Actually, though a lot of the credit was
going to be aimed his way, more deserving was Max's now full-bloomed
discovery, his political columnist Wendy Parker. Over the last decade
her columns of gritty, personal commentary had acquired a well-known
and well-feared sting. She, as Max had predicted, hurled accusations
which other journalists would feel skittish about even thinking. Max, in
his own mind a patrician Tory with a mischievous streak, didn't give a
hoot about politics; but he found Wendy's throw-the-rascals-out prose
great entertainment.

Whether it was the editor who suggested Wendy consider following
the Kennedy campaign or whether the idea was Wendy's to this day
causes the two friends to raise their voices. However, both agree the
inspiration was malicious: Wendy would keep on his tail until she found
a way to deliver the kayo punch to the carpetbagger.

Except it didn't work out that way at all. Wendy found a hero.

Throughout the primary and then during the general election campaign Wendy filed articles that gushed. Week after week, Bobby was
portrayed in the pages of *City*, as "honorable," "saintlike," "moral," "a
defender of the liberal tradition," and "a champion of blue-collar work-
ers who also is at home with Camus." Her articles might have gotten a
bit tedious in all their uncharacteristic effusion, except Wendy now hurled
her zingers without mercy at Bobby's opposition; each week in the pages
of *City* they were "malevolent," "snide," "corrupt," "neanderthal," and
"betrayers of their working-class roots." Max, who really didn't care one
way or the other about Bobby Kennedy, printed all of Wendy's stories
simply because she was his political reporter. He wouldn't dream of
telling her what to think; only how to.

The day after Kennedy was elected, Wendy, near to bursting under the excitement, trundled into Max's office.

"I just got a call from Bobby," she announced.

The editor was immediately put off by the coziness he was expected to be a party to. "Bobby who?" he deadpanned.

"Cute, Max. You know, the senator-elect."

"Oh," Max went laboriously on as if it were all suddenly becoming clear, "you mean *Robert* Kennedy."

Wendy ignored the barb. "Anyway Bobby, or the senator if you prefer that, Max, called to thank me for what I had written about him during the campaign."

"You certainly were kind," Max agreed. "It didn't seem like you."

Wendy continued stiff-arming Max's little nudges. She went on: "The senator didn't call just to thank me. He wanted to speak with you."

"You know I don't like phones," Max growled. Somewhere Max had read or heard it was bad form to talk too often on the phone.

"That's what I told him."

"Good girl." Max literally breathed a sigh of relief.

"So you know what Bobby, I mean the senator, suggested? He said why don't I come down to the offices and meet the great Max Fox? That's what he called you—'the great Max Fox.'"

"This is getting to be a bit much, Wendy. I hope you explained to him how busy I am."

"I did like hell. I told him you'd be glad to meet him. He's coming here at three tomorrow afternoon."

"Jesus, Wendy."

But at 2:45 the next day Max was behind his desk. He had put some consideration into how he should present himself to a man who was a senator, a Kennedy, and who, if Wendy's published encomiums were to be believed, actually spoke from a political philosophy, not merely position papers. He was certain the senator was coming downtown anticipating a meeting with a rather scruffy bohemian. Max, however, played out a script designed to surprise the senator. The editor did himself up for the occasion like some stuffy banker in a vested, mournfully gray flannel, a correspondingly lugubrious bluish tie, and a white button-down. His brier pipe was filled with a blend he felt had the cool, manly air of the Scottish moors and set down inches from his left hand; at the first signal of the senator's arrival he would light the damn thing and pop it between his lips. And Max had also made sure an imposing number of galleys were spread in seemingly haphazard intellectual frenzy across the top of his desk; copy which the senator would intuit required the wise editorial touch of the "great Max Fox" before it could be printed.

It was a couple of minutes after three when Max heard some commotion outside his closed door. As he lit his pipe he could hear Phil the copy editor stuttering out, "S-s-s-so ve-r-ry glad t-t-to m-m-meet you, S-s-sen . . ."

Max never knew if Phil ever managed to get out the rest of his greeting. Before Phil could finish, Max, trailing an aroma of manly smoke, had decided to leave his office by a rear, rarely used fire door. It wasn't that he thought himself too good to meet with Bobby Kennedy, Max told himself as he hurried down the rear stairs. It was simply that it was . . . *unseemly* for him, an editor, to accept the public thanks of a man who, when you got right down to it, was just another politician. A gentleman runs his business the way he thinks proper; he doesn't require friendship or even thanks for doing his job. Such testimonial scenes are superfluous, even vulgar, Max decided as he took refuge in the luncheonette up the street. He was sipping a cup of milky tea and making small talk with the Greek counterman while the senator-elect from the state of New York, two of his aides, and an embarrassed Wendy Parker were wondering where in hell Max Fox had disappeared. And why.

THIS WAS THE well-known Max Fox as Russell Lewis, a pink-cheeked, still ripening twenty-two-year-old, first met him. Russ met a man whose portrait was ready for commissioning: The editor was already gray-haired, already intimate with success, already wincing whenever he thought of Janey, already looking backwards at fifty-six years— more than two-thirds of the territory the Bible grants as our just deserts —filled with poverty, vanities, carousing, and now reputation.

Who would have thought these two men, emissaries of different generations, would find their ambitions and their futures and their desires become so entwined?

TEN

IF RUSS LEWIS had shown the guts to get arrested, he
might never have met Max Fox.

This public disgrace began to play itself out during the unseasonably warm spring of 1969. The campus walks were lined with neat blocks
of bright yellow daffodils; there was a whiff of lilac in the Quad; fresh
purple wisteria was climbing amongst the ivy; life was still pass/fail; and
the action faction decided to celebrate by liberating the computer center.

Why did Russ Lewis wind up going along for the putsch? He wasn't
"political"; it was more his style to raise a mocking eyebrow than to
throw a rock. Nor was he, despite being a government major, the sort to
carry a placard; he was embarrassed by clichés. You couldn't even count
on him to march for peace; he detested the grim, self-congratulatory
pride that generally accompanied undergraduate protest. But Russ Lewis
was greedy. And he was a schemer. And the boy wanted to get laid.

The focus of his lust (and the cause of his brief radicalization) that
fine spring afternoon was a raven-headed textile heiress who owned, Russ
had estimated, enough cable-knit crewnecks to outfit the combined field
hockey teams of New England's most select boarding schools. After
having endured a soporific fifty minutes of Western Civ, Russ and Janet
were stretched recuperatively out, hand in tight hand, as they lay drows-
ily across the warm green grass fronting the main library. Russ was
searching for a suitably cajoling note to convince Janet to cut Feminist
Literature 101 ("What's up for Clit Lit this week? Oh, I can see it now:
A bunch of repressed sophomores sitting around debating whether Molly
Bloom was really faking it or not. And all the time they're wondering if
they have a date for Friday night," was his aggressive opening gambit)
and head back to his room with him when the bullhorn-wielding mob
assembled on the library steps.

That did it. Sex was nothing new to Janet, but taking a building
was. "Don't you realize, Russ, this is our chance to stand up and be
counted," she insisted.

"I don't want to be counted. And I don't want to stand up. I enjoy lying down. With you."

But Janet was the sort of confident rich girl born to give ultimatums: "Either you march with us, Russell Lewis, or this is the last time you'll ever see me."

So Russ went. He, truth be known, considered calling her bluff, but such a hardnosed attitude was quickly overwhelmed by the contemplation of what was at stake: Here was a girl who allowed him to zip around campus in her fire engine red Alfa Romeo with the Hermes scarf knotted around the stick shift; and softly well-mannered Janet, Russ had found out the night before, would come with the boisterously screaming delight of a preppy who has just learned she's been accepted by the college of her choice.

(Also, though Russ was unaware of it at the time, there was another inducement brewing. Janet's father was on the verge of the greatest breakthrough in contemporary garment district history—branding the name of a nice Jewish boy from Brooklyn on the rear of dungarees. Such a visionary insight into the insecurities of his fellow Americans—the well-known name on my behind loudly whines that I'm a class act—would propel an ingenious man from mere wealth into this country's aristocracy of foundation-endowing tycoondom.)

Conscripts motivated by less commitment and vaguer fumblings of the heart have found themselves at the front.

Yet Russ's enthusiasm soon faltered. After three fraternal hours in the liberated computer center he was getting jittery. At first he blamed his uneasiness on the lights and the noise. Long rows of harsh fluorescent tubing illuminated the mysteriously humming machines scattered across a static-free carpeted plain the size of a couple of football fields. The stark glow from this artificial light never varied; neither did the hum. He could feel the powerful technology working him over.

"You're just chicken," Janet taunted as he tried to explain his unease. A threat was made clear when she withdrew her pale blue Shetland arm from his. "A real coward."

Before Russ could argue, events seemed to prove Janet's point. An amplified voice that sounded as if it were calling from the depths of a stormy sea began chanting: "End U.S. imperialism now! . . . End U.S. imperialism now! . . ." When the chant reached a hold-that-line pitch, the rocks started flying. The broad picture windows of the Saul and Millie Abramowitz Computer Center were the targets. Glass fell in shattered acres. Russ flinched. Janet, beyond gestures, walked away. But Russ, made increasingly jumpy by the sharp, sudden sounds of sporadically breaking glass, remained puzzled: How would a windowless Saul and Millie Abramowitz Computer Center help end imperialism?

It was in these wired moments that Russ Lewis realized he was in over his head. I don't belong with this crowd, he decided. I don't think or feel or see like they do. I want out.

And yet, he was learning, it takes a certain staunchness to cut and run. So Russ probably would have spent the night in the computer center; but then he received his sign. It was right there on the cinder-block wall.

Chris, a genially oafish senior with dusty brown hair which fell with plumb-line straightness to his broad shoulders, had written it in foot-high letters with a can of red spray paint. The message was succinct: "U.S.— Get Out of Viet Nam." But it wasn't the philosophy that filled Russ with the fervor of detachment; it was the philosopher. One look at Chris's face, at the boxy chin, pug nose, and high, already lined forehead, gave him away. His was a youthful replica of the wooden face that talked tough on Cronkite and stared them down from the cover of *Newsweek*. Chris's father was the Secretary of Defense. If Chris wanted the U.S. out of Viet Nam, then he could have accomplished more by calling home —collect. Instead, Russ felt with some determination, Chris and he were participating in what really was just a rude, messy prank, a rite of spring that would be cleaned up by the campus maintenance crew in the morning.

That's when he decided to split. "You can finish the revolution without me," he told Janet. And, as the cops were threatening to pound down the front door, he hightailed it out the back.

The next day, though, Russ was cursing his decision. Not long after he ran, the cops made their bust. Eighty-eight students—Janet and Chris prominent among the chosen—were arrested and charged, after con-ciliatory deliberations between the provost and the more hard-line local authorities, with trespassing. The university was willing to shrug off the nearly $800,000 in damages to the building, and eighty-eight of his friends got off with misdemeanors. But, as testimony to their fervor, they had received rap sheets, pink badges of courage which they flaunted about campus with mirthful disdain. Janet, in fact, had bullied her father's attorney into procuring a copy of the mug shot snapped when she had been booked: Beyond the faint outline of the Cartier tank watch on her thin wrist, soft hands ending in manicured nails hold the row of booking numbers against her cable-knit chest. She hung the photograph over her toilet. A bit of camp.

The only thing Russ Lewis had to hang, it was clear from the abuse Janet and the rest of the action faction were dishing out, was his coward's head. Forget about his getting into bed with the sports-car-driving Rosa Luxemburg; Janet wouldn't even sit next to him in Western Civ. Russ had committed caste suicide.

His was a lonely, restless exile. Then, while planted in the library one night—what else was there to do now but study?—Russ stumbled

onto a plan for his deliverance. Throughout that tedious evening he had
been glancing up from his *Problems in International Relations* to stare
across the room at a hook-nosed girl with monstrous breasts. Now she
was taking a break, and selfishly covering his view of those amazing
breasts, by thumbing through a magazine. A copy of *City* magazine.
Instantly he stopped fantasying. With breathtaking clarity, a scheme
became clear: Russ Lewis, an upstart college junior, would describe for
this trendy, big-time journal all he had seen and felt that day when he
and his fellow crusaders had so destructively liberated the computer
center.

Never again would he write so easily. There was no pain, no false
starts. By ten the next morning a piece he titled "You Can Finish the
Revolution Without Me" was typed and ready to be mailed. He copied
the magazine's New York City address from an old issue; and then, after
scanning the masthead, he wrote as an afterthought on the envelope,
"Attention: Mr. Max Fox."

SUBMITTING HIS article to *City* was an inspired choice.
This was the era when reading the magazine was a political and intellectual act: *City* wasn't just hip; it made you hip. If you saw someone on
campus clutching a copy of *City*, you naturally assumed this was the sort
of person you'd want to sit around with for at least one beer.

Not that Max Fox, flushly conservative with success and tiptoeing
toward his old age, was an authority on this self-proclaimed New Age.
However, he still had his knack for assembling gung-ho explorers. A
young, eclectic crew had been recruited during *City*'s second decade: a
Maine-bred East Village superintendent who saw all that was nasty and
brutish about city life as an opportunity to spout off as an instinctive,
but aggressive autocrat; a Peace Corps veteran of fabulous inherited
wealth who chased about the country spreading her indefatigably beatific
radicalism; an Annapolis grad, a descendant of a flotilla of admirals, who
was born, instead, to raise self-posturing hell and then write about it un-
abashedly; a chubby kid from Queens, the son of a cop, who invented
the hermeneutics of rock 'n' roll; a former longshoreman who gruffly
relied on street smarts to grapple with existential despair as well as three-
horse parlays; and a renegade English lit instructor from Harvard who
had so conscientiously stuffed his mind with Dickens and his body with
assorted visionary pharmaceuticals that he could detect the most incredible nuances submerged in ordinary events.

Other than the ambition and ego that are endemic to all who set out to fill a blank page with words, these *City* writers had little in common. The levels of mutual antagonism were generally at a feuding pitch; yet, there was one common denominator that united these cantankerous spirits—their allegiance to Max. His control, his careful psychological manipulation of each of his chosen troopers, was complete. More than that, there existed a debt that each of these writers acknowledged: It was Max who had bestowed his editorial blessings on all of them, giving these unknowns the chance to strut their talents in public.

The setup, and this was also Max's inspired design, was feudal. The scribbling serfs, begrudged a bread-and-water salary reminiscent of the magazine's earlier down-and-out days, were granted fields of newsprint to plant and nurture with their words; Max gobbled up the profits from these fecund labors. Still there were few complaints; and it wasn't just that each of the staff writers knew his presence was solely at Max's grace and favor. Ambition had them looking toward the future. All these fledgling journalists sincerely believed that if they stuck with *City* they would eventually be discovered. The Big Time, the book or movie or play you *know* you have bubbling inside you, was just a Big Deal away.

THERE WAS ANOTHER reason why Russ mailed his article to *City*—Conrad Franklin. Conrad's by-line encouraged Russ's hope that something he wrote might find a place in the magazine. Each week, Conrad filed rumbling, personal reports about goings-on in the East Village, Vermont communes, and be-ins or smoke-ins. He didn't pose as a reporter; he wrote with the critical passion of a participant.

To thousands of readers like Russ, Conrad was a romantic figure, a writer caught up in the confusion and the ideals of his generation. Conrad was also, of all the young handpicked talents crowding *City*'s offices, Max's undisputed favorite. Such attention and affection encouraged a flood of jealous theories.

One particularly insidious explanation centered around the twenty-four-year-old's pedigree. Snobby Max, claimed those he ignored, was taken by one of his writers' being the son of an ambassador; the elder Franklin, an Indianapolis lawyer of long-forgotten peddler stock, now represented his government in Sydney. It was an explanation with a seductive morsel of truth, but the whole loaf was this: While Max was impressed by the authentic currency backing the Franklin name, what impressed him more was how the youth recklessly transcended the stuffy confines of his heritage.

Conrad served as Max's daring explorer of the sixties, the editor's personal emissary to the front. Deskbound Max, his bohemian decades of hanging-out long gone, now lived vicariously through the youth. And those were heady times; people used words like "apocalyptic" and "revolution" seriously. But before Conrad sat down at his typewriter, he would first deliver an oral report to General Max. The two would remain for hours in the editor's office, the door shut, until finally Conrad would emerge and set out on a marathon bout of writing.

"Conrad Franklin is the bravest boy I have ever known," Max told Wendy Parker, now his city editor, after one of these meetings. "He lives his stories. He takes risks. And he struggles until he can put into words exactly what he feels about his experiences. He's not afraid to turn any point of view inside out." Wendy realized this was the highest compliment Max could offer.

What went on at those closed-door sessions? How did Max crank Franklin or any of his young charges up? When queried about his editing technique Max would shoot you one of his infuriatingly complacent tight-lipped smiles; or, if the mood were right and the Scotch was making him warm and prankish, he would offer a parable of sorts:

"My wife, Janey," he would begin, "has a cousin. A very religious man." Max would invariably at this point in the tale shrug his shoulders in mock exasperation; we men of the world, he complained with this pantomime, realize religion is a very silly passion. "To appreciate all this, you should be aware he was from Brooklyn"—Max paused for an implied smirk at Janey's roots—"and he was having some sort of feud with his partner. They sold corsets.

"The partner was trying to force him out, I think. Anyway, Janey's cousin is becoming frantic. He doesn't know what to do. So someone tells him to see the Lubavitcher rebbe. The Lubavitcher rebbe is"—now Max, trying a bit too hard, has broken into a gross Yiddish accent—"da visest man. Da rebbe vill know vut ta do.

"So Janey's cousin makes an appointment to see the rebbe. It takes four weeks to see the great man and, for some mumbo-jumbo reason I'll never understand, the tradition is that the rebbe only grants interviews after midnight. But the month passes and at twelve fifteen Janey's cousin schleps"—the editor has slipped; he looks to see if you caught it—"to this synagogue in Williamsburg. He gets there and the place is mobbed with people. All sorts of rabbis decked out in long black coats and beards. He's told to wait. There are two people ahead of him.

"First a lawyer, and I mean a big-time lawyer, a partner in a major firm, goes into to see the rebbe. Fifteen minutes pass and the lawyer emerges and all the rabbis crowd around and demand, 'Nu, vut did da rebbe say?' and the lawyer looks at them and exclaims, 'What that man knows about law! He's a genius.' And the rabbis ooh and ah.

"Then the doctor, a heart surgeon, goes off for his interview. When it's over the rabbis again crowd about and the doctor tells them. 'What that man knows about medicine! He's a genius.' The rabbis are now oohing and ahhing to beat the band.

"It's nearly one in the morning before Janey's cousin is called for his interview, but he's very excited. He's going to get his chance to learn all the answers. He's led into a small room with one very faint light. The Lubavitcher rebbe, who looks about a hundred and twenty years old and has a white beard reaching halfway down his chest, is sitting behind a desk that's as wide as the room. The cousin sits down on a stool opposite the desk and, out of respect, waits for the rebbe to speak. But the rebbe is just smiling. Finally, not knowing what else to do, Janey's cousin launches into a precisely detailed account of all his business problems, of all the machinations his partner is pulling. When he's done, the rebbe speaks for the first time. 'Vell,' says the rebbe, 'I hope it vorks out.' The man looks at the rebbe expecting some insights, some wisdom. But the rebbe just smiles. Then the rebbe must have pushed some button because his assistant comes in and tells Janey's cousin that the rebbe has to go on to his next appointment.

"When Janey's cousin comes out of the office, all the rabbis crowd around and beg to know what the rebbe told him. Janey's cousin looks at them straight-faced and says, 'What that man knows about business! He's a genius.' The oohing and ahhing breaks out like crazy.

"Now," says Max with a pranky twinkle, "that's how I got my reputation as a great editor."

Conrad Franklin was one of the people who helped to make and spread that reputation. What would he have thought of Max's little parable? That remains unknown. But a story, no, actually a brief encounter, that Wendy Parker frequently describes offers an inkling of how Conrad might have responded. It took place on the last evening she ever saw Conrad Franklin alive.

Wendy was leaving the office for dinner and he was just settling down to write. Pocket-sized spiral reporter's notebooks were open and spread about his desk like secret maps. She remembered that when she passed by, he looked up, brushed his long blond hair off his forehead, and asked if she could lend him a couple of cigarettes to help get him through the night. He was down to half a pack. She remembered he was wearing a locker gray Michigan State T-shirt; the shoulder seam was ripped and exposed a sliver of pale skin. Wendy, shaking her head, recalled that often she had warned him he shouldn't smoke so much. Conrad was like that, she explained; you wanted to mother this achingly skinny, sleepy-eyed child and then you'd read his pieces only to realize there was a manfully wise, confident part of him none of us knew or saw. Except maybe Max. Anyway, Wendy said she sat with Conrad for a while. I've got to get home, she finally apologized. "Not me," Conrad told her. "This is my home."

CITY WAS TO become Russ Lewis's home, too. He wanted its sanctuary very badly. But it was never his wish to take Conrad's place in the household.

ELEVEN

T W O W E E K S A F T E R Russ sent his piece to the magazine, he received a thick envelope embossed with the *City* logo in the mail. Despair set in as he weighed the hefty package in his hand. His rejected manuscript had to be stuffed inside.

He managed to ignore it till evening. Then, figuring that life really couldn't get much worse than the vapid gloom caused by a couple of appetite-killing forkfuls of the university's sawdust mashed potatoes and tinny lima beans, he ripped the letter open. It was packed with surprises.

First, a check made out to Russell Lewis for $35 spilled out. Then, there were two sets of galleys (a moment before the word had not even been part of his vocabulary) of "You Can Finish the Revolution Without Me" in what was clearly the *City* typeface. There was also a note from a Phil Connett, who held the lofty title of managing editor, explaining that the article should be running soon, that Russ should go over the edited copy as soon as possible, and, by the way, "Max Fox wanted me to tell you that he particularly liked the piece and that you should keep an eye out for other stories you might want to submit."

Russ was high-flying. His first thoughts were of whom he would brag to. But a quickly restraining instinct told him it was shrewder to play coy. Let his former friends come to him once the article was published.

A long but self-controlled week later the piece ran in *City*. For the first time since freshman registration, Russ didn't cut a single class. Whenever he strolled around the campus, there was a notebook in his hand. Russ made a big deal about publicly jotting down his private observations. His new boldfaced by-line had given him, he felt, legitimacy. He was certain everyone now saw him as Russ Lewis, the writer.

The article was widely read on campus—and widely attacked. The piece had trivialized, a right-on assistant professor with a fierce Zapata mustache hectored Russ and the rest of the students in his Poli Sci 402 class, "important political issues." And the editorial in the student daily concluded: "Our revolution, a revolution of humanistic concerns, doesn't need cynics. We will be glad to finish our revolution without you, Mr. Lewis." But Russ had no time for such carpings. He had discovered the last laugh of celebrity.

And its rewards. His swaggering pen proved mightier than a whimpering can of spray paint. Janet, who had taken to having oafish Chris riding shotgun in her Alfa, once more became susceptible to Russ's *City*-sanctioned charms. He won the fickle heart (and a few other choice bits of anatomy) of his action-faction daydream.

The next two pieces he wrote for *City*, however, found their way back to his campus mailbox in depressingly slim envelopes. As senior year began he was forced to consider law school seriously. But not that seriously. He was not yet willing to resign himself to what he envisioned as a grim, gray adulthood. He was determined to lead a life as bold as the by-line on the framed *City* article above his desk. He continued sending pieces to the magazine. Finally, a short piece on the rigid hierarchy of schoolyard basketball, a class system he had spent his youth exploring firsthand, was accepted. This time the check from *City* was $45. After that his articles got much longer and the checks got somewhat bigger. By the end of the term he was reading Mailer, not law school catalogs. His confident mind was set. He would get a job at *City*. For starters.

A month before graduation Russ wrote a rather formal, but not particularly timid letter to Max Fox asking for a job. After all, Russ decided with self-affirming logic, four of his articles had already appeared in the magazine. Why shouldn't Max Fox want to hire him?

The answer came from Phil Connett. He apologized that Mr. Fox was too busy to answer all his mail; the editor had passed Russ's letter on to him. Connett then broke the news: The chances of getting a job at *City* were not too good. Of course Russ could continue free-lancing, they'd be glad to look at anything he sent in. But a weekly salary, well, that was another matter. Still, if Russ had the time that summer, he should come by the office and introduce himself. Mr. Fox, he wrote, would be glad to meet him.

Russ found the time.

He had been back from school a couple of hours when he called *City* and asked for an appointment to see the editor. The unexpectedly friendly secretary—she knew his by-line—said she would check Max's schedule and get back to him. Russ couldn't help but feel foolishly adolescent when he gave the bubbling secretary his parents' number. He sat by the phone the rest of the day. And the next morning. Then, restless and anxious, he went out.

As soon as he returned, Russ realized he should never have left.

"Russie," his mother announced, "there was a call for you from a Mr. Bear . . . no . . . a Mr. Fox. Not him, really. It was his secretary. She sounded very friendly. A real pretty voice. Anyway, she said you have an eleven o'clock appointment for a week from Tuesday. Such a nice girl. Her name's Margie. When you see her, give her a big hello from me. Such a pretty voice."

Russ felt ruined. Surely anyone who used his mother as an answering service would be off to a hell of an impressive start with the high-spirited folks at *City*.

I T W A S N' T M A R G I E'S voice, though, that caught Russ's attention when he introduced himself in the magazine's offices on that Tuesday morning in June 1970. It was her nipples. She was wearing a mauve diaphanous blouse. With nothing on underneath. Her nipples pressed against the fabric like the pert noses of two warm puppies in the window. *City*, he decided, could be a very interesting place to work.

But as soon as she spoke, he realized something was very wrong. Margie's flirty voice was oddly subdued. As was the mood in the crowded office. People were huddled conspiratorially together, slumped in chairs and clumped on desktops: conversations in hushed tones. Something was up.

Margie didn't offer to explain anything. She simply suggested, "Max might be tied up today. Maybe you should speak with Phil Connett instead."

A disappointed Russ knocked on the managing editor's door. He was first taken aback by Phil's stutter, and then by his news.

"Y-you p-p-picked a bad day to v-vis-ss-it," he said. "T-there's been a d-d-death in the fam-m-ily."

Phil, very somber and precise, said Conrad Franklin had died yesterday afternoon. After a moment, the managing editor began a long, slow account. He spoke to convince himself of a reality he still perceived as impossible; Russ Lewis just happened to be there.

Conrad had left on Friday to go camping with some friends in the Adirondacks. Copping a line from Frank O'Hara, he had explained to Phil that he needed to look at the sky more often. Yesterday, his last morning in the woods, Conrad complained to his friends he didn't feel like sitting around the lake. He was going off exploring. He promised to be back for lunch. When he didn't return, they went out looking for him. By six that evening they had found his broken body. He had apparently fallen to his death.

Since the day they made camp, his friends remarked, Conrad had seemed challenged by a dark, hump-shaped cliff reaching up from the horizon across the lake. Conrad took to imagining what the view from its summit would be like at sunset. For most of the weekend Conrad had tried to coax his friends to climb up its sullen precipice. They wouldn't buy it. It was more a mountain than a cliff. Very rocky, very steep, very dangerous. It was certainly impossible to climb.

They found his body draped across a mossy rock at the bottom of the cliff; he lay there peacefully like a coat thrown over a chair. When they turned the body over, they discovered that his head was smashed. He had apparently fallen while working his way up the easterly side of the cliff. His friends never did learn how close he had gotten to the summit. He had been crazy to try was all they tearfully said.

When Phil finished, he sat at his desk looking out the window. A taxi had stopped traffic by letting off its passenger in the middle of the block. Horns were honking. Phil turned a pencil in a sharpener. Russ stood by the door not knowing what to say, where to go.

Finally, awkward and self-conscious, the boy broke the silence: "I'm very sorry. I really am." Phil continued to stare out the window so he added, "I guess I should come back to see Mr. Fox another time."

Phil didn't seem to be listening. Russ started to leave his office.

"W-wait a minute," Phil called as the boy turned away. "I-I'-d b-better check with M-Max."

Phil returned after a long while. "It's b-b-business as usual. T-that's what M-Max w-wants. He'll s-s-ee you n-now." Despite the deceptive hesitancy of the stutter, Russ had no doubts Phil had argued strongly against his meeting with the editor that morning.

But minutes later Russ Lewis was shaking hands for the first time with Max Fox, editor and founder of *City* magazine.

TWELVE

HE'S OLDER THAN my father. That was Russ's initial surprised reaction as he sat in the metal chair across from Max Fox's desk. He had not expected the editor of rebellious *City* to have gray hair.

Curiously, Max's mind was mulling not dissimilar thoughts. "How old are you?" he asked as he filled his pipe from a worn leather pouch.

"Twenty-two."

The editor lit the pipe.

"Twenty-three next month," Russ added.

"You look younger." The way Max said it sounded like a criticism. Russ wished he had a pipe.

"Clean living," the boy answered defensively.

Max, though, let the remark pass. He puffed busily on his pipe.

"Well," the editor finally said, choosing to follow another track, "there were some nice touches in those pieces you sent us in the last year. You've a good eye."

"Thank you."

"However that doesn't mean you should begin everything you write with I."

Max smiled and Russ was glad of the opportunity to laugh. Even if it had to be at himself.

"You just graduated? I think that's what your letter said . . ."

"Yes." Russ wondered if it would help to mention how well he had done.

"What do you plan to do now?" Max asked. "Graduate school? Law school?" A thumb was exploring the watch pocket of his vest.

"That's not for me." Russ hesitated and then added, "I'm going to try to become a writer."

Max gave Russ a wary look. It was apparent he had heard that ambition too many times before. The boy wanted to walk out of the office, away from the bored, patronizing old man sitting across from him.

Max, however, once again abruptly channeled the conversation in another direction. "Are you from New York?"

"I was born in the Bronx. My parents live in Westchester now."

". . . Yes," the editor said to nothing in particular. Then he asked, "You went to high school in the Bronx?"

"No." Russ mentioned the name of the private school he had attended. He considered mentioning that he had been on scholarship.

"So you're a rich kid."

Russ didn't like the way Max said it. Besides, one of Russ's chief disappointments was that he was not rich. "My parents aren't poor," he answered. He just didn't feel like taking this old man's crap.

"You're lucky then," Max responded. "I'm glad you've got the sense to admit it."

The editor's soft probing continued: "What about your father? What does he do?"

His father sold insurance. But Russ was not that forthcoming. "My dad's in business," he answered. Let Max Fox fill in the blanks any way he prefers, he figured.

"Why do you want to be a writer?" Again the sudden change in directions. Russ now realized the editor's mind was not merely wandering. Max Fox was running him through a very personal checklist.

Sensing the play of the older man's mind, Russ began to share a secret with Max that he had never told anyone before. As the words tumbled out, the stray pieces of his own ambition fell into a philosophy of sorts. No one was more surprised than Russ.

"Because," he said with conviction, "it's the only sort of life that seems to make sense to me. At least now. I don't want a structured, nine-to-five life. I feel I'm different. Better than that, I guess. And I want to prove it to myself. I want to find out if I'm up to the challenge. You know, the responsibility to fight my fears . . . to make my life different from the one I was brought up and then schooled to live."

"What if you're not?"

"What if I am?"

Max puffed deliberately on his pipe for a few moments; clouds of private thoughts were swirling amidst the smoke. Russ wondered where all this was leading.

"You say you're twenty-two?" the editor asked.

"Yes." Russ decided there wouldn't be any point to explain for the second time that he'd turn twenty-three next month.

"You look very young." Max bit down on his pipe. "Even Conrad Franklin looked older than you." There was a narrow pause before he slipped in, "Did you know Conrad?"

The way the editor's voice was sounding, Russ thought it would be better not to say anything about Conrad's death. "I never met him. But I read all his pieces. He always seemed to be in the midst of all the excitement."

". . . Yes," said Max. "Conrad certainly covered the sixties."

It was envy that made Russ add, "He took a lot of chances."

"A lot of chances," Max repeated mechanically. "It had to take its toll."

And then, without warning, the editor's eyes started to cloud. He turned away abruptly, but he knew the boy had seen his tears.

"Excuse me," Max said after a moment. His back was still turned, but Russ realized he was rubbing his eyes with his white breast-pocket handkerchief. A minute passed. The rustling of the handkerchief seemed very loud.

"You'll have to excuse me," Max eventually managed to say.

". . . sure . . ." Russ got up from his chair. He didn't know if he should shake the editor's hand. He decided just to leave the office.

Max, though, stood up. "As long as you're here, why don't you speak with Wendy Parker." He spoke as if the idea were an afterthought.

"I'd like to meet her." Russ stood by the open door of the office.

"I'll call her and tell her you're coming."

It took Russ a while to find his way to city editor Wendy Parker's cubicle on the floor below; but by the time he arrived, Max still had not called her. She politely offered the boy a chair, though. And she talked about Conrad Franklin's death. She said Max had phoned her at one this morning to give her the awful news. He had sounded very upset. Max and Conrad, she explained, were like father and son. She was very concerned how the editor would take Conrad's death. Russ never thought to share with her how upset he knew the editor to be. That was, he instinctively realized, their secret.

In the middle of the conversation Wendy suddenly asked, "Just how old are you, Russ?"

"Twenty-three."

"Well, you look much younger. Anyone ever tell you that?"

"Yes." He was about to tell her who when the phone rang.

As was her habit, Wendy hunched protectively over the receiver. She didn't want anyone listening to her conversations. This one was brief and muffled.

"That was Max," she explained as she hung up the phone. "Are you a relative?"

"No," he said with a laugh. His grin made it clear he didn't know what she was talking about.

"Well, he likes you. He said I should give you an assignment for next week." Russ was trying to take all that in when she added, "Since we don't give assignments to free-lancers, I guess that means you're being hired as a staff writer. Congratulations."

Russ was excited, but confused. Had he been hired or not? He didn't know whom to ask. Things at *City* were, he was discovering, very loose.

Wendy didn't waste time, though, in finding him a story. After scanning a page she had been typing when Russ had first interrupted her, she said, "There's a gay rights march starting at Sheridan Square on Saturday night. Why don't you cover it?"

"I'll be there," he said immediately.

She rummaged through a cluttered drawer of her desk until she found a small green plastic card. "You'd better take this," she said as she handed him the card. It was a New York City Police Department Reserve Press Pass. The green card was very official looking. On the line headed "Media," the word *City* had been typed in capital letters. He felt as if Wendy had awarded him the Congressional Medal of Honor.

That was Russ Lewis's first day at *City*. He left a bit confused over whether he had actually been given a job. But he was certain he had an opportunity. He was determined to make it work. Still, as he took the train from Grand Central back up to his parents' house in Westchester, he wondered what his father was going to say when he announced that he was going out Saturday night to attend a gay rights march in the Village.

All Norman Lewis said was, "Be careful." It proved to be good advice. The march exploded into a riot after a line of club-swinging cops tried to quiet some militant lesbians. And Russ's piece wound up on the cover. After it ran, he asked Wendy about a check. "The staff gets paid on Fridays," she explained. Yet it wasn't until Russ picked up his payroll check that he was convinced he had been hired. By the next issue, someone had decided to put his name on the masthead along with the other staff writers. Agate type had never seemed so large.

And so Russ began to settle in. He couldn't believe his luck. He just about lived at the magazine. There was one large room across from Wendy's cubicle where each of the half-dozen staff writers had a desk and a phone. In those days it was an incredible luxury. Except there wasn't a desk for Russ. Of course, there was one empty desk but he didn't dare take it. An additional desk, Wendy promised, had been ordered, but it was taking a long time in coming. Finally, one night when he was on deadline and looking for a place to type, Wendy said Russ might as well use the empty desk. He was too anxious and too pressed by a piece that was due in a couple of hours to argue. And by the end of the summer, when Russ Lewis found himself pitching for the magazine in the softball game which would change the entire course of his life, Conrad Franklin's desk had become his.

PART II
The Poverty of Romance

ONE

THEY MET AT A softball game in Central Park. Here one must congratulate the ingenuity of fate; for while the park is a cluttered refuge on a bright summer's afternoon for people pedaling bicycles, hurling Frisbees, jogging in seemingly endless circles, or knocking around with bats and balls, Russ Lewis and Kate Warner were probably the last two ambulatory New Yorkers to be caught up in such public fun.

Yet there they were at a softball game in a dusty corner of the park's Sheep Meadow on that August day in 1970. Russ was on the mound, a pitcher; Kate, a Heineken in her hand, sat Indian style on the third-base line, the perpetual observer.

Despite the sweat Russ was working up, they both had really come to observe: *City* magazine was playing *The New Yorker*. The downtown "I's" of new journalism were taking on the uptown royal "We's." All of the young, struggling, and—pain of unarticulated pains—unknown *City* writers were eager to see firsthand just what kind of supernal stuff those that had made it to the *New Yorker* team were made of: a grudge match of ambitions.

Russ, who hadn't touched a bat and a ball since summer camp, fast-talked his way to the mound. He was counting on facing, say, the rangy first baseman named Updike, or the magician at shortstop with the name Barthelme on his jersey, or their legendarily cunning manager Shawn.

But this was not to be. Those big leaguers didn't hang around softball diamonds; round tables remained the fields for their particular sport.

Instead, the uptown team was manned by a chinoed and madrased crew with rhyming Junior Yacht Squadron nicknames like Muffy and Buffy and Skip and Chip. With the energy of a Greek chorus, their suburban voices filled the Sheep Meadow with constant competitive and decidedly uncool chatter: "Okay, now, Skip baby, burn it in there"; or, "C'mon, Muffy, show 'em what you got."

It didn't take the *City* team long to discover what their opponents

had. They were all plebeian toilers in the underbelly of the great magazine, cute well-bred elves who labored as "fact checkers" and "O.K.ers"
for the actual wordsmiths. (In the scrupulous uptown world of journalism, Russ learned with some amazement at that softball game, a fact was
not a priori; rather, it was checked and then O.K.ed before a reader was
offered the opportunity to engrave it into the stone of his mind. At *City*
they were more, well, indiscriminate.)

After nine innings of sloppy, uninterested play, the *New Yorker*
team wound up celebrating a 24–3 romp. But that didn't faze any of the
downtown athletes. They dealt with defeat at the hands of these decidedly
ordinary nine-to-fivers with conspicuous disdain. After all, the *City* play-
ers were *writers*.

That's how Kate Warner and Russ Lewis happened to meet at a
softball game in Central Park. And that improbability was only the beginning. They shuffled through an initial encounter which, right down to
the dialogue, might have been cribbed from a corny half hour of "Happy
Days." Look at the uncharacteristic parts they found themselves playing:

Our hero, after a shell-shocked inning on the mound where he gave
up five earned in addition to seven unearned runs, trots off the field.
Swinging a bat with what he hopes resembles professional determination,
he waits in the on-deck circle. An idea occurs. Perhaps his swing would
be more powerful if he were not constrained by his dungaree jacket.
With a cavalier toss he hurls the denim jacket—yet one senses it is one
of his most cherished possessions—down the third base line. Then he
steps up to the plate to do his duty. Three pitches later, he grounds out
to the second base woman. Score that 3 to 1, sport fans. He now trots,
though a bit hangdog, to his teammates assembled around third base
only to find a girl—our heroine!—wearing his beloved jacket.

Girl: Sorry. Guess I borrowed your jacket. It was getting kind of
cool.

Boy: Yeah, the way they're scoring, this game could drag on all
night.

Girl: I know. They're taking all this pretty seriously. (She starts to
remove the jacket.)

Boy: No, no. Keep it. It'll probably snow before this game is over.

Girl: You don't mind? (But she is already putting her arm back in
the denim sleeve.)

Boy: No problem. By the way, I'm Russ Lewis.

Girl: Oh, I know your by-line. (He throws her a delighted smile:
the triumph of recognition. She continues.)

I'm Kate Warner, the—

Boy: The dance critic? Hey, I've read your column. It's good. (Of
course we realize he has never read the dance column; but does she fall

for it? Suddenly an offstage voice calls, "C'mon, Lewis, the inning's over. Time to face another forty batters.")

Boy: Well, back to the battlefield. (He offers her a resigned shrug as we watch him hustle offstage left.)

And we viewers yearn impatiently for the more creative drama of a commercial.

SUCH WAS THE banality with which the essential, predisposing relationship of both their lives began. Fortunately, though, there survives a photograph that must have been snapped only instants after this momentous exchange. Duke, the magazine's diligent and maniacally omnipresent photographer, standing behind home plate and aiming his long-lensed Nikon up the third base line, succeeded in capturing most of the *City* crew. Despite the crowd of people, two faces stand out; and even a quick glance at this forever frozen moment illuminates a telling bit of what Kate and Russ first saw in each other.

For weeks a 14 × 11-inch blowup of the photograph hung in the newsroom of the magazine. When the valuable public space it occupied was claimed for a trendier wanted poster of Abbie Hoffman, Russ appropriated the photograph for his own collection. For years it hung above his desk, a black and white remembrance of things impossibly past:

Russ is standing on the mound, right arm swung back like a pendulum, about to hurl a pitch. His getup is zanily eclectic: part sportsman, part activist, and part biker. There were Topsiders on his feet and a once white tennis hat on a black-haired head; remember, the boy had prepped. Ballooning about his legs were baggy khaki fatigue pants picked up at an Army and Navy store near campus a couple of years earlier when it looked like some sort of revolution was imminent. And on a tight black T-shirt the script logo "Norton" was inscribed across his chest; as in Norton 500, the monster bike he had borrowed from a friend the summer before and ridden throughout New England with cleansing cathartic fury after his decisive breakup with Janet of the many sweaters.

If clothes make the man, the catholicity of Russ's outfit was proof the job was still undone. Russ Lewis was too obviously just a twenty-three-year-old kid. And it's certainly a kid's face in that photograph. Years later Russ would still look cumbersomely young. But back then there was more than mere youthfulness smiling in that photograph: An indulgent daddy might want to pat this fresh-faced boy on the back for successfully avoiding any hard traveling; a wiser friend might want to warn him.

Kate's picture told another story.

With her knees raised up to her ample chest—her private dilemma, Russ would learn: a Bauhaus intellectual's mind trapped in a carny bimbo's body—she sat on her blue-jeaned haunches; there was a Heineken raised in her right hand as if for balance. But she needn't have worried. Even in that randomly captured moment, a stern, self-contained quality is apparent; no wind of gusting fad or fashion is going to blow this gal over. Her clothes—straight-legged Levi's, a striped boat-neck T-shirt, and dirty sneakers—are classic, comfortable, and decidedly unhip. Like the lady.

True, she's not pretty in an achingly ain't-she-sweet cosmeticized way. But she was precisely what Russ was unconsciously looking for. Kate, then twenty-eight, five large and full years older than the boy on the mound, seemed already a woman, a careful adult who had deliberately and perceptively plotted out the drama she was walking through.

Russ, now starting out to make it in a grown-up New York, was ready to cast off from his four-year string of casual collegial relationships: girls who had dropped the accusatory word "supportive" as frequently as the name of the blond-haired hunk in their English class they had hoped you'd be competitively jealous of; girls who had thought it was the height of sophistication to cross their sevens because they had spent a semester of their junior year abroad; girls who had hurried to take you to bed because they believed a repressed hour between the sheets was necessary and sufficient proof of their liberation; and girls who had felt spending the hours approaching dawn in a darkened bedroom listening to James Taylor's melancholic crooning was where modern angst was at.

Kate, one deep look told Russ, was his antidote: a worthy, thoroughbred muse.

Also, it would be wrong to think Kate was unattractive. She wore straight curtains of chin-length wispy brown hair parted right down the middle. It was a timeless no-frills style that exposed a brow which seemed broad enough to house the collected knowledge of all twenty-four volumes of the Britannica. Complementing this was just a snap of a nose and slim, sensible lips. And there was a sizzling, even tacky lushness to her body. Certainly, though, her most striking feature was her eyes—no one ever saw them.

Like an indicted labor leader, Kate habitually wore dark glasses; except her shades, an affect of quirk, not style, sported pentagonal-shaped frames. Day and night, she viewed the world darkly. There was, Russ would exasperatedly learn, neither a furtive nor a medical logic to her wearing dark lenses. Her particular logic was more offhanded: Years earlier she had lost her clear prescription glasses and—so Kate—she never found the time or, more accurately, the energy to replace them. For over a decade she simply made do with the pair that remained.

But these dark glasses, like the tinted windows of the limos rock stars tool around New York in, were an appropriate symbol for the woman: She looked out, but you couldn't see in. There were impenetrable walls of both resilient ego and, not as contradictory as it sounds, tender insecurities built up high around her.

Yet despite these defenses, despite the concealing dark glasses, Duke's wide-angled photograph reveals one truth as clear and as startling as any epiphany: Amidst all the hubbub both on and off the field, Kate is staring directly, and lovingly, at the boy on the mound.

TWO

"I HAVE A CAR," Russ suggested to Kate as she returned his dungaree jacket when the ball game was over. "Maybe I can give you a lift?"

Kate, as always, was more direct: "It's early. Would you like to get something to eat?"

They walked toward 67th Street where his Volvo was parked. Evening was beginning to trickle over the Sheep Meadow. Quickly they agreed on a place in Little Italy. And then they stopped agreeing.

An unexpected, yet rapidly escalating no-holds-barred scrap started as soon as Russ absently turned on the car radio. The radio had been set to an FM rock station. With the first loud beat, Kate contrived an even louder moan.

"I can't believe you listen to that junk," snarled Kate. Experience had taught her there was an advantage to controlling any situation.

Russ, though, was also not without ego. Having been raised in a family that valued manners ("There are two little words that can open any door you please," his mother had incessantly reminded him, "one little word is 'thanks' and the other little word is 'please'"), he would normally have politely switched to another station or even turned the damn thing off. But also having been brought up in a family that took little truck with being high-hatted ("Everyone's shit smells," was his worldlier father's didactic epigram), Kate's raised eyebrow routine had him digging his heels in.

But Kate was not the type to give up, either. She responded with another even more haughtily agonized look—the kind of contemptuous stare New Yorkers flash at the idiot who insists on honking full blast when traffic is obviously going nowhere. And that did it.

An indignant Russ became the freeway Philistine. The boy and his Volvo were suddenly bugalooing down Broadway. Sam and Dave came loud and clear from the radio, but they had nothing on his wailing, funky tenor. An insistent hand thumped across the dashboard, sashaying after the song's bluesy rhythm. Russ was having fun getting down, all right.

"Jesus," Kate finally screamed. "That's enough of that idiocy."

She gave the radio knob a decisive twist, stopping when what sounded like a violin concerto filled the tense car.

"Now I can hear myself think," she said with the sort of sighing gratitude which might have been expected to come from someone rescued from a burning building. And then she waited in silence for his counterattack.

Mr. Soul, though, turned surprisingly mellow. He was busy plotting.

Russ's angry mind was playing back at 78 RPMs the scratchy LPs they had forced him to listen to in Music Appreciation. Just one knowing remark about the obscure music squeaking from the radio would put this sophisticated miss in her place. He'd pull her advantage right out from under her pretensions. Except it didn't work out that way. He didn't have a clue. They were playing her song, not his.

So much for revenge.

Instead, like any competitive kid who has been admonished by a hoity elder, Russ sulked. He figured he would just eat and run. It was apparent an unbridgeable gap wider than simply the FM band stretched between the two of them.

Then, with the Volvo trudging down a crowded 7th Avenue, a bulletin hurried from the car radio:

". . . the reports we're receiving seem to indicate that a full-scale riot has broken out in the Bedford-Stuyvesant section of Brooklyn. Teenagers, protesting the shooting of a twelve-year-old bystander by police making a drug-related arrest in a crowded playground, have stormed down Atlantic Avenue hurling stones at store windows . . ."

Russ cut in over the announcer, "What kind of cops play shoot-'em-up in a playground full of kids?" There was a contentious, know-it-all swagger to his question; two months with a *City* press card had filled him with authority.

"Quiet," Kate instructed as she turned the volume up.

The announcer continued in his unflappably smooth FM voice: ". . . first reports tell of isolated instances of looting. Youths have been seen running from stores carrying television sets. According to the information we have received, tactical police squads from all over the city are being rushed to Bedford-Stuyvesant. The mayor's office has issued . . ."

In a moment the bulletin ended and the music—Beethoven's Violin Concerto in D, the announcer revealed—resumed.

Now it was Kate's turn to interrupt. "What did you mean by that?" she demanded.

"Huh?"

"About the shooting's not sounding right?"

"Well, look at it this way," he said, quickly scrambling to string his unformed thoughts together as the car now broke out of the downtown traffic. "I bet you wouldn't see cops rushing, guns drawn, into a playground full of kids in, oh, Forest Hills or Sheepshead Bay. Or any white middle-class neighborhood, for that matter." The car was zipping along and, the product of twenty years of protective schooling and sixties syllogisms, so was Russ. "Cops think twice before they put themselves in the sort of situation that could start a shootout in a white neighborhood. But I'm willing to bet they're not so careful in Bed-Stuy. I gotta believe they figure they can get away with playing by a different set of rules."

She responded to this enthusiastic argument with a tiny—oh, so sublimely delicate—nod. But Russ was not to learn if this faint gesture indicated either agreement or dispute. Instead, Kate lapsed into a long and bewildering silence. They had brusquely once more become two strangers. Classical music booming portentously all around them, they continued downtown without a word.

By Houston Street Russ was thinking about switching the radio dial to a rock station. Anything to shake this moody woman out of the silent treatment she was giving him. But his peevish scheme was sidetracked. A more practical concern popped up—parking.

Little Italy was jumping, a merry festival teeming with the hungry presence of an invading double-knit army. Scores of husky and jolly troops filled every outdoor café; they marched shoulder to beefy shoulder through sidewalks lit by low-hanging arches of multicolored electric bulbs; and, bumper to shining bumper, their large cars lined the streets. It was as if every gargantuan Cadillac and Lincoln Mark IV with New Jersey license plates had answered a warm weather mating call, rushing to claim its place this August evening in these narrow, twisting streets.

"This isn't going to be easy." Russ was talking about finding a space, but he might just as well have been talking about what remained of their evening together.

They were stopped at a light, the dented Volvo idling with the fitful grace of a choppy ground ball hit hard up the middle. "Then let's leave," she said.

Kate now turned to face him; he wondered if she was measuring him behind her protective dark glasses. Feeling outflanked, he let loose, abruptly defensive and tough: "Oh? Where the hell do you want to go?"

Of course as soon as Russ asked the question, he knew her answer was going to be a succinct "home."

Of course he was wrong.

"How about Bed-Stuy?" It wasn't a suggestion; it was a challenge. She explained: "I've never seen a riot before." It was the sort of comment some women might deliver with a coy flutter; but Kate was detached, cynical, curious—and rarely coy.

"You know it could be dangerous."

Such concern, Kate instantly was convinced, was indictable. Wielding a well-honed rhetorical knife, she started whacking away. "What kind of reporter are you? Here I've been thinking that maybe you were onto something about what happened when that poor kid got shot. What if there's a story in it? And now you're backing off because it could be dangerous."

Russ, wounded, answered her parry with a thrust: His Volvo accelerated through the red light. It was only as he was speeding toward the Brooklyn Bridge that he realized he didn't have the slightest idea where in Brooklyn, a borough as vast and as strange as a foreign country to this youth raised in Westchester, he was going to find Bedford-Stuyvesant.

BY THE TIME THE ANEMIC Volvo had found its way to Bedford-Stuyvesant, the riot had tucked itself in for the night. The helmeted, nightstick-clutching blue targets on nearly every corner were only artifacts of the short-lived trouble. Other than the police, the streets were empty. And eerily quiet.

"Why don't you ask one of the cops what happened?" Kate demanded. Just as she had insisted on announcing directions as soon as they had crossed the bridge. Her directions were spoken with authority; and they were wrong. It took them nearly three hours (and, finally, the help of a friendly gas station attendant across the borough in Coney Island) to complete what should have been a twenty-minute trip.

"I feel sort of foolish asking him if he's seen a riot around here lately."

"Then don't ask."

God, she was a ball buster; but Russ got out of his car and went up to two cops leaning against a schoolyard fence.

He was prepared for the usual good cop/bad cop runaround. But these two weren't satisfied to come off as Cain and Abel. They played Bob and Ray.

"Excuse me," Russ began.

"You're excused," said the cop whose face and neck had long ago been savagely nicked by a plague of acne.

This cracked his beefy, flush-faced partner up. "That's a good one," he said between applauding laughs.

"I'm from *City* magazine," Russ grumbled, displaying his Police Department Working Press card. "I was wondering if you could—"

"You still run those ads?" interrupted Scarface.

"Ads?"

"You know, those massage parlor ads," said Big Red. "Have lotion, will travel."

"Obedient pupil required for French lessons," the other gleefully chimed in.

"Or Greek. Don't forget Greek," rushed out Scarface, giggling while he nudged his buddy with his nightstick.

Russ turned from the two laughing policemen and looked across the street to where Kate, still in the Volvo, was trying to discern the joke. What's up, she pantomimed with a large, impatient shrug of her shoulders. He realized the only thing more humiliating than putting up with these two cops would be to return to that woman without a definite answer. There was no choice but to press on.

"Hey," Russ said testily, "I'm just trying to do my job. I was wondering if—"

"Sorry, sir," said Big Red with theatrical contrition.

Scarface followed: "At your service."

"Okay," Russ said warily. "Now, I was wondering if you could give me some information about the riot that broke out this evening. I heard a report on the radio . . ."

"A riot?" questioned Scarface.

"This evening?" asked Big Red.

"Yeah, the radio said there was a shooting in a playground and looting all along Atlantic Avenue and . . ."

The two cops nodded knowingly at each other and then said in unison, "Oh, *that* riot."

"Yes, there was a report of a drug bust . . ."

"You missed it, kid."

"Happened hours ago. Kid was shot at five. It's now eleven o'clock."

"I know, but . . ."

"The *Daily News* got here in time."

"Channel Four made it."

"Sure, but . . ."

"The *Times* showed up."

"Channel Seven, too."

The cops were enjoying giving Russ a hard time. He considered returning their verbal jabs, but then decided a lot more than his ego could wind up getting busted. Instead, he found the control to retreat across the street to his car.

"Hey," the heavy cop called after him, "next time we get a riot we'll try to keep things hopping until you get here."

"Don't worry," called his buddy as Russ opened the car door. "You can do what all the other creeps from your rag do. You can still make it up."

Their hoots kicked the quiet out of the Brooklyn night.

"What's so funny?" asked Kate as Russ hurried to start the reluctant car.

"We are. It seems we missed the story by about six hours."

"I guess we are," Kate agreed.

And then they, too, started laughing.

THUS DID THE BEGINNER'S luck (a necessary ingredient in any love potion) of their first date start to brew. They had not simply crossed a bridge into Brooklyn; Russ and Kate had crossed into an intimacy that allows two stubborn people to laugh at each other. In their brief shared adventure, however piddling, however wrongheaded, lay, Russ was happily convinced, the promise of more expeditions and more laughter. And Kate must have thought so, too. With a conciliatory smile, she turned the radio dial. They rocked their way back toward Manhattan.

As they drove down Ocean Avenue, the car was abruptly forced to come to a stop. Suddenly, the wide street in front of them was blocked with hundreds of bearded, black-coated men. An exotic, lilting chant rose from the crowd.

"Another riot?" Kate asked hopefully.

Russ studied the scene for a moment. "I don't think so." And he listened; the language now fitted into a recognizable pattern. "That's no riot," he said with a smile. "There are fiddlers on these roofs. Not snipers."

"Come again?" said Kate.

"Those men aren't marching. They're dancing. It looks like some sort of Hasidic celebration."

Kate looked beseechingly at him.

"Why not?" he agreed.

The car was parked and the two uninvited guests approached for a closer look. Kate and Russ, now holding hands, stood outside a wide snaking circle of, they learned, wedding revelers. Old bearded men and young boys, all in long black coats, all in wide-brimmed black hats, weaved through the dark street across from a red brick synagogue.

They listened; a high-pitched Hebrew melody drifted through the night. Ancestral spirits were summoned. Russ's feeling of awe grew, and he looked at Kate and was convinced she also understood. The hymn and the atavistic powers it invoked hovered around them . . . as, Russ was certain, he and Kate were also blessed: They were now a couple.

Kate's head was softly leaning on his shoulder as, an hour later, they approached the Brooklyn Bridge. "You know we still haven't eaten," she all of a sudden realized.

"Your timing's perfect. Look what's on our left."

"Junior's?" she asked reading the bright sign, each giant letter formed with dozens of light bulbs.

"*New York Magazine* wrote it up last month. Claimed it had the best cheesecake in the world. I never thought I'd wind up in Brooklyn to see if they're right."

"Cheesecake?"

But it wasn't long before they were seated in the jarringly bright restaurant, and a gum-chewing waitress with a pin on her left breast informing them her name was "Betty" was hovering about, pencil poised, demanding, "Whatcha having?"

Kate was studying the foot-long plastic-covered menu. For the first time this evening, Russ thought with sudden amusement, the woman seemed perplexed.

"You order," she said. "I need another minute."

Russ didn't waste any time: a slice of the famous cheesecake and a large glass of milk.

"I really don't like sweets," Kate said somewhat guiltily.

A frowning Russ insisted, "You've got to try the cheesecake. It's helping to keep Brooklyn on the map."

"Okay. A piece of the cheesecake, please."

"And something to drink?" Betty dutifully inquired.

"Yes, please. A beer." But before Betty could run off, Kate stopped her with a loud "Excuse me," and, flashing Russ a what-the-hell smile, said, "It's been a long evening. Better make that a pitcher."

Minutes later Betty returned. As she served, she gave a straight-faced play-by-play: "Let's see now. That was two cheesecakes. A large milk for the gentleman. And a pitcher of beer for the lady."

Betty plunked the pitcher of beer in the middle of the table. This obtrusive centerpiece dwarfed Russ's prudish beverage. Russ instantly understood a bit of what he'd tumbled into: He knew he would have to do more than switch his drinking habits if Kate and he were going to stay together. But from the start Russ wanted to be with her very badly.

Yet just when he was wondering what they could talk about, Kate, another blessing, instinctively brought up the one person—a common acquaintance, but in time a shared friend—who would forever dominate all that would come from this unanticipated and improbable beginning.

"Tell me," she said in that straightforward, often prosecutorial way she had of asking questions, "how did you get to meet Max?"

THREE

RUSS REALIZED FROM the start he was not prepared for a woman like Kate. But he only truly began to understand the depths of what he was up against the night Kate suggested for the first time, "Why don't we go to my place."

The offer had been a wearyingly long time in coming. After their adventure in Brooklyn, they had begun seeing each other fairly regularly. It was a sweaty period of late-night clutching and kissing. They both knew where this wooing was leading, but Kate, in command as always, didn't seem to be in a hurry to get there; and Russ wasn't secure enough to press the issue. So in October when Kate finally popped the question after their fifth time-buying beer at a quiche-and-salad, red-checked-tableclothed Upper East Side saloon, he was eager. What red-blooded kid would have given a thought as to what her place would be like?

That was Russ's mistake. But just his first for the evening.

Kate's apartment was on the Lower East Side, so low and so east that the city fathers had run out of the customary numbered avenues that divide New York. Down here, they had to start in with letters. And Kate's squalid address, Russ learned with some apprehension, was at the tail end of the alphabet, just a toss of a garbage can's lid from the FDR Drive.

While he glumly looked for a parking space for his Volvo (all the while silently calculating just how much a new set of hubcaps was going to cost), Kate, not knowing the spoiled case she was up against, was still enthusiastic: "Wait till you see my place. It's a real New York apartment. The tub is in the kitchen."

Clearly, though, they had different ideas about what was a *real* New York apartment.

Kate, however, went unsuspectingly on. "I love it down here. I don't know where else in this city you can get a place for $107 a month."

As they walked down a block where, Russ imagined, the frolicking guys drinking from brown-bagged bottles were contemplating how easy it was going to be to extract his Moroccan leather wallet from the bulging back pocket of his chinos, he silently agreed with Kate: He didn't know where else in the city you could find an apartment at that price. But he was willing to look. Right away.

Kate stopped in front of a building she had once described to him as a walk-up. A realtor would have called it a tenement. But the petit prince in the dungaree jacket knew a slum when he saw one.

"Here it is," Kate announced. "Think you can make it up four flights of stairs?"

"Two at a time." This was no boast: Russ was that eager to get off the threatening street.

They walked up the stoop and immediately the front door was held open for them by a brown-skinned bare-chested Puerto Rican boy. He must have been eight years old; and the radio he was toting, Latin music blaring from both its twin speakers, appeared to weigh nearly as much as he did.

"*Muchas gracias*, José," Kate said to the pint-size doorman. He smiled; and Kate asked, "*¿Cómo estás?*" In an instant they were trading Spanish sentences at a rapid clip.

"Do you have to tip him at Christmas?" Russ asked as Kate started the long, steep climb to the fourth floor.

"Excuse me?"

Russ abruptly realized Kate didn't speak an uptown language where doormen and Christmas tips were part of the vernacular. Quickly, and now a bit contrite, he changed gears. "Your Spanish sounds like the real thing."

"Oh, I can get by." Guardedly, she added, "I lived in Madrid for a while when I was a child."

Russ caught the faint whiff of mystery, but decided now wasn't the time to press. The details could lie quiet. For the time being, at least.

Besides, Kate was off and climbing. By the time the huffing and puffing straggler made it to the fourth-floor summit, an unwinded Kate was completing the turning of a procession of keys through the complicated series of locks embedded into the metal front door of her apartment. A final twist of a final key; a shove of her shoulder against the reluctant door; and then, extending a hospitable right hand, she said with mock grandeur, "After you, sir."

Russ crossed the well-protected threshold as Kate, still trying to pull it off with nonchalant humor, added, "Be it ever so humble . . ."

But with just one step into the apartment, Russ moved beyond placating irony. A quick look proved to him she hadn't been exaggerating: The tub really was in the kitchen. Except the kitchen was in the living room. Which also, when you opened up the couch, became the bedroom.

Russ Lewis had read about the other America, but until that moment he had always thought it was for other people. The simple and irrefutable poverty of Kate's little home was a shock. This wasn't candle shoved in the Bolla wine bottle off-campus bohemianism. This was living down and out in New York.

His face gave his astonishment—and his snobby chagrin—away. But Kate didn't get angry. She got even. "Let me show you the TV room," she perversely suggested.

The TV room, of course, wasn't a room at all. It was a corridor about as long and as wide as a pinball machine; at one end was the bleak living/dining/bed/bath room; while at the other end was a closet-sized space which, in what seemed the apartment's only concession to the twentieth century, served to accommodate the remaining more solitary biological needs.

(Months later Russ would be calling this little passageway the Roach Expressway. In the course of a sleepy nocturnal trip to the john, you immediately realized you were treading on very queasy ground. A flick of the bathroom light illuminated hundreds of frantic cockroaches zipping back and forth, the vile creatures apparently caught up in all-night high-speed cruising down this linoleum drag strip. He would stand there mesmerized, just watching them go. But his coming up with that sort of interest was months of philosophical resignation away. At first, and for a long time past second, third, and fourth, he was simply disgusted and depressed.)

The most jarring aspect of the TV room, however, proved to be the TV. A genuine, but now cracked and splintered, hefty wood case surrounded a gray screen about the size of a teacup. Droopy tinfoil rabbit ears—clearly the creation of untalented toddlers fiddling during a nursery school play period—lurched up from its rear in a halfhearted attempt at an antenna. Though the set was from another era, it had a long beaten-up time ago bounced beyond any critical consideration as an antique. The pathetic device had crashlanded into another category—junk.

Kate caught what was lurking in Russ's once-over; and, vengeful, she began playing it straight-faced for the tourist trade.

"I found the set on the street," she explained. Then cranking herself up: "Can you imagine anyone throwing it away?"

Russ didn't answer, but his expression said enough: He couldn't imagine anyone even touching it. This only encouraged Kate.

"Oh," she said, "it doesn't get Channel Four. And on Two or Eleven it sort of looks like they're always showing a movie about a blackout. But Thirteen comes in really clear. Well, almost clear. And that's PBS. Nothing else is worth watching anyway."

Then all of a sudden she was down on her knees, turning the ancient knobs of the set and methodically covering all compass points with the tinfoil antennae.

"Wait," she said. "I'll show you how well it works."

"No. It's okay. I believe you."

"No, no. You have to see."

Russ heard before he saw. The noise coming from the set sounded like someone trying unsuccessfully to clear his throat. After a while this noxious gargle lapsed into a fuzzy but decipherable moan. PBS was in the midst of another tediously self-righteous fund raising appeal. When Kate held one tinfoil rabbit ear flat against the wall and manipulated the other to a precise 30-degree angle, Russ could see quite clearly that the man chiding him for not being sufficiently grateful for all the English productions the station was so creatively importing had four noses, two mouths, and, depending upon Kate's agility, either three or four pairs of eyes. Odder, the testy announcer was coming on so strong while standing unperturbed in the midst of an avalanche.

"See," Kate said triumphantly, "I told you it works."

And enjoying his discomfort, Kate began to settle in. "Come on," she coaxed. "Sit down."

Russ squeezed down next to her in the little passageway; the proximity, at least, was an inducement. He put an arm around her shoulder. Unconsciously, or so he tried to pretend, he traced a soft line down her neck with a slow smooth finger. That made her smile. He repeated this journey, but now paved the route with quiet, tiny kisses. Still, the sublime noise of his lips against her neck seemed very loud.

Then it was her turn. She kissed him on the lips. It was a precise gesture: a pact of commitment. He, less graceful, returned the pledge.

"Give what you can to public broadcasting," rumbled the well-manicured voice in the background.

"No. Give it all to me. I want it," Kate countered, breathing hard, pulling wildly. Her excitement, so rare, thrilled him.

Russ couldn't help feeling as if he were once more a teenager in a Mylar-paneled playroom grappling with his date in front of a booming TV. Except now there were no parents upstairs to break things up. That evening Kate, the older woman, was in charge.

She undressed first. Lying next to him naked, her breasts round and full, she gave instructions. "It's all right, you know, to laugh," she said. So he laughed. The tenseness slipped away; and while it wasn't very expert, their first time was wonderfully tender and loving.

In the morning an unashamedly naked Kate served a pot of tea, soft-boiled eggs in McDonald's glasses (mementos from college, she explained), and thickly buttered pumpernickel toast. They ate sitting in bed while classical music played from a radio that must have been manufactured a couple of years before her TV. The Cleveland Symphony sounded decimated, down to a fiddle or two, and only a triangle for fortissimos.

But that sweet morning he wasn't complaining. By then Russ Lewis was beginning to consider that there might be more to the good life than woofers and tweeters.

FOUR

"I GUESS I SHOULD apologize," Russ told Kate the next evening as they sat drinking beers in the TV room. "I gave you a hard time last night, didn't I?"

"I like it that way." A lecherous wink. "I'm expecting one tonight, too."

"C'mon Kate, I'm being serious."

"So am I.'

But when he refused to return even her smile, Kate retreated. "All right, babes, what's on your mind. I want to know. Really." She kissed him once on the forehead; a soft, tender truce. Her lips were wet and cold from the beer and Russ was chilled.

"Talk to me," she said.

He took a sip of his beer. Settling in, he stretched his legs across the narrow passageway toward Kate's antiquated television. Kate put her head in his lap.

"I want you to understand what I was going on about," he said. Russ moved his fingertips slowly through her hair as he started to talk. It was an instinctive rather than a romantic gesture. He was completely comfortable; she might have been a purring cat cradled in his lap.

"I took one look at that broken-down set of yours," he went on, "and all of a sudden so many things started rumbling through me. So much about my childhood, my parents, even about why I'm working for *City* started to become clear. I know this sounds ridiculous, but your TV was my madeleine."

"Who's this Madeline?" she challenged.

He laughed with her. And then, once more weighed down by his memories, he said, "You've got to understand, I was raised in a home with a TV in every room. Color sets. Hell, there was even a little Sony in the kitchen so my mother could follow Julia Child. But it wasn't a big deal. I thought that was the way everyone lived. Or at least the way everyone was supposed to want to live."

As Kate listened, Russ told her about the heavy heritage he had lugged up the four steep flights to the center lane of the Roach Expressway and had plunked down that first night in front of her TV. He explained that his parents were not rich; though by Kate's standards, they were. He told her that the TV sets were the prizes awarded by his father's company to the best-selling "Insurance Man of the Month." Go-getter Norman Lewis continually blew away the competition; and as he kept on winning, brand-new sets kept on filling the house.

But what he was intuitively trying to convey to her (though he was years of insight away from being able to articulate or even understand these truths about himself) was the reasons for his unsettled reaction to her squalid apartment; and yet, how at the same time he was excited by the adventure promised by a life like Kate's, the risk-filled artist's life: a world of ideas, not things.

Russ wanted her to know he wasn't totally his parents' son; the rumbles of rebellion were loud and clear. He had wound up at *City* largely because he wanted to lead an intellectual's life. And he had wound up in a Lower East Side tenement with an older, quirky bohemian woman because, despite his parents' best training, he had grown up a romantic.

Two challenges: to be an intellectual; to be a romantic.

What's an intellectual? Russ had always liked Wittgenstein's line: Someone who thinks about thought. And a romantic? Russ, prodded by the pain of experience, came up with this: Someone who thinks about thought wishfully.

The chronic problem with Russ's wishful thinking, though, was that he did not take well to the hardship or to the faith necessary for romance. His wishful thoughts required a comfortable cushion of tangible, immediate success. Russ's personal battle: the struggle to become a respectable match for his idealized dreams. He was the heir to ambivalent ambitions, a contradictory inheritance he would spend a lifetime trying to resolve.

But, while he did not realize all this at the time, in those first days together he did understand enough to tell her two small stories from his childhood. He gave her a glimpse—and, Kate would later understand, an unwitting warning—of his heavy heritage: schemes; and conflicting dreams.

RIDING TO SCHOOL in the morning the routine would always be the same.

"You sure you don't want to sit in the backseat?"

"Come on, cut it out, Dad."

"You know, maybe I could get a cap . . ."

"Please, Dad . . ."

"I just want to make you feel comfortable. Why shouldn't you have a chauffeur just like the other boys? No need to tell your friends I'm your father."

Norman Lewis would then start to laugh, but Russ never found the routine funny. Even a twelve-year-old knew that some sharp, serious truths were provoking this daily attempt at offhanded humor.

One truth: Norman Lewis was very impressed by the eight-thirty turnout at the fancy (his word) private school Russ was attending. And another: It *was* quite a scene. The row of double-parked limos depositing their young charges for a tough day at the Arsenal School gave the place the feel of the Metropolitan Opera on opening night—sedate stretch jobs bearing the heirs to the familiar names separated by commas in a half-dozen or so different Wall Street logos; a gigantic black Rolls (once owned, study hall gossip had it, by the Queen of England) which carted the kid who was the original inspiration for the Richie Rich comic books; and, in the school's gesture to open enrollment and a winning football team, a gleaming gold Caddy which delivered the muscular son of Reverend "It Ain't No Sin To Be Rich" Sam, star of the pay-as-you-pray gospel circuit.

Another formidable truth: Russ Lewis, son of the socially mobile insurance salesman, arrived in a two-year-old Pontiac. There was a rusting gash scratched along the driver's door. Russ sat next to his dad; the backseat was stacked with black loose-leaf books filled with actuary reports.

A look and you knew—scholarship kid.

Worse, Norman Lewis was convinced they (the chauffeurs and their pampered young passengers) were looking. Even worse than that—he also managed to convince his impressionable son they all were looking.

So, a twelve-year-old's insecurities grew. And an outsider's detachment was nurtured. Not to mention embittered: Russ wanted what all the other kids had. He was becoming his father's son.

AND THEN AGAIN, maybe he wasn't. There was a more private, solitary, even rebellious side to the boy. A side that secretly reproached all the glib values and tame aspirations that were being passed

on to him. A side that if followed would lead him away from his parents
and the Arsenal. A side that began to take hold after Russ Lewis was
kicked out of school.

His expulsion was caused by an editorial he wrote for the school
paper, *The Bugle*. To an uninvolved reader, the editorial, entitled "Too
Much Memorization," might seem interesting only for its best-little-boy-
in-the-world smugness. Its five rambling paragraphs contained a self-
righteous appeal that Arsenalians make their noble institution even more
ennobling by cutting down on all the useless memorization inflicted upon
their obviously Advance Placement minds: "It seems pointless that Arsenalians be required to memorize that Phee Nuee Nuee is Fegee for
whale, to cite just one of the pointless questions on last week's Fifth Form
mid-term exam on *Moby Dick*. Rather, students should be quizzed on
the great book's symbolism."

But the Arsenal English masters were anything but uninvolved
readers. They heard revolution blowing in *The Bugle*'s editorial wind.
The only fiitting response, these masters were convinced, was to squash
this challenge to their authority.

Mr. Roger Cow, the oily-eyed and liquor-breathed adviser to *The
Bugle*, did all the necessary dirty work. When he was asked by his fellow
masters how he allowed such nonsense to appear in *The Bugle*, he knew
what to say. Or, rather what to lie. I never saw that editorial before in
my life, he quickly decided. (A point of information: *The Bugle* was
only a student newspaper; in such an open society as the Arsenal every
word in the paper—especially editorials—had to be first read and then
approved by the faculty adviser.) Good God, then Lewis published this
ill-conceived hogwash without first showing it to you? That's what that
little rotten toad did, insisted Mr. Cow. A triumphant chorus filled the
faculty lounge: Now we got him good.

An anxious Russ was summoned to the headmaster's study.

"Young man," Dr. H. Pinker-Britt announced, "you are accused of
a very serious crime."

Russ, whose largest sin to date was apathy, began to shake. "Me?"
he responded with genuine bewilderment.

As the headmaster outlined the specific charges made by Mr. Cow,
Russ filled with panic. How would he explain this to his father? Now he
shouted: "That's not true."

"You will not interrupt, young man. Your time will come."

To this day Russ is still waiting. Dr. H. Pinker-Britt was a stern
judge and an unsympathetic jury. The boy's insistent pleas of innocence
fell on deaf ears. When Russ whined that of course he had submitted the
editorial to Mr. Cow and had received his uninterested approval, the
mealy-colored English mastiff sitting at the headmaster's feet began to

bark. So Russ wisely shut up. The verdict swiftly followed: Russ was suspended for three weeks.

Yet Russ walked out of the headmaster's study with his head held high: the strut of a criminal. A grown man, no, a *master* at the Arsenal School had considered him enough of a threat to lie about his actions. Not bad. And Russ could tell by the looks he was getting from both the faculty and students as he cleaned out his locker that Russ Lewis was now considered someone to be reckoned with. Sure, this might have been just a first offense, but Russ silently pledged that it wouldn't be his last. It felt too good. Another realization: If his parents didn't understand, then that would be their problem.

Russ Lewis felt his life was beginning to have larger possibilities; and it would not be long before he understood that to pursue these unmarked trails would require the courage to take giant steps away from the comfortable, dull geography where he was raised.

FIVE

RUSS'S ATTEMPTS TO MAKE HIS LIFE something more than it had been seemed to be getting out of hand when, in the fall of 1970, the Hells Angels burst into the *City* offices threatening to kill him.

There were three of them: a short man, tightly muscled, black hair —dark as ebony—greased straight back, sharp reptile eyes, and a small golden cross dangling from his left earlobe; a bearded giant, booming beer gut, forearms as thick as telephone poles and covered with a swarm of tattoos, and a tiny, comical porkpie hat on his bald head; while the third was tall, blond, and coolly evil.

The short Angel did the talking; his tone was not loud, but his manner was precise: full of demand. "Where the hell is Lewis?" he asked Margie, the receptionist.

"Do you have an appointment?" she challenged; she was used to dealing with people coming in off the street and insisting on meeting with *City* reporters.

"This Lewis wrote a pack of lies about us," said the short Angel. "We got to talk to him about it. Set the record straight." He turned to his friend in the porkpie hat. "He's got to print a retraction, right?" When the husky Angel nodded enthusiastically, the hat slipped so far forward on his head that its brim fell over his eyes. The blond Angel was expressionless; he leaned against the wall, arms folded across his chest.

"Maybe you could write a letter to the editor," Margie tried.

The short Angel bit down on his lip, as if considering her suggestion. "What do you guys think about that?" he asked his friends at last.

Without warning, the two larger Angels ran past Margie and into the classified advertising department in the next room. They did not speak. They went from desk to desk, hurling typewriters against the wall, smashing telephones to the floor, and throwing papers across the room with furious, overhand movements. One ad taker, a dropout from the Living Theater, started sobbing with fear; the others, though, simply watched, fascinated.

When the two men had finished their destructive spree, they returned, their rage spent, to the short Angel. He was sitting on Margie's desk. Now he reached out to her, took her face in his hands, and said, "You tell Russ Lewis we're going to kill him."

"Do you want to leave a name?" she answered back.

So the Angels left with a smile.

That night Russ Lewis bought a shotgun and two cartons of double O buckshot in a sporting goods store. "Duck hunting," he told the salesman.

"You can stop a bear with that ammo," the salesman warned. "Double O will rip a duck to shreds."

"Seen some pretty tough ducks in my time. Better safe than sorry," Russ explained as he hurried from the store.

The shotgun was never fired; it remained unloaded for a year in the back of a closet in Kate's apartment until, without even telling Russ, she shoved it down the incinerator. And the Angels never tried to kill him. But a pimp in a massage parlor did.

The Angels wanted to kill Russ because they felt he had betrayed their hospitality. Stretching across three pages in *City*, he had described a cruise around Manhattan he had taken with a boatload of Angels (Knights of the Kounter Kulture, he had dubbed them), a flock of groupies, and the Grateful Dead.

It had been a voyage full of fear. "I am wary of men who carry hammers and are not carpenters," he had written. "I become on edge around men who constantly crack bullwhips though they are hundreds of miles from the nearest bull. I am unnerved by men who brandish solid wood canes, but do not limp."

Before the trip was over, Russ had witnessed a man smashed bloody by Knights of the Kounter Kulture wielding their hammers, whips, and canes, a groupie stripped and gang-banged, and a man tossed overboard just for sport. The next week in *City* he shared what he had seen. That was why the Angels wanted to kill him.

The pimp wanted to kill Russ because he thought the reporter was a cop. For three days Russ had waited with two detectives from the Public Morals Division ("the pussy posse," the cops called it) in a cardboard-walled cubicle in a midtown massage parlor. They sat in the stuffy cubicle listening as Sherry in the next booth went about her work; after the first customer the background noises were unembarrassing. They were listening because Sherry's former pimp had promised to "cut her up" for leaving him.

On the third day of waiting, the pimp came looking for Sherry. The two detectives, guns drawn, leaned against the thin wall, alert to every word.

"What you do that for, woman?" Russ heard the pimp say.

There was silence. Then Sherry's voice: "I . . . I . . ."

Suddenly there was a loud slap. Sherry screamed. The two detectives, on impulse, busted through the thin wall.

"April fool, motherfucker," yelled one of the detectives. Both of them had their guns leveled on the pimp.

The pimp was startled, but only for a moment. He released Sherry and, all in one swift motion, pulled a derringer from his waistband. He got off a wild shot, the bullet going so close to Russ's head that the reporter swore he could follow its entire projectory, before the cops shot him three times in the stomach.

The following week, after Russ wrote a first-person account of the shoot-out in the massage parlor, the two detectives were reprimanded by the Chief of Police for allowing a reporter to participate in an investigation.

So the next time Russ saw a man shot there weren't any police around. He was at a "peace meeting" between the Ghetto Brothers and the Savage Skulls in a basement on Hoe Avenue in the South Bronx when someone pulled a revolver and shot Rob, the Skulls' president. Rob wasn't badly wounded. But Russ did see a dying man, his bloody legs severed from his torso, a precise, neat bisection as thought the wailing man was cut in half by design, on the day of the Fraunces Tavern bombing. Russ had by chance picked that week to ride around with the police bomb squad. He was the first reporter on the scene. Not even the ambulances had arrived. It must have been minutes after the bomb had exploded in the crowded restaurant. When Russ walked through the remains of the restaurant with the members of the bomb squad, bodies were wedged under the rubble; the arid smell of gunpowder floated through the dust and haze, sickening him; and, with his every step, another piece of shaky ceiling fell near his feet. Russ wasn't hurt, though. The only time he got roughed up covering a story was when he fought in the Golden Gloves. He got eliminated early in the competition, he had no talent for the sport, but he did come up with a neatly self-aggrandizing account of his life "Up Against the Ropes." A picture of him, boxing gloves held high and ready, appeared in the magazine; and Max, going along with the joke, wrote the terse caption: The author.

RUSS, THOUGH HE WAS NOT READY to admit it, was aware of the personality he was trying to manufacture for himself during his years at *City*. He understood that each week in the magazine, with every swaggering article implicitly boasting about the jeopardy he was exposing himself to this time, he was trying to take giant steps away from the pampered, TV-set-in-every-room world he had been brought up in. With a *City* press card, a rationale of sorts, in his pocket, Russ was trying to shape himself into a man who would take risks; for, instinctively, he knew that if he were ever to find the courage to deal with the intimidating freedom that is the realm of the true artist, he would have to find the capacity to become a new man, a man who could reject the dull and restrictive world his parents and his education had prepared him to occupy.

And as he moved away from his heritage, he became part of a communal *City* scene. He ran through so much that was new: the rainy afternoon when they all huddled in a rear office to take deep hits from a cannister of laughing gas; or the time Margie, the unflappable receptionist, put on a cellophane dress and absolutely nothing else and they all followed her down to Max's Kansas City only to watch her be attacked by a feverish, tongue-wagging German shepherd; or the evenings at the Lion's Head when they talked about point of view in contemporary fiction and the advances other people were getting; or the time a bunch of them crashed Bob Dylan's birthday party and rock impresario Bill Graham sauntered over to Russ and gave everyone (except his embarrassed victim) a quick laugh by announcing that "this kid is too young to be a reporter, he must be Max Fox's son."

And there was his new life with Kate.

Russ, less than a week after their first night together, moved into Kate's East Village apartment. Not that he had grown to like the place, but now he was willing to try. Sunny days, curiously, were the worst: On bright afternoons the claustrophic orderliness of Kate's apartment seemed unbearable. But there were also days filled with ordinary moments which fused their budding relationship tight: haphazard Russ sitting on his instincts as he helped her laboriously sort his books—alphabetized by author, not title, Kate insisted—into the homemade shelves which ran like untrained ivy along every wall of the apartment; or walking hand in hand to the corner bodega to buy a quart of leche for the morning coffee; or Kate grumpy in bed with a cold and the once careless petit prince not thinking twice about running across town to find a *New York Review of Books*, an *Art in America*, a *Dance*, and a Ray's pizza with sausage and mushrooms to cheer her up.

Russ's kindness, his budding love, did not go unrewarded. Quickly, thanks to Kate, a patient yet decisive teacher, they had reached the stage in a relationship where sex is simply fun. The clumsy newness involved in exploring a once strange body had worn off; and Kate now enthusiastically tutored her younger lover in the sweaty finesse of technique.

"Talk to me," Kate would coax, the words whispered like a snake's hiss. "Tell me what feels good." She worked to draw pleasures out of his deep, unacknowledged reservoirs of desire; and, liberated, he soon learned to be reckless. In those new, unbridled days, neither of them could even imagine a time when the anger or inertia of their lives together would be so overpowering that, fighting this war with outlawed weapons, they might hold back.

THERE WAS also Max.

The editor, as his magazine approached its second decade and really began rolling, was still proselytizing his rebel's theory of journalism. Enraged by the two times two equals four logic of the daily newspapers, Max was determined to have his writers rope larger and more interesting truths—truths with greater explanatory and prescriptive powers. Russ, still taking giant steps away from his past, became Max's obedient pupil.

The editor's breakthrough insight: It would be necessary to invent a new breed of facts to get at this sort of truth. A reporter would have to manufacture "facts" strong enough to split the final atom that lay at the core of an examined life.

And oh how liberating Max's notion of truth—like Kate's realms of pleasure—proved. Now Russ could truly describe, for example, the scene of what it was like to wait in a busy massage parlor for a pimp who had promised to cut up one of his girls. Russ was empowered to invent dialogue between the two detectives as they measured out three long afternoons; to combine background characters so that the hectic experiences of a half-dozen girls could be personified as only Sherry's; and he was able to compress time, condensing a series of long days into one swift afternoon. Russ's piece in the magazine—and Max realized this—was not true to what he saw; however it was true to what he felt; and now his readers felt it, too. The literal truth, both the teacher and his pupil agreed, would have been inadequate.

The editor had dared his charge to become a Foxier explorer; and so Russ took another heady giant step away from his puritanical schoolboy intellectualism; and got his final revenge on Mr. Cow. This teacher, enjoying a routine he had perfected after thirty years in small-time journalism, had a set lecture for his well-bred reporters: "All one needs to know about writing, writing of any sort, mind you, is contained in our school's motto—'Great is the truth and it prevails.'"

This insight was further reinforced with a cunning Hawthorne would have appreciated each day of the six years Russ put in at the Arsenal: *Magna est veritas et praevalet*—prep schools, unlike the modern church, still realize there is no authority in the vernacular—was inscribed in a semicircle across the patch sewn onto the breast pocket of Russ's school blazer.

It's a handy, heuristically optimistic sentiment; and at fourteen a youth could find worse epigrams to plan an intellectual and moral life around. But, just as with the boy-sized blazer upon which it was displayed, Russ found himself outgrowing the constraints of its one-dimensional logic.

Max Fox got him to bulk up. The editor, an instinctive epistemological rebel, refused to accept the authoritarian wisdom underlying a donnish standard like "Great is the truth." He saw exciting possibilities beyond such simple convictions.

A new journalism was born: Max dismissed mere truth as offhandedly as he dismissed mere beauty; he was convinced there was more his readers needed to know. According to the editor's self-styled motto, only interesting and relevant truths were "great." And, still undeterred, Max went even further. He posed genetic questions about the origins of commonly accepted truths, the previously unimpeachable veracities one would read over the morning coffee in the *Times* or *News*. Whose truth? Max demanded. Why are they telling me this? he wondered.

"Don't be afraid of putting yourself into the story," he lectured Russ as he rejected the reporter's first version of his trip with the Angels. "You went on that boat ride. You were scared. You saw them beat up that guy and yet you did nothing. You and your fear are the main characters. Don't just give me detached judgments. Give me *your* feelings." As Russ was walking out of his office, the editor added, "Don't take potshots at the Angels from the lofty perspective of an uninvolved third person. Have the guts to make yourself a character in the drama. That way you can really have your say."

Like Xenophanes who had played cantankerously around with this question 2,500 years before him, Max lectured that truth and knowledge are, at their roots, really instances of guesswork. "Facts, and now I'm talking about difficult, insightful facts," he would tell Russ and the rest of the *City* crew as they sat assembled around his desk during a typically meandering Monday evening session after the magazine went to bed, "are really values dressed up in their Sunday best hoping they'll pass."

"Screw these so-called facts . . ." A deep puff from his brier pipe as his protégés, daring the smoke, lean closer, each of them as eager as the trained pup in the old RCA Victor ads who was so intent on hearing his master's voice.

". . . Just give me writers who don't try to disguise their point of view. Writers with values. And ideas. Any ideas. They don't have to be cut of my cloth. I'm no policeman."

He let that sink in; he wanted to show them he meant it. And then: "So, I disagree with you. That's my problem. Maybe we'll never have a drink together. But when I'm sitting at this desk, when I'm making decisions as an editor, all I care about is that I'm reading someone who thinks. That there is a philosophy, a point of view running through the article.

"And don't let anybody tell you that only seeing is believing. If you believe something that you haven't seen, then it's still your job to make your readers see it. (As Russ did: he had described what was going through the minds of the victims of the Fraunces Tavern bombing in the moments before the bomb exploded.) You have one large responsibility as a writer: To make your report true to the way you believe things really are." There was a strut in his voice as this tweedy Patton issued his final command to his troops: "Don't get bogged down in facts. Bring me *ultimate* truths."

There was another unspoken, yet perhaps more dangerous, underpinning to the battle orders General Max issued as he moved to take over a distant ridge of journalism—vanity. The editor believed he could meet someone, check out the cut of the newcomer's jib and the toothiness of his smile, and, with a flick of his analyst's mind, Max could have a pretty good idea of how to go about discovering what made this suspect want to get up in the morning. More precarious, he was convinced all his carefully selected soldiers set out on assignments with this same (or at least a functional reasonable facsimile of his) secret weapon.

Max also took on the tight-assed structuralism that Mr. Cow insisted was mandatory journalistic behavior. He righted the inverted pyramid that housed classical reporting. It was suddenly acceptable to put the spire of details up front; the bulky informative base could now follow. Another insight: Truth, like a man's memory, is not linear.

This was Max Fox's—and *City* magazine's—theory of journalism: *his* new journalism. What was so new about it? It wasn't that the questions he was dispatching his reporters to answer were new. Like Mr. Cow, Max remained curious about the oldest act in journalism—the Five W's; Messrs. Who, Why, What, Where, and When. Except Max didn't care if his emissaries invented answers to these restraining questions. Their authority would be vested in the totality of their vision. He granted his writers a teleological suspension of everyday journalistic manners and ethics. They could lie, steal, and cheat in the telling of the story if this were necessary, just so long as, in the end, the readers were delivered ultimate truths.

Max taught all this to Russ Lewis. Yet, throughout these lessons, a small yet potentially fatal misgiving lingered in the editor's mind (as a similar pang would occasionally sneak up on Kate as she considered the zeal of her quick-learning pupil): Would Russ Lewis develop the strength of character and the discipline of commitment not to abuse such freedom?

Max Fox, unlike the woman who had been conned by love, was never fooled: The verdict on Russ's future was still out.

FOR RUSS, THOUGH, in those exciting days, the future seemed wonderfully simple. Not long after he had moved in with Kate, he had started working on a piece that would eventually run in the magazine under a headline Max wrote with his tongue deep in his usually cynical cheek—"The Red Menace." The story was not about politics, but about old men who had chosen when they were young to be as brave as their idealism demanded. Now bald or toothless or their lives tottering under larger infirmities, these old Communists talked of all they had given up to chase what was, for so many of them, an unrewarding dream. Wives, children, jobs—all had been sacrificed. For years they had been chased and harassed by the FBI; and they had run until they were forgotten. Russ spoke with men who cooked on hot plates in shabby apartments, passed their afternoons in lobbies of fleabag boardinghouses, or were confined to nursing-home beds. He listened to men who had discarded their beliefs only, in the end, to discover themselves terminally alone. They had few expectations; except, perhaps, that death would bring more solace than life. Russ would come home from these interviews and rush to hug his Kate, his brave ideal. Back then it seemed so simple: Together they would escape such a narrow, lonely fate; a couple, their dreams intact, they would grow old together.

SIX

RUSS SHOULD HAVE REALIZED, though, such contentment is a fragile gift.

Kate and he had been together for a couple of months when the opening act of what would be their long-running, soul-searching calamity began to play itself out. It was late one peaceful evening. They lay together in bed, Kate's head resting on his chest as he settled into those smooth moments before sleep. Suddenly, though, Kate rose to her naked haunches and announced, "I want to show you something."

She got out of bed, scooting across the room to a chest of drawers she had found years ago on the street and had attempted to rejuvenate with a coat of bright red paint. Russ, now almost awake, followed her walk. Like a sly, peeping adolescent, he was excited by the unfettered bounce of her full breasts as she rummaged the top drawer. He felt possessive. He was glad she quickly found the slip of paper she had been looking for and, eagerly pulling back the covers, he welcomed her back to bed.

Snuggled next to Russ, Kate extended the paper. She held it out, only two of her short fingers gripping a corner; it was as if she were afraid of being burned. The paper, Russ now realized, was actually a photograph, a snapshot not much bigger than an index card. She still had not said a word.

Russ was drowsy and unprepared. He glanced absently at the photograph. He saw only a man and a woman; the man standing very erect, the woman in a ball gown. Another longer look and Russ realized the man was in a uniform. He was tall and his features were chiseled. On the sleeve of his uniform was a swastika. The woman's gown fell off her shoulders. She was smiling. She was standing in front of a portrait of a man with an unmistakable moustache. The man in the painting was Adolf Hitler.

"What's all this about?" Russ demanded, no longer sleepy. But, oddly, he still hadn't caught on; or perhaps he had and was giving Kate a last chance to invent an innocuous lie.

Not Kate.

"Russ," she said, "I want you to meet my parents."

"I JUST THOUGHT you should know," she began later that night as, each with a fortifying beer, the couple tried to sort through the ruins caused by Kate's bombshell. They were sitting across a yellow Formica card table. Kate, in deference to the occasion, had gotten dressed—a bit. She had put on a blue and white *City* T-shirt. Russ, more formal, had thrown on a pair of chinos and a faded work shirt.

Hesitantly, Kate continued: "After our first night in Brooklyn I knew I had to tell you . . . I was just waiting for the right time." Russ pulled a face; and she admitted, "I know. There is no right time. But I figured it was time to get it over with."

"And you think handing me this photograph wraps the whole thing up neat and clean? Am I supposed to say, 'Gee, Kate, you've got your father's chin. Hey, I didn't know he was a Nazi.' And then go back to bed?"

"Russ, he wasn't a Nazi."

"Then his tailor was."

"Russ, you're not letting me explain. I don't want to keep any secrets from you. At least not important ones. I want to trust you. And I want you to trust me."

"Look, Kate, if you're building up to telling me your mother's first name is Eva and that guy in the portrait behind her—"

"Goddamn you, Russell Lewis. Will you shut up and listen."

So he did.

Kate's father had been a twenty-three-year-old architectural student from Heidelberg. He spent his summers climbing mountains, and he looked at the opportunity to learn to fly as an even larger adventure. When Hitler invaded Poland, the Luftwaffe trained him to fly fighter planes, and the student became a first lieutenant. Now an officer, he married his twenty-year-old childhood sweetheart.

It didn't take Kate's mother long to realize her husband was never going to survive the war. Each day seemed to end with the same ritual: she would put on her one black dress to call on the wife of another pilot in her husband's squadron, a young wife abruptly made a widow. She tried to convince her husband to stow her in his plane and fly to Switzerland. As an act of faith in their future, she became pregnant with Kate. But there was no escape and no future. The architectural student from Heidelberg was shot down in a dogfight over Czechoslovakia four months before his daughter's birth. His body was never found.

"He wasn't a Nazi, Russ," Kate continued, a plea ringing through her words. "My father wasn't a Party member. He was a student who wanted to learn to fly. He was going to be an architect just as his father and his grandfather had been architects.

"Here," Kate said, waving the photograph in Russ's skeptical face, "look at my mother. She's a pretty girl in a lace gown. She was twenty years old. She was in love. She didn't know about politics. She didn't know that within a year, when she was only twenty-one, she would be a mother and a widow."

Russ thought Kate was going to cry, but she managed not to. He sat across from her watching her bite down hard as she struggled for control.

In a minute, her voice was steady. "Now do you understand?" she asked.

"Sure."

"You don't sound sure."

"How do you want me to sound? You tell me your father's dead. That he wasn't a Nazi. He was only a Luftwaffe officer. Yes, Kate, I understand."

But of course he didn't. Yet for the sake of Kate, for the sake of their life as a couple, he tried to pretend the past could remain forever in the past. He behaved like a patient who on being told his body had been invaded by cancer cells somehow summons up the necessary optimism to convince himself the fatal diagnosis is in error—life will go on no matter what. With that photograph, however, a lethal current began silently metastasizing through their relationship. Their life together went on; but it was never the same.

Kate, foolish with love, also was eager to believe her candor was more powerful than Russ's misgivings. After they settled into bed for the second time that evening, Kate risked sharing all that remained of her secret. In her broad, matter-of-fact way, she began to tell Russ the story of her life.

When the war was over, Kate's mother traveled throughout Europe and America as a reporter for a German daily. Sometimes Kate would be taken along. Mostly, the young, cranky child remained in Heidelberg with her doting grandmother. When Kate was six, her mother married an ex-GI she had met in Berlin. This free-spirited veteran took the entire family off to Madrid, where he had found work teaching mathematics at a high school for foreigners. In Madrid precocious Kate learned to ride horses and speak Spanish. When she was nine her family moved to Buffalo, her stepfather's hometown. She spent the next decade living in a downtown apartment with cracked casement windows looking out on a block lined with blighted elms. Kate, in time, learned to be confident enough to stop signing her school compositions Kate Warner, German immigrant; collected Elvis Presley records; wore white lipstick and a beehive hairdo; and perfected her unaccented English. She gave up the lipstick and the beehive during her first scholarship semester at Wellesley. After she graduated Phi Bet, she gave up all but the most formal contact with her mother and stepfather. She had left school six years ago and gone straight to New York, certain she would become a writer. She had been on her own ever since. She had worked as a governess, a travel agent, a salesgirl at Bloomingdale's during the Christmas rush, and in a Madison Avenue antiques shop. All this was before Max Fox had hired her for the heady but low-paying job of dance critic for *City*.

Someday, she said, lying once more close to Russ, her arm curled across his smooth back as they finally settled down to sleep, she would write a novel. Then she told him another secret: She would dedicate this book to her stepfather, Frankie Warner.

"Why him?" Russ tried not to sound jealous.

"Because he made my mother happy."

"You don't believe that. If you did, you'd visit him. And your mother. Hell, you don't even call."

"It's not that I don't love them. I just don't want to get too close to them. It's too painful."

"I don't understand."

"And I don't know how to explain. At least not now." She caught herself starting to yawn, controlled it, and then asked: "Haven't I told you enough for one night?"

He was saved from having to answer because moments later she was asleep.

THE RING OF THE phone at four in the morning is chilling.

Russ awoke on the first sound and reached for the receiver. Kate, always gung-ho, beat him to it.

She listened for an attentive couple of minutes; and when she spoke her voice was precise, almost pedantic, the words falling into a rhythm more natural to someone's giving tricky traffic directions to a lost motorist: "Okay . . . okay. I understand . . . Now you'd better go home . . . No, there's nothing you can do . . . Yes, go home . . . Yes, I'll be up . . .

Right, there's a bus that leaves at six and arrives at around three in the afternoon. You got that? Three o'clock . . . Fine. You meet me at the bus station. Now go home. And go to bed." Then she hung up.

"What's that all about?"

"It's Frankie. He was drunk for a change." She sounded calm, but only for a moment. Her lower lip started quivering. And as she tried to speak, tears fell full force over her words. This was the first time Russ had ever seen her cry. At first he was more astonished than concerned; it was so unnatural, he felt, for Kate not to be in total control. Soft, deep sobs continued to break through her words: "Frankie says Mommy's in the hospital. She was drinking. She knows she's not supposed to. She knows that. I guess they both must have been drinking. Frankie says all of a sudden Mommy started coughing blood and then she fainted. He took her to the hospital and Dr. Palmer says there's nothing he can do. Her liver and her kidneys can't take it anymore. The doctor said she's going to die. Oh, Russ . . ."

Russ could do nothing but hold her in his arms; after a while she was able to stop crying.

"I feel so silly when I cry," she said as he handed her a tissue. "I get these little pink pig eyes." Russ kissed her tenderly on one pig eye and then the other. His lips tasted the salt of her tears.

"You have the cutest pig eyes I've ever seen."

Kate blew her nose into the crumpled tissue and then tried to giggle. She didn't want to be afraid. Russ's hand was squeezing hers.

"I have to get up to Buffalo. Frankie won't know what to do. He's lost with her, but he'll die without her. I have to go up there to help him."

"I'm coming with you."

"That's silly, Russ. This is not the time for a visit. It'll just be depressing."

"Then it'll be my job to cheer you up." Russ went to work right away by making a loony, bug-eyed face. It didn't get a smile.

"Don't worry about me. I can handle it. I've been preparing myself for my mother's death for the past three years. The doctor warned her if she didn't stop drinking this was going to happen. I guess she just didn't care enough to stop."

"Look," Russ lectured, turning stern, "I'm not going to let you go through this alone." And with all the conviction he could wake up at four in the morning he told Kate, "We're a couple. And we're going to handle this as a couple no matter how it turns out."

But that was before Russ Lewis knew how it was going to turn out.

SEVEN

''KATE! Over here, Kate.''

As soon as Russ and Kate got off the bus in Buffalo the next afternoon, they could hear Florence, Kate's eighteen-year-old stepsister, doing her best to let them (and the rest of the city) know her whereabouts. The girl was standing less than a yard away.

Kate rushed ahead and was immediately enveloped by her larger sibling. Russ remained guarding their bags, taking it all in with some astonishment. The two girls didn't look like any sort of sisters. Flo was an athletically heavy girl, generously padded with the sort of bulky musculature that comes from routinely chopping a cord of wood or running dozens of miles before devouring a lumberjack's breakfast. As Flo reluctantly released her bear hug on Kate, Russ decided (with a temperament made prickly by a nine-hour bus ride that had stretched, thanks to the unanticipated snow, into a stifling eleven) it was only a wide and constantly flashing smile that saved Flo from looking too much like one of those severe East European shotputters who made the headlines by flunking chromosome tests.

"How's Mommy?" Kate asked as she led her beaming sister toward Russ.

Flo flashed a jack-o'-lantern smile before answering, "She's resting."

Kate knew her sister well enough not to press for details; and she was relieved simply to know her mother was alive.

As they approached the bags, Kate said, "Flo, this is my friend Russ Lewis." Flo let loose with another grin.

But not Russ. He was instantly put off by Kate's unembroidered description of their relationship. A "friend" seemed like someone who sat next to you in school, not in bed.

Still, Russ decided to behave. "I'm sorry to have to meet you in these circumstances," he said and extended his hand.

"Hi," said Flo.

But the one syllable was offered with so much singsong good cheer that an accurate transcript of the encounter would require a huge have-a-nice-day circle rather than a demure dot above the "i." Her grip was equally hearty.

Flo, oblivious to Russ's protests, grabbed their two small suitcases and started leading the way to the exit. It was only at this moment that Kate thought to ask, "Where's the car? And what happened to Frankie? I thought he was going to meet us?"

This was a toughie: a six-grin question. Straight off, two bright smiles while an answer was being formulated. Then: "Frankie has the car." A series of rapid, toothy flashes. And on to the punch line: "But Frankie's in jail." Clearly delighted by the skill with which she had handled this mind-boggler, Flo celebrated with another full-mouthed display of her sparkling smile. And still another.

Kate finally had enough. "Goddamn it," she wailed, slamming her purse to the depot floor in disgust. All sorts of things—bobby pins, an address book, birth control pills, rubber bands, pencils—scattered about the cement like souvenirs from another, more rational life.

"Now wait a minute, Kate."

But she cut Russ off. "I told you not to come, I told you it would be crazy." She was both embarrassed and a bit hysterical.

"Look," he tried, "let's calm down and figure out what's going on." He looked imploringly at Flo. She was on her hands and knees shoving the wide-scattered junk into Kate's bag. She returned his interest with an excited smile. Russ immediately conceded it was his fault; by now he should have known better.

"Come on," he said, turning his attention to the older sister, "let's sit down somewhere. I'm sure if you go over it slowly with Flo you can get to the bottom of this."

They sat down on a wooden bench in a corner of the depot as Kate, with a patient, loving calm, managed to extract a somewhat fuller report from Flo. It seemed Frankie after calling Kate last night had not, despite her instructions, gone directly home. He had stopped off somewhere—Flo was a little cloudy on the specifics—and through luck or force of personality had managed to attract the protective attention of Buffalo's finest. In what Russ imagined must have been a moment of true desperation, Frankie had used his one call to contact Flo. His request was simple enough: She should hightail it to the Central Street Station with $50 for bail. These instructions, though, were too demanding for Flo. She decided to await her big sister's arrival. She was convinced Kate would sort things out.

It was a sketchy tale, but there was enough for Russ to latch onto. "All right, here's what I think we should do," he said, assuming command. "I'll go bail out Frankie. Kate, you and Flo go to the hospital. I'll get Frankie and we'll meet you there."

"You're sure you want to get in the middle of this, Russ?"

"Why not? I never bailed out anyone's father before."

Kate was past shooting him looks. "Well," she agreed, "I should get to the hospital. Someone should be with Mommy."

So they hailed separate cabs in front of the bus depot. Kate and a still smiling Flo headed off to their dying mother; while a rather curious Russ drove across town to meet his lover's incarcerated stepfather.

AS SOON AS RUSS got into the cab large, wet snowflakes started swirling through the soot-gray Buffalo evening.

"We gonna get a shitload of snow," the driver said cheerfully. "Where to?"

"Central Street Station, please."

"Son," the driver said, now turning to look at the passenger in the backseat, "you don't want to go there." He was a very black man with a shiny bald head surrounded by a wispy border of gray hair. When he spoke, a mouthful of gold teeth twinkled at Russ.

"Yes I do," Russ persisted.

"It's your money." The cabbie drove with one hand on the wheel, held at eleven o'clock, and the other stretched across the front seat as though he were cuddling with his lover. As the snow began to do a treacherous job on the downtown traffic, he continued his argument.

"These here Buffalo cops don't like nobody. They don't like black folk like me. They don't like longhairs like you. Shee-it. Them mothers got it in even for little babies."

"They sound like a happy bunch," Russ joked; but he also tried to slick down his hair.

"Shee-it. Only one thing make them happy."

"One thing?" Russ asked as a quick look into the rearview mirror showed him that, despite his efforts, his scraggly hair had an unruly mind of its own.

"Yeah. Kickin' ass."

The cabbie's warning came as he pulled up to the precinct house. Russ trudged anxiously up the long, snow-covered steps. Obsessively, he kept on trying to shove his recalcitrant hair behind his ears. But it wasn't much of a disguise. Nobody seemed to be fooled. The cops kept on staring at him. Russ forgot about Frankie. He was wondering what was going to happen to Russ Lewis.

He entered a room as dark as a cave and, too late now to cut and run, approached an intimidatingly high front desk. A green-bonneted lamp shone on the flat-topped head of the desk sergeant. He seemed to be looking down four or five stories at Russ. Jack Webb playing Zeus.

"Yeah?" the sergeant demanded as Russ, straining his neck, was forced to look heavenwards.

"I'm trying to find a Frank Warner. He was arrested last night and I've come to bail him out."

"Yeah?" the sergeant repeated. Except now he rolled his ballpoint restlessly through his fingers. Russ imagined the officer's wishing it were a nightstick.

Russ pushed back his hair and tried again. "A Frank Warner. He was arrested last night."

The sergeant refused to acknowledge the question. Instead, using his ballpoint as a marker, he glanced down a row of names in the ledger opened in front of him. Halfway down the second page he brought his ballpoint to an abrupt stop.

"Franklin A. Warner you said?" His voice filled the room the way air fills a balloon.

"Yes sir."

"He's in on a D and D."

"D and D?"

"Yeah, drunk and disorderly." He took a clipboard off the desk and thumbed through a thick pile of pink sheets. He found the page he wanted and read silently for a moment.

Suddenly the sergeant let out a yell: "You know what that fucker did?"

"No," Russ said meekly, but he quickly imagined the worst. His imagination fell short.

"He attacked a bunch of nuns."

". . . Oh."

But Russ's consciousness was jumping: What had Kate gotten him into? A father who was a Nazi? A stepfather who attacked nuns? At least, Russ decided, knowing it was unfortunately only partly a joke, Kate's mother's taste in men was consistent.

"You related to this Warner?" sneered the desk sergeant, interrupting Russ's rushing thoughts.

"No. Just a friend of the family." He immediately regretted saying that.

The sergeant stared down hard at Russ as though the boy had made a rude noise, and then continued reading silently from the clipboard. Russ watched his lips move.

Finally, he spoke. "This Warner owes St. Mary's some money, all right. Seems he put a fist through a rectory window. Stained glass it was."

"Uh huh." This was the man to whom Kate planned to dedicate her unwritten masterpiece?

"I tell you, kid, if it were up to me I'd lock this Warner up and throw away the key."

"Yes sir . . ."

". . . but it isn't up to me."

God bless America, Russ silently intoned.

"No matter what kind of scum he is, he's entitled to his day in court," announced the sergeant with flag-waving conviction.

". . . Yes sir." But Russ didn't sound convinced; and he certainly wasn't eager to find out what kind of scum Frankie Warner might be.

But, for Kate's sake, he paid the bail money. The sergeant directed another huge cop to lead Russ to a room in the rear of the building that was as airy as a meat locker. Russ passed the time wondering if the dark blotches on the wall were dried blood. It must have been nearly an hour before still another towering, crew-cutted officer brought the prisoner into the room.

Frankie Warner was a letdown. Russ had expected Attila the Hun. Instead, this drunken defiler of the church looked more like a sherry-sipping professor, a man more likely to be busted for civil disobedience than D and D. Oh, Frankie was a big man; Russ immediately knew where Flo had inherited her bulk. But along with his size, Frankie Warner had a wonderfully intelligent black-bearded and almost owlish face. Jet black hair, combed into a neat thick forelock, fell over a wide brow. And his tortoiseshell bifocals, while perhaps an incongruous touch on most attackers of nuns, seemed to fit with the rest of Frankie's outfit: a blue-checked button-down shirt, a square-cut wool tie, a bulky cardigan, and rumpled brown corduroys.

Russ went up to the prisoner and, not really knowing where to begin, said, "Mr. Warner, I'm Russ Lewis."

Frankie Warner reached out to shake Russ's hand, only to draw sheepishly back as he realized he still was handcuffed to the officer. In a moment, though, he was free and he greeted Russ with a firm handshake and a small victimized shrug. Then, taking a deep, soothing breath before he went on, he announced in a curiously soft, almost childlike voice, "Welcome to Buffalo."

RUSS HAD A LOT of obvious questions, but on the way to the hospital Frankie did all the interrogating. Frankie was very anxious to find out about his wife. Russ answered Frankie as optimistically as he could, but all the time he was really waiting for the opening to try out the one question that was on his mind. Except he didn't know how to bring it up. Politely. It didn't seem proper to ask your girl friend's stepfather, "What's this I hear about your going after a bunch of nuns?" Even if you did bail him out.

The closest Frankie had come to an explanation was when they were on their way out of the police station. The two men were walking through the snow to Frankie's red Honda when he suggested, "You'd better get in on my side."

The door on the passenger side of the tiny car looked like it had gotten in the way of a powerhouse of a cosmic jab.

"What happened?" Russ asked, crawling across a front seat littered with beer cans. He tried to sound naive.

"It was a long night last night," Frankie said with a bedraggled nod of the head. And that, clearly, was all he was going to offer on the mysterious subject.

So, maintaining a correct silence, they headed off to the hospital. Except Frankie first wanted to stop for a newspaper.

"I'm sure we can get a paper at the hospital," Russ suggested.

"Yeah, but I got a favorite newsstand. Always get my papers there."

It wasn't until after they parked that Russ realized why this was Frankie's favorite newsstand—it was next door to Polish Mike's Bar and Grill.

"C'mon," Frankie said in his whispering voice, "just a quick one to warm you up. I owe you anyway."

"Kate's waiting at the hospital . . ."

"We'll get there. C'mon."

Russ considered arguing, but he decided it wouldn't have done much good. Besides, it was clammy and cold standing in the falling snow. Russ hoped Kate would understand; and if she didn't, what could he do? Frankie was running this show.

About a half-dozen men sat slumped on stools along the bar; above them a digital clock embedded in the mainsail of a plastic schooner read 7:11.

"Hey Frankie," called out the man with a mushy, pink-fleshed face behind the bar.

"Mike," Frankie replied in his decorous voice, as he took a corner stool. Frankie motioned for Russ to grab the stool next to him.

The bartender rubbed hands the size of catcher's mitts on the once white apron which was having a hard time trying to cover his belly. Russ figured this had to be Polish Mike.

"It's a bitch outside," said the bartender. "The usual?"

"Please," said Frankie.

Polish Mike turned to Russ. Russ, with a shrug, decided when in Polish Mike's . . .

"I'll have the same."

Polish Mike quickly produced two large foamy mugs of beer and two shots of whiskey. Frankie grabbed the shot glass, offered a ceremonial "cheers," and then drained it in a gulp. He chugalugged the chaser. Russ, always competitive, tried to imitate Frankie's bravado performance. There was a lot of coughing. But he got it all down. A nod of Frankie's jet black head and another round materialized.

They finished the round before Frankie decided to speak. "So you're Kate's boyfriend," he said as if he were considering the alternatives to a rather weighty dilemma.

"Yes," Russ answered with tipsy pride.

That pregnant exchange satisfied Frankie. He returned to his drink. The liquor, though, had emboldened Russ.

"Mr. Warner," he began.

"Frankie," the older man corrected.

"Frankie . . ." Russ agreed with a conciliatory smile; and he instantly hoped he didn't seem as silly as Flo. Then, egged on by his drunken courage, he decided there was no point in turning back. "Frankie," he repeated, "the desk sergeant told me you attacked a bunch of nuns. Any truth to that?"

"Is that what he told you?" Frankie, speaking in his soft, harmless way, seemed genuinely shocked. "I can't believe he told you that."

"Well, he did," Russ insisted with rather shrill conviction; the boilermakers were taking their toll.

Frankie didn't respond. He mulled over something that, if his concentrated gaze were any clue, seemed to be swimming in the bottom of his beer. After a while his attention returned to his drinking partner.

There was a weary, defeated strain to his words. "I guess if that's the story they're dishing out, I should tell you what actually happened." But Frankie waited until he ordered another round before sharing his tale:

Not long after Frankie had finished talking with Kate, he got it into his head that his wife shouldn't die without a priest's giving her the last rites. "I know Helen's not really a Catholic anymore and I haven't believed in anything for longer than I can remember," Frankie told Russ. "But for some reason last night it seemed extremely important to me to get a priest to come to the hospital." The embarrassed shrug of his broad shoulders implied the obvious moral: What makes sense when you're tight doesn't necessarily make equal sense the morning after.

But, following the logic of the moment, Frankie began hunting at 4 a.m. for a priest. He drove up to a darkened and locked St. Mary's. Straight off he made the first in a series of errors which would lead him away from religious fervor and into criminal mischief: The door he was knocking so imploringly upon was not part of the rectory—it was the front door to the nuns' residence.

"When no one answered, I got pretty angry," Frankie recalled. "You know, there I was yelling, 'I need a priest,' but the priest wouldn't even turn on the lights. I was really annoyed. Then I hear this woman yell from an upstairs window, 'Go away. You're drunk. Come back in the morning.' Now this really ticked me off. I figured the priest was too busy shacking up with some floozie to come down to the hospital to give Helen her last rites. It never occurred to me it was a nun yelling from the window. I guess I was too angry to think clearly. And . . . you know, a little drunk.

"Anyway, let's just say I got sorta carried away. I decided to crash the door down and drag that no-good priest down to the hospital. The next thing I know my fist is going through a pane of glass and a couple of cops are pulling me away. I'm yelling at them at the top of my lungs, 'I need a priest,' and they're putting me in the back of a squad car." This recalled image made him break out in a long, wheezy, admonishing laugh. "And that's how things were until you rescued me," he concluded, hoping, Russ imagined, that the long swallow of beer he was now taking would permanently wash the memory away.

"Well," Russ said, "at least I feel a lot better knowing I'm not drinking with someone who molested a couple of nuns."

"You believed that?"

". . . Well, I had never met you before and . . ."

"And you still drank with me?" Frankie's voice was a sudden, terrifying bass. His eyes narrowed as if taking a bead on a target. Russ suddenly had the uneasy feeling that the quiet professor was about to turn into the Incredible Hulk.

"Geez . . ." Frankie spit out. And he stood up. Was he about to square off?

"Look, I apologize if—"

But Frankie wouldn't listen. "Let's get the hell out of here. I don't feel like drinking anymore. Besides, it's time we got to the hospital."

And without waiting for an answer, the man who had spent the night in the Central Station drunk tank stormed indignantly out of Polish Mike's, leaving his savior, now tipsy and confused, behind.

EIGHT

"WHERE WERE YOU?" Kate asked as soon as Russ entered her mother's hospital room. She hurried to him and took his hand. "I was worried."

Russ knew this was neither the time nor the place to tell Kate she couldn't have been nearly as worried as he had been. Not that things with Frankie hadn't worked out all right. Frankie had remained sullenly quiet until they reached the circular drive leading to the hospital. But, with the looming white-brick building in sight, he lightened up, turning on the radio. Classical music; a reminder of Kate. Russ was further cheered when Frankie began in his meek, professorial voice:

"Well, I'm glad I cleared up what happened last night. You understand now, right?"

Russ answered immediately: "No problem."

"Good." There was a sweet, calm smile. And he added, "I'll drop you off before I put the car in the garage."

"Please." Russ hoped it didn't sound like he was pleading.

"Oh, one other thing . . ."

Russ waited anxiously.

But Frankie was simply coy: "I think maybe you'd better take a couple of these." He handed his passenger a pack of Certs. "No sense letting the girls know you've been drinking."

I've been drinking? But Russ knew he was too close to the hospital to blow it now. "Our little secret," he volunteered, popping a couple of mints into his mouth.

"Good," Frankie agreed. "And, here we are." The car stopped in front of Buffalo General. "Tell the girls I'll be right up."

So a couple of minutes later when Kate asked him where he had been, Russ figured it was best to circle the truth. "Well, things took a while and then . . ."

His voice trailed off as he focused for the first time on the woman lying in the hospital bed. A plastic tube was in her nose. Another ran

from her arm. Her skin was chalk white. But her eyes were bright; and
she tried to smile when she caught his glance.

"Mommy's much better," Kate said as she led Russ to the bedside.
"Dr. Palmer told me she gave him quite a scare last night, but it looks
like she's out of danger."

Russ stood by the bed trying not to look too much the worse from
an eleven-hour bus ride, a couple of hours with the Buffalo cops, and an
hour of fun at Polish Mike's. He took a deep, calming breath before
speaking. "I'm so glad you're better, Mrs. Warner."

"And I'm so glad to meet you, Russell. Kate has spent the whole
time telling me about you."

Listening to her words, Kate was once again flooded with a painful
concern: Her mother's voice was so tentative, so frail. But Russ ignored
this. He concentrated on what he considered a more disturbing symptom:
Helen Warner's heavy accent. His Kate had not even a trace of German
in her speech; her mark of Cain could remain a deeply buried secret. But
her mother—almost his mother-in-law!—sounded like Dr. Strangelove.
Of course, he instantly realized, she should; Helen Warner had spent
most of her life in Heidelberg. But it simply had never occurred to him
that she would sound this way. And as soon as Helen Warner had
spoken, the ghostly pale woman in the bed had been transformed by
Russ's stern mind: She was the young girl in the off-the-shoulders ball
gown standing in front of a portrait of Adolf Hitler.

"Russ," said Kate, calling him back to the present, "maybe we should
let my mother rest for a while. And I wouldn't mind a shower and a nap.
We'll come back in the morning."

"Sure. A little sleep and a shower sound great." As did avoiding
another confrontation with Frankie.

They said their good-bys and were walking to the door when Kate's
mother called after her. The voice was tiny, yet brave.

"I'll get the elevator," Russ suggested. "You see what your mother
wants."

Russ went out to the hall and rang for the elevator. Two came and
went before Kate joined him.

"My mother was very glad you made the trip," Kate said as she once
more took his hand. "You know what she wanted to tell me?"

Russ shook his head.

There was a shy, self-conscious fluttering giggle before she spoke.
"Mommy said she hopes I make her a grandmother soon. She told me,
'Russell will make a good father.'"

Russ didn't want to answer. Fortunately, he didn't have to. The
elevator came and Frankie got out. Kate and her stepfather embraced;

and Russ was suddenly alone, left to wonder: Kate, my uncommon Kate, what has my love for you gotten me into?

THEY SPENT A TENSE, snowy week in Buffalo. Kate's mother, though still looking as starkly white as the stiff hospital sheets which covered her brittle body, was definitely on the mend. She would survive this bout with gin, but the doctor warned—and Russ and Kate instinctively knew—a grimmer prognosis would certainly be found at the end of the next lost weekend.

Russ accompanied Kate to the hospital each day. Helen Warner's increasing strength helped her make elaborate resolutions as to how, once fully recovered, she would fill her days with energetic projects; and never, no, never touch another fateful drop. Kate pretended to the family—and to Russ—that she was cheered by her mother's newfound resolve. Yet they both knew Helen Warner's conviction would soon be floating away in a clear glass of gin.

From the dreary week Russ spent in Buffalo he could understand what Helen Warner was up against; and he could understand why Kate, without so much as a nostalgic look back, had fled to New York after college. He saw what a now stoic Kate must also have seen painful years ago: Helen and Frankie Warner were mired in a small, hopeless life that neither of them had any use for; and from which at this late date there remained no possibility of escape—except death. Alcohol would numb their pain as it eased the way.

Yet what made this so chilling for Russ (just as it had, years ago, started to tear Kate apart) was that one could not help but like a sober Frankie Warner. In many casually evocative ways, in fact, he reminded Russ of Max. Except Frankie was a warning, the dark down side of Max's thoughtful bohemian temperament. Frankie was what Max, the Max Fox who had spent a decade or so hanging out at the Cedar, might have dissipated into if the incipient editor had not possessed the courage to try to grab the life he wanted. And the luck.

Russ, who had just gotten used to measuring his future against the grace and charm of Max's fulfilled example, realized after the grim days in Buffalo that success wasn't necessarily so easy. He would have to come to grips with the lessons lurking around Kate's stepfather; and, in time, Frankie, even more than joyfully unencumbered Kate, got Russ thinking about applying the brakes to his romantic ambitions.

The devastation surrounding the Warners helped Russ appreciate the logic of the warning implicit in his parents' narrow lives: Play it safe —the odds are never in your favor. Norman Lewis, the insurance salesman, and his wife, Rachel, lived their lives without large gambles, without large thrills. They never expected much. It wasn't that they didn't know what they were missing; they felt it wasn't their place to miss it.

Russ had grown up wanting more. Yet the youth who had felt so triumphant in his landing a flashy job at *City*, so superior to his parents who sat complacently on the sidelines of life, was now forced to consider what Frankie's wishful thinking had gotten him.

Frankie had hung around Europe looking for the lost generation, and he got lost. He had tried running after the bulls with a bohemian crowd, and he got trampled. He had met a foreign woman, fallen in love, had no trouble supporting a family in Spain with the luxury of inflated American dollars, and then returned to the oppressive snowbound city of his youth only to realize too late the fiesta years were over. The Warners, along with their expectations, were stranded in Buffalo. So now they drank to remember the old days; and then they drank some more to forget them.

The down side to all this wishful thinking was, Russ was beginning to realize, a long way down.

Still, he caught glimmers from the lost life Frankie would like to have led. Russ would always remember his peek into a corner of what might have been; from the open door of the bedroom he was sharing to no one's dismay with Kate, he had spied unnoticed one evening on Frankie in the living room:

It is an hour before their scheduled trip to the hospital and Frankie sits in a leatherette club chair. His stockinged feet are stretched in front of him and crossed at the ankles over a walnut brown ottoman; cotton stuffing sticks out from a large gash across its tufted lap. The gin and tonic is only the first, a restorative after his back-breaking shift in the steel mill. He is reading a thick hardback copy of *Principia Mathematica*. He pauses frequently, looking up pensively from his book; he requires each sentence to fall into its logical place before he will proceed.

Russ thought a lot about this brief, accidentally observed instance. At first Russ saw it as the indelible shadow of the academic ambitions Frankie had explained he had once held: in these few moments Frankie imagined himself the professor he once hoped to become. Yet, before the evening was over, Russ realized it was also parody: a calm before the inevitably dissolute storm.

Within hours that quiet interlude is devastated. Oh, all goes well for a while. They trudge through the snow to the hospital; and then, to placate Flo's sweet tooth, they hit Ho Jo's for the Hawaiian Pineapple

Sundae Festival. Foolishly—but Kate's admonishment came only with hindsight—no one argues when Frankie insists they all head to Polish Mike's to wash away the gooey aftertaste.

After an hour crammed with gin and tonics (Frankie thought they were the only suitable chaser to a pineapple sundae), the Hulk is on the loose. Russ and Kate exit with a smiling Flo while Frankie remains behind, determined to prove, despite two soberer attempts with nearly disastrous results, he can hoist a 175-pound woman over his head. One last look back before they leave: Frankie has decided it's the added weight of the woman's boots that is making his ridiculous enterprise an impossible one. "The goddamn boots," Frankie is yelling as he is trying to tug these bits of dead weight off the pickled woman's chunky feet. "Off with the goddamn boots."

And so it will go with Frankie day after snowy day, night after snowy night.

IT SNOWED THE DAY Helen Warner was released from the hospital. Though the radio was announcing all departing flights were grounded, Russ and Kate hurried to the airport. They would gamble on a change in the weather. A Greyhound to New York wouldn't do—they were that eager to break out and literally climb over the ruinous city.

There was an hour's delay, but they got lucky. The flurries eased a bit and the plane took off. It wasn't until they were high in the sky, the city below disappearing behind a thick layer of cardboard-colored clouds, that Russ, for the first time in seven days, felt unburdened. Kate must have felt it, too. She took a bright yellow comb from her bag and ran it through her hair making sure her center part was straight. It was, Russ felt, a sentimental gesture to the more orderly world to which she was returning. She continued running the comb through her brown hair; while she also combed out straight, careful thoughts from the week's tangled events.

"Enough with the hair, Rapunzel," Russ finally intervened. "Do us both a favor and take a break." And he added, "Maybe it wouldn't be such a bad idea to share what's going through your well-combed mind."

Kate laughed, a little embarrassed that her obsessiveness had not gone unnoticed. "I was just thinking," she eventually began, "how I would make things if I were running this planet."

"Now this I want to hear," Russ mocked.

"No really, I'm serious. If I were running things, I'd make it so children were given the chance to pick their parents. I'd give babies the opportunity to choose the kind of people they want to be their mothers and fathers."

"You actually think that would change things," he challenged. "I mean, suppose somehow you were given a choice at birth, how do you know you'd pick wisely?"

"Oh, you can bet I would," said Kate confidently. "Look how shrewd I was in picking a true love."

He kissed her on the lips and Buffalo seemed a million miles away, a million years ago.

"Yes," Kate continued, "things would be a lot simpler if we could have picked our parents."

The plane started its descent into a clear and cold New York.

"At least we have each other," Russ dared to say.

But neither of them dared to mention the parent they would have chosen, the audience before whom they wished to play out the rest of their lives—Max Fox.

NINE

KATE AND RUSS had been living on the Lower East Side for over a year when they decided to give their first dinner party. They had something to celebrate.

Actually, there were two fanciful decisions to toast. Russ, despite the misgivings that had begun fermenting in Buffalo, was at an optimistic age when making commitments seemed important; and so, like a child's wishes they kept pouring forth. Convinced he had quickly ballooned into a full-grown adult—he had a job and lived with a woman—Russ conscientiously began structuring his life around Dr. Freud's prescription for mature happiness: a tablespoon of *arbeit* between meals and a dose of *lieben* after.

It was all going to be so easy; work and love.

A fast-talking publisher made it seem even easier. At first. Edwin Brewster, a senior editor at a well-known publishing house, called up Russ after reading some of his pieces in *City* and asked the young reporter to come to his office to discuss an idea for a book.

It wasn't much of an idea. It seemed Brewster had been approached by the agent representing Rico Pelligrini, a small-time hood who claimed big-time connections. When the Godfather got angry, he hired Rico—or so the mobster and his agent claimed—to get even. All the hood, the agent, and the editor needed was a writer to complete the package. At first Russ was reluctant. The shoot-'em-up adventure inherent in the story, the offhanded approach to murder that made the editor's eyes twinkle with a rosy commercial sheen as he speculated about the book's appeal, seemed too calculated, too amoral. And a brief conversation with Rico ("When were you born?" Russ asked. "1946," Rico shot back. "I thought you're twenty-eight years old?" Russ continued good-naturedly. Rico, equally good-natured, responded, "Whatever age you want me to be, I'll be. Who's going to know the difference?" While Brewster interrupted, "See, I told you he'd be cooperative.") had convinced the budding author that nobody involved wanted to let the facts stand in the way of the best-seller list. Besides, even Russ was instinctively suspicious of hoodlums who had friends at William Morris. But Russ didn't walk straight away from the project. And he agreed when Brewster suggested, the newcomer loving the aggressive implications of the senior editor's verbs, that "we take a lunch and knock the idea around a bit more."

The lunch was in the Grill Room of the Four Seasons. This was Russ's first meal at the restaurant, and when he revealed this to the editor, Brewster began flexing all his gray-flanneled muscles to win the youth over. "Do you realize we're sitting in the second most powerful seats in the room," he confided with a dismissive laugh. "They really make the most outrageous fuss over who sits in what booth in this place." Brewster's nonstop cheery banter played to all silliness that accompanies these lunchtime expense-account rituals; however, he also made it clear to Russ that his was an insider's disdain, the mocking of privilege by a man who was secure in his social position. Even his clothes suggested his raised eyebrow view of the glamorous life he was leading: He wore a three-piece suit and white tennis sneakers.

Russ, a *City* certified outsider, felt it necessary to feign indifference, but the editor's casual intimations of power were corrupting. The reporter hadn't got past the flaky croissants in the silver bread basket before he was chafing to take a dinner, too. And it wasn't just the glasses of sweet white wine ("Please, you must let me recommend a wine. It's one of my small prides," Brewster had insisted) that had Russ imagining himself instead of the blow-dried newscaster, dribblings from his mustard shrimps bespattering his tie, enthroned in the rosewood booth at the head of this fast-paced clique.

Throughout the long lunch the editor worked his campaign well, mixing bursts of soft, flattering charm with his power sweeps. Brewster was proclaiming how avidly he followed the youth's work in *City* when, caught in mid-sentence he paused; intently focused his eyes on his guest, his pupils suddenly glowing disturbingly as if he had been clipped on the blind side by satori; slammed down his Kir; and then in a voice well mellowed in a bottom-of-my-heart sincerity that even a talk show host would find sentimental announced, "I swear to you, Russ, only *you* could write this book." It wasn't until months later that Russ learned why: Just about every published writer within commuting distance of the Four Seasons had already refused the assignment.

Yet Brewster didn't have to sell so hard. He could have had the maître shuffle Russ off to the third or fourth most powerful seat in the place and the contract would still have been signed on the dotted line. Edwin Brewster wasn't the only actor using this power booth for a stage. Same as Russ patted his belly in polite protest before giving in "just this once" to a fabulous chocolate and whipped cream concoction perched on the dessert cart, he also found it necessary to put up a struggle before biting into the tempting literary pot. There was no way, though, he was going to pass up the chance to do the book—any book. Ambition would always get the best of him.

"It might be interesting to explore the psychology of a mobster, to consider the motivations of a man who makes his living killing other people on command," Russ began theorizing as he ate greedy forkfuls of velvety moist chocolate. And, leaning across the table as if he were already on "Nightline" and confiding his inspirational wisdoms to millions of his culture-starved countrymen, he explained, "What really attracts me is the opportunity to tell a good yarn." Another intoxicating swallow of this unscrupulously luxurious cake and, Russ and his Advance Placement French feeling no shame, he gave the editor the full treatment: "As Stendhal said, *'Il faut que le roman raconte.'* "

Russ, much to his later embarrassment, would always remember that he spoke that line with a straight face. Like Hallmark cards, Kate had once teased him, he had a pretentious line for any circumstance. Worse, she added when she was really angry, Russ had a boorish tendency to take this veneer of memorized erudition seriously. But Russ wasn't ready yet to learn from Kate.

So he paid. Or, more exactly, didn't get paid. His bilingual display of undisguised enthusiasm had convinced the sly editor that he was dining with a fellow hustler. Brewster instantly decided he could get the young reporter for half the advance he had planned to offer. But when the editor leaned across the table and proposed $1,000 for signing and another $2,000 when Russ delivered the completed manuscript, Russ felt like picking up the tab for lunch. While $3,000 seemed in those unencumbered days like a generous sum to anyone living on a *City* salary, money wasn't the real come-on in the package. Russ was chasing literary fantasies. He already was envisioning the book's cover—with the author's name in big letters. His name.

"Okay," Russ announced after he had let the editor coax him into another portion of the chocolate cake, "it's a deal." Russ reached across the table to shake on it; and as the youth, filled with a genuine fervor for the occasion and the new task, wagged Brewster's icily limp hand, Russ's blazer sleeve lapped up the whipped cream of his dessert. Despite the attentive maître's deferential elbow grease not all the club soda in the grill room could wash out this damn spot. It was indelible. Russ shrugged off the consequences of his eagerness; and the symbolic import of this small accident escaped him. Yet even today there remain traces of this ghostly gray smudge floating about the row of three brass buttons on his ruined sleeve.

On the taxi ride home (Russ decided he had earned a treat), paths of literary glory were being cleared through his daydreams; and previous misgivings fell to a cocky eminent domain. But as soon as he shared the bubbling news with Kate, Russ began to simmer down. He went on about what a book he was going to write, about the complex psychological portrait of a hired gun he would create, about the finely detailed scenes in the streets of Canarsie or in the back rooms of social clubs in Little Italy he would paint. Kate quietly listened. And then with one well-timed judgment she laid him low.

"If you play your cards right," she said, "it might sell."

"You're just jealous," Russ immediately shouted back. "I don't see anyone asking you to write a book."

He turned away, wishing there were at least one door in their little apartment he could slam. His anger was beyond words. But he realized Kate's curse had power. From that first day Russ's book was doomed—doomed for success.

So much for the first celebratory decision they had to toast.

It was the second of Russ's momentous commitments, however, that finally got Kate on the ebullient bandwagon. Now, at her suggestion, they would go all out and invite Max and Janey Fox before hoisting a glass. This decision was actually *their* decision. Russ and Kate had decided to get married.

AFTER A YEAR TOGETHER, what made Russ and Kate suddenly decide to get married? It's funny, but one never goes through the self-affirming rigmarole of articulating reasons unless one has already made up some stubborn corner of his mind not to do the deed. It's never necessary to cough up a reason for something you want to do. You make lists of ponderous excuses for not buying the car, or not returning the call, or not spending the night. Negation is bound in careful logic; affirmation simply rushes out. Either you take the money and run; or you stay at home and think of all the reasons why you shouldn't.

That's how it was for Russ and Kate. It all settled into place on an autumn night while the couple were walking hand in hand down Second Avenue. They had just seen *Jules et Jim* at the St. Mark's and then, cutting it so close that they had to do without popcorn, hurried over to the Eighth Street to catch Bruce Lee in *Enter the Dragon*. Jeanne had broken hearts; Bruce broke only bones. The less subtle violence made Kate restless. Russ, though, insisted on sitting till the final kung fu. A placating beer at the Lion's Head, and they headed home.

The October night was prematurely cold; when they spoke they could see their breath, illuminated by the green glow of the "walk" light at the corner, hang in the air.

"There was no reason why we had to see two movies, Russ."

"You've never been to a double feature before?"

"Hey," she warned, "that's when you get two movies for the price of one. We saw one movie and a dubbed fistfight for the price of two."

"So it cost us five dollars to go to the movies . . ."

"That's five dollars apiece, big spender."

"And don't forget the buck for your beer," he added nastily. And instantly regretted it; he hated it when anger turned him petty.

"You want your dollar back . . ." Kate was reaching into her pea jacket.

"Come on, Kate, you know it's not the money. What's the big deal if I wanted to see two movies tonight? Is the extra couple of bucks going to bust us?"

"That's not the point. It wouldn't hurt us to try to save a little money."

"All we have is a little money. A little more is still too little to help us."

Kate knew Russ was right, so she refused to answer. But her mute concession only provoked him: "Anyway, how come my slum goddess is suddenly so concerned about saving money?"

Kate glared. "I'm going to get a six-pack," she announced with curious formality and walked off to the bodega on the corner.

"Maybe you should buy only a bottle," he yelled after her. "Got to start counting those pennies." Kate didn't look back.

He was left standing alone on the street. A flashing neon sign from a liquor store down the block caught his eye; at the time Russ thought he had found a handy place to get out of the cold while he waited for Kate. But perhaps his mind was already exploring the unspoken territory Kate's angry mood protected.

Russ walked in, pretending to consider the display of bargain wines as he warmed up. Then, oh so abruptly—was it whim or destiny?—he reached into the chiller and grabbed a bottle of Moët.

Russ paid and hustled from the store, catching up with Kate down the block. She heard his thumping footsteps, but Kate played deaf. She showed him only her back. Still, gently, Russ parted an edge of her curtain of brown hair and offered a small warm kiss on a bit of cold pink flesh just below her ear. His lips lingered.

"Should I scream for help?" she whispered.

"Only if you're playing hard to get."

". . . I'd just like to play."

Kate turned and wrapped her arms around Russ. It was then that she noticed the big bottle stuffed in the brown paper bag.

"What's that?" she asked.

"Three guesses."

"I give up." She peeked with exaggerated furtiveness into the bag. "So you're planning to christen a tugboat in the East River . . ."

"Close . . . but no cigar. I just thought I'd splurge for one last celebration before we start saving our money."

"What do we have to celebrate?" she asked.

"The same thing we've got to save for."

"Oh, Russ." She hugged him with all her might. They kissed like lovers.

"Wait a minute, will you," Russ said, breaking from her embrace. Then, on windswept Avenue A, he got down on one knee and asked with all his heart, "Kate, will you marry me?"

In a flash she was down on her knees, too, hugging him. "Yes, Russ," she said between kisses while a passing gypsy cab serenaded the couple with amused honks, "I'll marry you. Yes, I'll marry you."

TEN

"SALTED BUTTER?"

"Yeah, goddamn it. Salted butter."

"Well, if you want, Russ . . ."

"I *like* salted butter."

Kate made a small, weary face, but Russ hoped she had given up. He started pulling the other last-minute purchases from the shopping bag. The tenacious lady, though, was only regrouping.

"You realize this is a dinner party, Russ . . ."

"I'll brush my teeth, I promise."

"Funny. But it wasn't your teeth I was concerned with."

"Yet."

"Russ, one doesn't serve salted butter to guests."

"Why not?"

". . . It's . . . déclassé."

Slowly he turned, seeing red. Thinking black and blue. There clearly was not enough room in the tiny apartment for both their pretensions. Especially when neither side was conceding its own.

Things had been going like that lately between the two of them. Too frequently Russ found his mind sputtering a very dangerous question: What have I rushed into? And Kate, though still very game, found herself wondering: Just when will he grow up?

Russ's most recent doubts had started flowing as soon as Kate had begun talking around the idea of inviting Max and Janey over for dinner to celebrate the book and marriage contracts. These days, though, Russ was rapidly sensing both contracts were a long emotional way from being signed, sealed, and delivered. And even passive Kate could tell he was in no hurry.

Of course, the dinner was not the real cause of Russ's fears. Ever since they had decided to marry, Russ found himself pondering a more threatening cause—the photograph of his prospective father-in-law in a Nazi uniform: Though deceased he would forever be the natural grandfather of their children; and Russ's natural enemy. A chilling inheritance; worse, a secret shame.

Oh, theirs might become, Russ imagined on the days he was comfortable about traipsing through a future girded by the discipline required for the realization of serious wishful thinking, a relationship of significant accomplishment: the books they would write, the exotic places they would visit. When he descended, however, from these sentimental and impetuous musings into the grinding reality of their daily life, he had to trek through sufficient ill will to bring them to each other's throats.

Only on paper did it make wonderful sense. Conceptually, Russ loved every Platonic ideal his Kate embodied. He respected every intellectual goal she aspired to. But away from this romantic drawing board, all the little artless actualities of their stark Lower East Side existence turned him queasy. The sweet details of life—a whiff of perfume, freshly squeezed orange juice, a fluffy pillow, a lamp so one could read in bed—meant nothing to Kate. Yet how uncomforted Russ missed them; and simultaneously detested his bourgeois self for fixating on their loss. All these relinquished bits of yummy garnish went unmentioned; but they were not unnoticed, not unthought.

Russ's repressed antagonism and fear were forced, therefore, to burst out in more respectable arenas. Like fights over salted butter or Kate's hastily written dance columns or her fifth beer. And Kate, never one to give an inch, refused to surrender to his criticisms. Did they go at it! There are private truths that once said can never be taken back, small meannesses that once spoken corrode any relationship with a diligently furious acid. In these crude scenes, Russ was the more active villain. For while Kate would quickly turn poutish, scrambling with a nimble and haughty arrogance high above the fray, he would claw after her. Russ didn't just come armed with a temper. He had an insecure vicious streak, a kill or be killed mentality.

Russ was running scared. While Kate, adding indignant fuel to his self-righteous fire, refused to be chased. Such grudge matches cannot be won on points. Only a knockout will do.

Their dispute over the gastronomic versus the class merits of lightly salted butter was only round one of the evening. Russ kicked and groaned, but ultimately gave in (he wasn't prepared to risk appearing déclassé with Janey and Max Fox as the audience; and he filed away another bit of scrounged knowledge from worldlier Kate).

A bit chagrined, he agreed to forage the corner store for some sweet butter while Kate dressed. But when he rushed back with a couple of bars of the real thing, the marvel of a "done-up" Kate sounded the bell for round two.

With a tentative smile and her closely clipped fingernails gripping the hips of her skirt, the well-dressed Kate playing kittenish, asked, "How do I look?"

Now there are some questions you don't ask if you have a suspicion of being afraid of an honest answer. Or if you're conversing with a louse.

Still, only a gutter fighter refuses to accept noncommittal silence and, feisty and daring, repeats the challenge. As did Kate, popping up again, "Really, Russ, what do you think?"

The louse swung away: "It's not a costume party, is it?"

The fight was on.

Oh, Russ liked, even admired the way Kate looked when she didn't try; her instinctively plain, classically unembellished easiness. But when she tried! She, he was painfully convinced, had as much interpretive sense of fashion as did those totalitarian municipal architects who, inspired by the clever simplicity of international style masterbuilders, came up with frighteningly modern concrete and brick clumps; the amateur's rush after inspired elegance resulted in bulky parody. For Russ, who in his own laid-back way carried off a certain frumpy chic, the spectacle of a conscientiously done-up Kate was infuriating and depressing.

Here's what his judgmental gaze took in: Her toothpick thin stork legs were wrapped tight in a pair of bright red knee-high suede boots that might have worked, if you tended toward kinky tastes, with a pair of satin hot pants; but of course Kate had a mottled brown and white pony skin fringed skirt from Teepee Town (Dale Evans as the Happy Hooker?); and the chic got more confused as his stern eyes climbed up to the faded maroon turtleneck around her neck; except this cotton relic from a high school ski trip had been washed so many times that not only had its color drifted past shade into faint shadow, but also the elasticity in the neck had so long ago popped that now it flopped about as though designed for an unfortunate with a gross goiter; yet, because the turtleneck had years of embarrassing sweat stain under its arms, Kate demurely covered this up with an embroidered jacket she had found at a bargain shop in Chinatown; the shiny synthetic jacket, probably made in Japan, was obviously designed for some Oriental version of football, as its well-padded shoulders seemed to conceal a gargantuan pair of shoulder pads; and, if all this were not enough, Kate, the aspiring coquette, took one of the solidest, most honest faces ever molded, and above those alert green eyes that were meant to read all the Great Works of Western Literature she had rubbed globs of brown eye shadow (brown? it picked up the pony in her skirt, Russ guessed) so that she reminded him of a petulant raccoon. Did his cursory glance miss something? Oh, yes, the finishing touch: Her pentagonal framed shades perched jauntily high in her hair—the ominously dark glasses ready to be dropped like a visor at the first hint of combat.

Yet there was, despite Russ's smugness, a logic to Kate's fashion crimes. Kate Warner was simply displaying an immigrant's fondness for all the accumulated "things" she had acquired in her peripatetic life. These carefully preserved possessions had become Kate's roots, her psychological anchors. The western skirt, a present from her stepfather during her first Christmas in Buffalo; the Chinese jacket bought with her first paycheck not long after she had settled in New York City; the bedraggled turtleneck sent by a Heidelberg aunt; the silly boots purchased during a nostalgic college trip to Madrid—these were mementos, tangible and cherished pages from a childhood album she had stubbornly carted around the world.

Kate, conceived in war and raised in bohemian poverty, did not bundle up her collected keepsakes in some attic for a reassuring peek on a bleak, rainy day. That advantage was not hers; emotionally (and realistically; let's not forget money was a genuine part of the problem) she couldn't afford to. Alone, on her own since she went off to college, a true foreigner, she happily trotted out these eclectic souvenirs when an occasion seemed special. She chose to celebrate with old friends.

In those battling days when they were routinely going toe-to-toe, such understanding, though, was too easily consumed by vengeful candor. You know how it is: One week he was head over heels; the next he was in over his head. How was he to find the time to sort it all out?

Russ didn't even try.

"You look ridiculous," he decided, his study completed.

There was an anticipatory moment of silence as he prepared for her counterattack. It was long in coming. Then, to his surprise, Kate burst into tears.

"Now, now, baby," he said, surrendering and trying to hug her, but she backed away.

"I'm a jerk," he insisted.

Despite her heavy tears, Kate nodded in agreement.

"Come on," he said. "I apologize."

"You're a rotten bastard," Kate said, sniffling. But without conviction. And now she let him hug her.

"Look at me," she complained as she glanced at a small mirror on the wall near the bed. "I've got these swollen pink eyes." Russ also noticed her thick brown eyeshadow had been rubbed about her teary eyes so that she wore a mask like the Lone Ranger's. But this time he kept his cute remarks to himself.

"How am I going to look to Max and Janey?" she moaned.

"Don't worry," he insisted. "There's plenty of time before they come."

Just then the downstairs front-door buzzer interrupted them.

"Well, maybe not that much time," Russ weakly conceded. As he returned their buzz, he told Kate, "Go on, wash your face. They've got four flights to climb. I'll keep them busy till you're ready."

Kate stood there, grounded and defeated.

"Go on, baby," Russ said as he took a tissue from the pocket of his chinos and made a small attempt at drying two sloppy eyes. "Wash your face. I'll hold the fort."

Grimly, Kate went off to the bathroom and Russ went to struggle with the police bar and the complicated series of locks protecting the apartment. He figured it would be more hospitable to greet his guests on the threshold of the small battlefield he shared with Kate.

As Russ stood in the doorway he could hear Max and Janey laboriously climbing up the four steep flights. There was lots of heavy huffing and puffing. He could tell, though, whenever they reached a landing. They took advantage of this pause in their ascent to tear into each other.

"Get off my back," Max sneered from the second floor landing.

"Well fuck you," Janey vowed in reply.

Then after a bitter minute they continued their climb. Russ could hear Kate still frantically running water in the john behind him as he watched Max and Janey, red-faced and sullen, making it up the final flight of stairs. Then, pumping up his courage, Russ greeted his guests: "So glad you've come. Kate and I have been looking forward to this evening."

ELEVEN

KATE PAUSED AFTER LADLING out another generous portion of stroganoff and, reading her guests' minds, gave the murky platter a critical once-over. She shrugged in whipped resignation. But, a trooper, she attempted to salvage this bad moment.

"It may be gray, but it tastes good," she reported with cautious enthusiasm.

An earlier sample had been proof enough to Russ that this was a self-serving half truth. The concoction was only gray.

Kate, undeterred, passed the dishes around the table, making sure Max and Janey got the only two matched plates. Looking hopefully at Russ, Kate continued, "I used your mother's recipe."

Russ knew that was impossible: His mother's recipe called for meat, not plasterboard.

"It is good," Max agreed as he gallantly gulped down a forkful of the unchewable food.

Kate ducked the compliment with a brief smile. In fact, she had been ducking Max's conversational probes since he had arrived at the apartment. It was clear Kate, someone who could ramble on with oblivious self-involvement about a line in Edith Wharton or a dash of blue in a Tintoretto, was reluctant to gab with Max. In those days he was still her boss, not her friend. She didn't want to appear fawning. While Russ and all the rest of the *City* crew would find beckoning in one of Max's casual smiles a legitimate excuse to corner him and confide their heady secrets, Kate remained obstinately guarded. It wasn't, however, that she didn't want to spill her troubled or reflective guts to wise Max. Like all of them, she was under his spell. But proud, private Kate didn't want him to know it.

Her reasoning for not talking to Janey was different. Janey's most recent affectation was an interest in dance; and, like a hypochondriac's letting her fears fly at a cornered doctor, Janey Fox kept pestering her hostess, the professional critic, with earnest questions. Hostess or not, cantankerous Kate didn't keep it a polite secret that she was not in any mood to talk shop at dinner.

Janey, though, persisted. She might not have been hungry for the grim stroganoff. But she was starved for culture. And attention. Poor Janey: She was hoping to find in Kate the friend to whom, as she had read dreamily in Emily Dickinson, she could "talk as girls do."

"We went to see Nureyev last week," Janey tried this time. "He's so . . . thrilling. Why, after all those years he even executes his jetés with as much skill as ever. And oh the emotion . . . the grace. Don't you agree?"

"I guess so," Kate managed to contribute; people who gushed were spilling over the wrong woman. And she tried leveling her interrogator with a well-practiced enough-already look.

It didn't stop Janey. But it did give her husband pause. Max, who had probably sat in malicious critical judgment of his wife's deep pretensions as frequently as any veteran domestic backbiter, was taken aback. In this graceless confrontation his sympathies were with shot-down Janey. Even Russ found himself pulling for his boss's wife. Kate wasn't simply being uncommunicative; she was being irksome. After all, everyone at the table knew Kate had written a wonderfully wandering 2,500-word piece about Nureyev's performance at Lincoln Center for this week's *City*. What, regardless of her own convoluted logic, was betrayed by sharing some of her wealth of knowledge for a quick social moment?

Russ watched as Max wrote off Kate with one grumpily raised eyebrow. All evening Max had been playing with figuring out what Kate was up to; but at that instant he quickly decided she wasn't worth the effort.

Russ, though, knew there was more to Kate's laconic mood than simply an offensive desire to be curt. Bitter experience had taught him it was just her narrow way not to give when asked. Demands flustered this so very self-contained young lady. When Kate wanted to, then, and only then, would she be generous.

But Russ kept quiet, and tried to carry the social ball by making sure everyone's wine glass remained filled. It was busy work. Max kept on emptying his glass as quickly as Russ could fill it.

When Janey, still foolishly begging, threw out another careful question, Kate just let it go by. Then the hostess tossed a diversionary non sequitur in Janey's wounded face.

"I know," Kate suddenly burst out. "It needs color."

Taken aback, they all watched as Kate dashed over to the refrigerator. Actually, it was more a hop than a dash. The geography of the apartment could be sketched, you might recall, with references to proximity. To the east, the kitchen lay across from the small card table they were using for a dining room. While on the west, just a napkin's length away from the festive table, stood the bed. And north of this (and holding a scrawny brown-tipped philodendron in honor of the occasion) was the exposed bathtub.

Kate meanwhile had grabbed a Hellman's mayonnaise jar from the fridge. The jar was filled with once-fresh chopped parsley, the time-filling product of an empty evening a long while back. Like a manic Tinker Bell sprinkling fairy dust, she began maneuvering in the tight spaces around the table, dropping handfuls of this rather tarnished garnish on everyone's plate.

"There," Kate suggested as she approached her handiwork, "doesn't that look better?"

Russ kept quiet. The army manuals insist gray and khaki are effective camouflage colors, but, he learned much to his dismay, they were way off: He could still discern his dingy portion of stroganoff.

Max was also off on his own trip. "It's a nice wine," Max said as he extended his once again empty glass.

Janey decided it was time to get in some licks of her own. She went after her husband: "Haven't you had enough?"

Russ realized something no good was brewing and tried to stop it. Perhaps a light touch might work: "Yes, the Gallo brothers do marvelous things with grapes."

Max ignored the youth. "No," he said in whining mimic of his wife's fluttering voice, "I haven't had enough."

Janey coiled, preparing to strike.

Max stubbornly held out his glass, waiting for it to be filled.

Kate was throwing some more parsley around. "Oh," she noted to no one in particular, "a little color certainly improves things."

Max shoved his glass toward his host. The gesture was now threatening.

So was Janey's tone: "I think he's had enough, Russ."

Russ looked to Kate. "Some more stroganoff?" she asked. She ignored the heaps of stew which were already quickly solidifying into a tough gray mound on his plate. So much for Kate, Russ decided.

"Can't a man get something to drink?" Max mumbled.

Russ was unsteadily clutching the neck of the bottle. There stood only a blue casserole bubbling with fetid strips of dubious beef separating him from the vituperative Scylla of Janey and the acerbic Charybdis of Max. He realized it was a no-win situation. He would be loudly damned if he poured; and—worse—perhaps never again blessed with a benevolently damning look from his boss and mentor if he didn't.

But Russ knew where his psychic bread was salt-buttered. He leaned across the table to fill Max's glass.

Then it happened: *Splat!* Then again: *Splat! Splat!*

A large hot white blob of wax had landed in the center of Janey's plate. Warm gray gravy took to the air.

Russ looked up.

Splat!

He caught it on the forehead.

By now Max and Kate, hip to the evil accuracy of the dripping candles decorating the chandelier hanging menacingly over their heads, had pulled their chairs out of range. Janey, instead, panicked.

"What is going on?" Janey shrieked. *Splat!* A bull's-eye in Janey's wineglass was the immediate answer. Flying Gallo left its hearty burgundy mark on her white silk blouse. Furiously Janey rubbed the stain with her napkin. It spread across her silken chest like blood from an open wound.

"This is crazy," Janey cried. "We . . . we . . . can't eat like this," she screamed.

"It's nothing," Kate said, really believing it. She took a spoon and effortlessly scooped the clot of wax off Janey's plate.

Max, who at first was startled, now appreciated his wife's discomfort and laughed with sarcastic pleasure.

Good Russ the host (and bad Russ, the domestic warrior, sensing an opportunity to sock it to ungracious, uncommunicative, unhelpful Kate) rushed to explain: "You see, Janey, Kate has this thing about candlelight. She just loves to see this chandelier all aglow. She insists that we light it up whenever we . . . dine." He let the word "dine" sink in; and he made sure to poke forcefully the solid mass of stroganoff on his plate. The fork didn't break, but Max's sneer told Russ his point was well taken.

"Kate's parents bought this chandelier for their apartment in Madrid," he continued, hoping to suck them all in with his conviviality, "and they gave it to Kate when she moved to New York. She keeps on telling me candlelight makes this room romantic.

"I don't know." Russ shrugged, but he did gesture toward the tub; he would let his guests draw their own conclusions . . . or their own baths.

After a moment he went on, "You tell me if you think it's . . . atmospheric. But if you ask me, the only atmosphere Kate's recreating with her hot dripping wax is the Spanish Inquisition."

But Kate was too shrewd to let Russ walk away with this round. "You know, Janey, it's a fifteenth-century chandelier," she explained, simultaneously displaying her erudition and shaming Russ's barbs. "It's really a beautiful example of Moorish decorative art. The man who sold it to my parents said he had found it in a shack in Granada." Then, out to save her social hide and to give snide Russ a public beating, she decided to open up and go on with all sorts of fascinating details about Granada, the troubled fate of the city after the fall of the Moorish caliphate, the astonishingly rapid decline of Islam in Spain, and then the girl even lectured on the prevalence of pewter in Spanish decorative art. God, Russ moaned silently conceding defeat, that exasperating woman knows a hell of a lot. And when to let it show.

With this little offering of conversational generosity, Kate won Janey over. The two began talking nonstop; rather, Kate pontificated and Janey eagerly soaked it all up. And Kate kept sweetly pouring it on, knowing all the time she was getting in licks against Russ.

Without even trying, Kate also scored big with Max. The neat nonchalance of Kate's initial handling of this social disaster—the offhanded, unflustered industry with which Kate disposed of the wax drippings— had convinced him the girl was not just an ill-mannered recalcitrant, but genuinely quirky in her fierce detachment. Now *that* interested Max! (And Max, always looking to have something else on Janey, also figured he was in Kate's debt because she had exposed another curdled edge of his wife's middle-class hysteria.) He decided to cancel all previous judgments and explore what made this puzzling girl tick. She and her younger boyfriend would get the full treatment from this gray-haired Socratic seducer. Maybe he could be friends with Russ and Kate, after all.

Russ could tell by all the smitten glances turned on Kate he was rapidly losing his hold over the fickle audience. He hurried to get back into the game.

"I think I'd like," Russ began with a puff of formality, "to make a toast."

"Sure," said Max, amenable to anything that would get a little more Gallo into his glass.

Russ topped off everyone's glass and then went on: "I'm sure both of you are wondering why we decided to throw this little dinner tonight." Max shot him a twisted look as if to say, No, Russ, we all realize whoever is left standing by the end of the evening wins the right to go against Muhammad Ali for the heavyweight crown. Russ decided to ignore his boss. "You see, Kate and I have an announcement to make," he continued. "We're getting married."

To Russ's surprise no one muttered, "I'll believe it when I see it." Instead, Janey gaily spoke up: "Now that is something to drink to." Even Max looked happy.

Russ raised his glass and immediately three glasses tapped against it. The wine was halfway to everyone's lips when suddenly Kate shouted, "Wait."

Russ wondered if he were saved.

No such luck; the knife was only turned deeper. "Wait," Kate ordered with good-intentioned cheer. "We should also drink to the success of Russ's book."

"To Russ's book," Max agreed.

"And to their marriage," Janey added.

Russ was once again attempting to take his medicine like a man when, this time the Gallo flush against his lips, Max broke in. "I think we have something else to drink to," he said.

Russ didn't question the reprieve. Kate did. "Huh?" she asked.

Max looked conspiratorially at Janey. She smiled back at him. Then, their signals agreed upon, Max began, "It seems I also have something to tell you. I was going to let it wait until tomorrow when I plan to make a formal announcement to the entire office, but since we're in a toasting mood tonight maybe we can keep this just between the four of us. Okay?"

"Sure," Russ said easily. But his stomach was quickly rumbling with apprehension. He looked at Kate and could tell she was riding the same rough wave. "You can trust us with whatever you've got up your sleeve."

"Fine," said Max. "This is what's happening: I've sold *City*."

Kate managed to speak first. "Shit, Max," she pleaded as, in a gesture of contrition, she removed her dark glasses from her eyes. "You didn't."

Russ just looked at Max as though he would never understand.

"Now," the editor continued with jovial evenness, "let me explain. It's not as drastic as it sounds. Here's what's up . . ." But his voice trailed off and he was quickly correcting himself. "I think perhaps I should start at the beginning. You see, Janey had this dream about three months ago—"

"Don't start that dream crap again, Max," Janey interrupted. There was no mistaking the fighting edge to her voice.

"Well, it's the truth, goddamn it," Max shouted back. "You had this dream about my getting hit by a truck—"

"I'm telling you, Max, don't go blaming me for something you wanted to do," Janey hissed.

"And I'm telling you," he flew back at her, "that the only reason I sold the magazine was because you woke me up in the middle of the night to complain there'd be no money to support you and the kid if I got hit by a truck."

"Bullshit," Janey screamed.

"Are you going to deny you woke me up at three in the goddamn morning to share your goddamn dream?"

"That's not why you sold *City*," she countered.

"No?" he asked with loud meanness. "I never thought about selling until you starting bugging me about the future."

"Bastard."

"Yeah, but I made you a rich woman."

"Why . . . you . . ." At a loss for words, Janey grabbed her glass and, with a furious swing, hurled the wine toward Max.

She missed. But she never knew it. Abruptly Janey had stomped out the door and executed a perilously quick descent down the four flights. She probably never heard Max shout after her, "Idiot, you got Kate smack in the face."

For the second time that evening a runny brown eyeshadow mask had formed around Kate's eyes. Except this time Kate wasn't upset. "Girls will be girls," was all she said as she went once again to the john to reconstruct her makeup.

While Kate tidied up (and eavesdropped attentively), Max gave Russ all the inside scoop. There was nothing to worry about, the editor insisted. "I got an ironclad contract, so I guess you'll be stuck with my running things unless I really do get hit by that truck."

"From the way things sounded tonight," Russ dared to say, "it looks like Janey might be the driver."

"Tonight," Max said flatly, "was nothing. You should see her when she's really angry." He shook his head, a signal meant to convey that there was nothing he could do about his wife. And then Max tried out a playful afterthought: "Oh, there's one other little thing, I guess I should tell you. I imagine it'll be in the papers. The press likes that sort of lurid detail."

"What's that?"

"The price. We got ten million bucks. Jonathan and I split that fifty-fifty."

"So you got . . ." Russ began with unconcealed amazement.

". . . five million dollars," Max completed proudly.

"Now that's something to drink to."

Kate joined them and once again they lifted their glasses. The three, wrapping their budding friendship tighter, drank one deep glass to Max's newly minted fortune; another to the book Russ would write; and a third to the marriage that was to be.

How should they have known, as they downed the glasses of cheap wine, that in this moment of cheer lay all the large reasons for their future despair?

PART III
The Romance of Dreams

ONE

WHAT A DEAL MAX was convinced he had pulled off! And for two triumphant years following the sale of *City*, he had quite a comfortably giddy ride.

Nothing much changed at the magazine. The new owner, Preston Warren Vandermaeker, however imperious the image provoked by the harumphing sound of his name, remained a vague, only a titular presence. General Max, assisted by publisher Jonathan, continued to command: His eager, pen-poised young troopers still interpreted his looks for their battle orders, still fought out their literary hearts for a discreet instant of his praise.

While on his home front, Max experienced for the first time in married life a stability and confidence that was true emancipation. Conscientiously, Janey moved from the metaphor of silk blouses into the more tangible symbolism of insurable acquisitions. These accumulations, on their new lawyer's cautious advice, soon filled pages of an inventoried inheritance; a random scan through this thick list could isolate a heavy silver samovar, a richly hued Tabriz rug, a set of Mark Twain first editions, or an intriguingly moody shaded Rouault. Max even had his collection of antique clocks painstakingly restored; he was finally restful enough to admit to the passing of time. These heady days the hourly ringing of their bells and the clanging salutes of their chimes reminded him of how far he had traveled, of what he had become.

It was this treasure trove of possessions, Max concluded with an oddly impersonal fascination, that came the closest to giving his wife and him a shared life. Here was their common glory, their mutual accomplishment. They displayed their booty in a sprawling apartment taking up an entire floor of the "best" building in the Village; though Janey, spurred to efficiency by her bottomless checkbook, got carried away in the orchestrated meticulousness of its color-schemed interior decoration. Of course no mortgage for them; they paid in cash.

And oh how pervasive did Max find the comforting power and thrill of his wealth; on sleepless nights the habitual insomniac discovered himself lulled by complicated calculations of how much his fortune, diversified by expensively obtained Wall Street wisdom into such impressive categories as utilities, municipals, tax frees, and venture opportunities, had grown with just the passing of that single, effortless day. Convinced his secret fear of his own ultimate failure—forty years without even an inclination for serious work does leave its mark—had come up a resounding lie, Max now turned belligerent in his pride of his accomplishment. He believed luck, good or bad, could no longer touch him; he believed that at fifty-seven he could finally rest easy.

Yet all the time it was perking. The contaminating flaw in Max's success was waiting to catch up with him. From the beginning his decision to sell *City* was infected by his snobby refusal to take $10 million from just anyone. From the beginning Max Fox, the master manipulator, was suckered.

Just as from the beginning Preston Warren Vandermaeker set out to play a destructive sting: He intuited the socially ambitious Achilles heel lying under the old editor's argyle sock; and, devilishly, he took aim.

Ten million dollars is a lot of money. Yet Max Fox sold cheap; the gentlemanly con game into which he stumbled took him for everything he ever believed in.

The mahogany elegance of the Metropolitan Club was the setting for the opening scene of the cool, prospective buyer, Preston Vandermaeker's, manipulations. The two men sat facing each other on conspicuously worn chesterfield sofas; but Max immediately understood that each crease in the butternut leather was wrinkled with the glimmer of tradition, not the destruction of age. The whiskey, brought over on command from the decanters of Vandermaeker private reserve, was as smooth as a rich man's hands. Only after the third tumbler did it creep up on Max; and even then it only felt like easing that smooth hand into a velvet glove. Most appealing of all, though, was Preston. The young, softly handsome blond heir played his part with debonair perfection.

Preston led Max to believe he wanted something only the renowned editor could deliver. He led Max to believe he was a thirty-four-year-old suddenly chomping to channel years of stored-up energy and ambition. This was a mind-set that Max, the late starter, could uniquely understand; as Preston, who had done his homework, anticipated he would. Young Vandermaeker, letting it show that he was embarrassed by his presumption, pleaded for Max to save him from the aimlessness of his pampered life. Preston leaned forward as the polished leather beneath him squeaked and, locking his fingers together as if in prayer, told the flattered editor he was convinced his deliverance lay in the bohemian journalistic world Max had created. He pleaded with the older man for the opportunity to allow his fortune to sponsor, to nurture Max's vision. Perhaps someday, Preston theorized, with Max's tutelage he might even be a more active participant in the enterprise. A writer? An editor? The details of his ambition were, he admitted, murky. He simply wanted an opportunity to learn and to grow.

All this was a lie. But Preston's lies held a remarkably effective strength; just as his shifting character cut with a dangerous edge. His was a psychopath's power: Preston somberly believed his unconsidered ramblings at the moment when he spouted them. The unforgivable sin, though, was that there was no history, no future, no perspective in his words. He lived and thought in the existential now; the parameters of his forever stretched only as far as the moment. His opinions, his desires, his promises were literally here today and gone tomorrow. How was an honest man like Max Fox expected to anticipate—or even understand—such indulgent carelessness? How was he to know that spoiled Preston was not a man of ideas, commitment, or honor; he was merely a man of moods.

Max, in fairness, was also on the make. As soon as he strode into the Metropolitan Club and was welcomed by its stodgy Old World demeanor, he was ready to cut a deal. Not that Max started adding zeros onto his selling price; you can dismiss that. Once the word got around New York that *City*, a magazine that not only made money but also made political careers and cultural movements, was up for sale, there were plenty of bidders. The people wanting to make him a rich man were a dime a corporate dozen. Jonathan to this day insists his partner could certainly have bargained bigger bucks from at least a couple of the other perspective purchasers. Price, though, was not the bottom line in the deal Max was cooking up.

(Even before talking to any buyer, the editor had made up his mind to stick to a stubborn strategy: The $10 million selling price was non-negotiable. Max was determined not to settle for less or to demand more. Bad business? Perhaps, but he figured his $5 million share of the loot would work out to a conservative $3 million after taxes: a mil for Janey, a mil in trust for their son, and a mil left over for him. A family of millionaires was all he thought fair out of the deal; a sweeter pot might have appeared vulgar.)

Following that drink in the Metropolitan Club, Max, often accompanied by Jonathan, set out on more than two months of meetings with Preston. These well-mannered encounters reinforced Max's initial belief that the attractiveness of the Vandermaeker offer rested in its carrying an opportunity more compelling than mere money—the deal promised an association with a class, an aristocratic tradition, and a set beyond Max Fox's first-generation grasp.

Here canny Preston tweaked both Max's unspoken desires and presumptions with particularly incisive skill. The troubled young man doing his imploring best to wave all sorts of flags of emotional distress in the discerning elder's face made the prospect of friendship, of more than just a business relationship with the Vandermaekers, seem assured. Max, full of his accomplishment, got greedy: This was his chance to smash his own rules and get it all—money and class!—in one lifetime. And so, smitten like an ingenue who recklessly gives herself to a Hollywood star just so that she can somehow share the often imagined wonder of his make-believe world, Max fell for Preston.

The editor even convinced himself there was no risk to selling to Vandermaeker. Max reasoned he could control any sparks of temperament or stupidity that might burst out of the younger majority stockholder. He thought he knew the pattern: It would not be long before he had recruited another obediently awed protégé in Preston, another young man whose character he could needle and twist into its mature promise. Foolish, blinded Max. How could he shape what never existed?

THE MORNING AFTER Kate and Russ's bombastic dinner party, the entire staff of *City* was summoned to Max and Jonathan's small office to hear their editor announce the deal. Preston Vandermaeker, done up in a blue pinstripe suit offset by luminous black hand-tooled cowboy boots as a concession to the downtown crowd, stood limply behind Max's chair, a reticent guest of honor.

"Don't worry," Max assured the stunned and panicked faces after he had laid out all the fateful details of the sale, "nothing is going to change around here. Nothing. Except maybe I'm going to have to find a pretty shifty accountant." Only Jonathan laughed, and the testy suspicion implicit in this powerful silence seemed to shake Max up. The editor stared out at his staff. "Well," Max asked hopefully, "are there any questions?"

"How could you do this to us, Max?" Wendy Parker began, her voice teetering on the edges of control. "Didn't you realize what you were doing?"

"Now, Wendy," Max started, his tone as soft as the wisps of cloudy smoke floating from his pipe.

She interrupted him, pleading, "Didn't you think about what would happen to all of us?"

Max, uncomfortable with her anguish, turned gruff: "There's no talking to her when she gets paranoid like this," he said, looking to the publisher who was sitting on top of the desk catercorner to his. "You try, Jonathan."

Jonathan Trout, his legs pumping nervously back and forth like a boy on a swing, tried to be soothing. "Max has laid it all out, Wendy. We've told you all there is to know. The change of ownership doesn't mean—"

But now when Wendy interrupted, her words were hard bullets; an armory of hate. "What else would you two say." And she added crisply, "Perhaps it would be better to address our questions to the new owner."

Everyone's eyes focused on Vandermaeker. He pulled himself up from his casual slouch and offered a pleasant grin. He remained standing, though, behind Max's chair, a target trying to hide.

Wendy and the others waited for Vandermaeker to speak. When he did not, there no longer seemed to be an excuse for controlling their attack.

Russ, not realizing how deeply he felt both betrayed and abandoned by the secret sale of the magazine, surprised himself by being the first to talk out. "Just what do you intend to do with the magazine, Mr. Vandermaeker?"

Wendy quickly followed. "Yes, what made you buy *City*? What are your real plans?"

While Arlen P. Davis III, the admiral's son, jumped up from his chair, his mud brown pony tail bouncing as he snarled, "You might not realize this, Vandermaeker, but this is a writers' paper. And your ten million bucks didn't buy us. What we write can't be bought. Do you really understand that?"

But Max came to Preston's rescue. "Just hold on, now," he told Arlen. "There's no need to get nasty."

Arlen's hands rolled into tight fists, but he sat down.

Then Max, with a quick wink to Preston, told the new owner, "That's the way things get around here. Pretty hot and heavy most of the time." Preston's thin smile returned the editor's unspoken message: Let's not talk too much about the children while they're still in the room.

At that moment Russ decided that it might become very easy to hate Max Fox.

Max went on: "Maybe it would clear things up, though, Preston, if you explained to all of them what you intend to do with the magazine."

Preston moved forward from behind Max's chair. He reached into his suit pocket and took out a leather tobacco pouch. Methodically he filled his pipe, lit it, and tested the draw. Plunking himself on top of the editor's desk, he seemed very much in control. His back was to Max as he began to speak.

"To tell you the truth, Max, I must say I resent all this. I don't feel

I have to explain anything to anybody. I paid for this magazine. And, I might add, I paid a steep price. I don't think I have to offer any explanations as to my motivations."

"Hey now," Arlen called out, "no one gives a rat's ass about your motivations. Just tell us what you intend to do with the magazine. Play it straight. Tell us where we stand."

"Fine," Preston continued, "here's where you stand." But he paused to relight his pipe before going on, and in that moment Jonathan climbed off his desk and moved toward Max; he wanted to be closer to his friend when disaster struck.

"I'm a businessman," Preston said, informing Max of that possibility for the first time. "And I bought *City* as an investment. Max Fox and Jonathan Trout will continue doing what they always did—running the show. Except now they'll be managing my investment for me." Then Preston, unconsciously mimicking Jonathan, got up from the desk as he added, "I think that should answer all your questions."

No one said anything; until the staff, anger and fear fermenting volatilely in this still uncertain vacuum, began filing from the office. The lurking catastrophe had not been averted, most were convinced. Only postponed.

Even Max sat rigidly behind his desk, for the first time wondering if perhaps he had misjudged Vandermaeker. He tried to feel reassured when Vandermaeker sidled up to him and whispered in his ear, "I thought if I didn't lay down the law from the get go, they'd always be trying to walk all over me." Max nodded and Preston added a final comforting touch. "After all," he said to the editor, "I told myself that would be the way Max Fox would have handled them."

Later that morning a resolutely cheerful Max gave Preston a meandering tour through the *City* offices. Huddled sulkily in the back of his cubicle, Russ was still able to watch as the editor marched the fifth-generation heir to the Vandermaeker fortune about, waspishly blond and pale Preston the deferential model of a concerned dandy surveying the corner of bohemia that was now part of his portfolio. Max puffed on his pipe as young Preston thoughtfully puffed on his; the worldly upperclassman showing the respectful firstie about.

A beaming Preston whispered something as the two came out of Wendy Parker's office and Russ, overwhelmed with envy and resentment, cringed as Max started into a small series of strange, full laughs. Russ's angry mind saw two old boys getting off on the townie. The elder's odd, sneering, insider's laughter kept building until the thirty-four-year-old new owner offered Max Fox—the editor and founder of *City* magazine, goddamn it! Russ wanted to call out—a reassuring pat on the back. Russ was certain it was a placating, vulgar gesture; he was sickened by its presumptions. Max also shuddered under the young man's touch. The editor's laughter was abruptly cut off, but there were no protests. He only paused to look over his shoulder at huge Wendy planted in the doorway of her office. She looked hard and hatefully at the man she had once admired. Max rushed from the condemning slap of her stare. But there was an instant, before the editor hurried away, when Russ saw it clearly: Max wore the woeful, embarrassed look of a man who had been caught betraying a friend.

MAX WAITED NEARLY A WEEK before he tried to look to someone to help him struggle through the anxiety he was just beginning to admit to himself. Yet ever since the tense meeting with the staff and Preston in his office, the editor had been forced to confront the possibility he had allowed the flimsiest of ambitions to sway the most dramatic decision of his life; and with this sweeping act of faith in a man he hardly understood, Max had suddenly created a new force that had the power to puncture the delicate gravity that held his world together.

Max thought about sharing his fears with Janey. Ridiculous. She would only gloat. Maybe Jonathan? No, he decided, his partner might as well enjoy their success for however long it lasted. With no one else really to turn to, Max instinctively reached out for a new ally, someone who had popped up, he recalled with a measure of reassurance, as if providentially summoned on another afternoon when events were similarly despairing and had shown loyalty, tact . . . and a compelling streak of arrogance. The editor, a bit buoyed, walked to the door of his office and called out into the newsroom, "Russ, you got a minute?"

Max, seated behind his desk across from the reporter, took a while to get around to what was really on his mind. Finally the editor steadied himself with a couple of drags from his pipe and after some brief small talk about the ill-fated stroganoff debacle, he launched into a cautious monologue concerning another dinner: the one last month at the Sutton Place home of the Vandermaeker heir when Jonathan and he had signed the letter of intent to sell.

Russ listened as Max spoke fulsomely. But the youth was not a very sympathetic audience. He was still caught up in his bitterness toward the boss who had abandoned him; yet even reflective Russ was not aware of all the complications hiding in his envy of Preston Vandermaeker. Russ, though he never would have made the comparison, suffered like someone who has learned by glancing through the wedding announcements in the *Times* that not only has he been jilted, but that also his lover has made a hugely successful match in the process.

So Russ, wounded, held back. He was a polite but stony audience as Max slipped jocularly into the despairing heart of the story. It was only later that Russ realized Max, so uncharacteristically gabby, had been trying to talk away his own doubts.

"All of a sudden we were outnumbered," Max said as Russ, hands folded in his lap like a schoolboy, stared across the desk at him. "As soon as Preston led Jonathan and me into the dining room, I saw that. Sure, there were two of us and only one of him, but he brought three servants with him. Three! There was one of these obsequious footmen to pull out each of our chairs.

"Preston also had the terrain going for him," the editor recalled with a bemused shake of his gray pompadour. "What a room this boy eats in!" He tried out an admiring smile on Russ as his mind recalled the lay of the land, but Russ didn't respond. Undaunted, the editor continued: "I expected it to be large, I mean a man needs elbow room to cut his steak. But Preston could have had a dozen head of longhorns prowling the back forty of that room and still filled his table with the entire *City* masthead without anyone's bumping knees. And the view! Windows were stretched for miles along the East River. A man could get seasick.

"I'll admit to you, Russ, I was impressed. But what really got me was how Preston—" In a flash Max interrupted himself as he hurried to edit the frown of overwritten contempt that was blanketing his audience's face: "I know what you're, thinking, Russ—that this Vandermaeker is some spoiled richie. Now, Preston is a lot more complicated than that. Sure, he's had it easy, but he's got a first-rate mind. The kid is genuinely interested in journalism, in learning how this whole magazine works. You'll see that when you get to know him."

"Judging by the first encounter, I'm not so sure he'll ever give any of us the chance to know him," Russ said, holding his ground.

Max shrugged off such tiresome quibblings with a small shrugging gesture and steamrolled ahead with his story: "So we're sitting there and these black-coated gents keeping trotting out with maybe a dozen courses, and every minute or so someone is filling a fresh glass in front of me with a new wine, and Preston is all the time asking me about how it was in the early days at *City*. He's asking all these questions about all sorts of boring people I had forgotten had ever written for the magazine. It's obvious he's really impressed by what these people have done. What can I tell him? Am I going to reveal the truth: that any one of these names he is hurling so reverentially about would trade any of the books they had written for the opportunity to eat like this every night? I know Preston would never understand that. He thinks everyone eats like this every night. Yet I'm thinking, how would this kid ever understand that I didn't have an apartment with even a dining room until I was fifty years old."

"I bet your friend Vandermaeker never had a dining room with a bathtub in the middle, either," Russ countered with his best hearts-and-flowers whine.

"And Preston's candles don't drip," Max added nastily. The editor let it sink deeply in before he continued. "Anyway, all the time the meal is going strong and Jonathan with his plantation manners is hitting it off with Preston, I'm wondering what is this kid going to think when he gets a look at the motley crew around *City*."

"Thanks, chief."

"He lives in another world, Russ. Nothing personal. But I figured it was high time I gave Preston a feel of what it's like down here. So I start telling him about some of the gang. You know, how they carry Dot away fortnightly; or how Wendy Parker thinks the Rockefellers control everything from the price of bananas at Shoprite to who's going to be the next Pope; or how our stuttering friend Phil has written seventeen thousand pages on a kingdom ruled by chipmunks and he's still plugging way. I don't spare any of the weirdness. And you know what? Preston is loving it. He's eating it all up. I can tell he's waiting for his chance to come down here and be a crazy, too."

"Until he finally got down here and decided that maybe we were all just a little too crazy."

Ignoring the boy, Max simply continued: "When the meal is over, we go into his walnut-paneled library for brandy and cigars. And, I'm hoping, to sign the letter of intent. I mean, he hasn't mentioned business so I'm not going to be the first to bring it up. Why should we interrupt a pleasant evening to discuss a measly ten million dollars?" Max grimaces at the politeness of his foolish passivity. But not for long; he cuts this off before it can sink in.

"Now, the last thing I'm needing after all the wine is a drink. But Preston is a diligent host. We have a brandy and then some more brandy. And just when I'm ready to down still another, Preston says something about why don't we get that letter of intent out of the way. He reaches into a desk drawer and—bingo!—takes out this three-page single-spaced opus. 'It's what my lawyers drew up and your lawyers agreed to,' he says. By this point in the evening I'm too tight to walk, let alone read three pages of lawyer English. I tell Preston to let Jonathan give it the once-over while I excuse myself. I figure I'd better splash some cold water on my face pronto.

"So I head off looking for the john, making my way up a long spiral staircase. The stairs, given my condition, are a bit tricky. But I manage. I find a john soon enough. But I'm tight and I'm curious. I just want to see where all these doors lead. I start poking around. Russ, the kid's got quite a spread, that's for certain. I mean there must have been a half-dozen bathrooms upstairs. Now I'm really impressed.

"After a while I hightail it back to the library and I ask Jonathan what does he think. He tells me, 'It's what our lawyers agreed on, Max. No more and no less,' and he hands it to me to look over. If Jonathan says it's in order, that's good enough for me. But I give it a quick once-over. I don't want Preston to think I don't know what I'm doing.

"I fly through the pages and then I announce, 'Preston, I got one question.' Sure, Preston responds. So I give it to him straight: 'How many johns do you have in this joint?' Preston doesn't know whether to answer or to laugh. So I repeat the question. I'm serious, I tell him.

"'Well,' the kid manages after a moment of sincere thought, 'I guess there are maybe eleven. Yes,' Preston says, 'I think there are eleven.'

"Now, that's a staggering number of toilets for one man. So I turn to Jonathan and tell him in a confident voice, 'Preston here has eleven johns. I guess we can trust him not to piss over our little magazine.'

"And with Jonathan and Preston both looking at me like I've taken leave of my senses, I take my pen out of my pocket and sign the letter of intent."

A large silent moment; and another; but Max, suddenly looking and sounding as if someone has snuck up on him and popped him one from behind, struggled to go on: "That's how it was, Russ. That's how I finally convinced myself to sell my magazine to Preston Warren Vandermaeker."

And then as his dazed mind pondered another instant replay of that ridiculous scene, an embarrassed Max let loose with a volley of uncontrolled laughs; echoes of the deprecating sounds Russ had first heard outside Wendy's office. Except, Russ now realized, Max was laughing at himself. The editor continues laughing so hard his pipe falls out of his open mouth and bounces across his desk.

There was no choice but to join him. Russ, another frightened, anxious victim, started laughing away. He laughed along with his friend, all the time hoping the raw, tumbling laughter would coax the chill of panic to fly hysterically from their lives.

TWO

THE MARCH WIND kept pushing waves of dark hair over his eyes, and Russ was kept busy trying to brush it all back into place.

"Just let it be, babes," Kate suggested, teasing his vanity. "I like your Heathcliff on the moors look."

Russ smiled, but still played with his painfully thin, unruly hair. They continued walking through the park for a while until, trying to emphasize the solemnity of his resolve, he reached for Kate's hand. At his touch, she knitted her fingers tightly about his.

"I'm going to talk to Max. It's time I tell him what I think," Russ announced.

"That's good." But Kate's voice was dry and distant. She brought him no peace; and yet her approval seemed very necessary if there were to be some solid ground under his conviction.

When she held back, Russ abruptly released her hand. They strolled ahead in silence, Kate setting the pace. It was one of those unseasonably warm days promising an early spring.that hits New York in March; the kind of bright, sunny day when you want to believe you can finally leave your parka and your scarf in the closet for another nine months. Kate had suggested they celebrate the returning sunshine by taking the subway uptown to the Central Park Zoo. She still took an out-of-towner's joy in all the postcard spots of New York.

She led the way until they reached the circular pool in the middle of the zoo. Kate, excited, leaned over the chest-high iron fence. An attendant in a forest green uniform was feeding the seals. Every time the man pitched a silver-bellied fish into the air with a lazy, underhand toss, a delirious barking seal would jump high to grab it. Russ, though, stared only at Kate.

"Max is being taken for a ride," he said at last. When Kate didn't respond he added, "A chauffeured ride, but still it's going to end in a crash."

"That could be," Kate admitted. She remained watching the seals.

"And that's why I'm going to sit down with him and have it out. Tell him about the silk noose Vandermaeker is shrewdly fitting around his neck. Convince him before it's too late. Too late for Max . . . and for all of us at the magazine." He felt triumphant with his conviction.

Only now did she turn toward him. "You know what's wrong with you, Russ?" she challenged.

"Why should I guess? I'm sure you'll tell me."

"You're an egotist."

"I knew I should have listened to my parents and become a lawyer instead."

"I'm serious," she said, her quiet tone meant to cut through his contempt and despair. "You really want to change everyone you love. Me. Your parents. And now Max. When are you going to learn to let people be the way they are? Instead of trying to make them the way you want them to be."

"When I stop caring about them."

"Look, Russ," she lectured, while tenderly taking his hand in hers, "I love your wanting to believe that you can change people. I really do. But the truth is, babes, you can't."

"I don't want to change Max . . ."

"No, you just want to tell him Vandermaeker is up to no good and he'd better stop cozying up to that upper-class snake. Listen to you: You've decided you have the right to tell a sixty-year-old man that he should get his act together and stop lusting after the aristocracy like some lady in a beauty parlor reading *Town and Country*. No, you don't want to change Max too much."

"Just what the hell do you think is brewing between Max and Vandermaeker?" he yelled, sounding as in control as one of the wild seals honking in the background. And once more he pulled his hand from hers.

"Oh, you're probably right. Max, Vandermaeker, the magazine— they're all on a collision course," she admitted softly.

"And you just want me to sit by and wait for the crash? I happen to love that magazine—and what it represents."

"It's not that I want you to, but I know you don't have much choice. What makes you think you can say anything that would convince Max?"

"He'll listen to reason." But as soon as he said the words, Russ had his doubts.

"For about thirteen seconds. Then he'll blow his top. And I tell you, Russ, he'll blame the messenger for the news."

"So you'd walk out on a friend?"

"That's not the point, Russ. What I'm trying to tell you is you can't save anyone. Here you are, all breathless with your daring. The importance of your mission. Did you ever stop and think that the true friend is a witness. That's it's more heroic to stand back. And that kind of control and loyalty require a more solid, a more disciplined courage.

"Please, Russ," she went on gently, "you've got to learn that people have to find out things for themselves. The most you can do is be there after they screw things up."

Russ paused; he would at least try to think through her passive logic. But Kate, sensing a victory, became bold.

"Another thing," she began, trying out a theory packed with too much explosive truth ever to be released between friends. "Did you ever stop to consider that maybe you're jealous of Preston? Of his relationship with Max?"

"That's a lot of shit," he erupted. "Save your fucking Psych One insights for your goddamn column."

"Now, babes—"

But he cut her off. "Look," he decided, "you can think whatever the fuck you want. But I tell you I'm not going to stand by with my hands in my pockets and watch a friend's life be ruined."

"Maybe. But fools rush in . . ."

". . . where cowards fear to tread," Russ taunted.

"Fine." She shrugged. "Do what you want."

Russ stared moodily at the pool filled with splashing seals.

"Come on," Kate offered as she once more took his hand. "Let's go feed the chimps some peanuts."

But Russ had had enough of the zoo for one afternoon. And enough of Kate. "No, it's getting cold. I'm going home. Anyway, there's that piece on chickenhawks I'm supposed to be finishing."

"The chickenhawks will wait. That's all they ever do. Please, babes, let's go see the monkeys. They're a lot more appealing."

"You stay if you want to. I'm going."

Russ, wanting to demonstrate his anger and his sense of mission, turned and walked quickly off. Kate, shaking her head at his silliness and vanity, went to the monkey house. She decided she knew better than to stop Russ; while he hurried through the park only wishing that she would.

''WANT SOME COMPANY?'' Russ offhandedly asked as Max was leaving the office the following evening. He had deliberately waited around hoping to bump into the editor.

The victim was all unsuspecting cheer: "I have to hurry home to change. My cultured wife is dragging me to the Philharmonic tonight. But you're welcome to walk with me."

They were heading across the Village toward Max's new apartment. Russ had planned to ease into his interrogation, but he immediately lost control. "What makes you think you can trust Vandermaeker?" he blurted out.

"His check didn't bounce."

"You know I'm not talking about that. What do you really think are his plans for the magazine?"

"It doesn't matter what his plans are," Max shot back a little too quickly. "I still run things. And I'll continue to. I have an ironclad contract."

"Sure," Russ weakly agreed as the pair crossed University Place. "But you realize, don't you, that Preston's going to want something for his ten million?"

"Jesus," spit out Max, coming to a halt. "He has something, goddamn it. He owns a magazine that's making him money."

"Come on, Max. When someone buys a magazine they want something more than just a return on their investment. Shit, if Vandermaeker wanted simply to make money he could have bought General Motors or kept his cash in the bank and collected the interest."

"What the hell do you know about making money?" Max suddenly screamed. "What the hell do you think you're talking about?" Max stood in the middle of the street and began jumping up and down on his toes in anger. His face had turned a bright red; and the traffic light turned green. Cars, honking ominously, began zipping around them.

"All right," Russ offered, hoping to placate his editor at least long enough to lead him from the middle of the road. But Max wouldn't listen and he wouldn't move.

"Goddamn it," Max went on shouting. "I tell you there's nothing to worry about. Preston worked out a hell of a deal. He bought a proven money-maker cheap. That's all he wanted. Are you able to understand that?"

A honking Pontiac passed wickedly close. ". . . Yes." But Russ was simply eager to calm Max down and escape from the rush of traffic.

"Okay, now I don't want to hear any more stupid questions about Preston. You're no different than Wendy—you're both paranoid," Max said after Russ had led him to the sidewalk. The youth nodded mutely.

The pair walked the rest of the way to the editor's building in silence.

"Well, I'll see you tomorrow," Russ tried as Max headed for the front door.

"Yes," Max said peremptorily; his anger still warm.

Russ walked off, but had gone only a few sulking steps before he heard Max call. He hurried over.

"Look, Russ," Max said, his voice restored to its familiar, worldly calm, "there's nothing to worry about. I tell you I can control Preston. Preston and I are friends. And regardless, the magazine is protected. I've told you I've got an ironclad contract. Okay?"

"Sure."

"Good," Max said. "Now just stop your worrying."

As Russ watched his friend walk through the impressive lobby while the liveried attendant holding open the door intoned, "Good evening, Mr. Fox," he wondered if perhaps Max were right. Maybe the editor had come up a winner. Maybe nothing could touch him or his success.

God, how they both tried to believe that.

THREE

"REMEMBER THAT ironclad contract?"

"Is that you, Max?" Russ said into the phone as he pulled himself from a foggy sleep. And a fear was quickly thrown away: Thank God it wasn't Frankie. Then his eyes caught the luminous dial of the clock on the nightstand: It was after one in the morning. "What's this about a contract?"

Max said something Russ couldn't make out. There were some busy rumblings in the background. "We must have a bad connection," the sleep-filled voice complained.

"Hold on a second. Let me just close the door. There. Any better?"

"Loud and clear. Where the hell are you, Max?"

"A rather friendly bar on Thirty-fourth Street."

"Uh-huh." The pieces were rapidly tumbling into place. "What was that about a contract, Max?" he asked, trying not to give in to panic.

"You remember—my ironclad contract."

"What about your ironclad contract?" Russ begged. Kate, still asleep, was stirring beside him. He reached out for her, girding himself for the bad news.

"It sprung a leak."

"How big?" For the first time Russ hoped he wouldn't be able to say I told you so.

"It's lifeboat time," Max said with a delighted, tipsy giggle. "Women and editors first."

"Jesus, Max . . ."

But the editor cut him off. "You were right, Russ. More than a year ago you had Preston's number."

"Forget that." It no longer seemed important to be right. "What do we do now?"

"We celebrate."

"Celebrate?"

"Yessiree. A man should celebrate his retirement."

"Where the hell are you?" Russ didn't like the sound of Max's voice at all.

"Costello's. Thirty-fourth and Seventh."

"I'm on my way."

"You can't miss it. Big neon sign. Pretty dark, though. Just look for the only drunken millionaire sitting at the bar. You'll find me."

Max hung up the phone.

"What's wrong?" a drowsy Kate asked as Russ got out of bed.

"It's Max. He's drunk," he said as he pulled on a pair of khaki chinos.

". . . He'll live." Kate wrapped the blanket tighter around herself.

Russ was busy hurrying to undo the intricate procession of locks on the door. "Well, there is something else." At last the door was open and he added, "It seems Max says he's out of a job."

Kate abruptly sat up in bed. "Call me as soon as you know what's going on," she insisted. Russ nodded; blew her a kiss; and then slammed the door behind him.

When he arrived at Costello's, despite the ominously dim lighting Russ had no trouble finding his friend. Max Fox may not have been the only drunken millionaire in the place, but he was certainly the only man wearing a three-piece suit and a tie. And for that matter the only man who looked like he had shaved in the past couple of days. A few steps into this smoky darkness left Russ overpowered by the bar's aged, rancid stench.

"Nice place. Come here often?" the youth asked as he took the wooden stool next to Max.

"First time. I guess you could say I just stumbled in." Max grinned at his predicament. "Glad you could make it," he added, offering Russ a paternal pat on the back. "What are you drinking?"

Russ shrugged. "Same as you, I guess."

"Bartender," Max said with some authority, "Two more Jamesons. Neat. And two more drafts."

The shots of whiskey came quickly and Max downed his in a gulp. Russ took a swallow and then broke off into a volley of breathy coughs; the liquor had gone down, he recalled with an ironic shudder, just as smoothly in Buffalo.

"Takes some practice," Max said as if to comfort his young drinking buddy.

"No wonder you got it down perfect."

Max sidestepped his rancor with another dopey smile; raised the beer toward Russ as if in salute; and, in a series of swift swallows, drained the mug.

"Hits the spot, huh, Max. Now could you just drag yourself away from your drink long enough to tell me what the hell is going on?"

"Relax, Russ. We got time. All I got is time. And five million bucks. Another round?"

Max didn't wait for an answer. "Bartender. Again, please."

They were served two more whiskeys. Max attacked his in a gulp; he rolled the thick shot glass between his palms as he waited for the youth to catch up with him. Russ, now wary, went after his drink in judicious measures. It took a while before Russ's final sip, but only then did Max ask softly, "I guess you're curious about what went on tonight?"

"I didn't come here for the atmosphere."

"You don't like it?" Max pushed his elegant gray pin-striped arm through the stale smoke clogging the air; it was a facetious attempt to display the marvels beyond their stools—two men slumped like bookends over a pair of round wooden tables, and a jukebox that flashed a thin white light.

"Max!" Russ insisted. The liquor and lack of sleep were proving an explosive mix. He was also scared: his future was at stake, too. And, Russ thought with a twinge of bitterness, he didn't have $5 million to fall back on.

"Maybe you're right," the editor conceded with overdone regret. "It isn't much of a place. I guess I might as well get on to the evening's entertainment. I wouldn't want you to think I made you run uptown for nothing." He took a fortifying gulp from his mug of beer and announced with inflated cheer, "Without further delay, then, here is the story of the decline and fall of Max Fox, former editor."

In the same soft, self-conscious tone that he had been hiding behind earlier in the evening, Max began with a confession: His contract was iron-clad, all right. Except it was only for two years. After that it was understood, he explained, Preston and he would simply ink another two-year pact.

"Understood?" Russ interrupted.

"Well, Preston's lawyer said anything longer than a two-year contract for Jonathan and me would have been . . . how did he put it? . . . 'cumbersome' . . . that was his word. He said suppose, for example, Jonathan or I had a heart attack and was incapacitated. It would be bad business to continue to pay us to run things. The lawyer's attitude troubled me at first, but Preston said not to worry. I would be the editor of *City* for as long as I wanted the job. We had a gentleman's agreement on that." Max considered what he had just said; and then, slicing the words with a smirk, muttered, "Some gentleman's agreement.

"What's that old joke about an oral contract?" he asked. "That it's worth the paper it's written on? Well, this gentleman's agreement was worth the hand it was shook with."

Still, Max admitted to only vague, unarticulated doubts for nearly two years following the sale. "To tell you the truth, Russ, I figured everyone was a little envious of the money I made. I never paid too much attention to the carping."

But that was before the unreturned telephone calls. It seems, Max explained, that starting a few months ago Jonathan had begun placing calls to Preston's secretary and leaving a succinct message: The two years would soon be over; let's get together and renegotiate the contracts. But Preston never called back.

"Now, that's when Jonathan started getting antsy. But I told him to relax. I said Preston is probably skiing or scuba diving or he sprained a finger clipping coupons. When the contracts expire, he'll get in touch with us. He's not going to let us walk away, I argued. Hell, he hasn't even come around the office more than twice in the past two years. All that talk about his getting involved in the magazine was just that—talk. How's he going to run things without us?"

Max breathed deep. "Russ, I think that was the first time in my life my imagination failed me."

The sore opened by this recollection proved painful; another round of Jamesons and draft chasers was ordered in a further attempt to cauterize the wound.

"Bottoms up," Max saluted before swallowing his shot. He waited until the whiskey reached a warm spot in the very bottom of his stomach before he tried to pick up his story.

"Jonathan finally convinced me," Max said with a wide, mournful shake of his head, "that it would be . . . oh, businesslike to get the contracts out of the way. That's when I decided to put in a call to Preston. I was certain he'd get back to me. After all, we were friends. And, sure enough, within a week he did. I was tough with him. Told him it was rude not to return Jonathan's calls. Straight off he apologized. Said he had been traveling, first Aspen, then in Europe. His secretary never told him that Jonathan was calling about anything urgent. Preston just thought he'd ring us when he returned to New York. When he got home, there was so much backed-up business to take care of that he never got around to returning the calls till now.

"Maybe my anger was too easily assuaged. I guess, in retrospect, it certainly was. But at the time I told him, Fine. Why don't we set up a meeting right now to get the new contracts signed. Just give me a date when you're free and I'll check with Jonathan. I thought it would be that simple.

"Preston must have been laughing at my naiveté all along. I mean, I remember as soon as I asked for a date, Preston got very silent. But I still didn't catch on. I figured he was checking his calendar. Some calendar! No, Preston was just getting up the courage to drive the knife in. When he finally spoke, it wasn't his words but his tone . . . his remarkably tentative tone that made things clear.

" 'Max,' I can still hear him saying, 'I think it would be more valuable to have a meeting without Jonathan.'

"And that's when I blew it. I should have shouted, 'Over my dead body,' and hung up. But I didn't. Instead I asked, 'How come?' Right then and there Preston must have realized he was in control. His voice suddenly had this tenor of authority. He just told me, 'Max, I think it would be more productive if we met alone.'

"I have to admit—" Max started to go on. But he broke off when Russ—by now hopelessly deep in his cups—released an ear-shattering burp. Russ giggled dumbly, and Max stared in reproach. Then he picked up his tale.

"I have to admit," he repeated as Russ struggled to muffle the next burp, "that I was taken aback. All I could stammer out to Preston was that I would talk with Jonathan and see if he agreed to my meeting Preston alone. I told Preston I would get back to him. But he was insistent. 'I'd like to meet today, Max,' he said before I could hang up. 'Say about seven in my lawyer's office.' That's when I knew everything was lost. Preston wasn't suggesting the Metropolitan Club or his home. We had gotten down to lawyer's offices. Still, I didn't crumble. I told him I'd check with Jonathan and get back to him.

"Jonathan was furious. He wanted to get our lawyer to call up Preston's. Maybe he was right. But I calmed him down. Look, I told Jonathan, it's Preston's magazine now. He paid ten million for it. Let me see what he wants and then we'll decide what to do.

" 'If that's what you think best,' Jonathan agreed. And so with Jonathan standing next to me, I telephoned Preston and told him I'd meet him that evening at his lawyer's. He hung up before I could say good-by."

Max had been sitting at the bar for hours, but he still refused to make any concessions to either the alcohol or the surroundings by as simple a liberating act as loosening the knot in his tie. It hadn't taken Russ long, though, to get into the swing of things. "Another round, barkeep," he barked out. Both Max and the bartender looked at him strangely.

Max actually felt himself being sobered by his story. After Russ's outburst, he continued his account with a grim relentlessness:

Max arrived for the meeting at Preston's lawyer's 51st Street office a little after the agreed upon seven o'clock. Preston didn't appear till seven thirty. It was in this half hour's angry wait in the reception room that Max realized the only possible thing he could walk out with would be his dignity. He had sold everything else he owned for $10 million. Max resolved to hold on to this sense of honor; he would be too proud to fight for anything else.

When Preston entered, Max was finally led into his lawyer's office. The editor had met this lawyer before—an elderly, liver-spotted though unstooped Brahmin with a correspondingly stiff formality to his demeanor and speech that always struck Max as deliberately patronizing. Max, sensitive in the company of ruling-class Protestants, was particularly goaded by the rigid three points of starched white handkerchief that invariably rose a precise inch from the breast pocket of the lawyer's suits. But the fourth man in the room was the surprise.

Preston immediately gestured toward the balding, rumpled-nose man with looming thug's eyes already seated in the cordovan wing chair across from the lawyer. "Max," he said, "I'd like you to meet Ross Clark." At that instant the purpose of the meeting became clear. So when the lawyer added as Max stiffly shook Clark's hand, "I imagine, Mr. Fox, you are presently wondering why Mr. Clark is in attendance," Max didn't answer.

There was no need to. He knew Ross Clark by reputation: Clark owned a constantly expanding nationwide chain of singularly undistinguished newspapers and magazines. At their worst, the Clark publications were gossipy and sensationalistic—"Oedipus Spills All: 'I offed my dad and did my mom dirty,'" might read a typical Clark tabloid. At their best they were not much better—"Blindness Is No Deterrent: Will Oedipus Strike Again?" might be the cover story of one of the chain's more highbrow magazines.

Max had little doubt as to what Clark was doing in that office. His only question was whether it was too late: Had Clark already obtained control of *City*?

The answer came with a vengeance.

"You might be aware, Mr. Fox," the lawyer started in confidently, "that ever since Preston first approached me with the idea of purchasing a controlling interest in your magazine, I was never very enthusiastic about the endeavor."

"That so?" Max said in a tone so unheated and remote that the lawyer couldn't determine if he were being goaded.

After a moment the lawyer decided it would be wiser to proceed obliviously. "I'm sorry to say," he went on evenly, "that my fears proved justified. The magazine has not been generating sufficient income. This circumstance coupled with liquidity problems resulting from certain other of Preston's investments has caused us to reevaluate the extent of our participation in *City* magazine."

It was at this point that Max felt he had put up with enough. He turned to Vandermaeker and asked, "Preston, what's up?"

"Well, uh, Max, uh, it's like this," Preston began, stammering as though he were a schoolboy explaining a bad report card to his father. "It's just that I never got a chance to really get involved in the magazine. I wanted to, but . . ."

"Preston," Max ordered, "where do things stand? Exactly."

"I've sold seventy-five percent of my majority interest in the magazine to Clark Publications."

"I see," Max said, straightening himself up in his chair.

"All it means, Max, is that we have a new controlling partner. Nothing changes at the magazine. It's a simple business deal," Preston said eagerly.

"Is that the way you see it, Mr. Clark?" Max asked the silent man sitting portentously in the corner. "Do you think it's just a simple business deal?"

"Well, maybe it's not that simple," Clark said, showing a row of nicotine-yellowed teeth as he gave an impish smile.

"I see." Max took the shot on the chin but he kept swinging. "What about our new contracts?"

Preston hurried to answer: "It's like this, Max—"

"I'm asking Mr. Clark," Max interrupted.

"I've heard so much about you, Max—you don't mind if I call you Max, do you?"

When the editor offered no immediate response, Clark merely went on: "Well, what I'd like to do is to renew your contract for another two years. At a raise in salary, of course. It'll take two years before we know if we can work together."

"Together," echoed Max. "You honestly think we can work together, Mr. Clark?"

"I'd like to try," said Clark sincerely.

"With me as editor?" Max asked.

"Whatever title you want. Titles aren't important to me." Clark was trying very hard to be friendly.

"And I would have final say in all editorial decisions?" Max pressed.

"Well, let's say we'd have final say together. I'm sure we'd agree on most issues," Clark suggested in his soft, airy way.

"I see," Max said. And he stared with unforgiving fury at Preston.

"What about Jonathan's contract?" Max now felt remorseless.

"Mr. Trout's contract," the lawyer started to answer, "raises certain issues involving the future of the publication—"

"I was speaking to Mr. Clark," Max interrupted. Looking the new majority stockholder of *City* straight in the face, he repeated the question: "What about Jonathan's contract?"

Clark didn't blink. "I don't want him. I hope to make *City* a national magazine, Max. There's no place for a Jonathan Trout in a big operation like that."

Max rose from his chair. He walked over to Ross Clark. "Thank you for your candor, Mr. Clark. And your offer. But I would never work at *City* without Jonathan Trout. Nor, for that matter, could I see myself after all these years consulting with someone else before making an editorial decision. I'm afraid I'll have to decline. I wish you luck with the magazine."

And then Max turned to Preston Warren Vandermaeker. With that perfect calm that comes from resigned anger, Max said the last words he would ever speak to the young heir: "Preston, you're a spoiled, gutless man. I feel sorry for you."

Max Fox then turned away and, aware he should not seem to be in too much of a hurry, walked out of the office. Once on the street, the cool night air sent him reeling. So this is how it was meant to end, he thought; and he felt almost amused at how neat and simple a victim he had been.

He walked aimlessly, not really thinking or feeling anything, for a couple of blocks and then he spotted a bar. He didn't stay there long. Not as long as he stayed at the next bar, a joint he passed on 38th Street. Costello's was his third stop on the way downtown. He had been there for about half an hour before he figured he was drunk enough to call Jonathan. But as soon as he put the dime in the phone he realized he wasn't up to it. He needed to start off with someone easier. Max called Russ Lewis instead.

When they left the bar a little after 5 a.m., both Max and Russ were drunk enough to be convinced the past was assuageable. As for the future, Max's view as the taxi let him off in front of his apartment house was equally fatuous: "Don't ask me what happens now, Russ. I'm retired. I got the rest of my life to sit back and wait to find out."

FOUR

SIX NIGHTS AFTER he had weaved his way out of Costello's, Max Fox, now joined by Jonathan Trout, began formally packing up his life's work; the two men, once partners, still friends, were cleaning out the small office they had shared for almost twenty years.

Getting Max to return to empty his desk took some convincing. He was quite willing to leave everything behind. "There's nothing there I need. *City*'s over for me. Clark can have it all," he said flatly; and Jonathan found his absence of bitterness both genuine and astonishing.

The former publisher, however, was less accommodating. In fact, Jonathan's belligerence was becoming a preoccupation. Max listened patiently at first. Yet by the end of an angrily repetitive week, his compassion became shredded; and, with a grimace not a grin, Max now anticipated his friend's wounded refrain: "I'm not giving Ross Clark anything for free."

"Oh, he paid," Max finally shot back. And, though he would have jumped up and down in protest before admitting it, Max took pride in Preston's selling only 75 percent of the Vandermaeker interest in the magazine for $12.5 million; his own vanity was flattered by Preston's turning a quick $2.5 million profit in two years while still holding on to 25 percent of his stock; for, undeniably, it was Max Fox's original vision, energy, and judgment that had made this incredible multimillion-dollar windfall possible.

"Well, I'll be damned if I'm throwing my files in for free."

"You do what you want," Max said carelessly.

However when Jonathan, reading beneath his friend's mood, suggested they enter the building at night to remove their mountains of personal papers, Max gave in. The former editor in chief simply had not wanted anyone to see him walking out like some seedy pensioner with a carton full of memories; he didn't want anyone's pity.

They returned to their offices on a Sunday night, a calm, darkly quiet interregnum in the magazine's hectic schedule. Russ Lewis, at Max's suggestion, was brought along as muscle, recruited to carry the heavier cartons down to Jonathan's station wagon. Yet while he was glad to help, it didn't take Russ long to decide he didn't belong. He didn't want to intrude on their grief; or be privy to its dimensions.

The three of them entered the eerily empty *City* newsroom a little after nine o'clock. As soon as Max began the familiar ritual of turning his key in the red metal front door, he realized it had been a mistake to return. The place was no longer his. He walked through the offices as a stranger, feeling somehow furtive. He was determined to escape as soon as possible; and to leave the key behind.

It did not take Max more than a half hour to finish haphazardly stuffing three deep cardboard cartons with the papers from his desk and files. Jonathan, though, preferred to linger. Each scrap of paper was studied, and if it triggered a particular memory, read aloud to a conspicuously uninterested Max. As the hours passed, the maudlin curve to Jonathan's enthusiasm became steeper; as did Max's impatience.

Russ, with single-minded determination, set about carrying the cartons down to the street. He wanted to do his job and then go. He knew nothing good would come out of the way this evening was moving: Too many reminiscences, like too much alcohol, will turn any wake nasty.

What Russ didn't know—and could not have understood—was that Max and Jonathan's friendship was never at risk. More than two decades of shared experiences has molded a beautifully immutable allegiance. Consider this: It never occurred to Jonathan to criticize Max for pushing the deal with Vandermaeker; and Max never for even the briefest instant weighed Ross Clark's offer of a job while Jonathan was turned loose. A pool of nonjudgmental affection and respect buoyed this relationship. But that Sunday night, caught up in the emotions of their own particular styles of mourning, Russ was an uneasy witness as they were plumbing its depths.

Jonathan was having a rough time. His sweet run with the magazine had ended too suddenly. Without warning. He found it difficult to accept. More destructive, he felt he was at fault, that he had somehow failed to see through Vandermaeker, to check Clark; and, reeling with this culpability, he took to recalling headier moments when, in the groove, he had knocked the hell out of insurmountable odds and obstacles. Desperate and sentimental, he luxuriated in these memories. He searched for clues, answers, even excuses. It didn't work. The wise momentum of his former life seemed once more a secret rhythm: beyond him. The publisher, now fleshy with middle age, was terrorized. The future was intimidating. Only the past—a lucky hand?—was consoling.

Max, though equally daunted by the swiftness of his fall, took the end of his career with more relief. He refused to look back; his arrogance forced him to be brave. For Max Fox, his accomplishments were his capital—something never to be touched; their value largely resting in the reassuring awareness he would never be required to test his luck again.

There was another large sore spot between the two friends: While Jonathan found the sale to sleazy Clark Publications particularly infuriating, the fatal debasement of the magazine he had devoted his adult life to, Max managed to reap some perverse pleasure from the deed. To his literary mind, it gave the dignity of a cyclical historicism to his decline— here was a tale of classic degeneration. If Preston Warren Vandermaeker alone had chucked him out, Max's fate would simply have been sneered at by those envious of the big bucks he had pocketed. Now, however, Max's journalistic ambitions were elevated when viewed from the perspective of Ross Clark's trendy cultural manipulations. And, hugging his millions and his sixty years, Max relished his new image as the forthright elder statesman: the founding father put out to pasture because he refused to travel with the slick and the shiny.

Throughout that night Russ, too self-centered to appreciate his former bosses' separate but equally destructive postures, kept his distance. Yet the conflict between restful Max and restless Jonathan continued building. Until it burst.

"Hey, look at this," Jonathan called across the room, interrupting Max, who had been stuffing the contents of his desk rather relentlessly into a deep cardboard carton. "Remember these things?" He held up for his partner's inspection the charts a once ambitious publisher had designed in the midst of the newspaper strike more than a decade ago; the red Magic Marker arrows zooming to the sky still thrilled him, a souvenir proving the power of his accomplishment.

"Will you throw those goddamn things in the box," Max growled. And immediately decided he was through packing. He grabbed his trench-coat from the chair. "Let's get the hell out of here."

Jonathan, though, was reluctant to relinquish this corner of the past. "Remember how one week we were struggling with only 6,756 news-stands sales? Look right here, Max." Jonathan pointed to the numbers exactingly printed in a corner of the chart. Max was pulling his trench-coat belt tight, preparing to knot it. But Jonathan, never noticing, went on: "And then, oh boy, did things start taking off." *Bang*! Three fingers slapped an onomatopoetic echo against the cardboard. "15,896." *Bang*! Another swift slap. "23,331." *Bang*! "35,7—"

That's when Max decided to drag Jonathan into the present. "Okay. I've had it. I'm leaving."

"I'm almost done . . ."

"Take as long as you want. I don't give a damn. Russ'll help you lug all your crap to the car. Right?"

"Sure," he answered quickly. There was no way Russ would allow himself to get caught in the middle of this.

"Can't you just wait another couple of minutes?" Jonathan asked, almost pleading. "I had hoped we'd walk out of here together." The poignancy of this request unnerved Russ; the youth knew he wasn't meant to witness this.

"You feel we should walk out together, that's fine with me," said Max sternly. He began to move away from the desk. "But the time to leave is now. Look," Max explained in a reassuring voice as he stood across the room from his friend, "we don't belong here anymore. Our time is over. Done. I say we get the hell out. Now."

"What about our papers? All these cartons?"

"I'll load 'em in the car and drop them off at your house," Russ volunteered. Just get out of here, he wished.

"See. No problem. I say we leave now." Max stared at Jonathan waiting for an answer.

Finally, Jonathan managed a small, quick nod of agreement.

Max walked swiftly across the room. "Let's go, then," he urged. And, as if to make it easier for Jonathan, he linked his arm through the taller man's.

Arm in arm, like two carefree boulevardiers, they strolled out of their office and then, unconsciously slowing down a bit, across the empty newsroom. Max held the red metal door open, but Jonathan, with the look of a child afraid to jump into the water, hesitated.

"You know, Max, I never thought it would come to an end."

"And I never thought it would ever get off the ground."

Max linked his arm once more in Jonathan's. "Come on," he said without a trace of irony. "I've had enough of this place to last me one lifetime."

The two men walked out without saying another word; there was not even a final, greedy over-the-shoulder look. The huge metal door slammed firmly shut behind them.

That was the last time Max Fox ever set foot in the offices of *City* magazine. He never again read another issue. He never again even walked on the block where he had worked for so many years. His decision to cut himself loose from both the realized dreams and the tedious burdens of his past was that tenacious.

THREE MONTHS AFTER Max and Jonathan had walked out the door, Russ followed. General Max had issued a farewell command that none of his young troops should desert. He didn't want any fuss. Or any responsibility. But despite these orders, soon his most loyal soldiers started marching off. Some left with a lot of huffing and puffing, writing angry letters to Clark or, as in one particularly symbolic burst of self-righteousness, even tearing up a paycheck in his face. Russ stuck around longer than many of his more quick-tempered and theatrical colleagues. And when he left, he departed without much ceremony. Truth is, Russ didn't mind Ross Clark that much. Oh, it didn't take Clark long to start tinkering with the loose, bohemian style of the magazine, but Russ Lewis was never as hip as the rest of the kids at *City*. And there was something else, a nagging bitterness that slowed the boil of Russ's loyalty: Max had not considered the consequences lurking for his staff when he had cut his own secret deal, pocketing $5 million. Russ took his time in leaving. But his loose anger was eventually washed over by sentiment: Without Max, the young reporter's heart was no longer in the magazine; it seemed dishonorable to stay on. With $1,123 in savings and a rough outline for a book now long overdue, Russ Lewis quit the only job he had ever wanted.

Kate, though sympathetic and in her own no-nonsense way steadfastly loyal to Max, hung in adamantly at *City*. She argued publicly (never knowing that she mirrored Russ's private broodings) that he had sold to Vandermaeker without worrying about her; similar self-interest insisted she hold on to her column. There was also a larger, but unarticulated practicality keeping her in tow: Despite her self-assured air, Kate had more fears about her talent than she would admit. She simply did not believe any other magazine would be willing to print her work.

Perhaps a kinder lover might have been able to piece together or even assuage the deep, unspoken insecurities grounding Kate's refusal to walk away from the magazine. But their life together had reached the tight, angry point where neither of them was forgiving or understanding anything. Kate remained aloof, beyond explanations; while Russ scurried acerbically about, looking for excuses. So for every week Kate's column appeared while Russ remained out of tangible work, for every week that she received a paycheck while he continued pursuing only the nebulous prospects of a book on gangsters, his anger at her complicity in the undermining of all Max Fox had worked to create and his certainty of her disgrace increased. Kate, Russ rushed to convince himself, had committed sins he could never forgive.

FIVE

EACH FECKLESS DAY as Russ struggled with his book, he also waited for the inevitable interruptions; and they always came, busting up his routine, putting a soapy head on his anger. Twice every day, before heading off to *City* each noon and first thing on coming home each evening, Kate would strip—her body was her magnificent weapon—and step into her bath. And straight across the narrow apartment there would be Russ, not more than a flick of a towel away, glued to a Naugahyde-covered bridge chair trying to keep his eyes and thoughts on the yellow pad propped demandingly on the rickety card table in front of him: the writer in the sanctity of his study.

Kate, a worked-up Russ was convinced, had no right. Couldn't the girl show him some consideration? You try concocting a yarn about a hitman when the only rubout on your mind is going on with a scratchy towel in the tub in front of you.

But this easy, convenient anger, even he had a notion, was little more than a makeshift disguise for the more accurate causes of his anxiety: Russ Lewis was scared stiff.

Three months ago he had marched self-righteously out of *City*—only to start cowering once the door was firmly slammed behind him. He had discovered being a free lance was a little too free; like Hobbes, Russ had been overwhelmed by the brutishness of his permanent state of nature. Suddenly there was no office mailbox stuffed with phone messages or press releases; no quick-witted, sassy colleagues handy to kill an hour discussing Dave Debusschere or Tom McGuane; no pride of a weekly by-line; and no pleasure of a weekly paycheck. Most disconcerting, though, was what happened to the magazine: *City* managed to come out each week without him.

Russ was on his own. Each lonely hour of each unemployed day as he sat struggling to write sentences about shooters and shoot-outs became the ammunition for an escalating parade of miserable thoughts: What if he never had another by-line again? What if the book was never finished? What if he somehow finished it, only to have his unamused publisher rip the unworthy manuscript into little pieces with a cruel, deprecating smile?

Doubt was scaling his cocky dreams down. Once unthinkable suspicions about the ineluctable pattern to his life were being thought: He was, no matter how he struggled to transcend it, his father's son, not Max's; it was Norman Lewis's uncontested failure, his dad's ulcerous victimization, his dad's untested hypotheses that he was heir to. Another familial vision: Russ would strand Kate just as woeful Frankie had stranded her mother.

Fate, slinking in the background for his first twenty-six years, he was now convinced, had finally decided to get around to Russ Lewis.

YET EVEN THE PROSPECT of a finished manuscript, however unlikely, loomed as little comfort. Russ had just begun to realize what it would take to pull the book off; or, more exactly, what sort of underhanded compromises would be required to pass off the speck of an idea he was dealing with as a story—a true story. After a half-dozen nonproductive sessions with Rico Pelligrini, Russ no longer had any doubts his kinetic, loquacious hitman had more imagination than experience.

There was no denying, however, that jumpy Rico was an enthusiastic collaborator. He was already anticipating his celebrity; and if he had to deep-six his seedy past as a bit player and reinvent himself on a grander Cinemascope scale to ensure a future jingling with gold chains and first-class trips to Vegas, Rico was game.

"Hey, Russie," he would cackle as he checked in with his Boswell in a typical 4 a.m. phone call, "did I ever tell about the shake 'n' bake jobs I did for Ike the kike?"

"Ike the kike?"

"Hey, Russie baby. Nothing personal, Gombah. It's just street talk. The creep was a loanshark. For all I know he wasn't even a Hebe . . . or a Jew . . . or whatever you call you people. The guy just had a lot of money on the street, so we called him the kike. Kapeesh?"

"Sure, Rico," he said flatly, "just like I'm Russ the kike."

"Hey, Gombah, what are you trying to cop an attitude or something? You're a writer. You got smarts. Don't go comparing yourself to some sleaze bag who got a rap sheet a mile long."

Still, the writer with the smarts couldn't help wondering how much time Russ the kike would get for passing fiction off as truth. At the very least, Max and Kate would throw the book at him.

But Rico jumped in. "He-ey R-rus-sie," he shouted into the phone, like a fan at a football game. "What's in a name? You don't like Ike the kike, I can understand that. I got feelings too, you know. Let's call him Mike the mick. Hey, make him Tony the Wop for all I care. Kapeesh, buddy?"

Russ decided to sidestep the issue for the time being. "What's a shake 'n' bake job?" he asked instead.

"Don't you know nothing," Rico complained with an evil laugh. "Now suppose," Rico lectured professionally, "you got money out on the street and some sleaze bag decides he can skip out on paying the weekly vig. You can't let that go on. That'd be bad business, right?"

"Right."

"So that's when a shark like Ike the . . . or whoever comes to me and says, 'Rico, baby, I got a little problem collecting. I think a shake 'n' bake job might persuade 'em.' So then I send word to the sleaze bag who ain't making good on his debt. I tell him to meet me at Joey's bar on Mulberry Street. And he comes because he thinks maybe we can work something out. Anyways, Joey's got this microwave oven. You ever seen one of those things?

"Sure."

"Yeah. Real fancy fuckin' contraptions, ain't they? Anyways, before the sleaze bag can realize what's happening I got his hand shoved in the goddamn microwave. I mean, the mother's turned up to 450 degrees or so and the sleaze bag is shaking to beat the band. Shit, I mean you can smell his flesh baking. And that's when I lay it all out to the tough guy. I tell him, 'Hey, sleaze bag, either you're going to pay what you owe or I'm going to stick your whole fuckin' head in the goddamn microwave.' Shit, Russie, you'd be surprised how quick they pay."

"Jesus, Rico, you ever really do something like that?"

"Hey, you like the story or not?"

"Like the story? What the hell goes on in your head, Rico?"

"Slow down now, kid," Rico said threateningly. "A story like that gotta sell books, right?"

Russ didn't answer.

"I mean that's what we're doing this for. To sell books, right?"

A moment passed before Russ conceded weakly, "Yes."

"Okay now," he said more amicably. "Now you're back on the right track." And his tone became easier, almost honey-coated as he added, "Just remember one thing: When you put all this into the book, I want it done so I look good. You know, so people think I'm tough. That I don't take any shit. But that Rico Pelligrini got a heart. Kapeesh?"

". . . Yes," Russ said, understanding too well what he had gotten himself into.

SO IT WAS EASIER for Russ to carry on about Kate's baths. And, as the hapless, unproductive days passed, these sudsy impertinences became only a jagged edge of the large, destructive grudge he was furiously inventing. Each long day soon acquired a melancholic structure—an order largely defined by how he perceived Kate's provoking his antagonism at a particular time.

Every morning Russ would be up at eight and by eight thirty, after a cup of instant espresso to jump-start his consciousness, he would be seated at the card table staring hopefully at a blank legal pad. By quarter of nine, however, he would be staring at the bed—there lay Kate, the scratchy blue blanket snuggled around her, blissfully sleeping away. She had her nerve! It wouldn't be until around ten when she might, after happily rousing herself with a series of languorous, loud, and provocatively graceful arching stretches, consider rising. Then she'd skip naked out of bed, kiss him lightly on his creased forehead, only to grab the newspaper and dive under the covers again. God, he cringed silently, the time that wanton girl had the luxury to kill! There wasn't a story in the *Times* she found too inane, a dateline she found too obscure—each day she filled a solid hour reading the damn thing. And next—all the time the up-and-at-'em author across the room still trying to pretend the next sentence was only a quick thought away—she'd grab the ballpoint off the nightstand and have a go at the crossword puzzle. She'd have inked the whole thing in—even her small successes got to him—before, the clock now striking noon, she'd get out of bed and splash about in her morning bath.

Russ, seated at his front row desk, observed each daily levee as though he were a spy in her court; each of her indulgences hardened his heart for the inevitable rebellion. His mind, conveniently forgetting hers was the household's only paycheck, argued for equality and fraternity: If they were setting out on a partnership, why should he be the only one struggling? Especially when, as the wasted days dragged on, he was starting to realize *Hitman!* was a phony, worthless task.

Once dressed, her second mug of milky coffee finished, Kate would greet the afternoon with another display of her happy freedom; and her treachery. "Bye, babes," she would say with an innocent smile; a token soft kiss on his by now more deeply creased forehead; words of sweet advice: "Write well"; and then, the door slamming behind her, she'd be off. To the office. Russ would try each afternoon to take advantage of this anticipated privacy, but it wouldn't be long before the sentence that was developing in his head had wandered off. To the office. Her office. The office Max had been forced out of. The office he had walked out on. There was no way he was ever going to allow her, so unrepentant, so guiltless in her easy pragmatism, to scramble away from the full force of his disdain.

Envious and brooding, Russ would sit impotently studying his pad as the afternoon meandered on; now and then he gazed inattentively out the apartment's dirt-streaked windows. As soon as the East Village street turned dark, his mood would lighten; at least he had gotten through another day without cracking. A scene from *Hitman!* might start to swagger into his mind. But the words never made it to the page. Kate never failed to bump them off.

She would return home and jump into her recuperative evening bath. She tried to be considerate. She wouldn't talk, attentive not to disturb her struggling hero. She would quietly strip and, with the utmost luxury, take a long, silent lounge in the tub. And Russ would sit across the room rigid with anger.

"Well, how did it go today, babes?" she would finally ask as, unembarrassed as a cat licking herself, she sprinkled her luscious body with talcum powder.

"Same as always," Russ would announce with deceptive cheer. He wasn't going to let her know he was getting nowhere.

And she would constantly plead: "When are you going to let me read it?"

"Soon." But to himself: As soon as anything is written.

Such was the joy Russ Lewis found in the writer's life he had always dreamed of living.

SIX

TWO OR THREE MORNINGS a week at precisely nine o'clock, Max, hurrying to map out some sort of schedule for his suddenly vague, overlapping days, would ring up Russ and ask if he were free to join Jonathan and him for lunch.

"You feel like taking off from your writing?" Max would ask, always solicitous of the grand endeavor he imagined his young friend was wrapped up in.

"I guess I could use a breather," Russ would decide, trying to lace his voice with guilty reluctance.

"Well, if you're working, Russ . . ."

"No, no. Let me finish this page and I'll meet you around one-ish." And then he would stare at the clock until it was time to leave.

Not that any of the three friends found these lunches much fun; and it wasn't simply the lingering dispirit caused by their still unfamiliar unemployment. Their woebegotten moods fell even lower as soon as they entered Mario's—a grimy and grim Italian joint in the windowless basement of a Village brownstone.

At Mario's the cockroaches were an accepted part of the ambience; the vermin either succumbed under the passing splatter of tomato sauce or were ignored. Still, each lunchtime the same assortment of pensioners huddled around the restaurant's curving, flamingo-painted bar; merrily they swilled their Manhattans as soap operas muttered from a black-and-white portable suspended from the asbestos-tiled ceiling. The two corner seats at the bar, choice because of the easy viewing angle they offered at the TV, were habitually filled by a thickly powdered woman sporting a jauntily perched plaid tam o'shanter and her competitively made-up friend, this woman's outlandishly curly helmet of fire engine red hair a garish beacon in the dim surroundings. "A pair of well-swung swingers," Russ suggested acidly to Max. "Just what any bar needs."

But what attracted the sprightlier, unemployed trio's steadfast allegiance to Mario's? The blame was entirely Jonathan's. He insisted they put up with all the culinary, aesthetic, and moral indignities of the place simply because he knew not a single penny of his bill was going to be used toward buying an ad in *City*. As publisher, Jonathan had tried for futile years to persuade the restaurant to take an ad in his magazine; now that the magazine belonged to Ross Clark he took comfort from the knowledge that Mario's wouldn't advertise in *City*.

These days Jonathan Trout was in a wild state. He would start in on his companions even before the menus came. Between compulsive gobbles of sesame breadsticks, crusty Italian bread, and pumpernickel rolls —each week he puffed up larger before their worried eyes—Jonathan would suggest the same destitute plot.

"We could do it, Max. We could start a new magazine. We could drive Clark out of business."

"It wouldn't be easy." As long as it was not real, Max would play along with his friend.

"No, we could really do it. Just like the old days. We could get the writers and the ads and . . ."

"The old days were a long time ago," Max gently reminded Jonathan, while he sneaked Russ an exhausted look.

"But I bet we could do it. We did it once. We could do it again."

And when Kate would join them for a lunch—neither the former editor or publisher ever judged her hanging in at the magazine as harshly as Russ did; and that really scuffed her resentful lover's sense of justice— Jonathan turned all his attention to her, waving manic questions in her face. What was the circulation of the magazine last week? Are subscriptions up? Newsstand sales? Who got a raise? Who got fired? When was Clark planning to launch the national edition? Kate tried to be kind; she invented answers and gossip to placate Jonathan. She fed him phony intelligence. She saw no harm; she assumed he was only sharpening his avenging sword to wave at corporate windmills.

But when the plot became dangerously real, Max rushed in to put a stop to it. Here's what happened: Nearly six months had passed since the two founders of *City* magazine had been forced into retirement. With Russ Lewis as their guest, they gathered for another glum lunch at Mario's. That afternoon, though, as soon as they sat down at the round table in the corner which both the waiters and the trio had now come to think of as "theirs," Jonathan, with an oddly triumphant flourish, waved a piece of paper under his companions' eyes.

"I wonder if either of you has any idea what this is?" Jonathan challenged.

Russ automatically shrugged; the success he was having with his book was making him the life of every party. But Max, while pranky, was game: "I got it! You're going to wrap up the rolls? Sneak a few dozen home to nibble on when you can't sleep tonight."

Jonathan Trout had spent a very contented lifetime ignoring Max's taunts. He wasn't about to be deterred now.

"I think I'll just tell you," Jonathan decided with his usual good nature. He searched for a pair of ebony-colored bifocals amidst the clutter of papers filling his inside breast pocket; rearranged his bulk in the chair so he could hold the official-looking sheet just inches from his eyes; and then in a proudly stentorian tone he read: "Be it resolved that as of the 17th day of May, 1974, in the state of New York, a private corporation is established in the name of Downtown Magazine, Inc.—"

That's when Max cut him off. "What the hell is going on?" he shouted.

The blast of Max's fury startled both Jonathan and Russ; and even one of the pensioners at the bar hissed an admonishing "ssh" at this young rowdy.

But Max was livid. Russ thought he would shatter the stem of the cocktail glass he clutched in his already white-knuckled fist. "Just what the hell do you think you're up to?" he said in a chilling voice which filled the entire restaurant.

The bartender retaliated by turning up the sound of "General Hospital." And, Russ noted with amazement, the coy thing in the tam o'shanter flashed Max a provocative wink.

Jonathan backed off. He tried, cautiously, to offer Max some placating logic to latch onto. "Well . . . I thought that . . . I mean if we're going to start a new magazine . . ."

"I'm not starting anything," Max said firmly.

"Well, we have been talking about it . . ."

"*You've* been talking about it, Jonathan."

"Okay," he conceded, still thinking he could avoid a scene. "But I thought it couldn't hurt to be prepared. Now if we want to talk to investors, we won't have to wait to get a corporation set up."

"You want to talk with investors," said Max with utter contempt, "talk with investors."

Jonathan attempted to speak, but Max rode over him in a booming voice: "Raise all the money you want. Start any kind of magazine you want. *But—count—me—out.*" It was at that moment that the beveled stem of Max's cocktail glass finally snapped off in his hand; three green olives tumbled from the teetering martini and bounced softly against the tablecloth with the symbolic solemnity of muffled drumrolls at a state funeral—the end had been tolled.

Still Max continued lashing away. "You think I want to go through all that again?" he asked, his florid face distorted into a mean sneer. He ignored the small wet disaster spilling across the table, and which had begun to drip steadily onto his blue worsted trousers. Jonathan, the perfect victim, also didn't budge.

Only Russ, grateful for the opportunity to avoid Max's glare, fussed with a napkin in a busy attempt at a mop-up operation; until Max, full of red-faced anger, decided, "The hell with that." He pulled the martini-soaked cloth from the youth's hand, only to hurl it with wits' end fury at Jonathan. A soggy bull's-eye: Max got him in the chest.

But even this bit of violence didn't pique Max's rage. The tirade continued pouring forth:

"I don't know what the hell you're trying to prove, but I'm too old to get into a dogfight with Ross Clark. Besides, I've had enough of all the crazies at *City*. Why would I want to have to deal with them again? They're Clark's problem now, thank God. He can have them. I'm out. O-u-t. Out. That part of my life is over with. I just want to sit back and grow old gracefully. Understand?"

"I'm beginning to understand, Max." The words were spoken slowly and succinctly, a peal of destitute pride ringing in Jonathan's acquiescence.

"Good." And a more compliant Max added, "You know, you don't need me to start up a new magazine."

"I realize that," he answered with deadly courtesy. After a moment Jonathan began folding the incorporation notice into precise thirds. He stuck the paper inside his sport coat pocket; and, the disruptive document out of sight, asserted quickly, "But I really don't think I'll be starting anything."

"That's your decision," Max answered with careful firmness.

Russ rushed in to head off the next round: "I'm hungry."

"I'm ready to order," Jonathan agreed.

"And I could use another drink," said Max, letting loose a small, weary sigh.

BY THE TIME the meal was over, Jonathan and Max were playing buddy buddy again, two old friends lackadaisically holding forth with the small talk of daily life. Russ, however, remained impressed. Not so much that the battle was gone and forgotten; but rather, that Max had managed to fight it at such a fever pitch.

Since the relinquishing of his editorship, Max, Russ had been observing with some concern, had taken to going with the flow of events;

and, if the vapid lunches at Mario's were any evidence, these days the flow seemed to be a river of martinis. Max Fox, retired and settling into his sixties, was apparently ready to accept that all the major scenes of his personal drama had been written and acted; he would shuffle through the coda which remained.

Yet today's lunch, however sourly combative, was a performance worthy of the old editor—General Max once more taking command, once more manipulating his loyal troops. Russ silently cheered as therapeutic his friend's prescriptive anger; and he hoped it would shake Max up as much as it had shook up Jonathan. Further, Russ marveled at Max's continuing resourcefulness: The young man, a fellow actor, suspected Max's glass-breaking bugged-out rage (or at least its steep edge) was trumped up—an instructive mood pulled out of a sly editor's hat.

As the three friends walked from the bleak restaurant into a startlingly crisp spring afternoon, Jonathan announced he planned to head uptown to track down a French-English dictionary for the twins. Russ and Max preferred to stroll through the Village. They hadn't gotten a block when Russ, still distrusting the remarkable pitch of the lunchtime histrionics, risked calling Max on it.

"You weren't really that angry at Jonathan, were you?"

Max tried fending off the question with a twinkling smile but it came out more coy than cryptic. He realized this and, a gesture of apology, turned candid. "Things were getting out of hand," he said without emotion. "The time had come for Jonathan to stop kidding himself. I know—you're going to tell me I got carried away roughing him up. Maybe. But he had to admit once and for all that he was never going to start another magazine." A self-deprecating sigh, then: "Both Jonathan and I are too old to confuse delusion with ambition."

They continued their aimless, postprandial walk. Max, flitting back to his role as a retired gentleman, extracted an impressive-sized cigar from a monogrammed black leather case; since leaving the magazine he had been filling some of his time by acquiring new affectations. A minute of intense open-air concentration passed while he snipped off one end of the cigar with a gold clipper, made sure his match didn't singe the tobacco, and pensively executed a couple of smoky puffs to check out the draw. The Dunhill glowing away, he felt comfortable enough to clarify the lingering issue. He spoke with deep intensity: "Look, I'm not complaining . . . and neither should Jonathan. We had a good run. That should hold any man for one lifetime."

The two friends' meandering route now had them crossing through the heart of Washington Square Park. The park was jammed, the cheery spring weather bringing out squads of New Age athletes going about their fun with kamikaze zeal: Spacy kids zipped along on swiftly snaking skateboards; sliced Frisbees as deadly as any guillotine through the pot heavy air; pummeled barrages of volleyballs into the spacious sky; and roller-skated wildly, boogying to the beat of a shouting chorus of ghetto blasters. Max surveyed it all with narrow, rebuking eyes. Russ, though, was not so cool. He saw danger everywhere.

Russ was right. While the short man toked obliviously on his snooty cigar, a zonked-out skateboarder, his lanky body collapsed into a killer crouch, came hurling toward Max's kneecaps. That's when Russ jumped in. In one swift, graceful motion, he pushed a startled Max aside, and swung his right arm in a tight, forceful arc. This forearm block caught the moon-eyed assailant precisely at his red bandanna covered Adam's apple.

Immediately the skateboard skidded into a crowded volleyball court; its pilot, praying "Hey m-a-a-n-n" as he catapulted through the zenith of his trajectory, crashlanded into a row of prickly hedges. But, apparently, there was no permanent harm done. The kid's rapid descent was buffered by a happy cushion of pharmaceuticals. He lay smiling in the bushes. Max, meanwhile, tried to disguise his shock. "Was that really necessary?" he suggested without any real concern. But Russ was too puffed up with silent pride to argue. He let the question fade away. Russ was certain he had done his duty: He had protected Max.

While Max, despite his carping, was grateful. And impressed. He walked ahead, making a big display of the relighting of his cigar. His mind, though, traipsed elsewhere. He was grappling with whether or not the moment had come for him to do his duty: Should he try to rescue Russ?

Max's concern was not simply spurred on that afternoon by a notion of reciprocity. This mission had been tugging at him for a while; just as he had long known the day would come when he would have to set Jonathan straight. For months of lunches he had been observing the wistful evidence: Russ Lewis, his unwritten book clearly whopping the will and ambition out of him, was crumbling. But, as was his detached way, Max had been reluctant to meddle; and there was always the time-honored hope things would work themselves out. Yet, by now even Max had finally come around to acknowledging that the hope in this degenerative case was looking pretty slim.

They had safely passed through the Washington Square Arch and were heading up the sedate, residential corridor of lower Fifth Avenue when Max found his resolve.

"How's the book coming?" Max asked, trying to sound offhanded.

"Slow." But Russ caught himself: ". . . and steady."

"Good." Max nodded coolly. He was puffing away on his cigar, yet both of them knew he wasn't the only one blowing smoke. "That's good."

"Okay, okay, we both know I'm lying," Russ said, surrendering plaintively. Then, as if liberated, he burst out with the thought that had been torturing him for months: "I'm never going to write this book."

The words finally spoken, Russ waited for the slap of Max's reprimand. Instead, to the young man's amazement, the retired editor was genially complaisant. "What are you going to do instead?" was his only response.

It was a simple, obvious question, yet in all the months of his self-centered misery Russ had never thought things through to such a rational, estranged end. A choked realization: "I don't know."

"You could call up Clark. Maybe he'd give you your old job back at *City*."

Russ answered immediately: "No way." Just as Max knew he would. The editor was counting on the energy resting in his young friend's strong pride.

So Max kept on tugging softly. "All right," he said amicably. And then in that same even tone he added, "Russ, you know you don't have to be a writer. There are a lot of other things you could do."

Russ listened; and, though he wasn't aware of it, Max was creeping under his mood: Russ's sullen, defensive radar had been fooled. He was caught up in the logic of Max's unaggressive argument. Sure, if he couldn't write, Russ couldn't be a writer. He had to be something else. Russ could be his father. Or he could be Frankie.

And while these impossible thoughts swirled through Russ's mind, the gray-haired pest kept at it: "What the hell do you want to be a writer for anyway?"

"You know that's the same question you asked me . . . when was it . . . how many years ago? Four? On that first day we met."

"I've always liked that question," said Max with the quick laugh of a magician being called on the card up his sleeve. "Still do."

Max recovered, though; and even dared to pretend he was asking a question to which he didn't know the answer. "What did you tell me then? That first day in my office, what did you say?"

"I don't know . . ." said Russ, searching his memory. ". . . Oh, I think maybe I said being a writer was the only thing I wanted to do . . . the only life I could dream of living."

"And today? Would you still say the same thing?"

Russ began thinking it through; but with the abruptness of just a moment, he came to a realization that left him shuddering with both fear and excitement: There was truly nothing he had a fair chance of accomplishing that would make him prouder. "Yes," he said at last. "Yes I would."

"Then do it."

Max Fox made it sound so simple.

"Listen, Russ," he explained, "you're lucky . . ."

"If this is luck . . ."

"Perhaps for at least today we could do without your customary sarcasm," he said severely. Max accepted his friend's somber nod as an apology; and he continued:

"Yes, you are lucky. You're lucky because you know what you want to do. When I was your age, I just drifted. Nothing seemed like a satisfactory alternative to drifting, to hanging out. Then, when I finally got a hold on something that excited me, I was forty years old. And scared stiff. Like you. I never thought *City* would work. I never thought I had the wisdom . . . the stamina . . . even the luck to make it happen. There were plenty of times in those early years when I was moments away from throwing in the towel. From telling Janey and Jonathan that this was it.

"But I didn't. You know why? It wasn't because I stopped being afraid. It wasn't because I became more confident the magazine would catch on. Just one instinct kept me from giving up—I figured this was my shot.

"All you can ask out of life, Russ, is opportunities. Opportunities you believe in. Maybe you won't be good enough for them. That's too bad. Then you're a loser. But worst of all, Russ, is not to chase these chances. Not to run after them with all you've got.

"Look, Russ, I can't tell you if your book will work. Who knows if you possess the talent? But it looks like you have an opportunity. And if you do, you're getting it young. If this is really what you want to do, then you'd be a coward not to throw yourself into it. If you don't try, Russ, that's the disgrace. Walking away from any challenge is worse than failing." He let that sink in before adding in a voice packed with warning, "It's fear, not failure, that makes life impossible to live."

They turned the corner, walking past the ivy-covered brownstones on 10th Street in silence. Yet in this short block a misunderstanding took hold that had the power to wreck lives.

Max was talking about accomplishment—not merely success. He was urging, in his own nondirective way, the pursuit of authentic triumphs, leaps of faith after uncompromised dreams.

Russ missed the point. Down and out and—more damaging—feeling it, he could dream only of winning. He could not see past conquering his heavy fears; he disregarded the unworthiness of his shoddy, fraudulent book. If only Russ had understood the unspoken warning in Max's lecture: Dignity follows only pride; and pride rests in integrity.

But Max had succeeded at least in energizing Russ. When the older man, still in no hurry, suggested they stop for a beer, Russ declined. He was eager to return home.

As soon as he got back to the apartment, Russ sat down at his make-shift desk, the blank legal pad in front of him. He busily sharpened pencils; and then stared out the window. For a while it seemed as impossible as ever. Perhaps, he considered, his long-sought-for opening scene might be found in the notes from his interviews with Rico. No, these dull truths would only slow his imagination down. Then suddenly, from out of nowhere he decided with a tickle of amazement, an invented episode popped into Russ's mind: the gruesome, bullet-splattered execution of a disloyal Mafioso as he drove his Caddy through the soapy confusion of a carwash. He tried writing the first sentence. Another smoothly followed.

It wasn't until Russ began rereading the ten pages he had so quickly written that he realized Kate had already come home. And it wasn't until he looked up and watched her stepping into her bath that he suddenly realized the heartfelt inspiration for the bloody opening scene of his book.

SEVEN

FOR THE NEXT eight months Russ sat at his rickety card table and worked away. Not that writing *Hitman!* always proved easy. But after that first chapter the task began to seem real, the action started to clarify, and the implacable anxiety which had unnerved him for so long gave way to a delicious and challenging excitement: Could he pull it off?

Discipline set in: three pages a day, seven days a week—a rhythm of eighty-four longhand pages a month. And as his writing gathered momentum, so did his resolve. The future loomed less tentative. His expectations, like his optimism, were once more wide-eyed. Russ felt he was on his way.

But before he moved on, he was determined to leave something behind. Here, too, the book became his solemn weapon. He sensed it would be the Big Get Even. That year as day after day he remained grounded in the bleak apartment, as day after day the pile of pages and completed chapters grew, Russ found the confidence to convince himself of the one perception that is liberation from even the most emotionally sticky of relationships: he no longer needed Kate.

Russ's complicated, inchoate feelings about Kate finally dared to harden. Reserves of intimate, unconfined pleasures slipped, amazingly, away. Stiff, foolishly proud lines were drawn in cold anger; and kindness became impossible. He twisted it all: What was became what was meant not to be.

There had been a time when, loving and concerned, Russ had tried to cajole her into cutting down on her two daily packs of Marlboros; now her stubborn adamancy enraged him; her dirty habit choked his air; and the trail of gray smoke, he decided as he gave the simple evidence a mean enough twist to turn it into a symbol, left a sickly dry shadow to even the touch of her lips. And, oh, there had been a time when he shrugged indulgently at the gnawed run in her chartreuse tights or her wearing the same dress for days in a row; now, indignant, Russ took her unconcern as a personal affront—*she didn't care enough about him to make an effort*. There had been so many times.

Every moment they were together Kate was paraded before Russ's warped mirror: Her taste for classical music was dismissed as out-of-touch fogeyism; the pedantic, multilingual deft to her careful pronunciations—he cringed everytime he watched her pucker up to roll out the syllables in charcuterie, zúppa di pesce, or even Isaac Asimov—was now pretentiousness; her swift opinions were now arrogance. It was a time of building, rattling fury; the bursting point could only spill forth in strokes of vengeance—then the letting go.

NEARLY FOURTEEN MONTHS to the day after Max's fateful, energizing lecture, *Hitman!* shoved its contrived way onto the nonfiction best-seller list; and finding a comfortable niche near the top, took up residence for a grand, high-flying while. The spoils—there were hefty contracts for a paperback edition, foreign versions, and even a mini-series—began pouring into Russ's checking account. So zing went the strings of his other-directed heart; and a remarkably self-satisfied Russ convinced himself he had pulled it off.

Who could blame him? The grab bag of delights seemed bottomless: There was William, the well-starched, imperious doorman of the "best" building in the Village who now jumped into action as the new tenant approached, greeting him—at twenty-eight!—"Good evening, Mr. Lewis"; there was the lavish thirty minutes of intensely polite book chat with Phil Donahue as millions attentively listened in; there was his new toy, a silver 911S Porsche, complete with push-button electric sunroof, Blaupunkt stereo radio and four-speaker cassette system (no Targa top or spoiler on this classically clean machine; Russ knew from tacky); and then there was the rainy summer weekend when everyone seemed to need a good read to take to the soggy beach, so *Hitman!* jumped over a celebrity workout book and a no-money-down real estate investment guide to become the nation's number-one best-seller.

But in all these unanticipated and wonderfully comforting riches, there were two triumphs that genuinely convinced the young author he had made it; yet these two victories carried with them a trapping from which he would never recover—the final justification for his smoldering desire to cut and run from Kate.

RUSS LEWIS MADE IT into *People* magazine.

Sure, a smugly fetching John Travolta was on the cover; but in supermarkets and beauty parlors around the country anyone could turn to page 38 and see a full-page picture of Russ Lewis—a portrait of the commercially successful artist as a young man. Though fatuously young and chubby-faced (his immediate resolutions: grow a beard or at least a mustache; jog; stick to apples when he got the munchies), Russ, all done up in his folksy writer's garb of wide-wale cuffed corduroys, plaid Viyella shirt, and Bean Ranger Oxfords, strode earnestly across the full page. While on the top of the facing page, there was a happy four-column shot of the author and his mistress—Russ, beaming with a proprietary nonchalance, slouched toward the camera, one arm draped around Kate and the other trailing over their newly acquired black marble mantel.

The editors of *People* saw this second part of the spread as a small, homey shot. Yet for Russ this photograph—surely as much as the snapshot of the toothsome, uniformed Luftwaffe Leutnant Warner who had piloted across generations to send shivers through a young man's romantic idealism—served to demystify, if not signal, how unreachable it had all become.

The way he saw it, anyone taking a moment to study the page in the magazine would hold him blameless. The malicious incongruity jumped out at you. Kate and he might just as well have been posing for one of those children's games in the Sunday funnies: Circle All the Things That Don't Belong in This Picture.

Not that this came as a surprise. There had been enough minatory warnings the day of the photo session to suggest how the finished product would turn out.

"Okeedokee, now, you love birds," the *People* photographer had chirped as he commenced to order Russ and Kate about ruthlessly, "here's how I see it." Then for tedious hours this blue-jeaned elf of a man with a white-on-white silk foulard wrapped loosely about his neck sent the couple scurrying about their new apartment as he searched for the properly artful poses.

"We're talking youth. We're talking writers. We're talking Greenwich Village. That's what this shot has got to say. Come on now, people. Cooperate!"

He instructed Russ to grab a pencil and sit at his new stripped oak desk; Russ went behind the desk. He had the author pensively searching through the volumes arranged in his expensively carpentered bookcases; Russ perused with thoughtful intensity. Ordered into the narrow kitchen to crack an egg into the gleaming copper frying pan, Russ obediently decimated a carton of Jumbo Grade A's as the high-speed Nikon searched for frames depicting domestic bliss. While in each of these shots, a stolid, unamused Kate stood with rigid detachment on the periphery of the camera's eye.

The Nikon clicked portentously away, but still the photographer fretted, "It's not right, people. It's not telling me what I want to hear."

"He's an artist," a patient Russ explained to a simmering Kate.

"Youth. The Village. Love," the photographer exuded. "Come on now, give it to me."

"He's an asshole," Kate corrected, her assessment prompted more by exasperation than by venom.

But Russ, knowing that the woman was also implicitly digging away at him, sharply challenged: "All right now, Kate, you gonna cooperate or what?" And he continued with snide, unremitting fury, "It might be wiser to keep your smartass comments to yourself. I mean you can't expect everyone to be a hotshot dance columnist making seventy-five bucks a week from Ross Clark."

Kate, quivering with anger, fell into place. After place. She was grim, but obedient; while the photographer, haphazard yet omnipotent, continued commanding. Finally, his foulard now undone and the unchic collar of his T-shirt exposed, he gave in to his frustration:

"You know what the problem is? I'll tell you what the problem is— her." He pointed a tiny finger at Kate's breast. Russ's irate, accusatory look only strengthened the indictment.

Quickly Kate tried to charm her way out of this one. "Me?" she asked.

"Hey," the photographer warned, clearly not falling for it, "can't you smile, girlie?"

And then she no longer cared: "The name is Kate."

"Wait a minute, now." Russ jumped wisely in to referee. "Will you just smile, Kate? Let's get this thing over with."

"I'll try. It's just that I'm not used to having my picture taken."

"Okay, okay, I understand. But, believe me, there's nothing to it— *Kate.*" The photographer spat out her name; and then licked his lips like an unrepentant brat who has gobbled down the last piece of cake and wants you to know he'd do it again if he had the chance. Russ also sent out his warning: another tough, shape-up look.

"I'm gonna help you along," the photographer continued. "We got a few shots left on this roll and we're gonna make them work. Right, people?"

Russ nodded enthusiastically; and, he noted with satisfaction, Kate at least was noncommittal.

The photographer arranged them in front of the fireplace.

"Let's see now. Hold hands. That's it. Yeah, that's right. Hold hands. We're talking young love."

Kate twined her fingers through Russ's; her touch was light, as though she was preparing to run.

"No. No. That's not it. Try this—Russ, you put your arm around her."

"Good. Now . . . *Kate*, you look at Russ. Come on. Like you mean it."

Russ crooked his head toward Kate. Defiantly she returned the gesture.

"Good. Good. Now smile."

Russ, the genial celebrity, beamed. Kate, forever Kate, was more restrained.

"Hey. Could you just give a little smile. Please."

Kate tried. A little.

"Bet-ter. But come on. Let it all hang out when I say, 'Cheese.'

"Cheese," he shouted. The camera's shutter whizzed away.

"Good . . . good . . . now you're cooking." Then a new come-on to coax even more enthusiasm from his models: "Mon—ey." The camera charged ahead with a rapid series of clicking noises.

"Just one more." And as a conciliatory gesture, the photographer added, "Hang in there, Kate." Then with a full-throated burst that can come only from genuine fervor, a shout so fierce, so earnest, so reverentially tremulous that a Baptist minister on the revival circuit would have envied his pitch, he delivered his ultimate inducement: "Suc—cess."

His camera captured the moment without a slip.

And that was the shot which ran innocently on page 39 in *People* magazine. Russ is there smiling proudly as if to say, "Okay, Posterity, make room for another comer." And there is Kate, the grip of Russ's unyielding arm about her shoulder holding her in place, looking up at her captor. But she is not smiling. She is slack-jawed, as if in mid-sentence. Russ was convinced you didn't have to be a lip-reader to get her drift. She is telling him while all the world looks in, "You phony."

Russ studied the photography in the magazine for hours, his anger building until he wanted to shout—Grab your crayons, kiddies. Draw a bright red circle around What Doesn't Belong in This Picture. Cynicism. Envy. Disdain. Who needs this? Or this girl?

THE TRUMP CARD, though, that really brought home the reality of his success was played out in a telephone call; a call that finally gave Russ the opportunity to draw his isolating circle in deep and indelible strokes around Kate. The caller was Ross Clark. The new owner of *City* magazine. And the man who had just fired his dance columnist, Kate Warner.

About a week before the unexpected call, Kate had returned to the apartment in the middle of a bright afternoon and announced to Russ with quiet resignation, "I won't be working for *City* anymore." Then, without either another word of explanation or even a shrug of disappointment, she retreated to the kitchen.

Russ put down the copy of *Publishers Weekly* he had been skimming ("Edwin Brewster—The Editor Who Shaped *Hitman!* into a Hit" was this week's bittersweet industry profile) and hurried after her.

"What do you mean you won't be working at the magazine?" he demanded.

Kate, her head stuck deep into their new stainless steel refrigerator as she searched for a Heineken, answered, "Just what I said. I'm done with *City*."

"Goddamn it, Kate," he said as he grabbed hold of her thin arm and pulled her forcefully from the depths of the refrigerator, "what the hell happened? Were you fired?"

"Not exactly," she said with dismissive nonchalance and, raising the beer she had triumphantly extracted, asked, "Join me?"

"I can't believe it," he said with gloating fury, not slowing down even to acknowledge her offer. "You got fired. You refused to quit the goddamn magazine and then Clark goes and fires you. Serves you right."

"I didn't say I got fired." She made a big show of hunting for a bottle opener; they both knew, though, she was trying not to cry.

But Russ was not to be deterred. "Like hell you weren't."

The sustained force of his vindictiveness helped Kate to level her mood: tears would only reinforce the cackle in his last laugh. So she took a few slow swallows from the bottle of beer, and then hoisted herself onto the butcher block island in the middle of the kitchen. In a calm, oddly disinterested way, she told him what had happened.

That afternoon when Kate had picked up the new issue of *City* and saw that for the third week in a row her dance column had not been included, she decided it was time to find out why. A spur of the moment strategy jumped up at her: There was Ross Clark, head arched high in the air, hurrying with his hasty, sloppy steps across the newsroom. Kate, always the fatalist, cornered him. Without breaking stride, his grumbling eyes still aloof as though he were attempting to scan a 10-point headline hot off the presses in some distant corner of his empire, the publishing mogul made his position clear: The column did not run because dance did not interest him; it was unlikely it would ever run again. "I understand," said Kate, finding the dignity not to argue; and with a scruffy nod from Clark as he rushed on, her days at *City* were over.

"So what are you going to do now?" Russ, remorseless, taunted as she finished her account. "Where do you think you'll be able to get a job?"

Kate hopped down from her butcher block seat and just before leaving the kitchen stated with simple ease, "Oh, I don't want to get a job."

"Then what the hell are you going to do?"

She was already in the living room when, without looking back, she announced, "I've already decided. I'm going to write a novel."

He shouted after her, "I'll believe it when I see it."

So a week later when he picked up the phone and the softly confident caller identified himself as Ross Clark, Russ thought the publisher was telephoning Kate. But Clark immediately set him straight.

"Let me get to the point," the publisher blurted out with hatchetlike deliberateness.

"Please," said Russ icily; this was, after all, the man whose purchase of the magazine had forced Max Fox to retire.

Still, Clark was taken aback by the young man's crispness. "I want to tell you straight off how impressed I am by the way you've spent your time since leaving us," he said, now covering his words with a mossy friendliness. "I started reading *Hitman!* and I couldn't put it down. It read like a novel."

"Thank you," said Russ quickly; the implications of that particular compliment always made him uneasy.

"I even gave a copy to my wife. And she loves it. You know, Russ, I made a mistake by letting you leave *City* so easily. I was wrong. We need your kind of writing in the magazine. We need someone who can take a routine story and get right down to the nitty-gritty. Who can make it come alive . . . seem real . . ."

"You mean, you need someone who can hoke it up," Russ interrupted.

Clark laughed. "Maybe that is part of what I mean," he said, as though sharing a happy secret. "But we both know the first thing a writer has to do is to get people interested, to make them want to keep on reading."

"I'll go along with that," Russ conceded.

"You can't sell magazines if people won't read what's in them," Clark went on in his agreeable tone. "And that's the business I'm in—selling magazines. Anyway, I think I've come across just the story that will give *City* the circulation push it needs. And it's a story that, I got to tell you this, made me think of you right away. Russ, you could write the daylights out of this one."

Clark now paused dramatically. "Russ," he asked at last, "have you been following the Son of Sam case?"

Five minutes later it was all arranged: Russ would rejoin the magazine as a free-lance correspondent assigned to cover the investigation into the ongoing Son of Sam homicides. His fee: an astronomical $1,500 an article. Still, the best-selling author, despite Clark's urging, refused to take a permanent position with *City*. He felt he owed at least that much to Max.

Clark, however, thought the young man's reluctance was prompted by another loyalty.

"I saw a copy of *People* the other day," he began after the deal had been completed and his new correspondent had agreed to have lunch with him later in the week. There was a measure of apology in his voice as he said, "I never knew you were married to Kate Warner."

"I'm not."

"Well, whatever, that you live together," Clark said with a twinge of embarrassment. "Look," he explained, "the trouble I had was with the column, not with her. In the old days, *City* had a small, select audience. Now we're trying to attract a broader readership. And if I'm going to get these new readers and keep them, there's no way I can justify giving space each week to a dance column. People want to read about other things. They want trends. Scoops. Gossip. They want to know what's the biggest and the best. And, I'll tell you this: Dance columns don't sell magazines. But I'm certain there are other areas she could write about for *City*. Why don't you have her call me?"

"Mr. Clark," Russ said sternly, "I have my career and Kate has hers. What happened between you and her doesn't affect me at all."

"That's fine with me," said Clark with relief.

And it wasn't until Russ had hung up the phone that he realized what he had just made public. From that moment on he had nothing to hide; and nothing to protect. Russ Lewis was only waiting for his chance.

EIGHT

THE LETTER WAS Ross Clark's idea. Russ thought he was joking.

"Sure," Russ told him as they sat in the office that had belonged (though without its veneer of creamy walnut paneling, tufted glen plaid couch, and matching Barcalounger) to Max Fox and Jonathan Trout, "I'll just begin 'Dear Son.'"

"No," Clark said after some earnest consideration, "that wouldn't be right."

"Fine," continued Russ, still going along with what he thought was the joke, "we'll make it more *Times*-y. You know, 'Dear Mr. Sam.'"

"That won't do, either," Clark firmly decided.

"I got it," Russ let out with a playful whoop, "'Dear Sonny.'"

"Too flippant. Why don't we just play it straight? Dear Son of Sam. Keep it formal. Classy."

"Classy? A classy letter to a homicidal maniac?"

"Trust me, Russ. It'll sell magazines."

So the week after Virginia Voskevichian—the fourth victim in the past two months—was shot dead by a .44 Charter Arms Bulldog revolver as she left a Queens discotheque, a letter addressed to "Dear Son of Sam" appeared on the cover of *City* magazine.

It was a public appeal inflated to the breaking point of good taste by its rousing sincerity; and, clearly, just a dash of cold-blooded empathy was considered a sufficient emollient:

"... I can imagine the dark monsters demonizing your soul, chasing you through the hot, mean streets of this city as you struggle against unleashing the only antidote to your horrible pain—killing young women. Yet if you come to me looking for the help you so desperately need, your life and the lives of who knows how many young, innocent women will be saved. ..."

The letter was signed in unembarrassed bold 14-point italic type by "Russ Lewis, Special Correspondent for *City* Magazine."

The Son of Sam never answered this or any of the two additional "calls to surrender," as the subsequent headlines heralded them, issued under the special correspondent's by-line during the next month. However, these letters did not go unnoticed.

A former *City* colleague, the vitriolic Dickensian who had ripped his salary check up in Clark's face rather than work for the man who had pushed Max Fox out of a job, sent a terse acknowledgment of Russ's new role as the magazine's special correspondent. "Nazi collaborator" was scrawled in thick red letters on the back of a postcard.

Then there were the comments by Matt Waldmann, the original "Hip Talk" columnist for *City* who had disappeared years ago only to bounce back these days as the gossipmonger for the Channel 7 Live at Five News Team: "In media circles the talk is all about how Ross Clark is tarting up everyone's favorite old bohemian, *City* magazine. This week's issue is a lurid case in point. Check out the cover where young best-selling author Russ Lewis—he made a bundle with *Hitman!* and if you didn't read the book, don't worry, you can catch the miniseries next fall—returns to his old radical stomping grounds with—do you believe this!—an open letter to the Son of Sam. Well, we all wondered when Clark bought *City* what audience he'd try to reach. Now we know—the homicidal lunatics."

While Kate, after the first letter appeared, left a note pinned to Russ's pillow: "Dear Son of Norman," it began, "I'll surrender to you if you agree to give me a fatter split on royalties (say 60-40?) than you gave that two-bit murderer Rico Pelligrini. It's only fair—I've killed more people than he did. And oh yeah, I want a percentage of the gross on all movie deals. . . ."

But when his second public letter was also featured on the cover of the magazine, Kate's good-humored indulgence hardened. "How can you sign your name to that drivel? You and Clark are daring that madman to go out there and kill someone."

"You're just jealous," he responded, wishing it were true.

And fortunately Max Fox, the judge to whom Russ ceded the ultimate verdict, was, the young man convinced himself, more amenable.

"What did you think of my letter?" Russ asked Max first thing as they sat down in Mario's a few days after the issue had appeared.

"I won't read that magazine."

"I thought maybe now that I'm writing for them you'd make an exception."

Max, his voice steady with conviction, not anger, said, "You want to write for Clark, I can understand that. But don't expect me to change the way I feel.

"Besides," Max continued, "who cares what I think anymore? Clark is running the show. He's the one whose opinion matters. Was he impressed with your epistle?"

"He was wild about it," said Russ, full of pride and enthusiasm. "He said it should sell tens of thousands of magazines."

"That's just what I imagined he'd say," Max said evenly.

BUT WHILE THE Son of Sam was giving Russ Lewis his chance, it was Mandy Reed who finally grabbed it for him.

Mandy was the staff photographer recruited by Clark to work full-time with his special correspondent. "I'm counting on you two to keep our readers on top of the biggest story in a decade—the tale of a city brought to its trembling knees by a killer with a .44," Clark explained after he had summoned Russ to his office to introduce Mandy. "And I think you should appreciate, Russ," the publisher went on with the same easy flowing graciousness he could just as neatly employ as a weapon, "just whom you're working with." While Mandy, in a slim dungaree skirt riding careless above her knees, sat silently, all crisp confidence, Clark detailed the highlights of her impressive résumé: Though only twenty-six, she had worked as a free lance for dozens of publications, won a handful of awards in the process, and—this is what brought her to Clark's narrow attention—recently made a splash with her book of endearingly madcap portraits of male rock stars and their children, *Pop Rocks*.

But during that summer of 1977 Russ Lewis would spend enough time with her to learn a few other things: Mandy rippled her sentences with emphatic "quite truly's" and "quite frankly's"; still wore, a superstitious accommodation, the same gold shell earrings that she had first put on as a senior at a New York private school; always made sure to get a bikini wax during the week following Memorial Day; on Sunday mornings drifted into reminiscences about the art history professor at Vassar who had returned to his wife; displayed a "Support the E.R.A." button on her Hunting World camera pouch; and, as the saying goes, had more movements than a Swiss watch.

Mandy would walk down one of the long fluorescent-lit aisles in the newsroom Clark had expensively redecorated as though she were prancing along a catwalk. Her thin summer skirts were as calculated as her candor; and when her stiletto heels tapped toward the picture desk you could just hear the drums going *boom! ladelada boom!* Mandy attracted quite an audience. And Russ—though she pretended never to notice—was one of her biggest, silently cheering fans.

Despite this ripe interest, Russ, disciplined more by shyness than any commitment to professionalism, walked a responsible line for the next awkward month. Mandy and he had a job to do; they were a team. And that's how they happened to be together late on a Saturday night in August at the Son of Sam task force headquarters off Main Street in Jamaica, Queens.

They were hanging out waiting for somebody to be murdered. Four victims, mostly unsuspecting couples trapped as they necked in their parked cars, had already been shot at point-blank range on hot weekend nights over the past two months; the *City* team did not want to arrive late for the gory spectacle that would, inevitably, surround the fifth. And they weren't alone. That summer a lot of newsmen passed a morbid weekend by keeping close to the red brick police station which served as task force headquarters. There was even a lottery: The reporters had a few bucks going on guessing the exact date and time when this killer would blow his way into the headlines again.

But on that Saturday night, just like the long hot night before, as the thick sweaty hours slowly passed and there was still no cry of alarm, it didn't seem likely that anyone who had put his money on the sixth of August would be a winner. Not that Russ felt much relief at the young lives being spared. His reaction was more self-centered: Clark wanted another Son of Sam story—"something new, something everyone will talk about," he had insisted—by Monday's deadline; what the hell could he come up with?

By midnight an anxious Russ, a new angle to the story still escaping him, was finding the precinct house, its air conditioning chugging along at a slow, institutional sputter, oppressive. There was no longer any point in talking to the task force detectives; they were only sharing the identical clues and confidential theories they had already revealed, despite their flattering displays of conspiratorial allegiance, in similar hushed voices to the rest of the notebook-toting press corps. Russ became convinced he would not find his story if he remained grounded at headquarters. The Son of Sam was somewhere out there; and so was the story. And with that realization, an idea started forming. He let his imagination run with it and then, excited, he tried it out on his sidekick.

"Mandy," he said after she had clip-clopped with him to a discreet corner yards away from the crowd of eavesdropping journalists and across from the detention cells, "I think I just might have found the angle we need."

"Shoot."

"That's dangerous talk in this place."

"Not as dangerous as some of the proposals I'm getting."

Russ, with a pang of admiration, had observed both cops and reporters coming on to her aggressively all evening. But he had assumed the little coquette with the wide ultra-suede blue eyes and the E.R.A. button had been enjoying it.

"Want me to defend your honor?" he offered, trying to affect a gallant air. But when she didn't even offer a smile to thank him, he played it serious: "No reason you should have to put up with that kind of crap."

"You're a dear, Russ. But, quite frankly, I think I can handle myself."

I bet you can, he imagined in a secret rush.

And, hurrying to avoid the disturbing places this quick fantasy might take him, he announced his plan: They would check out all the local lovers' lanes. Think of the pictures she could get—dark streets rumbling with danger and sex. And his interviews—what reckless thoughts would spill forth from adolescents sufficiently red-blooded and existential (just saying the word put an imitative strut in his voice that he never realized only Mailer could carry) to fumble through a couple of hours in the backseat despite the well-publicized threats of a murderer?

"These kids," he went on, "are playing chicken with the Son of Sam. It's a hell of a story. Are you game?"

"Quite frankly, anything has to be better than spending another moment in this stuffy place." She pantomimed her discomfort by tugging at the scalloped top of her sundress, fanning airless but otherwise apparently quite healthy breasts. It was a brief joke, but it confirmed a theory Russ had been avidly formulating all evening: His photographer wasn't wearing a bra. And it also was sufficient proof of its corollary: Mandy was game, all right.

So they were quickly off. The silver Porsche, the special correspondent at the wheel, the award-winning photographer with her sweet legs splayed over the black leather bucket seat, varoomed through the nighttime streets of Queens. (While a self-congratulatory thought passed through Russ's mind: He had come a long way from the days when Kate and he had sputtered late to the scene in his bedraggled Volvo.)

They drove across the borough, guiding the car down one quiet street after another, hunting for young lovers. It wasn't long before their luckless search had led them into the tranquil, tree-lined residential neighborhood of Forest Hills Gardens. Russ heel-toed it as he approached a stop sign. The streets, lined by huge, bulky Tudor homes, were dark and deserted.

"Seems pretty calm," he observed.

"Yes," she agreed. And as she faced him her pale blue sundress rode up high. A fleshy glimmer of tanned thigh was exposed. But she didn't notice. Or maybe she didn't care?

"Nothing suspicious at all." Except that Russ let his hand so very casually drop to her ripe knee.

But this didn't seem to alarm her. "No, it's pretty tame tonight." She made this sound like a complaint; and his blood raced.

"Doesn't look like we're going to come up with much of a story."

Mandy concurred with a disappointed nod. Then unconsciously, or so she made it seem, she crossed her knees; Russ's hand was delectably sandwiched.

And she offered a suggestion: "Perhaps we should pull over and wait for some kids to park," she said breezily. "You know, a stakeout."

Reluctantly he extricated his hand from between her knees. The car moved slowly down the empty block and pulled to the curb. A street lamp glowed through the latticed leaves drooping from a tall oak tree; and the silver car was lit by this diffused, shadowy light.

They sat there, feeling the silence, waiting for something to happen.

"What do you think the odds are on a couple of kids parking around here tonight?" he asked after a while.

"Quite frankly, not too great."

"For all we know, Sam himself could be driving by. And he must be angry as hell. Shit, his luck is as bad as ours tonight."

"You know, there's something in what you're saying," she began, throwing the reporter a curious smile. "Now just listen to me," she said as she raised a hand like an authoritative traffic cop at a red light. "Just think about this for a minute before you say no: Suppose we try to lure the Son of Sam to us."

"Lure him?"

"Well, if we were to . . . ah . . . pose . . . as a couple of kids parked in a car, quite frankly I don't think he'd know the difference."

"Oh, that's a great idea," Russ said with facetious enthusiasm. "And what are we supposed to do when he comes by? Do we get him to pose for some pictures? Or maybe we just capture and rehabilitate him. That'd be a good story, huh?"

"Come on, Russ. Do you have a better idea?" And the scent of her perfume as she swayed closer to him was meant to add some force to her argument.

"Mandy . . . this is crazy . . ."

"Strictly professional," she insisted, as she leaned toward him. Yet in an instant her swift tongue was dancing in little madcap circles about his ear. Then suddenly it was whirling like a dervish in his mouth.

"The things we do for a story," Russ managed to get out.

While one hand went off to discover that there was a lace border to her panties, the other contented itself with a nipple as long and as firm as the eraser on his favorite number 2 pencil.

". . . that's it . . ." she moaned.

His fingers softly at first, then with authority, invaded her.

". . . yes . . . yes . . ." she insisted.

"The dealer promised that the seats fold back," Russ offered provocatively.

Soon her thin dress was dangling from one of the cramped car's rear speakers; pink silk panties covered the other like a mask. She stretched out naked and abundant on the black leather seat.

". . . mmn . . . Russ . . . we got to make this look real. Come to me," she coaxed. "You've got to play, too."

It was a bit awkward climbing over the stick shift, but Russ manipulated his way into her waiting arms.

"Verisimilitude," he puffed out.

But even with her enthusiastic help it was quite a struggle in that tight space to get his belt undone. Russ worried he could not contort sufficiently to get his pants down. At that cumbersome moment he would have traded his Porsche for a Volkswagen van. Mandy, though, was not willing to give in to his despair. She pushed and pulled frantically at his clothes, attacking buttons and zippers wherever she found them.

There was only a momentary pause as she worked out the logistics of what to do with his seersucker trousers—out the window they went. She was making small quick noises like a wounded animal. Her eyes were lost, dreamy.

"Russ," she asked in a throaty moan, "what if he really finds us? What are we going to do if the Son of Sam catches us here?" There was excitement in her voice.

"Quite truly I'm afraid, Russ." Her voice trembled, but Russ doubted anyone genuinely terrorized could devote such single-minded attention to tugging at a pair of jockey shorts.

"Throw 'em out the window," he instructed.

The shorts flew into the street.

"Really, Russ," she wheezed, obviously enjoying cranking herself up, "what if he catches us? How . . . mn . . . mn . . . oh Russ . . . how will we explain that to Clark?"

"If he catches us, we won't have to explain anything."

Such horrible logic made her play harder.

"Forget about Clark," Russ asserted, hoping to hit the chord of apprehension which would cause all the remaining tricks this talented and energetic woman knew to tumble out. "We could wind up getting blown away. Shot dead. *Boom!* A .44 bullet straight through the skull."

His graphic warning ran through her like an electric charge. In a sweet instant Mandy was beyond caring about explaining anything to anyone.

Fortunately, the Son of Sam didn't strike that night. Neither of them had to make any excuses to Ross Clark. But Russ did need to come up with a story for Kate when he arrived home at 6:50 that Sunday morning.

"Another wild night?" she asked, drifting out of sleep as Russ crawled into bed next to her.

"What do you mean?" he challenged a little too quickly.

"Did that lunatic strike again, that's all?"

"No." Russ wished she would doze off; that would put an end to all this talking.

But Kate persisted. "Then what kept you so long?" She seemed casual enough.

"Oh, I hung out at the station house. You know, waiting for something to happen. Just a waste of time, really." He was determined to end this conversation quick. A yawn and then, "Good night, Kate."

He couldn't tell if she believed him or not. But she was soon asleep.

For a moment Russ wondered if he would have a hard time falling asleep. It was the first time in five years he had told Kate a serious lie; and it was the first time since a softball game a lifetime ago that he had made love to another woman. But he drifted off deeply in a matter of guiltless moments.

The next afternoon when he woke up refreshed after a long, thick sleep Russ still couldn't believe how easy it had been to lie to Kate. He was now convinced that what remained to be done would be even easier. But first there was an article to write. He climbed out of bed and went to his study. He sat at his desk, and then with meticulous concentration inserted a fresh piece of paper into his typewriter. It didn't take him long to start pounding out the sentences that would be next week's cover story for *City* magazine: "I Dared the Son of Sam to Come and Get Me."

NINE

"I THINK WE should talk."

"I'm not interested, Russ." Kate continued doing the Sunday magazine crossword puzzle.

"Well, you'd better be."

Kate didn't look up. She was stretched across the chesterfield couch in their living room; her naked feet pointed toward the window, while, up north, the magazine hid her face. Madame, Russ observed (making sure the up and down once-over served as the strop for his hostility), was in her Sunday lounging attire. She wore an oversized yellow terry-cloth robe, a relic of his summers at Camp Mohonk which had lain crumbled on the floor of the closet until she had salvaged it; while underneath was her customary—these days they no longer slept in the nude—nightgown: an extra-large Mickey Mouse T-shirt her sister had brought back from Disneyland.

He strode across the sun-lit room and, with the authority of a colossus, positioned himself above her cushioned head. She still didn't look up. This made his manner even more self-assured: "Kate, like it or not, you're going to have to listen."

Russ was not about to be put off. He had just returned from jogging around Washington Square Park; and while he had circled the concrete park, a wheezing, though steadfast, mantra had circled through his mind: Today is the day.

For the past two months Mandy and he had been enthusiastically, and a bit obsessively, going at it. Not that they were ever in love. It wasn't even infatuation. Still, it hadn't taken them long to make their groping way to this what-the-hell level of compulsive pleasure. Russ was also hooked on the intrigue, the clandestine thrill of his furtive game: the plotting to sneak away unnoticed from the magazine or his apartment; the complicated ingenuity involved in politely cutting short an interview because the photographer and reporter had other things on their minds;

or even the spontaneous decision to take advantage of a stray sliver of time in their busy days by rendezvousing at Mandy's apartment on East 63d. There, under a Magritte print of a man in a bowler hat, and co-cooned in her soft floral Deschamps sheets, they explored excess.

Perhaps Russ and Mandy were searching for a suitable consolation from something bumpy in their lives; or maybe they just liked to screw. The result—and Mandy was never a cause; only an effect—however was unarguable. Russ's 6 rms., 3 bths. in the "best" building in the Village had become strictly a hard-hat area. And this lazy Sunday morning, he had decided, was the time to finish the demolition.

Russ, with self-serving logic, deduced the proper way out of this mess was to level with Kate. It was a song of honorable innocence he convinced himself he would be singing. Yet Kate was shrewd enough to realize it was one of Blake's more hellish proverbs that set the tainted rhythm: "A truth that's told with bad intent/ Beats all the lies you can invent."

"We have to talk, Kate," he once more insisted.

After a moment she looked up from the puzzle. "Another one of your stories?" His credibility, even he had to concede, had lately become a bit too obviously tattered; there had been so many abrupt disappearances to explain. "Well, I'm not interested." Kate sunk her head back into the Sunday magazine.

"No more stories. It's time to tell the truth." His righteousness made him solemn.

"The truth?" She sneered. "Don't burden me with that." She flipped over on her stomach. This uncharacteristic display of athleticism was meant to proclaim the end of the conversation.

Russ, though, was just starting. "Look, Kate, I want to be honest."

"It's a little late for that," she whispered into the magazine.

"Goddamn it, you're going to have to listen." And just to make sure he grabbed the magazine from her hands.

"I don't have to do anything," she said proudly. Abruptly she rose to her naked feet, haughtily wrapped the colossal terry-cloth robe around her, and walked out of the room.

Standing alone in the living room, Russ realized he could have left it at that. He knew he was being presented with a crucial moment when what he decided to do next would rearrange his entire future. The choice was clearly there. Kate was giving him a chance to slow down; and, still loving, she was holding out the promise they could continue. But as the coin of fate flipped through the air, he, with a quick shrug, judged it was too late. Heads, Kate Warner won; tails, Russ Lewis lost. So in an act as symbolic as it was petty, he ripped the Sunday magazine in half; and chased after the woman he had loved.

Kate had retreated to the bedroom—this lady was a much cuter symbolist—for her last stand. She had plopped down in bed and huddled under their powder blue down quilt. She was lying there with her eyes closed, a woman wishing she could simply vanish, when Russ caught up with her.

He stood at the foot of the brass bed. His mind was made up: He would not take no answer for an answer. "Kate, we're going to have to talk."

She held her silence firmly.

"Okay," he gave in, "then I'll have to do the talking."

Once more she flipped over on her stomach. But what had previously failed was certainly not going to work now. Russ began stalking around the brass bed like a Comanche circling a wagon train. Her eyes were still shut, but he knew she could hear his Adidases squeaking on the wood floor. It was a war of nerves. Until he charged:

"Kate, I'm having an affair."

". . . so . . ." It was a soft tentative comment; and she remained lying on her belly, her face pushed deep into the quilt: hiding.

"So?" he mimicked, the word a furious curse. "Is that all you can say? *So?*" His voice, even his manner was pitched to suggest that he was the injured party. "Can't you do better than that?"

But it wasn't that she couldn't; Kate simply wouldn't.

So Russ was forced to continue: "This is some relationship. How can it last if one of us is sleeping with someone else?"

"Then stop fucking around. It's that simple." She still was prone, but all of a sudden there was a slap to her words.

"But what if I don't want to stop. What if I want to keep on"—he stumbled for a moment over her word, ". . . fucking someone else."

That did it. In a flash she was sitting up in bed. Her brown eyes were sparking. Her fists were clenched. Russ would get his fight after all.

"You think I don't want to sleep with someone else?" she challenged, her words meant to cut sharply, to hit back at his meanness. "You think my idea of Heaven is going to bed each night with someone who parades around in a smelly green track suit? With someone who leaves his dirty underwear on the floor for me to pick up? Don't you think I've come across men who look a hell of a lot more attractive than you? Don't you think there are a lot of good-looking men coming on to me all the time?"

Russ was taken by surprise: He wanted names, details. But he refused to appear wounded. "Then why don't you go off with one of these" —he made certain to snarl the offensive word—"*attractive* guys?"

"Because," Kate explained quietly, "I love you. We're getting married."

"We can't get married, Kate." And once more, full of menace, he began circling the bed.

"Why not?"

"It wouldn't work." The squeak of his sneakers followed him as, still circling, he started to pull his argument tight.

"Why?"

"How could I let my children have a grandfather who was a Nazi?" He hadn't intended to hurl that particular knife; for so long he had been pretending that the weapon was safely sheathed and, anyway, its edge was dull.

"He wasn't a Nazi, Russ. He was a pilot."

"Who just happened to fly for Hitler." And, once unsheathed, he twisted its still very sharp blade: "You remember Hitler? World War II and all that? Six million Jews who carelessly got in the way while some people like your father were only following orders?"

"My father didn't kill any Jews. He flew a plane and got himself killed. It's absurd to blame the Holocaust on him . . . or me, Russ."

But Russ, hot with venom, could only allow emotion to lead him. He changed his route, scurrying now in wrathful counterclockwise circles around the bed. And along the way he found his original argument.

"What about my affair?" Once again he made it sound as if it were Kate's fault.

"Do you love her?"

". . . No."

"Then I don't care. Keep her. Drop her. Don't tell me about her. Just let's get married."

"Where the hell is your pride?" Russ exploded. He pounded on the mattress. A Kleenex box jumped. He pounded again. Kate twinged, but said nothing.

"Goddamn it, Kate. Don't you have any pride?"

She was trying not to cry. "What do you want me to do, Russ? Just what do you want?" Her voice was begging; this was, he knew, her way of giving up.

So he quickly reviewed the terms of surrender. What did he want? Russ didn't want too much. He simply wanted what he felt his success had demonstrated he deserved: more than he had. But Russ didn't go into that with Kate. He said, "I think we should split up."

"Is that what you really want?" The world had been smashed in two before her; and it was so utterly tragic that, she knew, tears would be incidental.

"It's best for both of us." Russ still thought she might believe he really cared about what was best for both of them.

"You . . . you bastard. Just go to hell." Now she had found her resolve; there definitely would be no tears. Dry-eyed and calm, she announced, "I'll leave, Russ."

"You will?" He was astounded it had been this easy. And, suddenly, afraid.

But it was too late.

Kate issued her orders with the flat voice of an officer assuming command: "Just get out of the house. Let me pack up in peace. I'll be gone before it's dark."

"I'll help you . . ."

"Go to hell." Her lips were quivering, but they trembled with anger, with pain; not doubt. "The only way you can help me is by leaving me alone. Just get out of here and let me pack."

"You're sure I can't . . ."

"Get the hell out of here," she screamed.

So he left.

Even though it was Sunday Russ thought about going to the magazine. For a moment he even considered calling Mandy. Instead he got into the Porsche and drove. He headed, more out of instinct than desire, up the Saw Mill River Parkway toward his parents' house in Mount Vernon. Yet when he reached their block and saw their car in the driveway, he made a quick U-turn and rode back to Manhattan. By the time Russ returned to the apartment, it was evening. Kate was already gone. He looked for a note, but there was none. Her closet was nearly empty, though. The phone rang a couple of times that night; Russ let it ring. He just lay in bed. The TV was on but he wasn't really following it. And then his eyes noticed the clock on the nightstand: It was after one. He turned off the set and shut his eyes.

Russ was lying there when he realized this was the first time in seven years he had ended a day without saying, "Good night, Kate." But after an uneasy moment the thought faded and he was asleep.

RUSS'S FIRST CONCERN AS he left Clark's office was, what would Max say? It had been a momentous week: first Kate, now this. But, before his wonder could inflate into anxiety or, more likely, self-protective spite, Max beat him to it. He telephoned first. "I've got some news for you," Max said mysteriously when he reached Russ that morning with an uncharacteristic call to the magazine. "And wait till you hear the news I've got to tell you," Russ countered, genuinely amazed at such por-

tentous symmetry. Max suggested lunch and his friend agreed, rushing to
take control of the details. Russ, full of worldly authority, said he would
make a one o'clock reservation in his name at the 21 Club; and he hoped
Max savored the statement implicit in such a self-assured demeanor—his
days at Mario's were over.

Max was seated at the corner table in the barroom that Russ, trying
hard to be a regular, had become accustomed to and was halfway through
a martini by the time the young man arrived.

"Sorry," Russ said as he took his seat, waved at someone across the
room, and continued chattering nervously. "It's been quite a day. So
much to do. But you, probably more than anyone else, will understand.
But let me start at the top . . ."

"How about a drink?" Max offered kindly. "And then maybe we
should pick straws to see who goes first."

The drink helped. As did the fact that Max still hadn't mentioned
Kate. They ordered and when the waiter brought another round Max
asked, "Well, who goes first?"

Russ was at that instant terrorized: He knew Max was going to tell
him something about Kate.

But Max saw only courtesy in Russ's silence. "Fine," he agreed, "age
before youth. Here's the news . . ."

Don't let it be about Kate . . . don't let it . . . Russ prayed.

"I'm coming out of retirement, Russ."

"Jonathan hasn't convinced you . . ." But he was filled with relief.

"Nothing that drastic," Max interrupted with a laugh. "Something
entirely new. A job."

"That's fantastic. Congratulations."

"Well," said Max, quickly applying some of his customary detachment even to his own enthusiasm, "it's not really a job. It's more a title
than a position. A friend I know from the old White Horse Tavern days
has made it big. Started out as a lowly book salesman and, to steal a line
from ol' G and S, he sold all the books so carefully, that now he's the
ruler of the whole book company. He wants to give me an office and
make me a consultant. He thinks an old man like me might be able to
attract some young talent. The legacy of *City* and all that."

"And just where do you expect to find this young talent?" Russ
asked as he made his eyebrows jump in a facetious vaudeville flip; and
in case his friend missed the hint, Russ, never subtle, pointed a butter
knife at his own puffed-out chest.

"Thirty isn't young," Max countered with enough gravity to turn
Russ somber. "Besides, I want to discover new blood. Not tired best-
sellers."

"You couldn't afford me, anyway," Russ shot back; half in jest, and half in revenge. "And speaking of money, what are they paying to lure you away from sitting at home with Janey?"

"Oh, you know how it is with money . . ."

Russ nodded because these days he genuinely did; and Max, with paternal pride in his friend's budding fortune, nodded back: a circle of magnificent complicity. Then:

". . . when you don't need it, people are always giving you ways to make it. Twenty years ago Janey and I couldn't have believed my ever receiving the kind of salary they're offering. Except now I don't need it. And I don't want to be tied up. So I turned it down. I told him I'll give the job a try for a dollar a year. If I bring in a book, then we'll talk."

"You always wanted to be the bohemian Bernard Baruch."

"Except he was Jewish," Max joked, and instantly regretted the quip. This sort of humor was a little too revelatory for the older man's tastes; embarrassed, he hurried to turn the conversation onto other matters.

"Enough about me," he said tartly. "Let's get to your big news. Let's see how it stacks up against mine."

"Oh, what I got's pretty good," Russ said with a dry smile.

But Russ held back for a moment; he didn't know how to begin.

"I'm waiting," Max pressed, suddenly sounding like an annoyed old man.

Still, Russ could only ease into his news. "I've mentioned to you how pleased Ross Clark has been with the pieces I've done for *City*, haven't I?"

"Yes," the former editor acknowledged.

"Well, today I found out why: Clark said my Son of Sam coverage increased circulation by twenty thousand last month. But even before that the magazine was starting to move. Circulation's up by seventeen percent since . . ." Russ caught himself, and allowed his voice to trail off. He hoped a gentle euphemism would make amends: "Since the old days."

"Yes, the old days," Max repeated evenly. And then added, the words burning a hole in the conversation as if distilled from acid, "When we all know hardly anybody seemed to read poor *City*."

Russ realized he had backed himself into a difficult corner; there was only one way out. And he'd be damned if he'd crawl. So he went on, hoping he could remember to keep a neutral smile on his face:

"Anyway, Clark called me up yesterday and said he'd like to see me this morning. I met with him at ten fifteen today and at first I didn't know what he was driving at. Straight off, right out of the blue, really, he tells me that when he had originally purchased *City* from Vandermaeker,

he had never intended to run it. Clark swore—and I think he was telling
the truth, Max—that he had genuinely hoped you would have stayed
around to supervise things—"

"Thank God I didn't," Max interrupted, this time without a trace of
bitterness.

"Well," Russ continued, "Clark said he had purchased the magazine
because he had always enjoyed reading it . . ."

"So of course he put all his energy into tampering with it."

"Come on, Max, he hasn't changed *City* that much."

"Is that what you really believe?"

"Look," Russ decided, "we can debate that some other time. Just
let me finish my story. Okay?"

"Fine with me," Max said in that hard, distant voice he used when
he had had enough.

"So here's what happened: Clark told me he had just bought the
controlling interest in a movie company—you'll see it in tomorrow's
paper—and he now has other priorities more demanding than *City*—"

"He didn't sell the magazine, did he?" Max blurted out with genuine
interest. His mind was racing: How much could Clark have gotten for it?

"The truth is, Clark told me he had thought about selling it. Said
he even had a few pretty good offers. But he decided not to. 'I buy things,
I don't sell them,' he told me.

"Instead," Russ went on, a bit hesitant since he knew he was coming
to his punch line, "Clark said he had decided to appoint a new editor in
chief; he'd keep the job of publisher for himself. He wanted someone
who would respect the traditions of the magazine, but who also would be
comfortable with the changes he had started making. Someone who could
maintain the caliber of the writing, yet could still fill the magazine with
the sort of articles people would be interested in—"

Max cut in again: "Someone who'd be literate, but not too literary . . ."

"Maybe," Russ conceded.

But Max wasn't done: ". . . just as long as this someone made certain
the circulation continued to rise."

"Max," Russ said, throwing in the towel, "he offered me the job.
Editor in chief of *City* magazine."

"And did you accept?" The question had rushed out. Max had never
intended to sound so interested . . . or so anxious.

Russ hesitated. He only wanted his response to be solid, to appear
firm. Still, the delay was theatrical; and this, too, rubbed against the
older man's mood.

"Yes," he said at last. "As of eleven o'clock this morning I'm the
new editor of *City* magazine."

THE EXCUSE OF EATING was welcomed gratefully. Both men, as though there had been a pact, went after their food with voracious, single-minded attention. Russ, never a big eater, got through a half-dozen briny oysters, a thick steak, and then insisted on a piece of cheesecake for dessert. Max watched this performance (and he never doubted that this was a performance) and appreciated the tacit script directing his companion's showmanship: Russ's appetite was as expansive as his fellowship; their friendship, if the older man was willing, could survive.

Yet Max, glad for the handy escape the sheer physical activity of eating offered, remained confused by his reaction to the young man's news. Of course *City* was the past, a career, a lifetime ago. Still, he felt an unanticipated wicked twist in the force of the boy's announcement: it was as though Russ had been plotting. It was not that he feared seeing his life's work, *City* magazine, further traduced by Russ's inevitably glib collusion with Ross Clark; sixty-three-year-old Max, already feeling the intimations of his own mortality, possessed enough philosophy to understand and accept the ephemeral. Still, in a flash of instinct, he felt Russ's plot, however unconscious, was ultimately vindictive: The boy was not out simply to outdo him, Russ needed to usurp him.

Or, Max wondered as he took a calming mental step backwards, did he see too many curves when all there really existed was an aggressive, misguided straightforwardness: your typical success story.

However uncertain he was about what lay ahead, Max knew, though, that for the time being his control (and today, threatened by a suddenly full-grown Russ, he acknowledged the power stored in his side of the relationship) was secure. There were still judgments to be delivered— on Kate, on Russ's new job. So Max, also eating heartily, bided his time: He knew he still held the cards.

When the check came, Russ, once more flexing his muscles, signed for it. And Max, taking the boastful gesture as his operative signal, started in.

"Janey and I had dinner with Kate last night," he began.

"Janey?" Russ repeated, taken aback.

"Sure. Janey's always been fond of Kate. Thinks she's quite intelligent."

"She is." Russ felt as if he had been forced to concede a point.

"We picked her up at Wendy Parker's. She's staying with her, you know."

"I sort of figured that."

And then Max, playing his hand well, offered an account of the evening. He went long-windedly on about the South Village Italian restaurant, what everyone ordered, what everyone drank. Max, as though constrained by the manners of friendship, gave the impression he was trying to talk around the real issue. However, shrewd Max was simply waiting: He knew Russ, impatient and guilty, would lead the conversation into the rougher arena.

"How is Kate doing?" Russ finally asked.

"She's fine. Maybe a little sullen. But she says she's not depressed."

"Kate's not the type to be depressed."

"I agree. But of course Janey is worried. She says Kate's calm is merely an act."

"Isn't it that way for all of us?"

Max only nodded. He wanted to make it seem he was not the one leading this conversation down private paths. But, setting his trap, he didn't get up from the table. Instead he lit one of his big Dunhills. He sat back, puffing pregnantly; Russ watched the smoke rise above him until it formed a hazy halo around one of the miniature football helmets hanging from the ceiling.

Russ, as Max expected, could not hold back. "I guess Janey blames me?" he asked.

"Of course," Max agreed with a smile. "She blames you and she blames me. She blames all men. She thinks we're all self-centered. She thinks we're all no good. You and Kate splitting up simply confirms all the horrible things she believes about me. You just gave her a fresh opportunity to displace some of her resentment."

I could live with that, Russ thought. But by now he was in deep, his curiosity and insecurities leading him to just where Max was waiting: "Kate must have let me have it good?"

"No, she didn't. She didn't even want to talk about you. Janey, though, kept on trying to work her up . . ."

"It's good to know there's something one can always count on."

Max shrugged; years ago he had given up apologizing for his wife's behavior. And he went on: "But Kate wouldn't have any of it. Finally Janey got a bit exasperated at Kate's playing the stoic. 'After the way Russ has treated you, after the way he's led you on, why don't you admit you hate him?' my kindly wife prodded. But Kate didn't flinch. Kate said she didn't hate you and she didn't want to discuss it. So that was that. Until we were walking back to Wendy's and I asked her, I mean she is a friend of mine, 'What are you going to do now that things are over between Russ and you?' And you know what she told me? She said, 'It's not over until I believe it's over.' "

"It's over," Russ said with what he hoped sounded like conviction.

"That's what I told her."

"Thanks, Max." You shit.

"She became enraged. She told me I would never understand. So I dropped it. Let her have it her way if it makes things easier." Max sounded bewildered, almost amused.

I could also live with that, Russ thought. So, dangerously naive, he figured in for a dime, in for a dollar.

"What do you think, Max?"

Max sent a whiff of smoke across the table as he considered how to phrase his answer. Then he took the cigar out of his mouth and bit down hard on his lower lip; perhaps it was an unconscious gesture, perhaps he was censoring a thought. He was locked in that pose for a long, silent moment. Then he spoke.

"You know I'm very fond of Kate . . ."

"I hope so." And at that moment Russ wished he could talk, as he would years later, in the third person. That he could tell Max, impersonally and objectively, about his life with Kate.

"Well, I am."

Max waited until he was certain Russ appreciated the pause. He was trying to make this seem very difficult. "To tell you the truth, and I've always thought this, Kate was never right for you. You really have very little in common. You two are too different."

Russ felt very relieved. He stood up from the table and confided in the man he thought was simply his friend, "I'm just sorry it took me so long to realize how different."

"And I'll tell you something else," Max continued amicably, as they walked through the glass doors at the front of the restaurant and waited under the portico for a taxi, "I think Clark made a good choice. He picked the right man for the job." The words were spoken so politely that it was understandable Russ thought his companion was praising him.

Free of self-reproach, the equilibrium of his personal achievement restored, Russ returned to the office full of his authority: The entire magazine, down to even the incongruously suburban glen plaid on the Barcalounger where he would now rest *his* feet, was no longer, as was his habitual adolescent way, a hypothetical possibility to moon about. The challenge had become real.

Except that night as Russ, still charged with the newness of his commission, lay alone in bed and thought about what Max had said, about Clark's judgment, and about the many ways Kate and he were so different, he suddenly understood what the older man had really meant. He suddenly understood that Max Fox had sat there at lunch and, with suitably understated irony, offered up a mercilessly condemning assessment of his misguided values and shabby character.

He felt totally deflated; but as he continued replaying Max's loaded words his mood chafed into anger: Hadn't Max, intent on making a fortune, sold out him and the rest of the *City* staff? Hadn't Kate, so prideful, yet so complacent, also let him down? Their fall was not just inevitable—it was deserved. Russ made a mental resolve: He, a winner, would have the last laugh.

Yet that night Russ Lewis finally had trouble falling asleep.

PART IV
The Dream of Romance

ONE

SO THEY DRIFTED APART. Eighteen raw months passed before they could pretend life was once more being lived at full pitch. But this, too, was only a parenthesis between what was and what was to come: The complex valence of the past, filigree often as transparent as a spider's web, yet just as intransigent, just as menacing, held true.

KATE MOVED further downtown. A new world; a new vocabulary: a return to old, familiar truths. She had discovered in the commercial, ocherous brick depths of lower Manhattan a defunct shoe factory that was being "recycled" into residential lofts. Recycled, though, was the developer's gentrified verb, an intransitive come-on to the urban pioneers. The reality was much cruder. The rent was startlingly cheap, but you got what you paid for—there was no kitchen, bathroom or, for that matter, plumbing, heating, electrical outlets, or even walls. That didn't put off Kate. This ramshackle, inchoate homestead intrigued her; as did the spiritual adventure of creating a home. She rushed about her task with single-minded devotion, as though with this placatory energy she could create a new world to replace the one she had lost. Her jeans became paint-splattered. Her speech filled with words like "raw space," "square feet," and "sheetrock." Her esoteric, newfound knowledge delighted her: where to rent a Black & Decker high-speed floor sander, the name of a reliable moonlighting electrician, a sculptor who did tapering. It was all very consoling.

Her new, rough home made her feel emancipated, free of the compromises Russ, so contradictory in his ambitions, so unassuageable in his worldly aggressiveness, had made her witness; and endure. In time she became comfortable with a personal feeling that Russ's outlook was too narrow, his values too tangential: He had really never passed the test.

There were new bars. She made new friends. She flirted. Yet for reasons she did a remarkable job in keeping herself from exploring, Kate never allowed these attractions to gather the momentum required for a serious affair. It was only when she convinced herself, with typically detached logic, that she was denying a necessary part of her feminine nature, that she was missing out on what was potentially a new adventure, then she allowed herself to spend a night with someone. And so another giant step was taken—the past, she was certain, receding under the pull of the present.

"No more heel-clicking doormen for me," Kate boasted to a skeptical Max who had come downtown to look at her floor in its initial decrepit state; from his impertinent glances one would never have thought he had once lived in a single narrow room improved only by its view of a cemetery and a collection of broken clocks. "Here's where I belong. Struggling artists. Unknown writers. A community. Back to life on the edge." And then a dig: "Like *City* was in the old days."

"Sure, and I imagine you'll put the tub in the middle of the room for old times' sake," he said, attempting to debunk her enthusiasm.

"That's not a bad idea," said Kate genuinely.

"Oh, it's all a great idea. Very gung-ho and bohemian. But how are you going to afford it?"

Kate, the practical, pragmatic immigrant, had it all figured: She would construct a wall down the middle of the floor and sublet half the space at three times the rent she was paying for the entire loft; therefore, if she amortized—where the hell was she picking up these words, Max wondered—the bank loan for the fixtures and construction over the next five years, her monthly rent would come to $97. "I'll do one free-lance article a month to cover my expenses and the rest of the time, who knows? Maybe I'll work on a novel," said Kate, making it sound so easy.

When Max, as much troublemaker as liaison, told all this to Russ, the new editor's reaction was one of prideful injustice. "Ninety-seven bucks? I pay more than that each month to garage my Porsche."

"That was always the problem between you two," said Max with I-rest-my-case solemnity. It wasn't just that he saw less of Russ these days, but also that his feelings were turning: Max felt he had to get one in for Kate; if not for himself.

But when cornered, Russ turned mean and petty. "If she's so happy downtown, why doesn't she take the rest of her stuff out of the closet in my place? I could damn well use the space," he said with almost enough conviction to persuade himself he wasn't being irrational.

"Oh, I'm certain Kate will get around to removing the rest of her clothes from the apartment," Max said equably. Yet in a premonitory flash he marked Russ's words. And it was only this mental vision, a faith in the poetic vindictiveness that lay in store for the young man, that restrained Max from immediately adding, "Don't worry, Russ, the time will come. You'll get your chance to be sorry."

AS FOR MAX, his life, for so long knocking about cramped corridors following his leaving the magazine, was beginning to open up. Even Jonathan, who had gained a gross fifty pounds throughout the nervous months of his brooding retirement and seemed bogged down as much by this new weight as by the unrequited past, noticed and envied the changes in his former partner. Max's dollar-a-year job as a publishing consultant was more than just revitalizing, it was transforming. The shy, defiantly privatistic editor who had sneaked out the back door rather than greet Bobby Kennedy had grown self-assured. It had taken Max Fox sixty-five reflective years, the victory of a realized vision and the reassuring cushion of a fortune, but he had finally succeeded in finding an attitude more naturally suited to his inquisitive nature.

The irony, of course, was that for all his trouble, his life, like Kate's, had not taken a very wide trip. Rather, he had gotten back to where he had started: The role he now played as a publishing consultant was not significantly different from the youthful posturing which characterized his aimless early Village days. He was still the intellectual handyman, a bar stool referee overseeing the human condition. Except the mind-set he now brought to the task ran easier: Cynicism was replaced by dry amusement; and his brittle detachment, while more resilient, gave way to a critical if not always entirely objective perspective.

The essential, the altering difference for Max was, after all those years, he finally felt a growing sense that he had earned the right to judge. As so many people were constantly telling him, he was the founder of *City* magazine—the man who had invented (more or less, he knew) the new journalism. This rightful ascent to a place in the real world was further reinforced, he could not help but feel, by the fuss his new colleagues made over him at the weekly round table editorial meetings: the respectful anticipation when a senior editor called upon Max Fox's reflective voice for ancillary judgment; or when an ambitious junior called conspiratorially for back up from his natural ally, the presumably still rebellious eminence grise.

Max got off on playing this emeritus role at the publishing house, cultivating a deliberate, but still instinctive image: the millionaire founder of *City* magazine whose spacious office was open to anyone's problem or idea. And it worked. He quickly learned that in the rigid declensions of business (and publishing at this house's determinedly best-seller pitch was certainly big business), the two cents he might add to any editorial discussion was multiplied a thousandfold by reverential inflation.

With such immediate respect and nothing at risk—not even a salary —he no longer felt it necessary to live life totally as an observer, the General Max of old, barricaded behind his desk as he reviewed the reports from the front. He emerged from decades of doubts and struggles with an eagerness to explore. The skeptical distances he had put between himself and daily events gradually narrowed. Reasons suddenly existed for involvement, activity, expeditions. Appointments dotted his schedule. It had all come late, this he still volunteered, but no longer with a miserable sigh; instead, he ventured to make the most of it before, he realized with a wry and long-repressed Jewishness, the punch line that was inevitably waiting for each of us at the end of the cosmic joke was delivered.

Yet as the tempo of Max's life increased, so did, by corresponding leaps and bounds, his wife's remoteness. The scraping tumult of their marriage had worn Janey's character thin. Understanding had been wasted years ago. To try to think through Max's bemused yet hectic immersion in events would have required a truce. But one was never offered; and Janey, battle-scarred, responded with sharp and relentless derision.

Max was branded by his wife as "a silly old goat." The sturdy row of engraved invitations paraded each week across the mantel in his den was mocked with a militant disdain; and every handwritten r.s.v.p., for Max, in public at least, was always *comme il faut* the gentleman, proved further confirmation of his social fawning. Or just let him try to float across the dinner table a stray remark about his new job, a wisp of office gossip about the size of a printing or the heft of an author's advance. Here was the call to arms that Janey awaited. Eagerly, she gouged away at her husband, chastising him, the old bohemian, for allowing his values to be overrun by the venal uptown world of commerce.

So while Max moved about town reconnoitering new varieties of foolishness, as he reversed years of adamant refusals and showed up at cocktail and dinner parties, Janey held out. Steadfastly she refused to accompany him. She insisted the social whirl did not interest her. More accurate, though, would have been an admission that she still did not feel ready for it: the years had brought her the benefits of her husband's success, not his confidence.

It further chafed at Max that his hosting a dinner party in his own splendid apartment—one of the self-made man's unfulfilled wishes—was never a possibility. Janey's undeclared argument remained too heavily drawn: To be either hostess or mistress would be capitulation. Max remained unmollified; and he no longer troubled himself with the reasons for his wife's behavior. When their son went off to college, Max suggested, laying the blame on his insomnia, it might be easier for Janey if he slept in the boy's bedroom. She did not protest; and they stumbled into the tight arrangement of separate bedrooms. Once that happened, their entire lives, as Max had wished, became secrets from each other.

Max also manipulated Russ, learning from him; and, at the same time, gathering evidence for the still unacknowledged case the founder of *City* was building against the friend who had so readily succeeded him. These days Max grew very interested in how Russ managed to do all his chasing around, how the youth managed to shuffle the different combinations of new women into his week. Sure, Max made a running joke of it: "Better tell the doorman whom to expect tonight, Russ. We wouldn't want him to let the wrong one up." Russ, boastful without ever possessing the simple, unjudgmental love of women so natural to the true tale-telling playboy, found himself goaded by Max's interest: He played vulgarly to this very curious audience. And there were other minor—though equally odd—interrogations: Max, making it seem like a sudden whim, wanted to know the trendier restaurants people were frequenting these days; or whether his tie was too wide; or was it really that expensive an indulgence to rent for just a careless evening's fun one of those limousines you see all over town; or was Paul Stuart a suitably decorous alternative to staid old Brooks Brothers.

The clues were mounting; but who would have guessed such knowledge, like the pleasure of confidence, would be, so very late in the game, a dangerous gift?

RUSS, MEANWHILE, guided by as preposterously simple a philosophy as the desire to succeed, set about to institutionalize his position as editor of *City*. Like Jonathan Trout's a generation earlier, his office became festooned with charts: professionally printed evidence (unlike Jonathan's amateurish handiwork) of the magazine's seemingly irrepressible growth. But even Russ would have admitted, if anyone dared or even cared to challenge him, the magazine's increasingly popular appeal was accomplished by a slick comedown in its aspirations. Russ, with an easy inventiveness that he was beginning to find disturbing, boosted circulation with such cover stories as "The Ten Best Chocolate Chip Cookies in New York," "How Much Do TV Weathermen Really Know?" and "The Lawyers Lawyers Go To When They Want to Sue." So much trendy nothingness, he knew; yet the magazine's circulation was at an all-time high: success!

And his own roll continued across the board: The miniseries of

Hitman! was being filmed in the streets of New York; a new paperback edition of the book with glossy pictures of the stars on the cover was ready for release; and Russ had signed a contract for a "six-figure"—to use the imprecise phrase his publisher found so handy to convey the bigness of any deal—advance for a sequel. This new work, *Targets!* (the publisher also insisted that the title ring with Russ Lewis's trademark exclamation point) would be the other side of his first book: the notorious stories of the corrupt and powerful men who were rubbed out by the mob. "Here's hoping Lincoln was wrong," said Edwin Brewster, his editor, when the deal was consummated in the most powerful booth (I've made it! The sweet seat of success, Russ rejoiced) in the Four Seasons Grill Room. "We're gambling you can fool all the people all of the time."

Russ had become, and not just by his own inflated estimate, quite a catch. And, as Max had picked up on, he was eagerly pitching whatever he had. Mandy had been discarded long ago. Even with all her spirited dedication to the task, she could not distract him from inextricably associating her with the woeful end of his life with Kate. He put up with some lonesome nights alone. But there were, in time, a flock of others; it was all very new . . . and very heady.

But, most surprising of all, just as he was midway through his second year at the helm of *City* magazine and the anxious editor was driving across town to an appointment where he hoped to convince an auditor from the Internal Revenue Service that his coal mine deduction was justifiable, his Porsche got caught in traffic on the corner of 52d Street and Sixth Avenue, and Russ Lewis fell head over heels in love.

TWO

REBECCA HOLLAND, wearing a knapsack and a bundle of colors, was standing on the corner of 52d Street trying to hail a cab.

Sitting behind the wheel of his Porsche, Russ Lewis studied this tableau for a thoughtful instant, then poked his head out of the sunroof and called, "Running away from home?"

She giggled delightedly, but took only a cautious step toward the car. Then: "Oh, it's you. For a moment I didn't recognize you."

Why should she? They had spoken only once before: a quick nice-to-meet-you in the midtown offices of the production company which had purchased *Hitman!* Russ was calling on the director who had "come in from the coast," just as Becky, a ceramic mug emblazoned with the face of a long-whiskered cat in her hand, was cutting through the lacquered Art Deco-ish reception area to the coffee urn. Their paths intersected, and the dowdy, cashmere twin-setted secretary guiding the author to the bicoastal honcho's inner sanctum had no polite choice but to make the necessary introductions. Not more than thirty seconds of hellos before they continued on their separate ways.

"That's an attractive girl," Russ observed; it was really just an attempt to strike up a bit of a conversation with the dour matron as she, with an intimidating sense of mission, led the way down the long corridor to Mr. Big's. Her response, however, held a curt warning: "Miss Holland's a reader."

"Uh huh," Russ answered; his deflated tone clearly a pledge to keep the barbed wire tightly coiled around the class barriers of success. And in a moment he was up to his Ranger oxfords in scarlet carpet as a man with a glistening bald head and a Buddha-like paunch blew him a kiss, motioned for his guest to sit on a legless couch, and attempted to win the new arrival's sympathies by executing steady encores of woefully raised eyebrows—all without once interrupting his phone conversation with, Russ was provided sufficient clues to understand, someone in London. Russ jumped into all this showbiz; and the attractive reader did not even linger as a memory.

But trapped solidly in a maze of midtown gridlock on his way to the IRS two weeks later, his head stuck out of the sunroof like a caged giraffe's as he called to the knapsack-toting girl on the corner, Russ saw something.

Oh, given the benefit of only a similarly brief glance other better-traveled judges might have dismissed Rebecca Holland as just another of a pretty type: the tallish, outdoorsy blonde with the big blue eyes and the terrific, promising legs. While a longer, closer perusal might simply emphasize how far short she fell from the one-dimensional freeze-dried perfection that has been enthroned as the haughty ideal by the reigning fashion magazines: Becky's thick hair, truly more a livid scrappy tawny than a shiny starlet blond, took off too wildly, the handfuls of bronzed ringlets falling willy-nilly: she always had the careless, refreshed look of a girl caught in a sudden summer shower; and the stray soft whispers from this marvelous mane twisted delicately along the baby's pink nape of her neck and skipped across a surprisingly deeply lined brow (yes, worry lines at twenty-four; however, Becky insisted with a convincing lack of vanity, she was proud to inherit the creased Holland forehead); and her nose, classical in shape and happily freckled from the sun, but still perhaps too big: a solemn presence; and her lips, certainly not the generous flesh of certain fantasies, yet since she had a habit of frowning intently while she mulled over an opinion or even followed the passing drift of a conversation, they seemed that much tighter, almost sullen in their thinness; and even her eyes, though there's no denying the force of their bold blueness, were deeply set, ominous, more messengers of outspoken candor than the lazy neutrality that rests politely in a deb's gleam. Yet, it was the powerful combination of these flawed traits that made her special, that gave her the uniqueness and subtlety which so shook Russ Lewis: True beauty rests in character.

There was also something else to Becky that rounded out the wallop of this first encounter: Her ricocheting laugh shoved away restraints. More: Her vivaciousness was electric; these sharp currents—of course they were as brazenly sexual as a majorette's strut—jolted through his very flesh.

So Russ—in just an instant!—decided she was beautiful. Beautiful? In his mind the meaning—also in that incredible instant!—loomed clear and irresistible: ram-hard excitement; and, along with that challenge, considerable terror—something beyond his reach he had to possess: a fitting consort.

Even from those first moments, though, Russ (foolish, but rarely naive) saw it all. Becky may have been a natural beauty but she was no novice. Her style was all very calculated. Scientists at MIT had theorized, Russ had read, that the human eye can distinguish between twenty thousand different colors and, taking Becky in, he now could believe it. She had set out to mix bright magic and, with what Russ felt was magnificent success, had knocked the spectrum for a loop. That morning she must have gathered up all the more flamboyant pieces of her wardrobe, tossed the bundle high, and, part of the experiment, let the kaleidoscope fall where it might.

But Russ was convinced she wore it well, from the white bucks on her feet to the red-winged Piper Cub barrettes barnstorming through her golden hair. A wonderfully spirited look: the sheer, shocking pink blouse (he now understood the sly hint in the radio forecaster's voice when he had described the weather as nippy); the glorious and bouncy chartreuse skirt with a purple sash wrapped round and round a narrow waist; bright, signal-yellow knee socks on her jogger's gams; the sky-blue cotton blazer, a mannish touch, yet decorated by a lapel pin showing—a grim warning? Or was it a campy appeal?—a broken heart patched with a Band-aid; and, of course, the bloated kelly green knapsack strapped onto her back.

That afternoon poking his head out of the sunroof at this blaze of exuberant colors Russ was suddenly poised on the edge of obsession. With just one short sentence, he took the first step toward tumbling over that rational border.

"You need a lift?" Russ asked.

"I sure do. Not much chance of getting a cab in this traffic."

With an easy efficiency Becky disengaged her knapsack, chucked it behind the black leather bucket seat, and then climbed into the car.

"Where you heading?" he asked.

"To the shoemaker's. Eighty-first and Amsterdam."

That was nearly thirty blocks uptown. On the West Side. Russ's appointment was across town. On the East Side. In ten minutes. So much for his appointment.

"I've been putting this off for months," she went on as Russ stared ahead, anxious for the traffic to part. "And just my luck that I had to pick this lunch hour to go to the shoemaker's."

"Look at this," she said with a bemused shake of her head, her wild hair flying about the small car until Russ was certain he could feel the flick of so many strands against his heart. Becky reached behind the seat and opened the knapsack. It was packed with shoes. She grabbed one from the top of the sack and offered it to him.

"A penny loafer for your thoughts." And she applauded her small joke with a loose volley of giggles.

It wasn't that funny, but her high, easy laughter was so joyfully unrestrained that Russ had to join in. When all of a sudden—and for a puzzled moment Russ wasn't sure that he had heard correctly—she purred like a cat.

"Excuse me?"

"A silly habit," she said without any embarrassment. "I sometimes think I'm a cat."

"Oh," said Russ, playing cool and a little on guard. "Feel free to meow to me anytime."

So Becky worked another angle. She checked the Rolex on her wrist and announced, "Doesn't look like I'm going to make it to the shoe-maker's and be back at the office by one. Not in this traffic." Her message was clear: the blame was Russ's.

She continued: "Maybe I should get out and at least get some lunch. Though I sure wish I could have made it to the shoemaker's today."

Her wish was Russ's command. "Hold on," he instructed. In a flash he had neatly swung the Porsche out of the stalled crosstown street, up onto the sidewalk, shifted into fourth, raced across a pedestrian plaza, and guided the swift little machine into the free-flowing traffic heading uptown along Sixth Avenue.

"Me-ow!" she screeched.

As they drove to the shoemaker's Becky chatted avidly about the preoccupying manias in her life—cats and sailing. "Of course I also care about movies," she explained, "but that's work."

Russ followed her conversation, laughing when she laughed, and even crossing his heart—she had insisted—after she had made him prom-ise to try to think of a suitable name for her new kitten. Mostly, though, he looked at Becky, and waited for the proper moment to ask her out.

The right moment didn't come, so Russ had no choice but to grab the final one. They had already pulled up in front of the shoemaker's.

"Well, thanks for the ride," Becky said as she opened the car door.

"My pleasure."

She was on the street and walking off, the green knapsack bouncing on her back. It was now or never. Once more he poked his head through the sunroof and tried his luck: "Would it be okay if I asked you to dinner sometime?"

She turned and smiled.

That was all the encouragement Russ needed. "How about tonight?" It was Friday and he already had a date, but what the hell.

"Why don't you meet me at seven outside my office." And then she disappeared into the shoemaker's.

THEY HAD DINNER in a candle-lit Italian restaurant off Lexington Avenue, but before the night was over Becky had left a trail of her delicious ruby lipstick on the rim of champagne glasses across Manhattan. They hit bar after bar; and they grew happily sloshed, but not talked out. Spinnakers and the kitty without a name and writing books and running a magazine: an incongruous, yet compelling affinity of ambitions.

When they stumbled out of the Bemelmans Bar in the Carlyle Hotel at a little after 3 a.m. Russ decided Becky was having a difficult time keeping her white bucks in a straight line, so he put a supportive arm about her purple-sashed waist. She returned the gesture, her hand reaching under his jacket, gripping his shirt, a forceful, kneading presence. He pulled her even closer. Their shoulders rubbed together as they walked down Madison Avenue.

"What a funny name for a bar. Bemelmans, schmelmans," she sang out.

"Actually it's named after the artist who did the murals. Ludwig Bemelmans."

"Really?" She sounded amazed.

Only now did the other woman intrude. It was as if Russ could hear Kate Warner's authoritative no-nonsense voice beginning to lecture: Ludwig Bemelmans, 1898 to 1962; Austrian-born American artist, illustrator, and author . . .

But instead the voice he now heard was Becky's. "Oh, Russ is there anything you don't know?" she crooned. So, suddenly feeling beyond the reach of the past, he leaned into her, his hands greedily pressing the ribs beneath her soft blouse, and kissed her with all his liberated heart.

". . . oooh . . ." she sighed, the sound almost theatrical, a contrived Eros.

Russ, easily flattered, kissed her again: a vow. Her strong hands clasped about his waist as if she were afraid of floating away: her acknowledgment. They held each other, wrapped tightly for a long moment. And at last she spoke one word of soft contentment—"Meow."

Later they circled the long way through the park toward her apartment on West 79th Street. She pressed a button on the dashboard and the sunroof opened. The full moon lit up her face and the wind ran unruly through her hair like an impetuous lover's fingers. It became chilly; from time to time, her hand crept deep into his blazer pocket to keep warm.

Russ double-parked across from the ivy-covered brownstone where she had a studio apartment.

"I had just the best time," she said.

"Me too."

Russ felt it would be silly simply to kiss her good night. He wanted to spend the night. And the next day. And the day after that. "Can I come in for a nightcap?"

She looked up through the open roof as though searching the stars for an answer. When none came, Russ pressed further. "What's the matter? Cat got your tongue?"

She laughed, not her limitless giggles, but in a more reflective, even wary way. Her voice fell serious: "Not yet, Russ. It's too soon."

She saw the profound disappointment covering his face and, a placatory gift, added, "I don't know if I could control myself if you came in."

"Would that be so bad?" he begged.

"Oh, you . . ." She was her old high-flying self. "Promise me you'll call me tomorrow."

"Cross my heart." The editor of *City* magazine made, to his amazement, an X over his heart.

Russ moved to kiss her once more, but she pecked him quickly on the cheek and hurried out of the car.

"Hey," he called after her. "I don't know your phone number."

Becky ran back to the car. "Give me your hand," she ordered.

As she fished a tube of lipstick from her purse, Russ obediently stuck his hand out the window. Seven red numbers were written across his palm.

"Remember you promised to call me tomorrow," she yelled, running from the car to her front door.

"You can count on it." And then he watched as she waved once more before quickly vanishing inside the building.

Russ, too giddy to sleep, was back at his apartment trying to decipher the smudged phone number Becky had lipsticked onto his palm when the phone rang. Who could be calling at 4:10 in the morning?

"Meow," said the caller; and Russ immediately had his answer.

"I was hoping it would be you."

"I just wanted you to know I've decided on a name for my kitty."

"Go on."

"Bemelmans."

And then she hung up.

THREE

WEEKS, WITH BECKY leading the merry way, scooted promiscuously by. So solid in her devotion to a good time, she coerced Russ into demanding one, too. Piles of American Express receipts, evidence reviewed in the thudding thickness of hung-over Bloody Mary mornings, soon became their only connections to the foggy nights before. Yet, as in any courtship where from the outset it is apparent the stakes are real, the battle for control was quickly declared. There were so many painful times when they parked outside her brownstone until Becky, always giggly yet firm, rolled out her trump card: "Why, I don't think I could behave myself if you came in. Now be a good cat and call me as soon as you get home."

Then one evening, the city sticky and redolent with the heat of summer, Russ picked her up outside her office and Becky asked if she could stop at her apartment before dinner.

"Sure. But you don't have to change."

"I'm not going to change, silly. I just want to . . . you know, uh, pick up something." She smiled like a child holding onto a secret and then laughed. A skittish laugh.

On the way uptown she did not say a word; and Russ was gentleman enough to pry silently into her intentions. He kept his suspicions to himself; and her mysteriousness, he was convinced, confirmed them.

"Just double-park," Becky said. And, with genuine fluster, she explained, "I won't be long."

Within minutes she was back in the car. Russ, though, kept his emotions at arm's length. He would follow her lead. "We could go to an Italian place on the West Side." Becky didn't answer. "Or maybe French? There's a place in the Village down the block from me."

"French would be nice."

They were near the restaurant when he tried, "I could look for a parking space. But I guess it would be easier to put the car in the garage across from my building."

"Whatever's easier," she agreed.

He didn't rush things at the restaurant, either. The rich meal, waxy and heavy in the looming heat, dragged on; when one bottle of champagne was empty, a slight nod of his head caused a fresh one to appear. After the check was paid, he continued to circle around the obvious. "Feel like a walk?" Becky let the suggestion run by, so he said, "Or we could go up to my place. I think I have some brandy around."

"A brandy would be nice."

Of course there was no brandy in the apartment; there was, though, a Billie Holiday cassette and a couple of Heinekens.

His first kiss was small and gentle. The second was also brief, controlled. But a rhythm, a soft, steady tattoo, was building, and they were moving into it. The wetness of lips, of tongue. The surprise of a sudden bite. He was becoming greedy.

"I could get the car out of the garage," he said, breaking away, but not letting go, "and take you home." She combed the fine black hairs of his eyebrow with a finger, her touch full of wonder: it was as if she had discovered this silky, curving ridge for the first time. "Or you could spend the night."

"I'd like that."

Russ took her by the hand and led her to the bedroom. He was eager to obliterate a night, no, weeks of restraint. Yet at just the instant when he was allowing himself to become easy, sweet, and comfortable with her intimidating flesh—the skin at the very ends of his fingertips was pitched to her mood like the finest of antennae—he realized Becky, without even a murmur, was pulling away: a sudden dislocation.

"Come on, baby, what's the matter?" he probed.

"The sheets."

"The sheets?"

"They look dirty, Russ. When was the last time you changed them?"

"They're fine, Becky. Really."

"I have this thing about clean sheets, Russ. I hate sleeping in a dirty bed. Can't we change them? It'll only take a minute."

It didn't take a minute. Becky also had this thing about hospital corners. And about a smooth top sheet. And about the spread being tucked in, too.

"There, isn't that better," she decided after her meticulous handiwork had stretched the sheets as tautly as desire was stretching Russ's sensibilities.

"Fine," he agreed. "Let's go to sleep." Impatient, even clumsy now, he grabbed her arm and tried to pull her onto the immaculate bed.

She screamed: "Russ." And then she shrieked: "I can't go to bed like this."

"It wasn't what I had in mind either."

"No, seriously. I can't sleep without a nightgown. Isn't there a nightgown around?"

"That kinky I'm not . . . even when there's a full moon."

"Don't be a silly cat. Didn't, you know, what's her name, have a nightgown or something?"

"Kate took her Mickey Mouse T-shirt with her when she left."

"What about a pair of pajamas, then?"

"Kate didn't wear pajamas."

"I'm serious."

So Russ found a pair of pj's his mother had bought for him when he had first gone off to college. Becky, oblivious to his rocky temper, held obdurately to her own code of sumptuary behavior: she changed in the bathroom; also, an added insult: she made sure to lock the door. It took her a while. There was lots of flushing and running water. Finally she emerged wearing his oversized pajamas and holding her clothes neatly folded over her arm.

"Is there some place I could hang these up?"

"Why bother? It's almost morning anyway."

"Russ, don't be such a silly cat."

So he showed her the closet. A short line of Kate's dresses still hung inside.

"Hello, girls," Becky, full of breeding, cheerfully greeted the older occupants. It took, Russ could not help but feel, an agonizingly long time for Becky to decide she was satisfied with the way her clothes were hung.

And then, to his relief, without any further prodding she got into bed. "I'm so tired," she yawned.

He quickly began to undress. A conciliatory gesture: Russ, accustomed to sleeping in the nude, decided to leave on his Jockey shorts. He was pulling back his corner of the spread when, again without warning, she let loose another of her beseeching screeches: "You're not going to bed like that, are you?"

He started to take off his shorts.

"Oh, Russ. Aren't you gonna wear pajamas, too?"

"I hadn't planned to."

"Please," she begged. "We'll be twin cats."

So he hunted for a pair of pajamas. But he'd be damned if he'd change in the bathroom. And he tossed his underwear onto an already cluttered chair in the bedroom.

Becky's rigid manners, however, required more. He couldn't get in bed until he had brushed his teeth (a suitable if not promising concession, even he realized) and had shaved (at 3 a.m.?). Still, she was miffed when he didn't have any after-shave lotion.

"A gentleman always wears after-shave," she revealed.

Russ just nodded and—at last!—made it into bed.

He reached over, more cautious than tender, to snuggle his pajama-clad companion. She became cozy. He kissed her along her neck; such a smooth, delectable trail. She purred. Pajama buttons fell open very easily.

Then the rain came.

Ping! The sudden summer thunderstorm pounded like so many brisk blows from a hammer against the metal of the air conditioner outside the bedroom window. *Ping! Ping! Ping!*

"What's that noise?" she demanded.

"Just the rain."

But she bolted straight up. "No. That noise. That horrible noise. What is it?"

He explained about the rain hitting the air conditioner.

"Well, I can't sleep with that racket. I hate it."

Ping! Ping! Ping! And with that rat-a-tat there followed, as if called up from a remembered dream, the echo of another noise: *Splat!* And another woman. And the ineluctable pattern that he was leading himself into became apparent: two women, so different, yet so irreducible in their obstinacy. So many battles ahead.

But before he could follow this troubling thought to its end, Becky got out of bed and took refuge in the quiet, non-air-conditioned living room.

He went after her. "Come on, Becky, let's just try to get some sleep." By now he was willing to surrender. "We don't have to make love if you don't want to."

"Oh, Russ. I simply detest that sound. It gives me the shivers." And she said, "Don't be a silly cat, of course I want to sleep with you."

"Sure. That's why you're sitting over there."

"Oh, Russ, you know I love you."

As soon as she said the words he realized how much he had needed that knowledge. Abruptly he was full of invention. He returned to the bedroom, but only for a moment. After a complicated struggle, he was back in the living room dragging the king-size mattress behind him.

"Okay," Russ announced as the rain continued to pour outside the window. "We'll sleep in here." He flopped the heavy mattress down in front of the fireplace.

Becky made a meticulous bed for the second time that evening. And for the second time that evening Russ climbed in next to her.

This time there were no interruptions. Things started to click. Soon they were both without pajamas. Then, a look of sheer power filling her eyes, she was straddling him.

"Touch my breasts." It wasn't a request; it was a command.

"See," she said as he obeyed, "a perfect handful."

She was proud of what she had to offer; and with the niggling grace of a stern philanthropist determined to supervise so her gift will not be squandered, she gave herself to him. His appreciation was her pleasure.

Neither of them went to work the next day. Sometime around eleven in the sunny morning Becky, after demurely putting her pj's back on, helped Russ haul the cumbersome mattress into the bedroom; and moments later she was also helping him as, once more in bed, he maneuvered to take the restrictive outfit off her. This time she was more demanding.

It was an afternoon filled with encounters. About three, though, they took a break. At Becky's insistence, Russ had the superintendent come up somehow to silence the offending air conditioner. Mr. Grazio, a lazy man who made it a practice to disregard the whims of his spoiled tenants, was clearly put off by the request; however, a generous tip gave him initiative.

"I'll think of something," he promised as he palmed the bills Russ had discreetly offered. And the superintendent returned half an hour later with a yard-wide scrap from a thickly piled royal blue rug. He measured it against the air conditioner, cut it down to size, and then glued it to the top of the metal machine.

"Pretty classy," Russ said to Becky after the amused super had left. "I must have the only air conditioner in town with wall-to-wall carpeting."

"It's such a pretty blue. You know the rest of the room would really look swell with carpeting." A proud blue vision instantly spread before her. "Couldn't we get a blue carpet for the bedroom?" she asked, excited. "Be a good cat and say yes."

"Yes." And Russ noted with silent glee she was already redecorating the place.

By the end of the week Becky was at his door with four large monogrammed matching suitcases.

"Hello, girls," Russ heard her say as she hung her clothes in the bedroom closet.

When she was done she came into the study. She was holding four or five of Kate's dresses.

"What should I do with these, cookieface?"

He considered the possibilities.

"Should I throw them out?"

"No. Just put 'em in my closet. I imagine Kate will get around to picking them up someday."

FOUR

MONTHS PASSED WHILE Russ waited for Kate to retrieve
her dresses. These stray souvenirs, however, remained; and, in time,
were shoved farther and farther back as the closet filled. Nearly every
day seemed to bring another delivery from United Parcel—a dress, a skirt,
or some other stylish goody Becky had decided she couldn't live without
and had promptly charged to one of his accounts. Still, he accepted it; it
was part of their becoming a couple: Dog-eared mail-order catalogs
spilled across the living room coffee table, her sharp tawny hairs were
twirled through his hairbrush, and the gay smell of her perfume welcomed you as soon as you entered the apartment. Yes, they were becoming a couple.

A couple of what?

We are most jealous of what we don't know. This is, perhaps, one
definition of love; and it also helps explain the magnificent power Becky
wielded over Russ, and a bit of what he sought in her.

He became her pupil. The diversion of glamour became an occupa-
tion. She demanded the luxurious and he rushed, pleased and eager to
please, to fulfill her requests. Occasional extravagances became, with the
benediction of one of her abundant smiles, full-time addictions.

Crazy days and crazy nights: They ran about New York ordering
champagne and caviar just for the thrill that accompanied the making of
such rich demands. Normally restrained if not shy, Russ turned another
corner, responding to Becky's encouragements by kissing her with outrageous public passion in restaurants. They kept the sunroof opened when
it rained, vain Russ coaxed to smile as his thinning hair got wet. She loved
to dance, there were so many new clubs, and he, catching her jumpy
mood though not her talent, never said no. Cashing in the fixed-rate
treasury certificates his accountant had suggested, Russ invested in the
flashier yields of diamond earrings and an emerald necklace; and his
lavishness was reciprocated in full, if not outdone, he felt, as he watched
Becky, braiding the gift box red ribbons through her flowing hair, out-

sparkle the gems. Reckless, they raced the Porsche through the late night streets of Manhattan, Willie Nelson blasting from the tape deck, warning all the mamas out there that their babies shouldn't be allowed to grow up to be cowboys. They went to bed early in the morning and woke up fuzzy-mouthed in the afternoon; why go to work when it's just as easy, especially if you're the editor in chief, to call in sick? And now when Becky purred at him, he meowed right back—another krazy kat.

Their outings had become their accomplishments: Becky paraded her beauty and Russ displayed his position for all the world to see and envy and judge—what a beautiful couple.

There were moments of private joy, too. Just watching the naturally graceful way she moved through so many small moments of the day brought him pleasure: the way each morning she strenuously, with so much wonderful concentration, brushed out the long wild strands rippling through her muscular hair; the way she tittered conspiratorially to each plant as she watered them; the way she would break away from a conversation, reach into her purse to extract her compact, and then paint a fresh playful cherry red over her lips; the way on a cold winter's night she would so precisely stack the logs and twist the paper kindling before she would light the fire in the living room—and then, the blaze ferocious, she would lie on her belly close to the glow, huge tortoiseshell glasses balanced on her nose, as she pretended to read *Bleak House*; or the way she curled her tongue, craftily circumnavigating the rim of a newly opened bottle of beer before she took a sip.

So many acts of simple elegance; still, Russ also filed away actions that hinted at a way he could never be or even understand: Becky, the girl who took the Tiffany catalog along with her to work for lunchtime reading; who called people eggheads; who subscribed to *Psychology Today*; who obsessively ordered patterned sheets and ceramic dishes from the large pile of mail-order catalogs she kept on her nightstand; who could spend entire afternoons window-shopping; who played Peter Allen on her Walkman while she jogged; who insisted on petting every puppy she passed on the street . . .

And it wasn't only that Russ couldn't see himself doing any of this. There was something else: He couldn't see Kate doing any of these things, either.

Kate was always in his thoughts: the other woman. She was always the unspoken comparison. There were days when he could almost hear her, so coolly understated in her sarcasm, so Kate, reproach what he had allowed himself to become, the easy compromises he had accepted, the opportunities he had ratted on.

But Becky had her wisdom, too. "Cookieface, you've really got to understand," she would say with last round introspection as she

bottomed-up another champagne cocktail and threw out her inevitable
challenge to his brooding mood, "that any day you can go out there and
get hit by a bus."

Except they never got hit by a bus; they simply slammed into walls
of blank days.

LIKE A BANKRUPT who continues bold and undaunted to
pay his way with empty checks, Russ waited for the moment it all would
catch up with him. And while he waited, the wrenching events were being
set in motion by, simply enough, a call from Max inviting Russ to dinner.

The two men had not seen much of each other lately. Their dis-
engagement had been unspoken and casual. Excuses came easy: Max had
a new job and a revitalized social agenda; Russ was busy running *City*
and being run ragged by Becky. Yet beneath the etiquette of their evasive-
ness there existed real, strong reasons, they both knew, for distance:
Max, from the first, had not been comfortable with Russ's easy ascen-
dancy to the editorship he had not only once held, but also had labored
so single-mindedly to invent; and Russ, feeling culpable but not contrite,
realized how his magazine, his book, his life with Becky must look to
Max's subjective eye: so much heralded achievement, so much sand.

So when Max caught him at home one evening before Becky and he
were heading off to meet a group of friends at Le Club, Russ agreed
readily enough, but his voice, however puffed up with goodwill, leaked
trepidation: "Great. Next Tuesday seems fine. It'll be good to get together again." And, no attempt at irony, he added, "Like the old days."
Immediately he realized how impossible that was, and so he quickly
pushed the conversation along; only, again, to emphasize how long ago
and far away the old days were. "But hold on a minute. Let me check
with Becky if Tuesday's good for her."

"Actually, Russ, I'd prefer if we did without Becky this one time."

"If that's what you want . . ." Russ knew fully well what the older
man thought of Rebecca Holland. Russ had introduced them about six
months ago and Max, after just thirty minutes of polite conversation, took
his friend aside and said, "Sure, she's beautiful. But is she anything
more?" Russ had never forgiven Max this restrained appraisal; or the
comparison it lay tacitly open: to a woman downtown in a loft, no
beauty, but certainly something more.

Still, Russ moved to hide his pique: "All right then, it'll just be the
two of us."

"Well," Max went on hesitantly, "there'll actually be three. There's someone I want you to meet. An editor I work with. Might be able to do your career some good."

"The only thing that'll do my career any good would be for me to get down to work. But I'll come if you want." And, as a sop for Becky's honor, he said, meanly, "Alone."

"Fine," Max answered; and Russ noted the caller was oddly unresponsive to his antagonistic manner. "Know a good place?"

"What kind of food are you thinking about?"

"Anything. So long as the restaurant is special . . ."

"Special?"

"Well, perhaps the sort of place Becky would like."

Russ mentioned a hoity Italian restaurant uptown on Second Avenue; there would be a hovering maître, flambéed extravaganzas shimering about the candle-lit room, hothouse flowers on the table, and only the Arabs would pay in cash.

"Are you sure it's the sort of place Becky would like?"

"I took her there on our first date. It seemed to do the trick." A purely capricious comment; but later, when the time would come to think this conversation over, Russ would be tempted to acknowledge that an instinctive prescience must have been leading him on.

"Perfect. I'll make a reservation for eight on Tuesday. See you then."

"Wait a minute. Who is this editor?"

"You'll meet her Tuesday night."

When Russ arrived at the restaurant a few minutes after eight, Max was already seated at one of the more prominently displayed tables. His only company was a three-olived martini.

"You got clout," Russ said with offhanded admiration as he sat down.

"Is it really a good table?"

"Head of the class."

"Good," he said with a contented smile.

"Seriously, Max, who do you know?"

"Well," he explained sheepishly, "I don't know anyone. I had one of the secretaries from the publishing house make the reservation. I told her to lay it on thick. I guess it worked."

"You think you can use your influence to get me a drink?"

"Wouldn't you prefer wine?"

Russ caught something hopeful in the suggestion. "Sure."

"Good," Max said, lifting a hefty leather-covered wine list from the table. "I don't know much about these things. You choose." There was only the slightest self-conscious twinge. "Don't worry about price. I feel extravagant."

Max passed his companion the dictionary-sized volume; and as Russ began to thumb through, he realized something that had been working on his mind since the moment he had sat at the table. He looked up and confirmed his suspicions. "A new suit, Max?"

Max nodded, unconsciously giving the tail of his tie an exaggerated pull as though he were opening up a curtain to put himself on display, and asked, "What do you think?"

The suit was a heathery glen plaid, nipped at the waist, and the lapels were sliced on the fashionable narrow. The paisley tie, which very deliberately caught the rusty tone running in the suit's plaid, couldn't have been much wider than Max's thumb. And the shirt, a field of mauve with a contrasting white spread collar, had a silky sheen.

"Polo," Max announced, the imprimatur thrown in to influence his companion's verdict.

Russ thought he looked like a dentist from Long Island who had just formed a p.c. and had bought an outfit to celebrate. "Polish?"

Max explained evenly: "Ralph Lauren."

"Oh." He put enough syllables into the word so that it was clear it didn't contain an apology.

But Russ felt he did owe Max this much: "Forget the clothes. You know me. I was always a sucker for your frumpy old tweeds. But, hey, *you* look great." And, truth was, Max, always lucky, had double-crossed time: His brushed back gray hair was full, and whatever wrinkles he had picked up over the past sixty-six years seemed to be the necessary ruddy testimony to his intellect, his presence eruditely fleshed out, completed; and while there was no denying the insomniac's indelible darkish circles, his owlish eyes still scurried about with—best of all—a vivid, curious glow: an impertinent, still—after all these years—shrewdly mischievous stare.

"Well," said Max with a consoling sigh, "I might as well drink to that." The martini was emptied to its olives. "Now what about some wine?"

"I'll pick the wine, all right. But only if you give me some hints about our mystery guest. There is someone joining us, isn't there?"

"You know women," said Max trying to affect the weariness of an expert, "always late."

"I'm not interested in women. Just tell me about this one."

Max gave a hapless, gig's-up laugh. "Well, I think this is one woman you might enjoy meeting."

But instead of talking about her directly, Max circled a bit, starting in, with an almost boastful pride that Russ found both revelatory and troubling, on her pedigree:

"She was born Jessica James. Old English county family. Her father was a peer. Died while Jessie was a child. Hunting accident or something. Mother didn't have a title, only money. But old money. They came here when her mother tied up with an investment banker. Jessie was six, maybe seven at the time. So she's very American in a Miss Poo Poo's sort of way. Anyway, when the banker kicked off a couple of years ago, her mother headed back to England. She's holed up, Jessie says, in one of those crumbling manor houses. Jessie likes to go on how they can't afford it. [A knowing snort of disbelief.] Says they have to shut down half the place each winter. Who knows? But let me get back to the lady in question. After college Jessie married an American. Porcellian but, she insists, not really like that. I'll tell you, though, he sounds like one of those lifeless Wall Street types to me. A Jeremiah Jones. That made her Jessica James Jones. At least she didn't have to change the monograms after the divorce. She and this Jones fellow split about two years ago."

Russ interrupted the story, strongly feeling the need for the solace of a drink. He decided, brightening up a bit, on a bottle of Sancerre. But his unarticulated joke was lost on Max: only on the Upper East Side of Manhattan are the Italian restaurants pretentious enough to stock French wines. "Pretty label," was Max's only comment as the sommelier uncorked the bottle with a well-practiced effortlessness.

Russ, always put off by the superfluous ritual, went through the quick motions of tasting and approving the vintage; just as he realized he would have to let Max, despite the clues bursting out all over the place, continue his temporizing.

Reining in his impatience, Russ tried to coax out the essentials. "So this Jessica James Jones is divorced?"

"Yes, I told you. For two years now. But listen to this," said Max with a punch-line smile. "When she separated from this Jones fellow, there was a fuss over the custody of their child, little Jeremiah James Jones, Jr. [A sardonic shake of the head; it said: imagine the staunchly inbred, alliterative legacy of these sort of people.] Oh, Jessie got to keep the boy, but in order to get alimony, I mean a *substantial* alimony, Jones's lawyer required that she sign an affidavit swearing she wouldn't establish a permanent residence with the child beyond a hundred-mile radius of Columbus Circle. Jessie read the document and then turned to the lawyer and said, 'Columbus Circle sounds so tacky. Perhaps we could change it to a hundred-mile radius from Bendel's?'"

Max smirked at this silliness, but part of his amusement, Russ felt, derived from the inside joke: that Max Fox, the kid from Roxbury, had made it into the world of such silliness.

No longer waiting for the waiter, Russ poured himself a third glass of the Sancerre. He topped off his friend's glass, too.

Max, though, gushed on: "She's one of these people who knows everyone. Tons of connections. You can imagine how valuable all that is in publishing."

Russ said nothing, so Max added, "That's why I wanted you to meet her. You two hotshots might be able to help each other. She's just the sort of woman you'd be interested in."

"That I'd be interested in?"

Now it was Max's turn to hold on to the silence; and he, pensive, let his grasp linger, cooling the mood at the table. At last he broke off, studying his watch. "Perhaps I should call her?"

Russ was willing to relent: "Another bottle of wine should keep us for a while. I'm not in any hurry."

Relieved, Max waved over the sommelier. Moments later both the wine and the lady arrived at the same time.

"A thousand apologies. Really. Things got terribly hectic at home. You know what I mean, jellybean?"

Jellybean? Even Preston Vandermaeker would never have dared that. Then, prodded by his memory of Vandermaeker, an unburied and unforgiven ghost from their past, Russ—in the suddenness of that recollection—understood for the first time some wisdom he had once read and dutifully underlined in Marx: History always repeats itself; first as tragedy, then as farce. And, observing the cozy scene across the table as the brittlely thin, clipped-featured streaked blonde took a seat next to Max Fox, Russ contemplated how incisively the prophecy of one Marx was reinforced by the wit of another: Who wants to join any club that will take me?

Russ's musings (and the self-denigrating path they might have taken him on) were interrupted, however, as Max took over his role as host. "Oh, I'm sorry. Jessie, you haven't met Russ. Jessica Jones, Russ Lewis."

She had a way of fixing people with her dusky blue stare before she spoke; it was, Russ felt, a strategy both feminine and submissive; and very contrived. "Max has told me all about you," she said, an engaging singsong lilt to her words, as they shook hands. "But I never realized you were so young. I imagined you were much older. But that's me—ol' oatmeal between the ears."

She took a sip of the wine, and, approving, went on to drain the glass. Russ refilled it, and Jessie took another deep swallow. "Well," she said, "I guess it's off to the races this evening."

Max laughed heartily.

"Now that I don't feel so zooey," she began as she turned her full attention to Max, "I really should explain why I was so late. My brother rang up from London just as I was about to leave. Bad news. It seems Mummy fell and broke her hip. A simple fracture, thank God. That is, if an eighty-three-year-old woman can even have a cold that's simple. Reggie, that's my brother you know, says Dr. Hartley insists she will be fine. Mummy is a tough old bird, it's true. But I can't help worrying. Except for a nurse and some help, she's stranded all alone in that monstrous house. She refuses to come down to London and camp out with Reggie. Not that I blame her. So Reggie wants me to come and stay with her. And I really feel I must. It might take me a few days . . . oh, perhaps a week to wrap things up, but I think I could get away from work for a spell. I'll just have to."

"How long would you stay in England?" he asked.

"I'm not certain, really. Jeremiah Jr. has his vacation coming up soon, and I rather think he would like to visit with his grandmother. He really should spend some time in England, you know. It's incredible how lush the countryside in Cornwall can be this time of year. All those strident blues and greens I just adore. And publishing is so very dead once the weather turns warm." Jessica seemed to be convincing herself while she talked. "Truth is," she decided, "I'm considering staying for the entire summer."

"It's a good time to be out of the city," Max said unconvincingly.

"Don't be such a silly rabbit. I want you to come and visit me. There's oodles of room. And you'll just adore Mummy." Then, a polite afterthought, Jessica threw in, "You must come, too, Russ."

Russ smiled and Max laughed: distraction techniques. But her invitation—and all it implied—reverberated through the moment like the exotic strains of a distant train's whistle.

"No, really, you both must come and visit. Please say you will," Jessie continued to insist.

"Sure, I'll just drop everything and head off to England," Max said, making the likelihood sound totally preposterous.

So now she turned and, challenging Max, focused, flirty and imploring, on the other man at the table. "Just because Maxie's trying to be an old stick in the mud, that doesn't mean you have to be one, too, Russ. Now tell me you'll come."

"Maybe I'll be able to get away from the magazine, who knows," Russ said airily. He understood the game Jessie was playing; and he had his own complicated reasons for giving Max a hard time. "Ever since I read *The French Lieutenant's Woman* I've been hoping for the opportunity to traipse through Cornwall."

"Don't you just adore Fowles," said Jessie. "I had dinner with him once."

"Really?"

"He wasn't at all what you would have expected . . ." she began.

Max, stranded between these two fast friends, their banter flying over his head as though he were the victim of a playful bit of monkey-in-the-middle, was aware that he was being coyly goaded and yet, simultaneously, he was turning deeply resentful: such is the strong, irrational, and malefic ambivalence that spreads through insecure lovers.

He turned on the threatening intruder. "When I was editor of *City*, it was a full-time job. In fifteen years I was never able to get away for a vacation."

"Maybe that was the problem," Russ shot back; his decision was immediate: he would punch, not duck. "You were always so on top of the magazine, you couldn't see how it needed to grow, to keep pace with the times."

"And running stories on the ten best house plants is keeping pace with the times?"

"Cut the crap, Max. You know I never ran that story."

"House plants? Chocolate chip cookies? What's the fucking difference?

"The difference," said Russ, his voice quivering over the injustice he tried to convince himself lay in Max's attack, "is that I'm trying to give people stories they want to read. Not esoteric articles that interest a few losers still trying to pass themselves off as bohemians."

"Bullshit. You're just pumping up circulation by pandering to the basest sort of interests . . . or is it cravings? You tell people what's chic, so they can wail if they don't have it. What the hell? I guess you're keeping Ross Clark happy. The formula keeps on raking in the bucks."

"Whatever you say, Max. But I think the truth is this: You're jealous because *City* now has twice the circulation it had when you were running it . . ."

". . . and half the readers. Most of your subscribers just thumb through your rag to check out the movie listings."

"You really can't stand the way things have worked out, can you? You think you can sit there, Max Fox the old wise man, and dismiss me and my magazine with your half-baked beatnik tautology: The only way to succeed is by selling out; therefore, anyone who makes it has sold out. But we both know the truth, Max. You were a coward. You were afraid of real success."

"You don't understand, do you?" said Max, a trace of compassion finally tracking through his anger. "I wasn't afraid of success. I simply was reluctant to make compromises."

That stung. Russ looked first to Jessie, who had sat mutely through this exchange, and he caught her excitement, the repellent morbidity of the spectator waiting for the first blood. And he looked to Max: smug, still at arm's length from the past. Russ, at sea, fighting for his dignity, suddenly found all his long repressed grievances flying from him.

"Except you weren't so reluctant," Russ, his voice a tempest, said, "when it came to feathering your own nest. You sold out to Vandermaeker and pocketed your millions. You didn't care what happened to your precious magazine . . . or any of us. So just bag your fucking principles, Max. You sold out everything for your pieces of silver. You betrayed all of us."

Max, to his credit, took his punishment. He did not flinch. He rigidly absorbed the devastating truth in Russ's words. He waited, and then when he spoke there was an evil precision, a decisiveness in his retort: "Betrayal is a subject, I would imagine, that you certainly know a lot about. Why, I'll vouch for your expertise." Then a final, inexorable lance was thrown: "And so will Kate Warner."

"Go to hell," Russ shouted, beyond reason, as he jumped from his seat and stormed, wild, quick strides, from the restaurant. Max and Jessica, a beautiful couple, were holding hands as they watched him leave.

THE LIGHTS WERE OFF when he opened the apartment door, so Russ assumed Becky was asleep. He tiptoed into the bathroom and began putting on his blue pajamas. Russ was brushing his teeth when she called out, "I bought you a new bottle of after-shave today." He finished washing up and found the small rectangular bottle in the medicine chest. Even unopened, it smelled sweet. He unscrewed the gold-colored cap and splashed some on his face.

He got into bed and curved around Becky. Her hair cascaded about his arm; he slipped his fingers between the bright strands.

"Are you awake?" Russ asked, pulling her closer.

There was no answer, but he needed to speak about the evening. "You're not going to believe this," he said, hoping to start with what would be easiest to reveal, "but Max is in love."

". . . mmnn . . . you smell good," was all Becky said. And then she turned over on her stomach and drifted further into sleep.

But Russ remained awake for hours, thinking in the dark. It had occurred to him earlier in the calmer course of the evening that his friendship with Max had gone full circle—the pupil was now teaching his mentor. But lying there, Becky's steady breathing the only sound in the dense night, he realized that Max, once again, had caused the climax and the focus: The past is never past. Lying there, really alone, a pattern spread before Russ: a timeless pursuit starting with a schoolboy's desire to write one true sentence . . . with the wonderful accident of true love at a softball game . . . and ending only with a dedication to an uncom-promised fulfillment of these authentic challenges. Or, in the doomed alternative: a futile lifetime of moving and calculating and destroying. So many diversions: the greedy pursuit of lopsided ambitions, the vain chase to become another beautiful couple.

A couple of what?

FIVE

RUSS DIDN'T SLEEP that night; however, with the new morning came the same old daydreams: He wanted to believe his love was true.

A deeper, more troubling truth, though, was he simply did not know how to share the implications of his newly found knowledge with Becky; and he remained afraid of where the pull of his convictions would have to take him: the tests of commitment, of talent that such deep resolve demanded.

He had no doubt Becky, with the irrefutable certainty of someone who believes all that glitters is gold, would ridicule his disappointments, his self-absorption: What did Russ Lewis, riding so high, have to complain about? But just as he was poised to sit down with her over one last champagne cocktail in an attempt to explain the fundamental falsities underpinning the life they were so carelessly leading, Becky stepped up to the bar and slapped his hesitancy silly. The final blow: Not how much Russ would never belong to her world, but how deeply she was a part of it. It all became brutally clear the day Becky took him sailing for the first time.

"HELLO, LUG," Becky called out.

"Hello, Mrs. Lug," the tow-haired man responded.

"Who's that?" Russ quickly asked. They were standing on the yacht club dock near her parents' Long Island home, waiting for the launch to pick them up.

"Mikey? The Lug?"

"That's the one."

"Oh, he's just a neck with legs."

Maybe. But they were the biggest legs and the biggest neck Russ had ever seen. The only thing small about him was his bathing suit. "Why did he call you *Mrs*. Lug?"

"Oh, that." Becky laughed. "We used to go out together." Her hand flew out in an easy wave, an attempt to dismiss the muscular youth; but Russ could only see a rug being thrown over an open trapdoor.

"For a long time?"

"You know, it was high school . . . I guess college, too. He was the big football star. And I was a cheerleader. I met him when he came to me for a haircut. I used to cut the hair of all the guys on the football team."

"A pretty serious romance, huh?"

". . . At the time . . . I mean I guess we were sort of engaged."

"Sort of?"

"I gave his ring back years ago, Russ. He's no one to be jealous of. You'll meet him at the party after the race. He's very sweet, but really stupid. Not like you, cookieface."

Russ was staring at him, thinking about how much Mikey was not like him when Becky called, "Come on, there's the launch."

A skinny, droopy-haired boy, perhaps fifteen, was driving the launch. He approached the dock at full speed, not slowing until the very last moment.

"Hi, Johnny," Becky said to the boy. "We're going out to Chip's boat."

"Sure thing, Becky." As she, lanky and elegant in a red one-piece bathing suit, climbed into the boat, Johnny let loose with a wolf's long whistle.

"Eat your heart out," Becky snarled at the boy. "You're gonna have to wait your turn." Everybody in the launch laughed. Except Russ.

And so it went for the rest of the bright afternoon. The starting gun was fired and a line of sailboats took off for an unseen buoy far out in the Sound. It wasn't much of a destination, or much of a race, but only Russ seemed to notice.

For hours the *Good Times*, a lovingly restored, tall-masted 1930s-design wooden boat, floated indolently in the becalmed water. Russ, the novice mariner, was becoming impatient with the repetitiveness of his first lesson at sea: just how hot the teak deck of a stagnant sailboat can get in the ferocious afternoon sun. Then all of a sudden there was a gust of wind; and Chip, the captain, who strode about the deck like a Viking with his shaggy blond hair and beard but who earned his living filming commercials ("I know a lot of writers," he confided to Russ. "A good friend of mine is the guy who came up with the line, 'Where's the beef?' "), was barking orders; Becky and Tommy (a childhood chum who on introducing himself announced with a deprecating grin, "I work at Manny Hanny") were busily changing sails; Judy, a giggly, booming-voiced redhead going through her second divorce at twenty-nine, was tugging at the rigging while demurely blowing kisses to the captain; and Russ, attempting to follow Chip's patient yet authoritative commands, was manically grinding the winch. The boat began slicing through the Sound at a thirty-degree angle and Russ held on tight, his back splashing against the water as the cool, refreshing spray sprinkled his face. It was all very exhilarating—for the three minutes it lasted. Then the wind died down and the flat hot pace continued. It must have taken the *Good Times* six relentless hours to reach a dull gray buoy and make it back to the yacht club harbor.

"Wasn't that fun?" Becky insisted to Russ, pulling herself away from her intimate, hush-voiced huddles with her friends for the first time that afternoon. Her oddly accusatory tone, Russ noticed, continued as the captain dropped anchor. "See," Becky said, "I told you we really know how to have fun."

Before Russ could respond, the fun kept on coming.

"Attack!" cried out Tommy.

A water balloon splattered at the captain's feet, making him spill his beer. Across the bow the Lug's ship was zeroing in on the *Good Times*. Another volley of water balloons splashed on the teak deck.

"Oh boy oh boy!" said Tommy.

"Oh boy oh boy!" said Chip.

"Meow!" said Becky.

Judy emerged from the galley with two large buckets loaded with red, yellow, and blue water balloons. "This time we're ready for them," she called out.

The battle was on. The colored balloons flew through the air, bouncing on the deck and splashing the crew. Only Russ remained dry. He knew he was being treated like an outsider, an unnatural target, but for once he felt secure in his detachment. Finally Chip, a considerate captain, crossed the sopping wet deck and armed Russ with a red balloon, urging him "to get into the swing of things." Russ purposefully hurled it high over the Lug's boat. The balloon arced through the sky and fell with a thud into the water; yet it remained intact, soon a red dot floating away in the distance. Russ knew it was only a question of how and when he, too, would escape.

After a drink at the club and a shower, Becky and Russ, both of them holding to an undeclared silence, joined the crews from the other boats for dinner at Judy's. Her home, part of the settlement from her recent divorce, was a rambling red-bricked and white-pillared colonial, very shiny and very new. The developers had positioned it on the crest of a stiff hill. As Russ wandered to the bar on the flagstone rear terrace, he discovered he could look beyond the vast freshly cut sloping lawn, over a rocky strip of beach, then straight off into Long Island Sound. Even without a drink he was full of whimsy. Immediately he began searching for an orgastic green light flashing in the distance. The reality—and here was a literary lesson he promised himself he would someday make good use of—was a much more appropriate symbol for the suburban fantasies he felt brewing around him: a white-lit tennis bubble spread like a huge, glittering cocoon on the inlet across the water.

It was a crowded, noisy party and Becky quickly revitalized in the rush of familiar faces. Russ, innately shy, trailed after her as she moved about. Becky made a point, though, of ignoring his presence, never bothering to introduce him to any of the attentive faces or garrulous clusters that welcomed her. Russ was put off not so much by her rudeness as by its abruptness and apparent tenacity; it implied that she, too, had reached a decision, and had no qualms about being the first to act: She had stolen his thunder. Then he heard Chip tell her there was a tiny split in the rear seam of her canary yellow pants. "What are you looking at my ass for anyway," Becky reprimanded. But Chip continued looking; just as, Russ could tell by the way she wiggled off, Becky had hoped he would. That's when Russ headed to the bar.

He set out to get drunk. He filled a plastic glass with a lot of dark rum, a little grapefruit juice, and a slice of lime—an aesthetic prerogative; he wasn't wild about the sweet taste, but he liked the way the concoction looked. But by the time the bar had run out of both grapefruit juice and limes, he was content to settle for straight rum.

It was in this drunken mood, complacent rather than combative, he would recall later, that he wandered toward the light of a bonfire on the beach. He found Becky sitting with Chip, Tommy, and Mikey the Lug. They were all huddled closely together. Chip held one of Becky's hands; Tommy held the other. Russ joined them, a drink in his hand. No one greeted him, so he kept quiet, listening as the Lug continued with his story.

". . . oh, he was the cheapest bastard you ever saw," said Mikey.

They all laughed.

"Yes, he was the cheapest little Jew."

They kept on laughing. Russ, suddenly sober, put his drink down on the sand.

"A real greasy Hebe, with one of those thick accents, and one of those bagel-baker noses . . ."

They kept on laughing. Including Becky. So Russ, very deliberate, very assured, rose to his feet, brushed the sand off his chinos, and walked over to Mikey and hit him with all his might. Square in the mouth. Then, without a word, Russ walked off.

When Becky caught up with him, Russ was in front of the house, leaning against his Porsche and trying to shake the sting out of his swelling hand. He was feeling contrite: perhaps his hand was broken; and perhaps he had let too much rum lead his insecurities out of control.

"I can't believe you did that. I should have let Mikey go after you. He would have killed you," she shouted at him. There was a savage lash to her words. "It was just a silly story. If you don't like what you hear, then you shouldn't listen."

That's when Russ knew he had done the right thing. That's when he knew he had finally broken through all her dithering, seductive hedonism. And that's when he knew—such was the gift of insight in this powerful moment—that the Mikeys were his real enemies: His work, both as a writer and editor, must stand up to their facile bigotry, their intellectual banality, their mainstream know-nothingism.

But Becky, unaware of the determined sweep of his thoughts, heard only his muteness. She misread his mood completely; and, full of this confidence, she set out to finalize what she thought was her advantage. Still, she was the one who first articulated the simple truth Russ had been trying to blurt out since his dinner with Max. "The problem is," she revealed with icy finality, "we have nothing in common."

Russ looked straight into her strongly beautiful face, straight into a face he had pursued, fantasized over, kissed, and now realized he could never again see in the same way, and said, "Thank God."

R U S S D R O V E B A C K to the city alone. He pushed the Porsche, ignoring the risk. The needle on the speedometer hovered around ninety for a stretch. He grew giddy, even triumphant, racing down the Long Island Expressway. The speed was helping to persuade him that it had been his decision to leave her. He was determined not to miss Becky.

But as soon as Russ entered the apartment, the smell of her perfume jostled his resolve. He hadn't counted on the argument in this lingering aroma; or the way her long tawny hairs would be stretched across his pillow, shiny place marks that had his mind turning to other nights.

When the phone rang early the next morning, Russ felt he shouldn't answer it. He had made a decision, and so had Becky. What else needed to be said? But each loud ring seemed to pierce his certainty. He grabbed the receiver.

"Yes," he said cautiously. He knew there would be a woman on the line, one he was trying to persuade himself he did not want to speak to.

He was right; and he was wrong.

"Russ," said Jessica Jones in her unmistakable singsong way, "I wonder if you're free for lunch today. Please be a dear and say yes. I've got a problem and I believe you're the only one who can help."

S I X

"AND I'D LIKE it monogrammed," Jessica instructed the salesman holding the cordovan leather suitcase. "The initials MF."

He nodded silently, and then, as if to apologize for this lapse, added, "Certainly, Mrs. Jones."

Satisfied, Jessica abruptly turned and walked across the store toward Russ. "I just adore the smell of fine leather, don't you?" The question was designed to draw Russ from the pinwheel display rack of silk ties he was turning. "It makes me feel quite extravagant. Even sexy." When Russ did not respond, she went on: "Do you think Max will like the case?"

"It's very handsome," Russ said, trying to curb his rising exasperation, "but not very subtle. He's too old to be coerced, Jessie."

"But not to be charmed," she said, her eyes fluttering with self-mockery. Yet in her retort, however mannered, Russ also read a condescension and a confidence: I know things about Max Fox that you will never know.

It had been like that throughout lunch. Jessica's problem, she had confided as soon as they sat down in the King Cole Room of the St. Regis, was Max. He remained adamant about not coming to England. Yet Jessica was convinced, she set about explaining at length, Max would change his mind if Russ also agreed to make the trip. Her logic hung on an unshakable belief that the two men, despite the vitriolic scene she had witnessed, shared an inviolable friendship; last week's outburst, a harmless explosion of mood and ego, she insisted, would be quickly set right in the restorative calm of the English countryside. There was also another turn to her argument. "If you'd come," Jessica concluded with a frankness which she felt required her to reach across the table and grasp his hand, "Max would feel as if there was something, oh, less impetuous about the trip. He'd feel better about the whole show. That it was a vacation. Not something more . . . well, let's say dramatic."

By the time the check arrived ("It's my party," Jessica announced, grabbing the bill before he could protest) Russ was feeling anxious, and somewhat baffled. He was becoming convinced that beneath her effusive, social side, beyond the fey banter compulsively sprinkled with an upperclass slang, there existed a determined, manipulative woman; the artifice, Russ was beginning to suspect, was a deliberately misleading disguise. More puzzling, though, was Jessica's provocative femininity: her lingering tactileness, her rush to meet his every comment with an applauding laugh, even the way she kept running a hand through her long blond streaked hair. Russ was flattered, and not uninterested; and yet, he could not help wondering if this, too, was part of her performance: a spurious come-on thrown at him as a further inducement to accompany Max to England.

It was in this guarded, reflective mood that Russ went with Jessica to Mark Cross to buy Max a suitcase; and then, enjoying the gleaming city day, agreed to accompany her as she walked along Fifth Avenue to her apartment opposite the Metropolitan Museum. Russ had not yet reached a decision about the trip. He told Jessica he did not know if he could get away from *City*. He even suggested that Max, whatever the impression created by his arm's-length arrangement with Janey, was still a married man. But if Russ had been more honest, he would have told her his greatest concern: He was certain Max, after their last bitter encounter, would not find his presence as a traveling companion much of an inducement.

"I don't want to sound crude," she responded sternly to his articulated doubts as they continued up the avenue, "but that shit simply won't flush. Max can placate Janey. No one's talking anything . . . drastic. She'll understand. We're all adults. You know what I mean, jellybean?" And, finding her more familiar lilt, said, "So don't you worry. And don't try to pretend you can't get away from the magazine."

"It's not that simple—" he started to explain, but she cut him off.

"Maxie's meeting me for dinner tonight and I'm going to tell him all about our little tête-à-tête. I'm sure he'll be delighted that you're coming."

"I didn't say I was, Jessie."

"Don't tell me it's that cutie you're running around with that's holding you back. Little Miss Va Va VaVoom seems to be leading you quite a life, the way Maxie tells it."

They were standing under the canopy of her building, across from the broad stone steps leading to the museum, as Russ told her an expurgated (minus, of course, the incipient understanding of himself; and the ethical responsibilities that accompanied this knowledge) account of last night's confrontation with Becky and her friends.

"So you're footloose and fancy-free," Jessica declared when he had finished, hoping to bolster her contention that there was nothing to keep him in New York.

"I guess that's true." Yet even as he said the words, he knew nothing could have been further from the truth: His heart had not been unencumbered since a softball game so long ago. And he quickly paid for this rash dishonesty.

For not more than a moment later, as he was saying good-by to Jessica in the lobby of her building, Russ, politely moving aside to allow a silver-haired matron and her tugging poodle to pass, found himself turning toward the museum; and in that brief, unpremeditated movement he could not help but notice an unmistakable figure climbing the steps.

"You know I think that's Kate Warner across the street," he said to Jessica.

Even with her back turned, Russ was certain he could recognize her assured gait, the straight curtain of neck-length brown hair that bounced about as she walked.

"What if it is, Russ?"

The woman had Kate's beaded Indian bag slung over her shoulder.

"Sure it is."

There was a tall man with lots of curly black hair walking with her.

"You can't tell from this distance," Jessica tried.

The man had his arm firmly around the woman's waist.

"Of course it's her."

And the woman had her arm around the tall man's waist.

"Leave her be, Russ."

But Russ wasn't listening. He was running across the street. He hurried past the gurgling fountains and, taking the steps two at a time, caught up with the woman near the huge entrance doors. He tapped her on the shoulder.

"Kello, Kate," he said.

At the sound of Russ's voice she quickly dropped her hand from the tall man's waist, and turned to face him. But she did not speak. She stared at him hatefully.

"I just wanted to say hello," he mumbled.

The tall man stood there, his arm protectively around her.

Kate nodded, stony and utterly remorseless; and then she turned and entered the museum.

By the time he had walked down the steep steps and returned across the street, Russ felt bereft beyond any sorrow he could have previously imagined. "You shouldn't have done that," Jessica said.

Russ did not answer. There was no point.

"I'VE GOT TO APOLOGIZE. Explain to Kate."

"I think a drink might be more in order," Jessica offered.

They had just entered her apartment, the elevator man leaving them at the twelfth floor landing which served as her entrance hall: the entire floor was hers.

"Flowers. I'll send flowers. A dozen roses. Where's the phone?"

Jessica, taking him by the hand as one would a confused child, led him into the library. The room shone at him; the walls were lacquered a bold Chinese red and the sofa, roomy and plush, was covered with a yellow and green floral chintz, the softer colors in the upholstery meant to play against the stridently golden carpeting. "You make your call and I'll make a pitcher of Gibsons. House specialty. We'll have you feeling better in no time."

Russ called his florist, another tony vestige of Becky's influence, and had roses sent to Kate's loft on Warren Street. When he put down the phone, he, as if on command, rose—such was the aimless, uncontrollable energy running through him—and paced about the room. He studied the Avery above the mantel, a beach scene. The painting, he decided, was chosen only because it picked up on the same colors already crowding the bright room. Looking at this arrogant attempt to reduce art to decoration, Russ could not help thinking about how he had similarly debased his great advantages: work, friendship, love. The renewed pain of these memories left him totally adrift: ruined.

Jessica returned to the room with a silver pitcher. "Now bottoms up," she ordered as she poured a Gibson into a long-stemmed glass and handed the drink to Russ.

She clinked her glass against his, the pearly onions bobbing, and he took a sip. It was a strong, cool drink. "I feel reckless," she said; and then, in a quick series of swallows, finished her drink. "Come on," she urged, "don't let me drink alone." He obeyed. "Well," she said, little-girlish with her narrow smile, "it looks like we're off to the races."

He sat down on the couch and, two fresh drinks in her outstretched hands, Jessica joined him. "Don't say a word," she said. "First one more quick one to ease the pain." They clinked glasses and tasted their drinks.

With this second strong Gibson, the liquor rushed to his head, encouraging his mood, feeding his deep despair. He thought of Kate: the standard by which he had always measured his life. He stared across the room at the trivialized painting: the emblem of what he had become.

Suddenly, he felt, it was too late to strive against the string of eroded opportunities that had brought him to this point; the only choice, his destiny, was to live with his real nature, however unscrupulous. And with that surrender, that hopelessness, came another impulse. He leaned across the couch and, without hesitation, kissed Jessica.

Her lips stayed with his. "My, my," she said when he eased away. But now she kissed him. Her arms pulled him toward her . . . and he allowed himself to fall on top of her, pinning her to the couch.

Her bra unclasped in front. It was lacy and white. As were her panties.

Her lips were all over him, so versatile. Jessica, playful, wanted him to follow her, to keep pace with her ingenuity. But he was full of anger, looking for consolation, graceless, without pride.

When it was over, really just a few moments of fury, he knew it was a failure: her femaleness, and, beyond that, her superior cool, had not been pierced.

"It must have been all the liquor," she chided. "Or maybe just a bad onion."

She wanted her taunt to burn, to reaffirm her power; but this was not to be. Instead it focused his shame: He suddenly had something to prove.

So, meanly, Russ shoved her off the couch, watching as she fell, a soft, cushioned drop to the carpet: pale skin and that goading triangle, curling bristles of tangy brown hair (unstreaked, uncosmeticized, unpampered—a pure natural cunt; at last he had her truly naked) on the chrysanthemum yellow field. A vertigo of sorts as he looked down at her; however, this small hesitation quickly fled. In its place: Excitement; an appreciation of what would be required. Now he eased himself on top of her, his weight on his palms, his head high, his thoughts focused like a spike, as his body went after her. He fell, calculating and skillful, into technique: a rhythm—beat after beat after beat after beat coaxing her to need him; and in the cadence of this time, ever so slowly, with a first small shudder, then another, breaking into a longer, fuller, more wonderful sound, until, fast and freely now, wailing, she acknowledged his control. Still, he did not stop; he sought to acquire her spirit. He would not give in, he would not allow her to give in, always commanding, taking her farther . . . only to pull back ruthlessly . . . and then all of a sudden once more unstoppable (her keen of sharp pleasure proved this was the surprise he had hoped it would be), his attentions again lavish and generous, the journey continuing . . . to some place unintelligible . . . until screaming, kicking her thin legs, heels hard against his back, no longer daring him, she came in a shriek.

His triumph, though, was short-lived; for just as he was enjoying a self-congratulatory thought, Jessica, as if reading his vain mind, articulated his very musings.

"Well," she said as they lay on the carpet, her head resting on his chest and her legs splayed across him, "you must feel very proud of yourself. Best-selling author; editor of *City* magazine; and now you've made an heiress scream."

It was all true; and it was all worthless. His predictability left him foolish. And full of contempt for her, for the vulgarity of her vision: the mirror of his. He hated her; as he hated himself.

But that, too, quickly passed. What remained was only Russ's passive submission to the grotesque coincidences plaguing his day; because at that moment Max was calling from the entrance hall. "Jessie, you around? The elevator man said he had just taken you up . . ."

And as soon as Max, unsuspecting, entered the library, a new world was created: something was done that could never be undone.

"THERE ARE NO EXCUSES," said Max.

Those were his first words. Max had left the apartment without speaking, ignoring Jessica as she, sobbing and inconsolable, called after him. When the elevator had come for Max, Russ rose from the carpet, got dressed, and, his calm immaculate, waited for the elevator once more to come up twelve flights and take him to the lobby. It wasn't until he was on Fifth Avenue that he started to run. He began running after Max. Russ caught up with him a few blocks downtown, Max walking with slow, ancient steps on the park side of Fifth Avenue. He must have heard Russ's shoes slapping against the concrete, the heavy breathing as he ran toward him, but Max did not stop. He waited until Russ was standing next to him and then, hard and angry, he turned to confront the friend who had betrayed him.

"There are no excuses," said Max. "No justifications."

Russ stood facing him. Silent.

Max looked through him. At last he spoke. "You bastard."

Perhaps it was because Russ did not answer that Max struck him. It was a quick, open-handed slap; a gesture of contempt.

Russ felt the sting, but stood his ground.

Max stared at him, the slap having blunted merely the edge of his anger. "The last time we spoke," he said, "you accused me of being envious of your accomplishments, your so-called success. Well," he went on, a hideous control wrapped about his words, "whatever envy or even interest I once might have possessed has been discharged. I now realize how totally your dubious accomplishments have destroyed your character."

Russ, like a prisoner who knows his only hope for redemption lies in his behavior before the hangman, answered, "I understand."

Yet at this, the sudden intrusion of the young man's listless voice, Max's steadiness fell apart. "No you don't," he screamed. "You don't understand at all."

Max took a sharp, menacing step toward Russ. Russ thought Max, his fists clenched so tightly that Russ could see the veins running to the older man's knuckles, was going to hit him. And a furious punch might have been thrown, but then Max—in the raging instant of that one small step—was made aware of what he was caught up in; and with this realization the moment was gone.

Now when Max spoke, he sounded weary, his words coming slowly as though each syllable was held down by a weight. "No," said Max, "there's no way you could understand. In that, I'm to blame. There are things I shouldn't have condoned. Things I should have told you."

Max started to laugh. It was the derisive sound of a man laughing at himself. "What you don't understand," he said, "is that we're two of a kind. We've always been two of a kind." Another short knowing smirk, and Max, as if defused, continued with the lightness of a man beginning a joke at a bar: "I never told you about the time Janey caught me with someone else, did I?"

Max told Russ about the icy night on a rooftop more than twenty-five years ago, a night when he had celebrated his fortieth birthday, a night when he had announced his plans for *City* magazine, a night when he had decided to get married. As he spoke Max started to walk downtown, toward the lights of the Plaza Hotel. Russ followed at his side. A stranger might have thought they were friends.

They were approaching the fountain in the middle of the concrete island across from the Plaza when Max, as if to signal that they had reached their destination, stopped and asked, "You know, don't you, why I've told all of this?"

Russ decided not to answer. The sound of water splashing in the fountain spilled into the silence.

"You realize this is the last conversation we will ever have. You've destroyed our friendship."

". . . Yes."

"Well, I want to believe that whatever was between us had its purpose. Perhaps—and maybe this is nothing more than an old man's farewell wish—our friendship was the price that had to be paid if the possibility was ever to exist for you to redeem what's left of your life. An expensive price for some cures; but then again, perhaps not for this one. The only problem is this: I can't tell you what the precise prescription should be. My wisdom is simply passive, a knowledge of my failures.

"That's why," Max went on, solidly, without emotion, "I told you about my night with Diane Farrell. That night I ran from the conclusions of all my passion. I settled on a compromise. I thought I could resign myself to Janey, to my work, and the rest of my life would take care of itself. I was a fool. No, worse. You were right: A coward. And I paid a price. Just as older but not wiser, I thought I could renounce my past mistake with more extravagant compromises—with Vandermaeker, with Jessie."

The mention of Jessica's name caused Max to pause, and he followed a private memory for an instant. He shook his head, an act of self-flagellation, and then continued: "To this day I don't know if I could have made a life with Diane Farrell. Or even if I would have wanted to. But I should have found out. I owed myself that honesty. But it's too late for me. And most likely it's too late for you.

"Oh well," Max said, turning affable and easy, "that's your problem." Max hesitated and finally said, "Perhaps I should shake your hand. But I won't. I can't forgive you. Now you're on your own." Then he turned and, without another word, walked off.

SEVEN

RUSS CHOSE A STOOL along the wooden bar that gave him a view out the window. He wasn't watching only for Kate; his silver Porsche seemed very conspicuous on this threadbare Tribeca street.

To fill the time, Russ ordered a Heineken. The bartender shook his head. "Bud or Rolling Rock," he said. Russ chose a Rolling Rock. The bartender put the bottle in front of him, no glass. There were horses' heads on the green bottle. And on the jukebox Sgt. Barry Sadler was singing "The Ballad of the Green Berets." Then the Vapors: " . . . everyone around me is a cyclone ranger; everyone around me is a total stranger. . . ." The bar was dark and smelled of stale beer. The music from the jukebox reverberated off the tin ceiling. He ordered another Rolling Rock and waited.

It had been Kate's idea to meet at Puffy's. For two rough days he relived in his mind all that had happened; and he struggled to find the courage that would help lead him in the direction Max had, in his enigmatic way, revealed was the only true, self-sustaining course. When he felt comfortable—not with the past, but with the possibility for a future—he wrote a brief letter to Ross Clark. And he called Kate Warner.

"How dare you?" Kate had thundered as soon as Russ spoke.

"I realize now it was wrong to have stopped you at the museum. I just thought I'd say hello."

"Like hell that's what you thought. You were trying to spy on me."

"It was a mistake. I'm sorry."

"And your ridiculous roses only made it worse. You think I'm that easy to manipulate?"

"I meant them as an apology."

"Don't apologize. Just leave me alone."

"Look, I'm not trying to manipulate anything. It's stupid for us to be mad at each other. We're not enemies."

After a moment Kate said, "I suppose you're right."

"No reason why we can't be friends."

"There are plenty of reasons."

"But there shouldn't be, Kate." He was begging. "Couldn't we meet for dinner? Just a friendly dinner."

"I don't want to have dinner with you."

"Then a drink?"

The question lingered; and Kate said, "There is something we should discuss."

"Fine. Let's make it tonight. Say six at the Carlyle."

"Are you crazy? The Carlyle? I hate going above Canal Street. I went uptown two days ago and look what happened. I'll meet you at eight at Puffy's."

"Just tell me where it is."

That had been earlier in the day, and now Russ was sitting in Puffy's finishing his second beer when Kate walked in. She caught the eye of a huge, bearded man hunched over a table in the corner, and he looked up from his sketch pad and waved to her, pencil in hand. Russ stood as she crossed the bar and Kate, without asking, took his stool. "Rick," she called to the bartender. "I'll have a Rock, please." Then she finally spoke to Russ. "What are you drinking?"

"I'll stick with beer."

"Make that two, Rick."

"I hear you, Kate," the bartender called back as he opened the cooler.

Kate put down a ten-dollar bill. When the beers came, she let the change remain on the bar.

She wanted him to begin the conversation. When he realized this, he said, "You seem pretty much at home here."

"It's a neighborhood place. A lot of carpenters who want to be artists; and a lot of artists who should have remained carpenters." A sip and she conceded, "Oh, some of them are serious. They've managed to hook up with galleries. But they only hang out at Puffy's to gloat . . . or to show that success hasn't changed them."

Russ sat there listening to the hard, artificial edge to her words, the distance she was clearly putting between them, and was overwhelmed by a sense of estrangement: what had been lost. His vulnerability only made it worse.

"And you?" he asked. "Have you changed?"

"Changed? Who knows? But I do know this: I'll never again let anyone do to me what you did." She played with her beer, running her fingers up and down the long neck of the bottle. "No, I haven't changed. I've just recovered my control."

"I guess it wouldn't help if I apologized . . ."

"You couldn't. There are some things you can't apologize for. Or that can never be forgiven."

Only now did Russ realize the obvious. "You've spoken with Max?"

"Yes."

(And she thought about what she did not tell him: Max sitting exactly twenty-four hours ago with her in this same bar, though at one of the wooden tables, had said, "I've got nothing left but my solitude. Russ, Jessie, even Janey—they're all out of my life."

"You still have me," said Kate.

He seemed amused as he played with an idea. "Maybe that's the way it always was meant to end up."

Kate also let the idea lead her on; until, wanting to believe it could be easily abandoned, she lied. "I think I'm a little tipsy."

"I know what you mean," he said, laughing.

So she laughed, too. And in a moment they were talking about a movie; and what had been left unsaid and undone would forever remain that way.)

Russ, grabbing her silent pause to pursue his own thoughts, looked out the window at his silver car. Drive off. Don't ask any more questions. Don't listen to any more answers. But, unlike Kate, he would not be satisfied by the consolation of a fictive reality.

So the question that had been lurking ever since she had sat down stumbled out. "What about that guy you were with . . ."

"Peter."

"Peter," he repeated. "Is he an artist?"

"A sculptor."

"Talented?"

"It's too soon to tell," said Kate in her habitually candid way. "Right now he's working his way through art history. He's got the desire, the discipline. We'll see if he has the talent."

One question remained: "Are you in love?"

"That's none of your business."

"I just want—"

Kate cut him off. "Look, Russ, you really want to know—fine. Right now I belong down here. Away from you. With Peter. Are we in love? I honestly am not sure. Like talent, love takes time to develop. We'll see."

Russ drained his beer. He had intended to tell her about his letter to Clark, but now decided not to. He rose from his stool, ready to leave.

But Kate, vindictive, was not done: "Since you're so inquisitive, I'll tell you about love, all right. Remember when you first moved into my apartment on the Lower East Side? I loved you then. We were broke, but I respected you so. I thought Russ Lewis was the bravest man I had ever met. You knew what you wanted, and no one was going to stop you from achieving it. Except yourself. And you really did blow it. Now you don't know what you want, do you? So you grab everything . . . and everyone. Shit, you're not ambitious, Russ. You're just greedy."

"I guess you've got me pretty well figured out," he acknowledged. "There doesn't seem to be anything else left to say." He started to walk away from the bar.

"There is one other thing."

Russ waited; he had asked for this.

"I'd like to come by the apartment and pick up the rest of my clothes," said Kate.

R U S S   W A S   N O T   H O M E when Kate retrieved the remainder of her clothes.

The next morning, after delivering his letter of resignation to Ross Clark, Russ bought a cellophane-wrapped carton of yellow legal pads, packed his duffel bag, and, no real destination in mind, drove toward the cool upstate air. It was only a matter of chance (that is, he was not conscious of the memory of another doomed spiritual son of Max Fox whom years ago he had replaced) that led him to the Adirondacks. Russ spent a night in a motel and the following day, after scouting through a local paper, rented a small cabin with a view of a diamond blue lake. He walked through curving trails sprinkled with pine needles; swam in the clear, cold water; drove around until he found a bar that had a roof antenna strong enough to pick up the Yankee games on its color TV . . . and before long an idea began to intrude with more and more clarity into his thoughts. He knew he would not write *Targets!;* he was determined to pursue a story that didn't rely on the shout of an exclamation point to reinforce its hokey, true-life drama. Instead, he would invent a fiction that would be true. But even as the mental scaffolding for this new tale became sturdier, he, cautious and fearful, held back. Then, as the moment inevitably comes for all writers, Russ decided he had no choice but to rip the cellophane off the carton, select a clean pad, and sit down to write the first lines:

> I stood on the beach with Betsy and searched the dark-
> ness: A white-lit tennis bubble spread like a huge glittering
> cocoon on the inlet across the bay. I should have known
> then that I was in for trouble—big trouble.

Of course these lines would never remain; in the morning they would be scratched out; and, in time, even their memory obliterated. Russ, though he had not realized it yet, possessed neither the voice nor the self-assurance to create a narrator who could speak in first-person revelations. But it would be wrong to call that first attempt, his first steps backward, a false start.

For Russ, the would-be novelist, was already getting closer to creating a character who could eventually reach an unsplittable atom of knowledge—We are always alone. All the rest, despite the sweetness of the writer's imagination, is deception, fantasy. A grim reality: Even in our closest moments, our lovers are not with us; and, however tight the urgency or the binding, we are not totally with them: I am always he; just as she unfailingly sees me as him.

And also with these first lines, Russ was starting out on a journey that would take his first-person narrator on a full grammatical circle. The writer—and his narrator—were setting off to mold a new person from the old: a being—and a point of view—not dependent upon the detachment of third-person insights or measured by these always inherently comparative standards of success. Both the man scribbling on the legal pad and the character staring across the bay, these two Russes, were destined to find in their shared history an ironic lesson: The realization of an uncompromised, authentic I would be the challenge they both would be pushed to confront; and, another irony, only in the realization of this true success, the triumph of a self-contained right-feeling I, is a We ever possible.

EPILOGUE
A Loft of Our Own

THE APARTMENT IS FINALLY EMPTY. Even the mantel is now bare. The last beer is in my hand. Only a sip or two remain; enough for a farewell toast. A toast to what?

My decision to move? Perhaps . . .

WHEN THE FROST was on the pumpkin, the TV at the local bar was picking up the Jets games, and by the time the boy staring out at the bay had been permanently established in the best apartment in the Village, I left the rented cabin in the Adirondacks. I stuffed the duffel bag in the trunk and on the leather bucket seat next to me I carefully placed the carton of legal pads. I wanted the pads where I could see them—the yellow pages were filled in longhand with my novel.

I didn't contact anyone when I returned to New York. For solitary weeks I remained in the apartment editing and typing. I was fused with energy.

Often, though, I would take a late evening walk across the Village to the newsstand at Sheridan Square; by 10:45 each night the early edition of the morning paper was available. Here, too, was further evidence of the neurotic planning which lay at the core of my discipline: If I read the *Times* before I went to bed, I could begin a day's typing as soon as I awoke.

It was on a wet snowy night, the damp flakes whirling through a starless sky as I walked toward the newsstand, that I happened to notice a man crossing Sixth Avenue. He was hatless; his oval bald spot a perfect target for the freezing rain. He moved hesitantly through the treacherous weather, his shoulders hunched, the frayed collar of a long black overcoat turned up around his neck.

There was a red light at the corner so I caught up with him. As I stood there, he turned and immediately tried to pull himself straight. "Good evening, Mr. Lewis," he said. The voice was at once familiar. "Good evening, William," I answered.

He headed uptown as I continued to Sheridan Square; but I remained thinking back to that first day when Max, Kate, and I had strolled through the lobby of the "best" building in the Village. How impressed I had been with William the doorman; so elegantly erect in his wing collar and velvet-trimmed coat, the neatly brushed back silver hairs protruding from his cap. So much artifice. So much, as Kate had seen from the start, pomp and circumstance. That snowy night I decided I no longer needed it.

The next day I called a broker and the apartment was put up for sale. Two weeks later, papers were signed. I had eight weeks to finish typing the book and find a new home.

WHERE AM I MOVING? There is a small story to that, too. Something worth, I believe, raising a bottle to. Perhaps the stuff of a farewell toast . . .

When the manuscript—typed, xeroxed, and creaking with so many hopes—was finally a finished work, I waited a day or so before turning it loose. There was still one last touch (or act of contrition?) required, and I wanted to be very certain of my motives before I made such a decisive, if not presumptuous, commitment. When I realized there was no retreating from it, I sat at my desk, put a blank piece of foolscap in my typewriter and typed a laconic, yet heartfelt dedication: For Kate. I hand-delivered one copy of the manuscript to my unsuspecting editor; the other was put in a manila envelope and mailed to a woman in a loft on Warren Street.

An anxious, though wistful week passed before Kate called.

She still had not learned to beat around the bush. "I think we should talk," she said flatly.

The hollowness in her voice unnerved me: an echo of our last meeting. "Fine."

"Someplace near you?" she offered.

"No. Puffy's will do. See you tonight at six."

This time she was waiting for me. The thick manila envelope containing my manuscript was resting on the bar. As I sat down she handed me a Rolling Rock; and she said one soft word, the fulfilling amen to all my silent prayers: "Congratulations."

"You like it?" I rushed out.

Forever my Kate, she answered, "I didn't think you had it in you."

"That's one of the reasons why I wrote it."

"You always were a snotty bastard."

"Hey, back off." She liked the book; I was swarming with confidence. "Save your wisecracks for Peter."

"Peter's gone. And he's not a bastard."

"What happened? He got lost while trying to find his way through art history?"

"You know, you really are a shit."

"So he walked out on you . . ."

"As a matter of fact, I walked out on him. He made a crack about my spaghetti carbonara and I suddenly realized he was too . . . inconsequential for me to have to take that kind of abuse."

I started laughing.

"What's so funny?"

I was enjoying the arrogant charm of a woman who could skewer a lover with the irrevocable epithet "inconsequential," but there was no way I would share that with her.

"I was just thinking," I said, flexing my advantage, "that you could have saved yourself a lot of inconsequential times if you had rustled up some of your renowned stroganoff for Peter on your first date."

"You don't let up, do you?"

So now of course I couldn't. "Was it one of your romantic, candle-lit dinners? Fussy Peter couldn't put up with a little hot wax in his carbonara?"

"Goddamn you."

"Hey, I hope Peter wasn't sent packing before he got the full treatment. You did show him the snapshot from the family album, didn't you? You know, the one where the dry cleaner sent your father the wrong uniform."

"You louse."

It was just like old times! She grabbed the hefty manila envelope off the bar and swung at me. *Caboom!* A forearm fended off the blow.

"And did Peter take time out from traipsing through art history to watch your remarkable TV?"

Caboom! The manuscript smashed against my shoulder.

"And I hope Peter got to meet the family. Nothing like having to bail out a man for attacking a bunch of nuns to make you feel at home."

I liked that one too much: I didn't see the blow coming. Kate let me have it with a fierce smash to the side of my head. *Caboom!* The envelope split in two; and hundreds of typewritten pages flew about the bar.

That brought us around; or at least shut me up. In a moment we were on our knees on the white tile floor trying to gather the far-flung pages.

Kate had tears in her eyes. "I haven't cried since I walked out of your apartment three years ago," she said, sniffling.

"See what you've been missing," I joked as I crawled over to her and tried to grab the tattered envelope out of her hand.

But Kate wasn't in the mood for jokes. "I hate you," she said.

We were both on our hands and knees facing each other like unleashed, scrappy terriers. Our noses were inches apart.

"Well," I told her, looking straight into the dark glasses shielding her eyes, "I love you."

"You do?"

"Yes. I always have and I always will."

". . . Oh, Russ . . . why do you make everything so difficult?"

I was on my all fours creeping along the floor of Puffy's when I asked Kate the same question I had asked her once before: "Kate, will you marry me?"

"Yes . . . oh yes. You know that's what I always wanted. What I always knew would happen."

"You did? You might've told me . . ."

"I just figured that was one of the things you had to realize for yourself."

I raised myself to my knees, put my arms around Kate, and kissed her on the lips. She kissed me back. I held her feeling the strength of a victory finally won.

"And this time, Russell Lewis," said Kate, now crying tears of joy, "you'd better go through with it."

"Just let anyone try and stop me." For some reason, there were tears in my eyes, too.

Kate and I will be married today in City Hall. Where will we live? I am moving from this apartment into Kate's loft, once more returning to her world; but this time determined to make it ours.

As I said, that's worth a toast. But now, as I prepare to leave this apartment for the last time, to walk out of but not away from so much history, I can't help but think another toast is really in order—to what is missing. Yes, I will raise my last bottle to a belief in the impossible; for I know—and I have spent my lifetime learning—that what cannot be undone, will be undone; and however impossible it is that Max and I will one day share a future, I remain confident in the absurd power of my newfound faith: Max and I will once more be friends. I'll drink to that. A toast to wishful thinking.

The End.

HOWARD BLUM, a former award-winning reporter for the *Village Voice* and the *New York Times*, is also the author of the national best-seller *Wanted! The Search for Nazis in America*. He lives in New York City and on a hilltop in New York State.